...g urban fantasy that will cement Holm's reputation in the field. 8/10"

SciFi Bulletin

"Holm's touch is deft and his language surefooted, a rare feat in the realm of dark fantasy. The best books combine the smart with the careening, and Holm does that so well."

Sophie Littlefield, award-winning author of Aftertime

"Exactly what the urban fantasy genre needs. It's an action-packed thrill ride that blends elements of the best urban fantasy, pulp crime, and adventure novels have to offer ... Highest possible recommendation."

The Debut Review

"The fight between heaven and hell takes a turn for the hardboiled in Chris F. Holm's fantastic debut novel, *Dead Harvest*, where he's created a character as pulpy and tough as anything Chandler or Hammett dreamed up in his doomed Soul Collector. Holm's writing is sharp, powerful, and packs a wallop."

Stephen Blackmoore, author of City of the Lost

"Fans of the Harry Dresden series and those who like their modern-day fantasy with a twist of hardboiled detective story will love this."

Ed Fortune

Also by Chris F. Holm

Dead Harvest

CHRIS F. HOLM

The Wrong Goodbye

The Collector Book Two

ANGRY
ROBOT

ANGRY ROBOT
A member of the Osprey Group

Lace Market House,
54-56 High Pavement,
Nottingham,
NG1 1HW, UK

www.angryrobotbooks.com
Soul man

An Angry Robot paperback original 2012
1

A catalogue record for this book is available
from the British Library.

ISBN: 978-0-85766-220-0
Ebook ISBN: 978-0-85766-222-4

Set in Meridien by THL Design.

Printed in the UK by CPI Group (UK) Ltd, Croydon, CR0 4YY

JUBILEEWOODS.ORG.UK

For Papa

"Hell is other people."

Jean-Paul Sartre

1.

Rain tore through the canopy of leaves, soaking my clothes until they hung wet and heavy on my limbs, but doing little to dispel the fetid stench of decay that pervaded every inch of this God-forsaken place.

Just keep moving, I told myself. It's not far now.

Mud sucked at my shoes as I pressed onward, swinging my machete at the knot of vegetation that barred my way. The roar of the rain against the leaves was deafening, swallowing the noises of the jungle until they were little more than a distant radio signal, half-heard beneath the waves of static. Heavy sheets of falling water obscured my vision, reducing my entire world to three square feet of vines and trees and rotting leaves. I swear, that dank jungle stink was enough to make me gag. Then again, that could have been the corpse that I was wearing.

See, I'm what they call a Collector. I collect the souls of the damned, and ensure they find their way to hell. Believe me when I tell you, it ain't the most glamorous of jobs, but it's not like I really have a choice. Back in '44, I was collected myself, after a bad bit of business with a demon and a dying wife. I didn't know it at the time, of course, but this gig of mine was my end of the bargain. Most folks think of hell as some far-off pit of fire and brimstone, but the truth is it's all around them, a hair's breadth from the world that they can see – always pressing, testing, threatening to break through. That hell is where I spend my days, collecting soul after corrupted soul, all in service of a debt I can never repay.

Which brings me to Colombia, and to the dead guy I was wearing.

One of the bitches about being a Collector is that even though you're stuck doing the devil's bidding for all eternity, your body's still six feet under, doing the ol' dust-to-dust routine. But a Collector can't exist outside a body, which leaves possession as our only option. Most Collectors choose to possess the living – after all, they're plentiful enough, and they come with all kinds of perks, like credit cards and cozy beds. You ask me, though, the living are more trouble than they're worth. They're always crying and pleading and yammering on – or even worse, trying to wrestle control of their bodies back – and the last thing I need when I'm on a job is a backseat driver mucking everything up for me. That's why I stick to the recently dead.

Take this guy, for example. I found him on a tip from my handler, Lilith, who handed me a clipping from a local paper when she gave me my assignment. "Honestly," she'd said, her beautiful face set in a frown, "I don't understand your morbid desire to inhabit the dead, when the living are so much more convenient and, ah, pleasant-smelling."

"A living meat-suit doesn't sit right with me. It's kind of like driving a stolen car."

"You're aware you're being sent there to *kill* someone, are you not?"

"Yeah, only the folks I'm sent to kill need killing." I waved the article at her. "The hell's this thing say, anyway? I barely speak enough Spanish to find the restroom."

"Says he's a fisherman. Died of natural causes – and just yesterday, at that. He's as fresh as can be," she added, smiling sweetly.

Fresh. Right. Just goes to show, you should never trust a creature of the night.

Turned out, Lilith's idea of natural causes included drowning. This guy'd spent six hours in the drink before they'd found him, washed ashore in a tangle of kelp a good three miles from where he'd gone overboard. I'd cleaned up as best I could in the mortuary sink, but no amount of scrubbing could erase the reek of low tide that clung to his hair, his skin, his coarse thicket of stubble. Still, if Lilith thought this guy would be enough to make me cave and snatch myself a living vessel, she was sorely mistaken. I'm nothing if not stubborn.

But the hassle with the meat-suit was nothing compared to the job itself. His name was Pablo Varela. A major player in the local drug trade. Varela's brutality was a matter of public record. In the two decades he'd been involved in the trafficking of coca, he'd only once been brought to trial. It was seven years back, and the Colombian government had turned the trial into quite the spectacle – TV, radio, the whole nine. Their way, I guess, of demonstrating their newfound dedication to the War on Drugs. Varela declined counsel, and mounted no defense.

After eight weeks of damning testimony from the prosecution, it took the jury only minutes to acquit. Some say Varela got to them – that he threatened their lives and the lives of their families if they failed to set him free. Others claim he didn't have to, that his reputation alone was enough to guarantee his release. Whatever it was, the jury made the right choice. Save for them, everyone who set foot in the courtroom over the course of his trial was murdered – every lawyer, every witness, *everyone*. Some, like the bailiff and the court reporter, got off easy: two bullets to the back of the head. The judge and chief prosecutor weren't so lucky. They were strung up by their entrails in the city square – their throats slit, their tongues yanked through the gash in the Colombian style. One week later, the courthouse burned to the ground.

Now a guy like Varela, I don't much mind dispatching. Problem was, the man was paranoid. As soon as he caught wind that I was looking for him, he sent a couple of his goons around to take care of me. That didn't go so well for them, so he sent a couple more. I'm afraid they didn't fare much better. That's when I slipped up. See, I'm not much for killing anyone I don't have to. You could call it mercy, I suppose, or whatever passes for a conscience among the denizens of hell. I call it stupidity, because the bastard that I spared spilled his story to Varela, who grabbed a handful of his most trusted men – not to mention enough firepower to topple your average government – and disappeared into the jungle. Not a bad play, I'll admit. Hell, the first day or so, I even thought it was kinda cute. But as the hours wore on, and the rain continued unabated, the whole affair sort of lost its shine.

Now it'd been four days since I left Cartagena – four grueling days of tracking Varela and his men through blistering heat and near-constant downpours, without so much as a moment to eat or sleep or even catch my breath. Varela's men were well-trained and familiar with the terrain, but they were also laden with gear and would no doubt stop to rest, so I was certain I could catch them. Still, October is Colombia's rainy season, and during that rainy season, there's not a wetter place on Earth. All I wanted was to turn around – to find some nice, secluded spot on the beach and watch the waves roll in off the Caribbean through the bottom of a bottle of beer. Which is exactly what I intended to do, just as soon as Varela was dead.

Woody ropes of liana hung low over the forest floor – clawing, scratching, winding themselves around my weary limbs as though they might at any moment retreat with me into the canopy, the rare unwary traveler too delicious a morsel to pass up. It was ridiculous to think, I know, but even the plant-life in the Amazon has a vaguely predatory air – from the strangler figs that choke the life from the mighty kapok trees to the thick mat of green moss that blankets every surface, always probing, searching, feeding. By the light of day, the jungle wasn't so bad. But as the last gray traces of sun dwindled in the western sky and the brush around me came alive with the rustling of unseen beasts, panic set in. My heart fluttered. My spine crawled. The bitter tang of adrenaline prickled on my tongue. My lips moved in silent prayer – a useless habit – and I quickened my pace, pressing onward through the darkness.

I never even saw the embankment coming.

One moment, I was slashing through the underbrush, the jungle pressing in against me, and the next, there was just a queasy, terrifying nothing. It was like scaling a flight of stairs in the dark only to realize there's one fewer than you remembered, except in this case, my lead foot never hit ground.

I pitched forward. My arms pinwheeled, and my blade clattered to the forest floor, forgotten. I fell for what seemed like forever. Then I slammed into the side of the embankment so hard it knocked the wind out of me, and snapped my jaw shut on my tongue. My mouth filled with blood. My lungs seared as they begged for breath that wouldn't come.

And still, I wasn't done falling.

I tumbled down the steep, muddy slope, clawing frantically at every fern and rain-slick root, but it wasn't any use. I tried to dig in my heels, but one of them caught on something hard, and instead of stopping I hinged forward, somersaulting. End over end I bounced, every inch of my borrowed frame erupting in white-hot pain.

Then, suddenly, all was dark and still and quiet. I was lying face-down in two feet of muddy water, its vegetal stink invading my nose, my mouth, my very pores. Arms shaking, I pushed myself upward, gasping as my face cleared the surface of the muck.

I was at the edge of a broad, shallow stream, which burbled a delicate melody as it passed along its rocky bed. Behind me, the embankment jutted skyward maybe thirty feet, more cliff-face than hill. From the dense bramble of exposed roots and the relative lack of greenery, I guessed it was the result of a mudslide, and a recent one at that. Not that it mattered much to me either way. I mean, a fall's a fall – and besides, I was way more interested in the fire.

It couldn't have been more than fifty yards downstream, nestled in a rocky crook on the far bank of the riverbed. The fire itself was lined with river rocks, and a makeshift spit of branches stretched across it, upon which roasted a goodly hunk of meat. Whoever'd chosen the spot knew what they were doing – the canopy was heavy there, providing shelter from the rain, and the stream supplied ample drinking water; the natural depression of the land hid the fire from view of anyone passing by above. Were it not for my fall, I would've walked right on past and never been the wiser. I allowed myself a smile as I pondered my sudden turn of fortune.

Though it had been days since I'd last eaten, and the aroma of cooking meat had set my mouth watering, I forced myself to hold my ground, counting to one hundred as I listened for any indication that Varela's men had seen me. I heard nothing but the growling of my stomach, and there was no sentry in sight. Given what I knew of Varela, the lack of perimeter guards was surprising, but maybe he believed the jungle to be protection enough from me. He had no idea how wrong he was.

I approached the stream at a crouch, suddenly grateful for the deepening twilight and the thin layer of mud that together served to obscure my approach. Water leached into my boots as I crossed to the far bank, mindful all the while for any whisper of movement that might indicate snake. With Varela finally within my grasp, the last thing I needed was to tangle with a deadly coral, or have this meat-suit squeezed to death by an anaconda. I might not be too fond of this job of mine, but I'd still rather be predator than prey.

Twenty yards out, I knew that something was wrong. There was no idle chatter, no rustle of fabric – no sound at all from Varcla's camp, save for a low, persistent buzzing, like a dentist's distant drill. From behind a massive kapok trunk, I hazarded a glance. Several men, their backs to me, were silhouetted by the fire, but all were as still as death. I watched them for a moment, wondering if this was perhaps some kind of trap – a dummy camp set up to lure me in. Then I realized where the buzzing was coming from, and I knew this was no trap.

I stepped clear of my hiding place and wandered into the camp. The buzzing here was deafening, and up close its source was clear. The entire place was swarming with insects – millions of them – all fighting for their share of the feast laid out before them. The corpses of Varela's men teemed with them – from tiny flies and gnats to massive, iridescent beetles the likes of which I'd never seen, all attracted by the scent of spilled blood and dead flesh, still too faint for my meat-suit's nose to recognize. I counted seven men around the fire. Five of them were riddled with bullet-holes, and abandoned among them was a Kalashnikov assault rifle, its action open, its clip spent. Each of the dead men carried a Kalashnikov of their own, strapped across their backs as if they were at ease when they'd been attacked.

By the look of the other two, I'd say those first five got off light. The first of them lay face-down a few feet from the fire. His rifle lay beneath him, as if he had been holding it at ready when he was attacked. No doubt this was the sentry I'd been listening for. It looked to me like he'd come running to help his buddies when the shooting started. An admirable reaction, to be sure, but apparently not the smartest play. I rolled him over with the toe of my boot. His neck flopped like a wet noodle, and his head lolled to one side. A crushing blow from a rectangular something-or-other had caved in his nose and made tartare of his face – all meat and teeth and glistening bone. A glance at the abandoned Kalashnikov confirmed the gunstock was to blame; it was caked with blood and bits of flesh. Whether the blow had been enough to snap his neck, or his assailant had done it afterward for good measure, I couldn't say.

"What the fuck *happened* here?" I asked of no one in particular. For a moment, I thought I might just get an answer – the sentry's ruined lips parted and emitted a faint, rustling whisper. Then a cockroach the size of my fist crawled out of his mouth, antennae twitching in the still night air. I eyed it for a moment, but if it knew what had gone down, it sure as hell wasn't talking.

The last of the bodies lay spread-eagle on the forest floor. His hands and feet were staked to the ground with knives no doubt scavenged from the belts of his dead companions. His shirt lay open at his sides, exposing his mutilated chest, now crawling with all manner of bugs. Unlike the sentry, his face had been spared, though I suspect that was more for my benefit than for his. His eyes were clouded and glassy, and his features were twisted into a rictus of pain, but still, there was no mistaking that face.

Varela.

I crouched beside him and lay a hand atop his bloodied chest. Insects scampered across the back of my hand and crawled up my sleeve. I ignored them, instead closing my eyes and extending my consciousness – probing, searching. But it was no use. There was nothing left to find.

Varela's soul was gone.

My meat-suit's heart thudded in its chest as the realization hit. Now, I don't know how the white-hats play it, but the souls of the damned don't just up and leave on their own. That means whoever attacked these men wasn't human – as far as I knew, there wasn't a man alive who had the means to steal a soul. That meant Collector.

Problem is, we Collectors ain't exactly the Three Musketeers. All for one and one for all sounds all well and good, but hell doesn't work that way. Varela's soul was *my* responsibility – no exceptions, no excuses – which meant if *I* wasn't the one to bring him in, then I had failed in my mission. And believe me when I tell you, my employers don't take kindly to failure.

I took a calming breath, and willed my racing heart to slow. The last thing I needed now was to freak. I forced myself to look over the scene, certain there was something I had missed.

Turns out, I was right.

It's embarrassing, really, because in retrospect, it was so damn obvious. But when I'd first approached the camp, I had no reason to assume Collector. I just figured one of Varela's competitors had beaten me to the punch, in which case Varela's massive chest-wound made sense – I mean, he had to die of *something*. But when you take a soul, the body dies. So, then: why the bloodied chest?

I retreated to the fire, toppling the spit and sending the hunk of now-charred meat into the flames. For the first time, I realized how recently this must've all gone down – the meat, though burned, had yet to cook off the spit, and though the air was hot and thick with moisture, the bodies weren't bloated, and showed no signs of rigor. Whoever'd done this had beaten me by a matter of minutes. Of course, that knowledge didn't help me much – a few minutes was plenty of time for any Collector worth his salt to disappear. I pushed aside all thought of pursuit, instead focusing on my immediate task. I shoved one of the support branches from the spit into the embers until it caught. Then I returned to Varela's body, torch in hand.

The flame danced in the sudden breeze as I swung the branch at the writhing mass of bugs that blanketed Varela's chest. Reluctantly, they parted, frightened by the fire but unwilling to relinquish their blood meal. As they shifted, I caught a glimpse of something odd – letters, three inches high, carved into the dead man's flesh.

I lost my patience with the flame and dropped to my knees, scattering the remaining insects with a sweep of my arm. Beneath them was a message, ragged and crusted brown with drying blood:

SAM –
WE NEED TO TALK.
YOU KNOW WHERE.
        D

That bastard, I thought. I should've known.

I must've spent a half an hour sitting there, marveling at the presumption, the sheer arrogance that pervaded every grisly slice. Eventually, though, I rose and left the camp behind, plunging once more into the jungle – this time heading south.

Toward Bogotá.

Toward Danny.

2.

The first time I met Danny Young, I wanted to kill him. I don't mean figuratively, like he was some jackass who rear-ended me at a stoplight when I was late for an appointment. I mean I literally wanted to wrap my hands around his neck and squeeze until his face went purple, his eyes bulged out of their sockets, and that incessantly wagging tongue of his was finally still, so I could sit and sip my drink in peace. Not the kindest of impulses, I'll grant you. But in my defense, I was having one hell of a lousy day.

It was the fall of '53, and I was in a dingy basement pub in Amsterdam, a few blocks south of De Wallen, where, in the shadow of the Old Church, prostitutes peddled their wares. Ten yards of earth and stone were all that separated the place from the canal beyond, which no doubt contributed to the damp chill that had settled in my weary limbs. Of course, it wasn't the ambience that brought me here so much as their reputation for a heavy hand with the jenever – a local spirit that tastes like gin and turpentine in equal measure. I'd had three of them, maybe four, and still I couldn't stop my hands from shaking. I told myself it was the cold, but I wasn't yet drunk enough to believe it. Not after the job I'd just pulled.

His name was Arnold Haas. A doll-maker by trade – and from what I'd heard, a damn good one. The way Lily told it, his dolls weren't the type you'd see dragged along the sidewalk by some jam-handed toddler – they were more the fetch-five-figures-at-auction sort of deal. Now, you might be wondering why I'd care about a thing like that, but normally, that kind of information is pretty helpful to a Collector. See, there's two kinds of folks who wind up marked for collection: contract kills and freelancers. Contract kills are the ones who went and made themselves a deal with a demon, usually chasing fame or fortune, or maybe love, or lust, or revenge. Most contract kills are decent enough people – they just want a better hand than they've been dealt. Believe me when I tell you, most times, it ain't worth the price. Freelancers, on the other hand, are a nasty lot. They're the ones whose actions are so heinous, hell won't wait around for them to die. Given the quality of Haas's work, I'd assumed he was the former.

I was wrong.

It was dusk when I'd arrived at Haas's house. Amber streetlights shone against a sky of deepening blue, and reflected off the still waters of the canal that ran parallel to Haas's street. The house itself was an elegant brick row house in the Dutch style, with tall, narrow windows and a gabled roof shingled in slate. The porch light was unlit, and the windows, save for one, were dark. I spent the length of a cigarette watching the house from beneath one of the many bare, skeletal elms that crowded the banks of the canal. Occasionally, a shadow would pass across the face of the one lit window – a bedroom, no doubt, as it was situated in the top-left corner of the house, just beneath the steep pitch of the roof, and three stories above the street on which I stood.

Good, I thought – that means he's home.

The lock was nothing to sneeze at: a thick, mean-looking

deadbolt I couldn't have picked in a week. But the door was inlaid with several squares of leaded glass, and those weren't so hard to handle. I wrapped a kerchief around my fist and knocked out the pane nearest the knob. In seconds I was inside.

I hesitated a moment, just inside the door, waiting for my eyes to adjust. The house, I realized, was cold – bitterly so. The air was thick with the spicy scent of potpourri, and something else as well, earthy and unpleasant. Beyond the entryway was a tidy living room – a floral couch, draped with lace; two high-backed armchairs, camel-colored and accented at the arms and legs with dark-stained wood; a thick mahogany coffee table, gleaming faintly by the light of the streetlights that trickled in through the sheer white curtains. A small iron fireplace sat unlit in one corner of the room, set into a rose-colored wall. But for that three-foot strip of wall, which stretched from mantle to ceiling, the entire room was lined with shelves – heavy, floor-to-ceiling shelves, stained so dark they appeared black in the dim light, and lined with thousands upon thousands of dolls. Some of them were made of simple cloth, with hair of yarn and button eyes, while others stared at me with eyes of glass, set in faces of ghost-white porcelain. All were resplendent in their Sunday best, an oppressive cacophony of bold prints and elaborate brocades, of chiffon and satin and lace. Their blank, implacable gazes unnerved me as I passed, cutting through the living room to the stairs that lay beyond.

I left my shoes at the foot of the stairs, and headed upward in my stockinged feet, as quiet as could be. The staircase walls were graced with floating shelves at irregular intervals. Too small to support whole dolls, these shelves were adorned with delicate porcelain hands and feet and eyeless heads – stark white and unfinished. Something about those empty sockets bothered me, though why, I didn't know. I ignored them and pressed on.

At the second floor, the staircase turned. The unpleasant odor I'd caught wind of downstairs was stronger here, but I was so focused on finding Haas, I didn't pay it any mind. Through the delicate balusters above, I caught a glimpse of a half-closed door, silhouetted by the light of the room beyond. I headed toward it. The landing floorboards creaked in protest beneath my weight, and I winced. But this Haas was a doll-maker, I told myself, not some hardened criminal – what did I care if he heard me coming? So like an idiot, I threw caution to the wind, taking the stairs two at a time, and sprinting toward the open door. When I reached it, I kicked it inward – and then I froze. Haas wasn't there. But what was there was so fucking awful that for a moment, I forgot myself and just stood there, agape and staring.

There were three of them, propped around a table laid with silver as though they were enjoying a midday tea.

They weren't.

The farthest of them, an older woman, sat across the table from where I stood and beamed back at me with an expression of charmed delight – or rather, that's what it would have been, were she not dead. The putrid stink of her was overwhelming, and it was all I could manage to keep my feet. Her silver hair was pulled back into a bun, revealing flesh the color and texture of old shoe leather, cracked and peeling. Her mouth was set into a smile, revealing gray-brown teeth and gums of withered black. What I first took to be dimples were, in fact, metal pins, inserted into the flesh to preserve her expression. Her eyes were not eyes at all, but large, vaguely iridescent buttons, an X of rough twine at each of their centers, affixing them in place. I had a shock of recognition, but disfigured as she was, it took me a moment to place her. Her photo sat atop the mantle in the living room. This was Haas's wife.

The other two sat on either side of the old woman, facing

each other across the table. They had the look of a couple in their thirties, and they were fresher, it seemed – their flesh less desiccated – but their treatment had been the same. Worse, in fact, in the case of the man – his eyes had simply been stitched shut, his smile painted on; and though his shirt was clean and freshly pressed, an ugly smear of brain and blood streaked across his forehead still. But the woman – whose resemblance to Haas's wife suggested daughter – was truly a masterpiece. Gleaming eyes of glass stared out from bloodied sockets. Red lipstick graced her lips. Her teeth he'd replaced with the finest porcelain, at least mostly. A plate of yellowed molars and a pair of pliers sat atop a brown-stained rag on the table in front of her, and beside her was an empty chair. I guess I had interrupted Haas's fun.

You want to know where I went wrong? I was so freaked out by what I'd seen in that room, I went and dropped my guard. A creaky landing isn't much of a concern when you're sneaking up on a kindly old man, but when that kindly old man turns out to be a human-doll-making nutjob, it's kind of a big deal. Which is to say, I should've seen that mallet coming.

Of course, I didn't know it was a mallet at the time. Felt like he hit me with a dump truck. All I know is one moment, I'm taking in this nightmare tea party, and the next, I'm on the floor. He hit me again, and I heard something snap. Pain blossomed in my head like a firework, and the room went white.

And then, for a while, there was nothing.

When I came to, my hands and feet were bound. My head was pounding, and my left eye was swollen shut. I raised my hands as one to touch it. The flesh was all hot and pulpy and wrong. I cast a glance at my fingers with my one good eye. More blood than I expected. If I didn't put pressure on that soon, I'd be lucky if I managed to stay conscious.

Then I saw what Haas was doing, and I wondered if lucky was the right word.

He was standing at a workbench at the far end of the room, stringing twine through a heavy darning needle and humming softly to himself. A small man, stooped and heavily lined, he wore a tweed vest over a blue Oxford, with matching tweed pants. His bald pate gleamed above a crescent of wispy gray. When he saw me watching him, he smiled.

"Ah, good," he said in lightly accented English. "You're up!" He riffled through his toolbox for a second, producing a handful of assorted buttons. "Tell me – which of these do you like best?"

I tried to speak, but my head was full of angry bees, and the words wouldn't come. The effort damn near made me puke.

"I rather think this one," he said, crossing the room and holding it to my cheek appraisingly. "It complements the gold tones in your hair."

He knelt beside me, sliding the needle through a button-hole and pressing the point against the lid of my swollen, ruined eye. "Do try to sit still," he said. "I'm afraid this is going to hurt quite a lot."

The needle pierced the tender flesh of my eyelid. I screamed in agony, and tried to pull away. Haas expected that, though – I was hardly his first, after all – and he held my head fast, one bony hand an iron grip at the base of my neck. Blood ran hot and sticky down my cheek, and with it came a fresh wave of pain – exquisite, clarifying. Suddenly, I realized what I had to do.

If back wasn't an option, I was gonna have to go forward.

I lunged toward him with all I had, driving the needle through the tender flesh of my eyelid and into the soft tissue beyond. Haas, startled, tipped backward. My hands were up in a flash. I landed atop him, the needle buried deep in my eye. Despite the searing pain, a manic grin spread across my face, so pleased was I my gambit had worked. Then everything went a little gray around the edges, and I realized I didn't have much time before this meat-suit gave out on me.

Haas struggled to get out from under me, but I had a good fifty pounds on him, so he wasn't going anywhere. My hands found his chest, and plunged inside. Suddenly, the room around us disappeared, replaced with a swirling blackness, a keening wail – the light and song of Haas's withered soul. I wrapped my fingers around my prize, and now it was he who screamed.

"Sorry," I muttered, "it's nothing personal." It's something I say to all my marks – my way, I guess, of reminding myself this collecting thing is just a job. This time, though, I wasn't sure I meant it.

I rolled off of him, yanking free his soul as I did. As it tore free from his chest, the darkness around us flickered and receded, and his song faded into nothing. My consciousness threatened to do the same. I mustered every ounce of strength this meat-suit had, and hurled my being toward Haas's lifeless form. But this body I'd borrowed was broken and bloodied. I didn't know if every ounce of strength it had would be enough.

Death, as a Collector, isn't final, but that doesn't mean it's a walk in the park. When a body dies, the link between soul and flesh is severed, and the soul – whether native or invading – is unseated. Now, for a native soul, the shock of being dislodged from its earthly vessel is considerable – and believe me, that's a good thing. Shock makes you numb. Shock makes you forget. But a Collector isn't afforded that luxury. We experience death in all its unfiltered glory, which means for us, it's excruciating. Plus, there's the added indignity of eviction. See, the body finds its native soul familiar, and will house it long after death if necessary until collection. An invading soul, on the other hand, is unnatural – unwelcome. The body's constantly trying to expel it – which is why a meat-suit pukes every time someone like me hops in for a spin. When a meat-suit dies, it sends any invading soul packing. But since we Collectors can't exist without a body, we wind up reseeded into another body at random – no big deal if it's a strapping young man with energy for future body-hopping to spare, but you get stuffed into an infant and it's nothing but diapers and puréed peas until they get strong enough for you to up and leave. Many a Collector's gone mad as a consequence of an unlucky reseeding. I'd really rather not be one of them.

It seemed like forever that I hung there in the vertiginous nothing that stretched between Haas and the mutilated corpse I'd left behind. There was no light to guide my way, no sound to mark my passing. I tried in vain with limbs I no longer had to reach for that fresh vessel, so tantalizingly close just seconds before, but now an eternity away. For a moment I thought I'd failed. Then the world lurched, and my eyes, uninjured now but rheumy with age, sprang open to reveal the bedroom ceiling some eight feet above. I swear I could've danced a jig.

Haas's body, though, had other plans. Its stomach clenched, and I doubled over, puking. You'd think I'd be used to that by now. It's sort of par for the course for possessions – the body's way of trying to rid itself of something that's not supposed to be there, I guess. Still, after the trauma of hopping bodies, it'll surprise you every time.

Once my stomach was empty, I wiped my mouth with the back of one liver-spotted hand, and took a look around. My last body was lying on the floor beside me, the darning needle buried a good six inches in his head. A puddle of blood expanded slowly beneath him like an oil slick, and the tiny swirling orb of Haas's soul was still cradled in his lifeless hands. I struggled clumsily to my knees, and then collapsed, Haas's limbs slow to relent to my commands. I tried again – the same result.

That's when I heard her crying.

It was the faintest of whimpers – so quiet, in fact, that at first I thought I had imagined it. But as the roar of my pulse in my ears subsided, there was no mistaking it. I cast my gaze around the room, looking for the source of the noise, but there was no corner of the room I could not see, no closet in which to hide.

There was, however, a chest.

It was an old wooden affair, glossy with layer after layer of honeyed lacquer, and fastened with an ornate iron hasp. A matching iron key lay atop its lid. I shambled toward the chest, my new meat-suit still sluggish and unresponsive, and pressed my ear to it. I heard a single, hitching sob, a sharp intake of breath, and then nothing. It seemed whoever was inside had heard me coming.

I snatched the key up off the lid and jammed it into the lock, hearing tumblers catch as I clicked it home. The lid was heavy, stubborn. I heaved it open with a grunt.

She was a girl of maybe three, dressed as the dolls downstairs had been, in a pinafore of purest white over a loud floral dress. White stockings adorned her legs, and her feet were clad in patent leather Mary Janes. Curly hair framed a delicate face far too young to be painted as thoroughly as it had. She was made up not like a woman would be, but like a doll, with circles of red at the apples of her cheeks, and her lips painted to appear permanently pursed in an expression of coy innocence. The illusion was shattered by the streaks the tears had made down her cheeks, and by the look of wide-eyed terror on her face. Instinctively, I reached out to her, but she recoiled, trembling. Of course she's afraid of you, I thought – you're wearing the flesh of the man who did this to her. I lowered my hand,

and told her softly it would be all right. Of course, being Dutch, she probably couldn't understand a word I said, but then, I wasn't sure that I believed it anyway. Whether she understood or not, it was clear *she* didn't believe it; she hugged her knees to her chest, and clenched shut her eyes against the tears.

As I sat there, looking at her, I couldn't help but notice the resemblance to the couple at the table – her parents, no doubt. Which meant this girl was Haas's granddaughter. I wondered all the sudden if, for Haas, hell was punishment enough.

Unsure what else I could do while in the body of her tormentor, I lowered the lid of the trunk, and left the girl in peace. I wrapped Haas's soul in a scrap of fabric torn from his dead wife's skirt and stuffed it in my pocket. Then I went downstairs and dialed the police. I told them in a whisper I was being held against my will, and gave them Haas's address. When they asked me for my name, I hung up. Then, with a silent prayer for the girl I'd left behind, I left the house, letting the door swing open behind me.

My head was reeling as I left the row house, and my stomach threatened mutiny. I told myself it was just the standard-issue hiccups of an unfamiliar meat-suit, but I knew that wasn't true. The job had gotten to me. Haas had gotten to me. After nine years of doing this, I didn't think that was still possible.

A few blocks from Haas's house, I stopped at the base of a gnarled old elm, and buried Haas's soul beneath six inches of chill black earth. Then I covered it over with fallen leaves and headed straight for the fucking pub. The night I had, all I wanted was a little peace and quiet in which to get stinking drunk. Thanks to Danny, though, I had no such luck.

"Pardon me, mate – anyone sitting here?"

Shit. I'd picked this place because the drinks were tall and cheap, but the trade-off was it was an old-school pub, with long, narrow tables and benches to match – the kind of bar where strangers sat together and left the place as friends. Only I had all the friends I could handle – zero, to be exact – and I wasn't in the market for another.

My would-be new acquaintance was a lanky kid of maybe twenty-five, standing at the end of the table with an expectant half-smile pasted on his face as he awaited my reply. British, by the accent, and a bit of a dandy, if his outfit was any indication. He was decked out in a darted charcoal sport coat over a crisp white dress shirt, open at the throat. Pale khaki chinos terminated in loafers the color of cognac. A tartan scarf hung loose around his neck, and a porkpie hat tilted rakishly atop his head. I fixed my gaze on him a moment, and then dropped it back to my glass, hoping he'd get the message.

He didn't.

"You're a Yank, aren't you?" he said, sliding onto the bench opposite me with a casual grace that spoke of moneyed arrogance. "You've got that look, like you think in English, or at least what passes for English on your side of the pond. I'll tell you, mate, I'm glad to have found you – I haven't had a proper conversation for bloody ages. I mean, yeah, most of these guys, they muddle through well enough, but you can tell by the way they screw their faces up when you talk to them they've got to concentrate, and they're not exactly *chatty*. Everything's all 'yes' or 'no' or 'toilet is jusht down ze hall'. It's nice that they try and everything, but you know what I mean?"

I said nothing. Just sat and stared at my drink.

"Or maybe you don't," he said. "Bloody hell, you ain't drinking jenever, are you? I wouldn't wash brushes in that stuff. I swear, I could murder a decent pint right now, but all they've got in this place is some God-awful Pilsner that tastes like rat piss. I'd have to be completely off my face to even get it past my lips, and even then, I'm not sure I wouldn't spew it straight back up."

I closed my eyes, and massaged the bridge of my nose with my thumb and forefinger. This kid was giving me a headache. If he noticed, though, he didn't seem to mind.

"So what brings you to Amsterdam? Business? Pleasure? A bit of both, maybe? Me, I just got off the train from Brussels. Thought I'd see the sights, maybe check out the Red Light District, know what I mean? After all, a man cannot live on bread alone."

I tossed back the remains of my drink and got up to leave.

"Oh, come on, mate, don't go yet – the night's still young!"

I shot him the kind of look I normally reserve for ax-murderers and pedophiles, and then made for the door. When I reached the table's end, he called to me.

"Hold on!" he said. "Don't go. We've a lot to talk about, you and me."

I turned and flashed the kid a rueful smile. "No offense, kid, but you and me don't have shit to talk about. I think you've got me mixed up with someone else."

"I do, do I?" He smiled, and raised his hands in mock acquiescence. "All right, Sam, if that's the way you want to play it. I just figured you might like a little company, now that the Haas unpleasantness is behind you. The job *is* over, is it not? Or did you decide to tie one on before disposing of his soul?"

I flinched as if stung. By the look on his face, the kid knew he hit his mark. I closed the gap between us in a flash, grabbing fistfuls of his shirt in my bony hands and hoisting him up out of his chair until his face was a scant inch from mine. "Who *are* you?"

"Easy, tiger! I'm a Collector, just like you," he said, his tone placating. "Name's Danny."

"Why the hell are you following me around?"

"I just wanted to talk to you."

"So what – you thought you'd swing by, swap some war stories or whatever? Well you came to the wrong guy."

"No," he said, not unkindly. "I don't believe I did."

"I don't care *what* you believe. Contact between Collectors is strictly forbidden. Do you have any idea what'd happen to us if our handlers caught wind of this? I ought to kill you just for being here."

"Perhaps you should, but I don't believe you will. It's my understanding you've got a certain affection for the living. You may wish to get rid of me, but I'm guessing you aren't going to sacrifice this perfectly good skin-suit to do it. Now, have a seat and let me buy you a drink."

"Why on earth would I do that?" I asked.

"Because the way I hear it, we ain't so different, you and me. We both know this job of ours is designed to chip away everything decent and human about us, until we're no better than the monsters we work for. I, for one, am shitting myself at the very thought of that, and I reckon you probably are too. Look, I know it's a losing battle, trying to hold on to what makes us who we are, but I also know that isn't going stop me from trying. And if I had to guess, I'd say you aren't going to, either. All I'm saying is, maybe it'd be easier if we weren't going it alone."

He was right, about the job part at least. See, this vocation is punishment for a life misspent – and as punishments go, it's a doozy. Every time we take a soul, we experience every moment that brought that person to our grasp – every kindness, every slight, every gruesome act our mark inflicted. Mind you, I don't mean we *see* those moments; we *live* them, with painful, blinding clarity. Over time, it wears on you. Breaks you down. Not to mention, every time you leave a vessel behind, you lose a little bit of what makes you who you were in life, until eventually there's nothing left. It was the thought of that happening – that, and the horrors I'd experienced collecting nutjobs like Haas – that kept me up at night. It was these that kept me talking to Danny.

"So what," I said, "you're asking if I'll be your *friend*?"

"I'm *asking* if you'll let me buy you a drink."

"You're fucking nuts, you know that? If anyone were to find out about this—"

"Oh, for Christ's sake, Sam, all we're talking about is a drink. What's the harm in that?"

What's the harm? I swear, over the years, I must've played that sentence back a thousand times. I'd like to think that if I knew then what I know now, things would've gone differently. And who knows? Maybe they would have. Or maybe I'm kidding myself, thinking I had ever had a choice. In those early years as a Collector, I was so lonely, so desperate – so scared of what I might one day become – there was really no other way for me to play it.

So yeah, I took that drink, and we got to talking. Turned out, we did have a lot in common. As I said, those who wind up marked for collection are either contract kills or freelancers, and since all Collectors were once collected, that means the same holds true for us. Now, I don't want to tell tales out of class, but the guy who collected me? He was a freelancer, and if that sadistic bastard is any indication, they're not a group you want to hang out with come the company picnic. Me and Danny, we were contract kills. The deal I made saved the life of the woman that I loved. Danny made his deal at the tender age of fifteen when, in the wake of the First World War, the British economy took a bad turn and left his once-affluent family penniless, and his once-loving parents hateful and embittered. He was but a child, and the only education he'd ever had was in the classics as had befitted his family's station; he hadn't the skills to reclaim their fortune by wits alone. So he sought help – help of the demon variety. The way he told it, if he had it to do all over again, even knowing what that deal would cost him, he would've played it the same way. Something else we had in common, I suppose.

As the evening wore on, one drink became three, three became five, and by the time we stumbled arm-in-arm out of the
pub and into the chilly November pre-dawn, me and Danny'd
become friends.

Was it stupid? I don't know. Fate? I couldn't say.

One thing I know for sure, though: right or wrong, things
would've been a lot simpler if I'd just killed him.

3.

The Plaza de Bolivar sparkled in the midday sun, still rain-slick from a spate of showers that had burned off when the first rays of morning light crested the Andes to the east. It was Sunday, and the massive square was flush with people: students, lounging on the steps of the old cathedral; lovers, chatting amiably as they strolled arm-in-arm; children, startling pigeons into flight as they splashed through the puddles that had gathered in the shadow of the capitol building. The scene looked like something out of a picture postcard, right down to the plaza patrons' unselfconscious good cheer. At the moment, I hated each and every one of them, traipsing about without a care in the world while Danny jerked me around like a puppet on a string.

Five days had passed since I'd received Danny's grisly message – five days since I'd left Varela's mutilated corpse, and the corpses of his men, to be reclaimed by the jungle they'd so wrongly sought refuge in. The first two of them I'd spent hiking to the nearest village, although maybe village was too strong a word. Really, it was nothing more than a handful of ramshackle huts clustered around a narrow dirt track that served as their only road. God knows what they must've thought of me, stumbling filthy and delirious out of the jungle and begging for food and water in broken Spanish. But whatever they thought of me, they took me in, giving me not only food and water, but fresh clothes and a bed to sleep in as well. The bus to Bogotá arrived two days later, looking – as all buses in Colombia seem to – like some crazy Technicolor school bus, its roof piled high with suitcases, wicker baskets, and sacks of grain. I boarded it with a full belly, a clear head, and an undeniable reluctance to leave after the staggering hospitality I'd been shown by these people who had so little to give. Of course, the choice to leave wasn't mine to make – Danny had made sure of that. I didn't know what he was playing at, snatching Varela's soul, and truth be told, I didn't care. All I cared about was taking back what was rightfully mine, even if I had to tear him limb from limb to do it.

I set fire to a cigarette, and then struck out across the square. Though the sun was bright overhead, the mountain air was cool and thin. After a week spent traipsing through the Amazonian lowlands, my lungs seared from the sudden altitude, and gooseflesh sprung up on my arms at the slightest breeze. I was dizzy and weak, and my muscles protested at the exertion required to remain upright and on the move. If this meeting of ours were to come to blows, I didn't like my chances. And with Danny, I really couldn't rule it out.

About a half a block from the square was a small sidewalk café – a smattering of wrought-iron tables beneath a black canvas awning, within sight of the twin spires of the cathedral. I took a seat and ordered a cup of strong black coffee, as much for warmth as to kill the time. The minutes passed by as lackadaisically as the tourists, as though both had nowhere in particular to be. When I reached the bottom of my mug, I signaled to the waitress for another.

By the time I finished my second cup of coffee, I was jumpy, and my palms were sweating. My waitress wasn't faring much better. When she brought my second refill, she shot off something in rapid-fire Spanish that I couldn't understand, but I think I got the gist: order something besides coffee or beat sidewalk. I tried to explain to her that I was waiting for someone, but that didn't seem to get much traction. Eventually, I acquiesced, looking over the menu and picking an item at random. That seemed to mollify her, because she snatched the menu from my hands and disappeared into the café, leaving me and my coffee jitters in peace.

"Hello, Sam. It's been a while."

Even though I'd been expecting him, I swear I never saw him coming. See, every Collector's got their type. Some pick meat-suits based on strength, or speed, or stamina. Me, I prefer the quiet of the newly dead. But Danny, he's got a whole 'nother set of criteria. Danny likes 'em pretty. Good teeth, a healthy tan, and ideally with a walk-in full of swanky clothes. He told me once in a moment of drunken confession that he clings to the creature comforts he enjoyed in life as a way of protecting against the erosion of self that comes from subjugating vessel after unwilling vessel, but I didn't believe him for a second. He does it because he likes the way the ladies look at him.

But that was then, I guess. Today, he looked like shit. Sunken eyes ringed dark from lack of sleep. Sallow skin beaded with sweat and streaked with dirt. There was dirt in his hair, as well, and his clothes were so covered in it, it took me a moment to recognize them as the same fatigues worn by Varela's men. So this is where the eighth man went, I thought – the one whose rifle I found abandoned alongside his dead compatriots. But that was nearly a week ago, and I'd never known Danny to stick with a meat-suit longer than a day or two. Something clearly wasn't right here.

"You ask me, Danny, it hasn't been long enough. Now where the hell is Varela's soul?"

He blinked at me for a moment as though he hadn't understood the question, and then dropped awkwardly into the chair opposite me. His eyes darted to and fro, never settling on anything for more than a second. His hands found the unused place setting laid out before him and began fiddling absently with it. His feet tapped out a twitchy, nervous rhythm from beneath the table.

"I wasn't sure you'd come," he said, his once lilting Queen's English now brittle, strained.

"Then you're an idiot. I *had* to come – your little stunt in the jungle made sure of that."

He recoiled as if I'd slapped him. His features twisted into an expression of hurt. "I'm sorry about that – really, I am – but I didn't know what else to do! I've got no one else to turn to."

"Sure you don't, Danny," I replied, my words dripping venom. "How is Ana, by the way?"

"Piss off, Sam, that was *years* ago. I mean, I'm sorry how that shook out, but I was hoping we were past that."

"Past it? Is *that* what you hoped? You *lied* to her, Danny. You betrayed me. You know damn well I had nothing to do with Quinn getting shelved – but hey, if pinning it on me means you and Ana get to ride off into the sunset together, then by all means. After all, what's a little backstabbing between friends?"

"Oh, for God's sake, Sam, we've been through this all a thousand times. I swear to you, whatever she heard, she did not hear it from me. How many times am I going to have to tell you that before you'll actually believe it?"

"At least once more."

"I think I'll save my breath," he said. "Besides, what I did or didn't tell her is immaterial. Ana's a big girl, and her conclusions are her own. You know as well as anyone that once she's made up her mind, there's not a force on God's Earth that's going to change it. Now, I won't deny that when she turned her back on you, it was me she turned to, but I can promise you there was no riding off into the sunset for the two of us. When Quinn got shelved, it shook her up pretty bad. And then *you* left–"

"*Left?*" I let out a single, barking laugh, shrill and humorless. "The way I remember it, you two abandoned *me*."

"Yeah, well, whatever you want to call it, it was the beginning of the end for Ana and me. We held on for a while – out of obligation, I suppose – but we were just forestalling the inevitable. Truth is, I haven't seen Ana in months."

I wasn't sure if I believed him. Then again, it didn't matter. After all, I hadn't come here to pick at old wounds. I had come here to take back what was rightfully mine.

I came here for Varela's soul.

"All right, Danny. Why don't you tell me what we're doing here?"

But Danny wasn't paying me any mind. Instead, he seemed suddenly transfixed by a spot over my left shoulder. His face contorted in panic, and the idle tapping of his feet ceased. I twisted in my seat to see what it was he was looking at, but it was nothing but a common crow, preening itself on a porch rail a couple doors down. Or rather, it *would* have been a common crow on damn near any other continent. As far as I knew, no one had ever seen a crow this far south, which made this one anything but common. But aside from Danny, who looked like he was going to crawl out of his skin – and me, I suppose – no one seemed to pay it any mind. Guess there weren't a lot of bird-watchers out that day.

Eventually, Danny realized I'd asked a question and got around to replying, though his eyes never left the crow perched behind me. "I'm in trouble, Sam." As he spoke, three more crows fluttered to a landing on the street beside us, picking at whatever scraps of food had settled in the cracks between the ancient cobblestones. He glanced at them, and the fear-lines in his face deepened. "I need your help."

"I'm listening."

"It's… it's about a job. A couple weeks ago, this was. The bloke was a mob enforcer out of Vegas by the name of Giordano. Nothing special about him, really – just your typical street thug. Or, at least, he *was*, until he cut a deal with a demon a couple years back and wound up a made guy. Honestly, you'd think if you were going to go to all the trouble of selling your immortal bloody soul, you might aim a little higher."

I thought back to my deal, to the wife whose life I saved. "Yeah, I guess I would, at that."

"Anyway, the collection went strictly by the numbers – he never even saw me coming. Only now his soul is missing. Stolen right out from under me."

I smiled, all teeth and ill intentions. "Seems there's a lot of that going around."

"Look, you can make your funny jokes, but I'm not fucking around here! I swear, I buried the bloody thing like I was supposed to, but by the time the Deliverants arrived to pick it up, it was nowhere to be found. Now I'm at the end of my rope, and my handler's getting really narky. Pretty soon, he's going to run out of bollocks to tell his bosses, which means if I don't produce something soon…"

So *that* explained the crows – who, by the way, had since been joined by several dozen of their friends, and now darkened every cornice, balcony, and parapet for a half a block around. Deliverants are the creatures responsible for conveying a soul to its ultimate fate. They're often mistaken for simple scavengers by the living, and the form they take is dependent upon the location of the collection. These ones must've had quite a flight, tracking Danny all the way from Vegas. As I watched, another handful of them fluttered to a landing atop the clay shingles of the roof across the street. Danny's missing soul was, by all rights, theirs now, and it looked to me like they meant to take it back. If I were Danny, it wouldn't just be our employers I was worried about. Though if his manner were any indication, I'd say the Deliverants worried him plenty.

"Look, I get you're in a bind," I said. "What I *don't* get is what the hell you expect me to do about it."

"I *expect* you to show some fucking compassion! I *expect* you to find it in that bitter bloody heart of yours to care! I *expect* you to help me figure out who did this before our bosses' bosses tire of my excuses and take matters into their own hands! I mean, for Christ's sake, Sam, I thought we were mates!"

"You're full of shit, Danny, and you know it. If you want to go on about friendship and compassion, that's your business, but if you believed a single word of it, then why'd you take Varela's soul?"

"I had to be sure you'd come, didn't I?"

"Yeah, I get that. But if you and I were really friends, all you would have had to do was ask. Only you and I both know that ship sailed a long time ago, so let's not pretend this is anything other than what it is. You took something that was rightfully mine. I want it back. Now why don't you tell me what I'm going to have to do to get it?"

"So that's it, is it – you think I planned to blackmail you? Well, fuck you, Sam Thornton. Fuck you very much. Of *course* I took your precious bloody soul – I knew there wasn't any other way you'd meet with me. You ever ask yourself why it is that after all these years, you're still so sodding mad at me? You tell yourself that I betrayed you – that I filled your precious Ana's head with lies and stole her away from you. Only she was never *your* Ana to begin with, was she? And anyway, I did no such thing. If you ask me, you're not angry because you think she never would've chosen me all on her own – you're angry because you suspect she *did*."

"Damn it, Danny, that's not what this is about!"

"Ain't it?" He fished a bundle of olive-drab cloth from his uniform shirt pocket and tossed it onto the table between us. "If it's your soul you want, then take it and go. Sorry to have troubled you."

I eyed the bundle for a second, and then picked it up. "Look, it's not like I don't see where you're coming from – I just don't know what I could possibly do to help. I mean, a year ago, maybe, but *now*? Now I can't. Not after what happened in New York. There's a war brewing between heaven and hell, Danny, and our kind are being kept on an ever shorter leash."

He guffawed. "You think you need to tell *me* that?"

"Apparently, I do. And believe me, *no one's* under more scrutiny right now than I am. I mean shit, when the dust from the Manhattan job cleared, there were two demons dead – dead by my hand. We're talking the first of their kind to be killed in *millennia* – the first since the last Great War. I'm lucky I'm not spending the rest of eternity getting flayed alive. Probably would be, if I hadn't gone all Dirty Harry on the bad angel and averted an apocalypse in the process. But it ain't like I'm getting a free pass in all of this. Lily's spent the past ten months watching me like a hawk to ensure every job is by the book – and there isn't an angel or a demon out there that wouldn't like to see me burn. Which means for now, I walk the straight and narrow. Hell, I'll be lucky if they don't shelve me just for *meeting* with you. I'm sorry, Danny, but my hands are tied."

At that, Danny deflated, the fight gone out of him. He looked suddenly small, and frail, and afraid. Despite everything that had come between us, I wished there was something I could do to help him – that there was something I could say to keep him from feeling so alone. There wasn't, though – or at least, that's what I like to tell myself. It sounds better than the truth. Better than *I didn't even try*.

Danny's gaze drifted over to the building opposite the café, an elegant Spanish colonial with balconies that overlooked the avenue below. A wan half-smile spread across his weary face. "It was a hell of a job we pulled in there, wasn't it? When was that – '81, '82?"

"'83," I replied, a smile tugging at my lips as well.

"'83, of course it was! Bloody hell, seven of them, all at once – that's not something that you soon forget. And the *fight* they put up – it's amazing we got out of there alive! I remember the last of them was so coked up, he laughed and laughed as, one after another, all his mates went down. When all was said and done, I was so exhausted I thought I might collapse, and Ana had to shower for an hour to get the blood out of her hair."

"I still remember the look on Lily's face when she found out I'd pulled it off – she thought for sure they'd send me packing. Of course, she had no idea I had help."

"We were thick as thieves back then, Sam. Where did we go wrong?"

I shrugged and shook my head. "Thieves steal, Danny. That's where we went wrong."

As soon as I said it, I regretted it, but Danny didn't bristle. And at that moment, the waitress returned, carrying a steaming plate of tortilla-like flatbreads piled high with meat and cheese. She set the plate in front of me, and addressed Danny in Spanish too fast for me to follow.

"Sorry, love," he said to her, rising from his seat, "I can't stop." And then, to me, so earnestly it broke my heart: "Thanks for coming, Sam. It was good to see you."

He turned and left, then, his shoulders hunched against the mountain chill, his hands stuffed into his pockets. He set out in a diagonal across the street, heading back toward the plaza. I just sat and watched him go. I wanted to call to him, to tell him that I'd help, but I didn't. I was too angry, I guess. Too afraid. Eventually, I lost sight of him within the crowded square, so I sat and stared at nothing.

And then, as one, a thousand crows took flight and followed.

4.

"Where the hell have you been?"

At the sound of Lilith's voice, I damn near jumped out of my shoes. Not that there was anything wrong with the sound of Lilith's voice. Lilith's voice is like a slow drink of whiskey – a throaty purr you can feel in your socks. The kind of voice that'd make a man do pretty much anything, provided she asked just right. And Lilith *always* asked just right. No, it wasn't the timbre of her voice that startled me. It was the fact that it was coming from about three inches behind me.

I tried to spin around to face her, but I'd been crouched low to the ground when she interrupted me, so I wound up landing on my ass. Said ass was now planted smack in the middle of Independence Park – several acres of rolling green criss-crossed with paths of brick, in the center of downtown Bogotá. After my meeting with Danny, I'd walked the streets for hours, trying to get my head straight. Eventually, I wound up here. Truth be told, the walk did nothing to sort out the jumble in my head, but at least the park afforded me the chance to inter Varela's soul. Which was precisely what I was doing when Lilith decided to pop by and scare the living shit out of me.

I propped myself up on one elbow, and willed the thudding

of my meat-suit's heart to slow. Lilith looked as beautiful as ever, her long red hair spilling down over alabaster shoulders to a scant silk dress the color of blood, of lust, of sin. Her long legs gleamed faintly in the evening light, and her bare feet did not disturb the grass beneath. By the smirk that graced her gorgeous face, I'd say her entrance had its intended effect.

"Jesus, Lily – can't you wear a bell or something? You scared this meat-suit half to death!"

Her perfect nose crinkled with distaste at my chosen epithet. "Watch your tongue, Collector. I've no patience for your insolence today."

"That implies that there's a time when you do."

"That's precisely the sort of comment it would be prudent to avoid," she said. "I assure you I've not come here to trade witticisms."

At that, she extended a slender, elegant hand to help me up. I took it, and she lifted me from the ground as easily as a parent might a fallen toddler. For a moment, we stood nose to nose. I was achingly aware of her breasts pressed tight against my chest beneath the thinnest wisp of claret-colored silk, and her scent was so intoxicating, I couldn't speak, or think, or even breathe. On legs unwilling, I took a couple backward steps. The fog cleared, but just a little.

"Then why have you come here?"

"Why else?" she asked. "I came about a job. Or, to be more precise, I came about *two* jobs – the one I'm to assign you, and the one you've as yet failed to do."

Ah, so *that* explained the grumpiness – she was pissed about the Varela job. See, every Collector's got a handler – someone who gives us our assignments, and cracks the whip when we step out of line. Lilith is mine. Near as I can tell, she's an oddity among handlers in that she's not a demon – at least, not exactly. See demons – or the Fallen, as they prefer to be called –

are angels who have turned their back on God, and Lilith is nothing of the kind. As to what she actually is, that's complicated. If you're inclined to believe the books, Lilith was the first woman on Earth, and she was cast out of Eden for refusing to be subservient to Adam – well, for that and her voracious sexual appetites. Now, they say, she rules the night. The southern wind. That she's a lover to all demons, and mother to all incubi and succubi. That she is seduction itself. Whatever else she is, she's my connection with the demon realm, my only formal contact to the hell in which I live. Since Collectors are forbidden from fraternizing with one another, and no demon not assigned to us would deign to associate with such lowly creatures as us, a Collector's handler is all he's got – his boss, his confessor, his corruptor, and his only friend, all rolled into one. You ask me, I think it's hell's way of keeping us docile and in line. Or at least their way of trying.

I tapped a cigarette out of my pack and lit it behind cupped hands. "I haven't *failed* to do anything," I said, exhaling a blue-white plume of smoke in Lilith's direction as I spoke. "The job just took a little longer than expected."

Lilith shot me a withering look from behind the veil of smoke. A sudden breeze kicked up from the south, and the veil lifted, scattered to the wind. "A little longer than expected? Is that what you call this? It's been two *weeks*, Collector. Two weeks since you were tasked with collecting Varela's soul. And in that time, I saw neither hide nor hair of you. I heard nothing by way of update – nothing I could pass along to explain your delinquent behavior. That is simply unacceptable."

"What can I say? Turns out Varela's a hard man to find. *Was*, anyway," I corrected, nodding at the fresh mound of earth that sat beside us at our feet. "Besides, the way I see it, taking a couple extra days to get the job done is a hell of a lot better than crawling back to you with my tail between my knees and telling you I couldn't hack it." I knew it wasn't what she wanted to hear, but it sure as hell beat the truth. The way I figured it, all delays aside, I'd gotten the job done, so any dressing-down I got for dallying was nothing compared to the shit-storm that would ensue if I told her it was a rogue Collector who'd mucked things up – one I'd been in covert contact with on and off for going on sixty years.

"I might accept that from some fledgling Collector, but it is shameful for someone of your talents to hide behind so paltry an excuse."

"Why, Lily, I do believe that was a compliment," I said, an amused smile breaking across my face.

Lilith colored, and screwed her face into a scowl. "I assure you, it was not intended as such. Tell me, Collector, in the two weeks that you've spent gallivanting around this country, have you perchance laid eyes on a newspaper?"

"Can't say as I have," I said. "If you recall, I'm not so good with the Español."

"Oh, I think the pictures would have been quite sufficient."

"What the hell are you talking about? Pictures of what?"

"The commuter train that derailed in Osaka, for one. Or the as yet unidentified plague that wiped an entire Bantu village off the map. And, of course, there was the explosion at the Vatican…"

"What's your point, Lily?"

"My *point*, Collector, is that ever since New York, the détente between heaven and hell has been crumbling around us. These petty skirmishes between the Fallen and their Chosen kin have only gotten worse of late, and both sides are itching for an excuse to escalate into all-out war. Even the mortal world can sense that something's wrong, though of course they've no idea what that something might be. So you see, now is not the time to stray from the straight and narrow –

now's the time to keep your head down and do your job. Maybe in so doing, you'll spare the both of us a world of hurt."

"Keep my head down and do my job? That's pretty fucking rich, coming from you. You think I've forgotten that it was *your* private little war on God that got us into this mess in the first place? That it was *you* who orchestrated the damning of an innocent girl in an attempt to jump-start the End Days? Just because the bureaucrats on both sides are convinced the insurrection died with So'enel doesn't mean that *I've* forgotten. So why don't you save your good little soldier speech for someone who doesn't know it's full of shit."

Lilith's eyes gleamed with rage, and for a moment, I thought she was going to hit me, but instead she took a breath, and the anger drained from her face. "Even if what you say is true – and I'm not granting that it is – your actions in thwarting the MacNeil girl's erroneous collection attracted no small measure of attention. Attention toward you, and by extension toward *me*. It seems to me that, all thoughts of revenge aside, only a fool would try to fan the flames of war while under that kind of scrutiny. Tell me, Collector, do you think me a fool?"

"No," I admitted. "I don't think you're a fool."

"Nor I you," she replied. "Which means that for the moment, at least, our motives are aligned."

"I suppose it does."

"I am glad you see the logic in my position," she said. "But let me offer you a word of warning: should I ever suspect that your motives and mine are no longer aligned, I assure you my response will be as swift as it is final."

"Of that, Lily, I have no doubt."

"Good. Now, let's get down to business, shall we?"

5.

"Hey."

The pale man's eyes fluttered for a moment, and then were still.

"Hey, buddy – wake up!"

His head lolled to one side, and his limbs twitched as if in a dream. A thin stream of drool extended from the corner of his mouth to the white tile floor below.

"I said *wake up*!"

"Hurm," he muttered, though his eyes remained closed. "Grah."

I looked down at my naked torso, at the stab wound an inch above my navel. Though I held my hands as tight to it as I could, blood seeped red-black between my fingers. The wound was muscle-deep, and burned hotter than the bile that still scratched at the back of my throat. The blood loss was making me woozy – if the pale man didn't wake up soon, it was going to be nap time for me as well, and I was pretty sure I wasn't going to like how that scenario played out. And since talking to him wasn't doing the trick, it was time to move on to plan B.

I tossed the sheet off of my naked legs and swung my feet onto the floor. Pain radiated from my stomach in nauseating waves as I sat up, and my eyes clenched shut as I willed myself not to puke. I'd already thrown up once – the channel that traced the perimeter of the stainless steel table on which I sat ran thick with evidence of that fact. But then, that's what happens when you snag yourself a fresh meat-suit.

Twenty minutes ago and a continent away, Lily and I were having our little powwow in the park. Now I was bleeding out in the back room of a mortuary in Aurora, Illinois. Most folks would probably call that a pretty unlikely turn of events. I call it an average workday.

See, the assignment Lily gave me was for a job in Illinois. Some kind of bigwig at the local state house. So when she and I parted, I made my way through Bogotá's evening rush to an internet café so I could find myself a suitable vessel.

Now I'll grant you, the hop from Bogotá to Illinois *sounds* impressive, but when it comes to possession, distance ain't the issue. Once you leave a body, the physical realm sort of drops away, so it makes no difference whether you're traveling three feet or three thousand miles. No, the issue is having a destination to focus on, which in my case means tracking down a fresh corpse.

Which leads me to this guy. His name was Jonathan Gray. An insurance man, according to his obituary. He'd died of carbon monoxide poisoning the night before last, thanks to a family of chimney swifts who'd taken up residence in his flue. I wondered if his company'd ever handicapped the odds against that one. Anyways, he was perfect for my needs, on account of he was brand spanking dead, and his manner of death meant no obvious physical trauma. You get a body that's too beat up, or one that's been embalmed, and you may as well be trying to possess a bean-bag chair for all the good it'll do you. Of course, what I didn't count on was his mortician being a night owl.

With one blood-slick hand, I snatched at the spray nozzle that hung over my head. Sluggish as this meat-suit was, the hose was hard to get a hold of. Eventually, though, I grabbed it, and turned it on my sleeping friend. His whole body went rigid when the cold water hit, and his eyelids sprang open like a pair of roll-up shades. Then he spotted me, and took off in a crab-walk away from me across the floor. Or, at least, he tried, but his hands and feet found no traction on the wet tiles, so he just sort of collapsed into a thrashing mound of knees and elbows.

"Good, you're awake," I said, marveling at the effort it took to form the words. "Now would you mind maybe stitching me back up?"

"B-b-but – I mean, y-y-you... you're..."

"Dead?" I offered. His head bobbed up and down. "Yeah, not so much. Now are you gonna be cool, or am I going to have to hit you with the hose again?"

"N-no!" he shouted, and then he gathered his wits about him and tried again. "That won't be necessary. Oh, God – your stomach!"

"That's what I've been trying to tell you. And what the hell are you doing here, anyway? It's a Sunday night, for Christ's sake!"

"I'm sorry, I – well, you see, I live around back, and some-times, when I can't sleep, I... oh, what's it *matter* what I'm doing here – you're *dead*! Or, at least, you *were*, until you sat up while I was making my incision so I could begin the em-balming process. I guess I must have fainted then, because the next thing I know, you're spraying water on me, and..." He trailed off, blinking hard a couple times as though convinced that with a little willpower, he could rid himself of this whole unpleasant situation. "This is all highly irregular," he added. I wished I could agree.

"Look, I–" I said, and then I paused, narrowing my eyes

appraisingly at the man before me. He was growing paler by the moment, and he appeared a little green as well. I worried he was going to faint again. If that happened, this meat-suit was toast – and if this meat-suit expired, God only knew where I'd end up. Which meant I had to keep this guy calm enough for him to stay conscious – and to do that, I had to keep him talking. "Hey, you got a name?"

"Ethan," he said. He swallowed hard, took a few gulping breaths. "Ethan Strickland."

"Look, Ethan, I understand this is a bit of a shock for you, but I could really use a hand."

"Yes, of course!" he said, rallying a bit. "We've got to get you to a hospital!"

"Not an option," I replied.

"But you're hurt!"

"I'll live. As long as you stitch me up, at least."

He shook his head emphatically.

"What's the problem? You've got needles, right? You've got thread."

"I can't. I'm not a doctor – I'm a mortician!"

"I didn't ask to see your degree."

"But I don't have any anesthetic!"

"You got any whiskey?"

He looked down, said nothing.

"I'll take that as a yes. Get it, and get it quick."

The pale man clambered to his feet, and disappeared from the room. Said room seemed to swim a little bit, and I wondered if he'd be back before I passed out. Then I wondered if he'd be coming back at all, or if he was off calling for an ambulance. But come back he did, with a pair of reading glasses in one hand and a bottle of Michter's in the other.

"Hey," I said, "far be it from me to criticize, but if you need glasses, shouldn't you have been wearing them already?"

"Most of my, uh, *patients*, aren't in a position to complain," he said, handing me the whiskey. I took a long swig straight from the bottle, and then offered it to him.

"That's probably not the best idea."

"Yeah," I said, "but at this point, it probably ain't the worst."

He pursed his lips for a second as he considered what I said, and then he took a pull himself. "All right," he said, as much to himself as to me. "Let's get started. I'm going to need you to sit as still as you can. This is probably going to hurt."

That, it turns out, was an understatement.

I'm not saying it was the worst pain I've ever felt, but that's more a commentary on the sum total of my life experience than it is on the matter at hand. What I *can* say is that from the moment he disinfected the wound to the tug of the last stitch being pulled into place, sitting still was a task akin to resting your hand atop a hot burner and keeping it there. To his great credit, my mortician friend soldiered on until the wound was scaled. When he finished, I collapsed sweating and exhausted onto the stainless steel mortician's table, but I'll be damned if the world didn't seem a little more solid than it had before.

Then again, I guess I'll be damned either way.

"Are you all right?" he asked as I lay panting on the table.

"I will be," I said.

"Yes, I think you will. The bleeding's slowed considerably, and you've got a little more color to your face than you did when you... awoke."

"Yeah," I said, smiling. "You, too." I took another slug of whiskey and passed the bottle on to him. This time, he didn't protest.

"I'm guessing you'd like some clothes," he said.

Truth be told, I had forgotten I was naked, what with the more immediate concern of not dying and all. But the air in the mortuary was cold and damp, and the chill of death still lingered in my meat-suit's bones, so all the sudden, clothes sounded like a fabulous idea. "I wouldn't turn them down," I said.

He nodded toward a garment bag hanging from a hook on the wall beside us. I unzipped it and found a black pinstriped suit, a dress shirt, a buff and blue tie. At the bottom of the bag were a pair of boxers and some socks, as well as a set of loafers.

"This stuff gonna fit?"

"It should," he said, surprised, "it's yours."

I dressed in silence. The suit fit well. The tie I skipped.

"So," he said once I was dressed, "is there someone I should call? If not a doctor, then your wife perhaps?"

"What? No! I mean, I'd hate to bother her this late."

"I think she'd like to know as soon as possible, don't you? After all, your return is nothing short of miraculous. I swear, in all my years, I've never seen anything like it! I expect the medical journals will be chomping at the bit to write about you – and let's not forget the media! No doubt they'll be sure to *growf!*"

I'm guessing the media wouldn't be sure to *growf* – that's just the noise the guy made when I snatched the sheet off the mortician's table and wrapped it around his head. He struggled against me, but I held it fast, twisted tight over his mouth like a gag. Eventually, he caught on he wasn't getting anywhere with his thrashing about, and he dialed it down to the occasional token kick.

"Listen," I said, my lips scant inches from his ear, "I don't want to hurt you, but if you force me to, I will. See, I can't have anybody knowing I'm alive, which means you aren't calling *anyone*, you understand?" At that, his thrashing increased, and he shouted some muffled *mmm-mmm-mmmms* into the sheet around his mouth. I tightened my grip on the sheet and forced him to the floor. With the gag in his mouth, and my knee in the center of his back, the fight once more drained out of him.

"That's more like it," I said. "Now, you've been decent to me up until now, and I appreciate that. But I've got some business to attend to, and I'm pretty sure the second I walk out that door, you're going to be on the horn to the cops. Maybe they believe you that I up and walked out of here, and maybe they don't – but either way, this body'll be missing, and they're going to want to find it. Which means I'm going to have to tie you up."

More thrashing and muffled screams.

"Hey hey *hey*," I said, yanking back on the twisted sheet like a rider reining in a horse. "No need to get touchy, OK? It might not seem like it right now, but I'm doing you a *favor* here. One way or another, *I'm* walking out of herc, and *you're* keeping quiet. My vote's for tying you up, but if you'd rather I left you laid out on a slab, it's your call. No? OK, then – put your hands behind your back, and keep still."

He did as I said. I left the sheet around his mouth, and wrapped each end a couple times around his wrists. Then I moved down to his feet. "Lift 'em up." He bent his knees so that the soles of his black loafers pointed skyward. "Attaboy," I said, wrapping his ankles as I'd wrapped his wrists, and then tying off the ends. The result was more or less your basic hog-tie, though I confess it probably wasn't as tight as it ought to've been. But like I said, the guy'd been decent to me, and besides, all I really needed was a few hours' head start.

"Can you breathe OK?" I asked. He nodded – or tried, at least. "Good. Now my guess is, you can work your way outta that in a couple of hours, and if you manage to, then good on you. In case you don't, though, I'll put in a call to the cops as soon as I get to where I'm going, and let 'em know where they can find you. Sound good?"

"*Mmm-mmmm!*" he replied, wiggling around in a manner that suggested he thought there wasn't much about this situation that sounded good to him. I tried not to take it personal.

"All right, then. Oh, and Ethan?"

"*Mmm*?"

"I'm afraid I'm gonna need a car."

6.

Scalding water beat down on my face, my chest, my injured stomach, pinking up my borrowed skin and washing the grit of this God-awful day from my weary limbs. Going on two days now, I supposed, since the midday sun was high overhead by the time I'd arrived at this shit-hole of a motel. But I hadn't slept a wink since the bus ride to Bogotá, a meat-suit and a continent ago, so the last thirty-odd hours bled together into a tangled mess of pain and guilt and shame. Then again, I guess the same could be said of the past sixty-odd years.

Snippets of my conversation with Danny kept running through my head like a record on repeat. Lilith's admonitions about the straight and narrow aside, I couldn't shake the feeling that I should have done something more to help him. But there wasn't anything I *could* do – and besides, Danny's problems were his own. After all that had passed between us, I didn't owe him a fucking thing.

Thing is, if I really believed that, why couldn't I stop thinking about it?

When the shower finally ran cold, I shut it off and grabbed the coarse white towel that hung from the ring beside it. The motel was a run-down little mom-and-pop place on the outskirts of Springfield, just off of Highway 55 – The Land of Lincoln Motor Lodge, according to the sign around front. The room was courtesy of one Mr Ethan Strickland, a little object lesson about the perils of leaving one's wallet in the center console of one's car. The car in question, a faded blue Fiesta two-door with all the roominess and pickup of a riding mower, was in a spot out back, out of view of the street in case ol' Ethan managed to wriggle free of his constraints and notify the authorities of its theft. The room I wasn't as worried about – the desk clerk wouldn't run Ethan's credit card until check-out, and since I planned on skipping out before then, I'd be long gone by the time the charge posted to his account. I know I told him I'd put in a call to the cops once I got where I was going, to let them know where they could find him, but after the day I'd had, I didn't think Ethan would begrudge me a few hours' grace for a shower and a little shut-eye. OK, that's not entirely true. I was pretty sure he *would* begrudge me that, but truth be told, I didn't care.

At least today's collection had gone well enough. Guy was a big muckety-muck at the local state house who, after an un-successful gubernatorial run back in '98, cut a deal with a demon to curse anyone elected to the post. He was allowed to stick around for long enough to see the next two dudes go up the river on corruption charges, but he won't be around to see what happens to the third. The guy was a politician to the last: when I showed up to collect him, he tried for half an hour to talk me out of it. Once he saw that it was useless, though, he didn't put up much of a fight. Eh – if it's true what they say about hell being a committee, I'm sure he'll feel right at home.

Once the job was done, exhaustion hit me like a cartoon anvil, and I set out looking for someplace to lay my head. Even when I've got the cash – which for the record ain't that often – I tend to avoid your nicer hotels, because their staffs are typically friendly and attentive, and I've got no use for either. Hence my shabby motel digs. But hey, the shower was plenty hot, and the bed looked soft, so shabby or not, it was good enough for me.

I dried off, and padded naked to the bed. Then I slipped my boxers back on and switched on the TV. CNN was covering a ferry accident somewhere off the coast of Maine. A dozen bodies had thus far been recovered, their skin stripped from their flesh by the force of the blast that had caused the ship to founder. The survivors they plucked from the chilly waters of the bay reported that immediately prior to the blast, two passengers had been heard arguing atop the upper deck. One of them was a local named Larry Thibodeau, though those who'd spoken to him that day claimed he hadn't been himself, and one obviously distraught witness said there was something wrong with his eyes – she claimed they flickered with black fire. I'm sure the authorities just assumed she was in shock, but my guess was, she'd caught a glimpse of a demon walking around in Larry's skin. The other man was a stranger to them, and apart from the fact that he was of average height and build, not a one of them could remember what he looked like. That's pretty much standard operating procedure for angels working out in the open; they're far too dignified to take human form, opting instead for a sort of vague sketch of a person that human eyes slide right off of.

Lily was right: these skirmishes between the demon realm and their angelic counterparts were getting out of hand. But right now, I was too tired to care, so I changed the channel in search of something I could ignore. By the way, you know there's a whole channel dedicated to game shows?

Anyway, I turned down the comforter and pulled back the sheets, wanting nothing more than to collapse into a nice, warm bed. And I would have, too, if the damn thing wasn't already occupied.

The occupant in question was a fat black beetle about as big as a deck of cards, sitting in the center of the bed as if I'd interrupted it mid-nap. Although on closer examination, it wasn't really *sitting* at all – it was sort of standing on its head, its ass-end propped up on what looked to be a wad of dirt. As I watched, its rear legs kicked out behind it, propelling the small earthen ball pillow-ward. Then the creature shambled backward after the ball, pressing onward until its ass was once more propped atop it.

The beetle looked like it was getting set to start its little maneuver all over again, but I'd seen enough. I grabbed the trash bin from the corner and used it to scoop up the critter and its payload both. Then I dumped them in the bushes outside my door and returned to my room, setting the chain behind me.

I thought about calling the front desk for a new set of sheets, but I really didn't want the attention – and besides, when you make your living inhabiting the bodies of the recently departed, bugs sort of come with the territory. Last year, on a job in Oxford, I found a dude on a tip from Lilith who'd been laid out on the floor of his apartment with the heat cranked for the better part of a week. Fucking meat-suit was crawling with flies by the time I got to him, and to make matters worse, in life the guy'd apparently been scared shitless of bugs. A phobia that deep-seated goes well beyond memory – that shit lives in your *bones*. So when I woke that meat-suit from his big sleep, he had a full-on, grade-A panic attack. I had to park my ass in the shower for an hour before my meat-suit calmed down, and even when I got those fuckers off, his skin never stopped crawling. I guess the moral of the story is one beetle does not a freak-out make. Well, that, or Lilith has one sick sense of humor.

Anyways, once I climbed into bed, the beetle was forgotten. Exhausted as I was, I fell asleep in minutes. Would've stayed that way, too, if the goddamn tapping hadn't roused me.

It was an odd, irregular sort of noise, quiet but persistent. At first I thought it was the television, which still prattled on quietly atop the dresser and bathed the room in eerie, blue-white light. When I shut the TV off, though, the room was plunged into darkness, but the tapping kept right on going.

I flicked on the bedside lamp and looked around. Nothing. Pissed now, I tossed off the blankets and swung my feet down to the floor, determined to find the source of the noise. But the faucet wasn't dripping, and as far as I could tell by pressing my ear to the wall, the rooms on either side of me were vacant.

That's when I realized it was coming from the window.

I yanked open the curtains, half-expecting to see a couple prepubescent pranksters, merrily tapping at the glass so they could rob me of my sleep. What I did see rocked me back. It was my little beetle-friend, paying me back for the kindness of not killing it by bouncing off of my window, over and over again. And the bastard had brought reinforcements. There were dozens of them – not just beetles, but also massive flying roaches, as well as moths and locusts, wasps and mayflies. The largest of them ricocheted off the glass only to regroup and try again, while the smaller ones slammed into the window like tiny kamikazes, splattering into oblivion against the pane.

I confess, the scene had me a bit unnerved, but what the hell could I really do? Persistent though they were, the little fuckers were outside, and so long as they stayed that way, they were all right by me. I shut the curtains and snatched my still-damp towel from where I'd let it fall beside the bed, twisting it up and laying it along the seam between door and floor by way of insurance against any future six-legged visitors. Then I climbed back into bed and pulled a pillow over my head.

This time, sleep didn't come so easy, but it eventually did come. I awoke hours later, my face still buried in the pillow, to the persistent buzzing of the alarm clock. Fucking thing must've been set by whoever stayed here last. After the night I'd had, they'd be lucky if I didn't hunt them down and throttle them for their thoughtlessness.

I pulled the pillow down tighter over my head, but it wasn't any use – that buzzing refused to be ignored. Fine, then – I'd just have to shut it up. I took a blind swipe in the general direction of the bedside table. A swing and a miss. I tried again. My hand whacked the corner of the table and came back smarting. The third time, I managed to give the alarm a good wallop, but the buzzing didn't stop, and why the fuck was my hand sticky?

I tossed off the pillow and looked around. Then my whole body clenched as revulsion washed over me. Every surface of the room was coated in a shifting mass of bugs – crawling, scrabbling, flitting back and forth with the electric hum of a thousand insect wings. They covered the floor, the ceiling, the bed on which I laid. A thick smear of snot-green flecked with shards of black encrusted the top of the alarm clock where I'd smacked it, and as I watched, the smear and then the clock itself disappeared beneath a teeming swarm of scratching, hissing, buzzing things.

It was then I realized that *I* was covered in them, too. Their tiny legs pricked against my arms, my chest, my back. I could feel them winding through my hair. When one sought refuge in my ear, I shuddered, thankfully shaking it free. I tried in vain to brush away the rest, but there were too many, and they just kept on coming. Thousands of them. Millions. They were pouring into the room from a vent high above the bed, its louvers bent out of shape by the sheer magnitude of the invading force. From the thick paste of carnage the creatures pushed through to enter the room, it was clear that thousands of them must've died in their attempt to gain entry – but why? What in God's name were they doing here?

The answer was right in front of me, but in my panic, I almost didn't see it. There, atop the shifting insect landscape before me, was my little beetle-friend. It drifted toward me from the foot of the bed as if by magic, its cohorts beneath it conveying it ever closer.

And with it, its payload.

Once the beetle and its earthen ball reached me, it stopped. The mass of insects beneath it still boiled with activity, all red and brown and iridescent blue, but the fat black beetle held its ground, regarding me with what I couldn't help but think was an expectant gaze. Then it nudged the ball toward me once more with one spindly, bristle-laden leg.

Gingerly, I accepted the proffered package, and the sea of insects seemed to calm a little – not receding, exactly, but quieting, as though waiting for my response. My heart was anything but quiet as it thudded painfully in my chest. What I'd taken for a ball of dirt wasn't dirt at all, though its surface was filthy enough that my mistake was understandable. No, what the tiny creature had been carrying was in fact a small bundle of cloth – once military drab, but now black from the dirt in which it had been buried.

I recognized that bundle. Of course, I *should* have – I'd buried it two days and a continent ago.

It was a soul – *Varela's* soul. And suddenly, the insects that surrounded me made sense.

These creatures were Deliverants.

They were Deliverants, and they were angry.

I wasn't yet sure why, but I was beginning to get an idea. Whatever was going on, Danny Young had set me up.

He'd set me up, and he was going to pay.

7.

That fucking son of a bitch. In all my time as a Collector, I'd never once had occasion to interact with my Deliverants, and now after my meeting with Danny, they flat-out reject the soul I'd buried? That was too much of a coincidence for me to swallow. The question was, *why* had they rejected it? What exactly had Danny done? I didn't know, but I had an idea how I might find out. So I left the motel in my rearview, and headed out into the night to get some answers.

I eyed the door before me. It was typical for the front door of an apartment – stainless steel, and reinforced, at that. But the jamb was standard pressure-treated lumber, and the building wasn't young, which meant that all that held this tank of a door closed was a latch installed in a plank of aging wood. Not great if subtle's what you're shooting for, but easy enough to pop if you don't mind a little noise.

Right now, I didn't mind a little noise.

I glanced back toward the front of the building where I'd left the Fiesta, but the night was getting on, and there wasn't anyone about. The place itself was nestled in an upscale residential neighborhood, and from the curb, it looked to be yet another in a line of neoclassical homes, all stark white and austere, with a series of four columns flanking its massive, transomed entryway. But the hearse in the large circle drive out front and the tasteful, somber sign beside it indicated otherwise. No, the only living going on around here was in the apartment tucked around back – and that's just where I was headed.

The first kick made a hell of a noise, but the door didn't budge. The second, and the wood began to splinter. If this were some cheesy dime-store novel, I suppose the third time woulda done the trick, but the fact is, I had to kick that fucking door a half a dozen times before it finally gave, swinging inward with a sickening crack and a hail of wooden shards.

I was inside in a flash. Ethan Strickland was cowering behind an upturned kitchen table, a Louisville Slugger in one hand and a cordless phone in the other. He was trying desperately to dial the cops, but his hands were shaking so bad, it was all he could manage not to drop the phone – that, or bean himself with the bat.

I spotted the base of the phone on an end table beside the couch, and I dove for it, wrenching the phone cord from the wall. Ethan stared in horror for a moment, and then leapt at me with a guttural – if not entirely manful – scream, his bat brandished high above his head.

I rolled. He missed. His bat instead met the floor with a *crack*, and Ethan yelped in pain and surprise as his wispy frame was wracked by the reverberations. He tried to wheel toward me, but I'd already found my feet, and I sidestepped the blow with ease. Then I wrenched the bat from his hands and drew it back to strike. It was instinct, nothing more, and when I saw him cowering on the floor, his hands raised to protect his tear-streaked face, I tossed the bat aside. Then I extended a hand to help him up. But he just lay there, cowering, and regarded my hand as though it were an asp about to strike.

"You OK?" I asked him.

He said nothing. I stooped a bit to bring my hand closer, and he flinched.

"Look, I'm sorry about the entrance, but I had a feeling if I knocked, you weren't going to let me in."

Still nothing – that is, unless you counted the sobbing.

"Damn it, Ethan, I'm not here to *hurt* you – I'm here because I need your *help*! Now will you take my hand so I can help you up?"

He blinked at me a moment, and then accepted my offer with one trembling, hesitant hand. I helped him up off the floor. He wiped the tears from his cheeks with his sleeve, gulping air all the while, and cast a sly sidelong glance toward the gaping apartment door.

"I wouldn't," I said, and he deflated slightly.

"P-p-please d-don't…" he stammered as he tried to bring his panicked breathing under control. "Don't tie me up again. I couldn't take it."

"Yeah, I'm sorry about that, but it was for your own good. As for whether I'm going to have to do it again, that's going to depend a lot on you. Besides, you look like you came out of it OK."

"Took me six hours to get out," he said. "My legs still hurt like hell."

"You call the cops?"

"No," he said too quickly.

"OK, I'll take that as a yes." His eyes bugged out in panic, and he went a little green. "It's OK, Ethan – I would've too if I were you. But it does complicate things a little. Which means you're going to have to make it up to me."

His eyes narrowed. He took a small step backward. "What do you mean, make it up to you? Make it up to you *how*?"

Fuck it, I thought. The truth was probably the safest thing I could tell him – after all, who in their right mind was gonna believe him?

"The fact is, Ethan, I am not the guy they wheeled in to your funeral home. That guy's dead and gone – I'm just borrowing his body for a while. As for who or what I *actually* am, that's complicated, and you're probably better off not knowing. Suffice it to say, I'm a guy who's got a job to do, just like you. Now, if you help me do my job, I promise you I'll walk out that door tonight and you'll never see me again. If, on the other hand, you *don't...*"

Ethan swallowed hard. It seemed he got the picture. Good thing, too, because that whole implied violence thing was nothing but a bluff – the worst I was going to do to the guy was tie him up again until I got what I came for. Still, this night was going to go a whole lot smoother if he'd cooperate, so I'm glad he was on board.

"W-what," he said, wincing at the quaver in his voice. "What is it that you need?"

"What I *need*, Ethan, is a body."

"You sure this is the best you got?"

Ethan shrugged his shoulders. With his willowy frame, he looked sort of like a twitchy scarecrow. "It's been a slow week, death-wise. Besides, uh, you, Mr Frohman's all we've got. He was the sausage king of Chicago!" he added helpfully.

"Yeah," I said, "he looks it."

Though the guy wasn't an inch over five-four, he must've gone four hundred pounds, and every inch of him was covered in a thick mat of hair – well, every inch that wasn't on his *head*. Even in death, his face had a sort of pinkish hue; I couldn't help but think it was his sausage subjects who'd eventually dethroned him. Eh, I thought, he'll do. And hell, it's not like I'd have to worry about him making a break for it.

I fished Varela's bundled soul from my pocket and picked at the dirt-caked twine until finally, the knot untied. The tiny orb swirled gray-black atop the scrap of fabric in my open hand, and Ethan stared at it, entranced. "What *is* that?" he asked, his voice full of awe and wonder.

"Gumball," I replied. The pale man frowned. He was standing at the corner of the mortuary table, scant inches from Mr Frohman's bald pate. I jerked my head by way of indication, and said, "You may want to stand back a little – this is liable to get messy."

Ethan took a big step back, and I drew in a deep, halting breath. Truth is, I didn't know if this'd work. I'd never done anything like this before – as far as I knew, *no one* had. But hell, a bad plan is better than no plan at all, right?

In one swift motion, I grabbed the soul from the fabric upon which it sat, and plunged it into Mr Frohman's meaty chest. For a brief moment, I was engulfed in a swirl of light and sound. Then the Frohman body gasped, and the world came rushing back.

The wooly mammoth of a man sat up, his eyes wide, his limbs flailing madly. Then he doubled over and puked. Ethan let out a whimper, and crumpled to the tiles. That made twice in two days. Still, you couldn't really blame him. At least this guy he managed not to cut.

Frohman/Varela's eyes were wild, panicked. His massive chest heaved as it sucked in breath after labored breath. His neck craned as he took in the scene around him: me, standing over him, expectant; Ethan, lying unconscious on the floor; him, draped in white as he floundered on a stainless steel slab. Despite myself, I felt a stab of pity for him – as I well know, that first wake-up is pretty damn traumatic. But when he decided it was time to flee, my sympathy evaporated.

I had to give it to him – for a big guy, the man could move.

He rolled away from me, the sheet falling from him as his feet hit the floor on the far side of the slab. He got halfway to the door before his limbs gave out on him. It's always that way with a fledgling meat-suit – it takes a while for the body to acquiesce to your commands. And never more so than your first time out, which is why I didn't even bother giving chase.

The big man hit the tiles with a *fwap*, and I was on him in seconds. I rolled him over with a nudge of my shoe, and slapped the look of blind panic from his face.

"*¿Habla ingles?*" I asked him, but he just let out a wail of confusion and panic.

"*¿Habla ingles?*" I repeated. "*¿Como te llamas?*"

He blurted out a couple nonsense syllables as he struggled with his unfamiliar meat-suit. Then he squinched his eyes and shook his head as if to clear it. I cocked my hand back to slap him a second time. It seemed to do the trick. He grabbed my wrist with one sausage-fingered hand to still the coming blow, and, anger glinting in his eyes, he finally found his voice.

"Listen, asshole, I don't speak Mexican, so slapping me ain't gonna help! You try that shit again, you're liable to lose your fucking hand, *comprende?*"

I stared at him a second, dumbfounded. "You speak English?"

"That a trick question? Yeah, dipshit – I speak English."

"I'm guessing your name isn't Pablo Varela then, huh?"

"Wow, a gold star for the good guesser."

"So who the hell are you?"

"Why the fuck should I tell *you?*"

I plunged my free hand into his chest and gave his soul a twist. The big man's face contorted in fear and pain, and reflexively, he released my wrist from his grasp.

"'Cause I'm the guy who rescued you from oblivion – and if you don't start talking, I'm the guy who'll send you *back.*"

"Jesus, dude – that fucking *hurts*. You try that voodoo shit again, I'm gonna break your fucking face."

Sure, his words were plenty tough, but they were betrayed by the frightened look in his eyes.

"Really? *That's* the way you wanna play it? Me, I'd prefer to keep this all friendly-like, but you want to play the bad-ass, be my guest – we'll see how far it gets you."

I drove my fingers into his chest once more. This time, he tried to fight, but it wasn't any use – with his soul held tight inside my fist, his borrowed body wouldn't listen. Once his thrashing died down, I let him go. He collapsed back onto the tiles, sweating and exhausted.

"Gio," he said, sucking wind. "My name is Gio."

At that, I deflated a little. I don't know what I was hoping for – some kind of clue, I guess, as to what Danny was up to – but the name meant nothing to me. "Tell me, Gio," I said, sighing, "you got a last name?"

"Gio *is* my last name. My first name's Francis, but nobody calls me that but my mother."

Suddenly, the pieces fell into place. "Gio," I said. "As in, short for Giordano?"

"That's right," he said, eyeing me with sudden suspicion. "How the hell'd you know that?"

I thought back to my meeting with Danny, to the sob-story he'd spun about his missing soul. "The bloke was a mob enforcer out of Vegas by the name of Giordano," he'd said. "Only now his soul is missing. Stolen right out from under me." But that wasn't exactly true, now, was it? Turns out, Danny had Giordano's soul the whole time. Which meant the whole fucking meeting was nothing but an elaborate bait-and-switch. He must've figured that when I buried Giordano's soul, his Deliverants would be appeased, and he could go about his merry way with his stolen Varela, leaving me to twist in the wind.

But why? What in the hell could he possibly want with Varela's soul? And more importantly, how the hell was I going to get it back?

"Hey, buddy," Gio said, "you still there?"

"What?" I said, snapping out of my reverie. "Yeah. I'm still here." For now, I added mentally – because once my superiors caught wind of the fact that I'd lost Varela's soul, they were going to shelve me for sure. Which meant I had to find that soul, and fast.

"You wanna tell me how you knew my name?"

"I know your name because I heard it from the guy who was sent to kill you."

"This guy," he asked, his face clouded with sudden anger, "he a friend of yours?"

"He *was*," I said.

"Yeah? The way you say that, it don't sound like you and him are very buddy-buddy now."

"No," I said, "it really doesn't."

"Well, it's a shame for him he missed me, 'cause now that fucker's gonna hafta pay."

"I hope that's true," I said, "but Danny didn't miss."

"The fuck're you talking about?"

"Look at yourself, man – this the body you remember?"

He did. It wasn't. He kinda freaked a little, then, but once I calmed him down, I explained as best I could. When I finished, he sat there stunned for a while, saying nothing, and occasionally shaking his head in disbelief. Eventually, though, he found his voice.

"So I'm dead, then, huh?"

"Yup."

"And damned to hell for all eternity."

"Yup."

"And *you* – you're some kind of fucking Grim Reaper!"

I let out a bark of a laugh, shrill and humorless. "More like
the devil's mailman," I replied.

"I dunno, dude – I think you're selling yourself short. You
gave me another body. Another *chance*."

"More like a short reprieve."

He considered that a moment. "So what's to keep me from
taking off? Making a run for it, and starting somewhere new?"

"Well, *me*, for one – I mean, you've got to know I can't just
let you walk. And even if I *did*, they'd hunt you down. Your
soul belongs to hell now – and believe me, these guys always
get their man. My guess is you wouldn't last a week. Besides,
you're not going to take off on me – not when we have a job
to do."

"*Really*," he said, his voice dripping sarcasm. "You and me
working together like some kinda buddy-comedy? I gotta tell
you, dude, I don't see it. I mean, ain't you one of the guys I
should be hiding from in the first place? What makes you
think I'd wanna help you?"

"Because the man who killed you also fucked me over but
good. Because I plan to hunt him down and make him pay.
And because right now, you're the best lead I've got. So you
tell me – you want to see the bastard hang?"

Hc seemed to mull it over for a second, and then he smiled.
"Shit," he said. "Just tell me where we start."

I helped the big man to his feet, and looked him up and
down. "Why don't we start by getting you some clothes?"

8.

"So how's this work, exactly?" Gio asked, tucking his shirt into his dress pants and straightening his tie. "How'm I gonna help you find this guy?"

"When a Collector takes a mark's soul, there's this *moment* – a moment when that Collector experiences the lifetime of joy and sorrow, of happiness and regret, that brought the mark into their grasp. The thing is, that moment cuts both ways, which means that once it comes to pass, the collected can forever sense the presence of the person who collected them. That isn't usually much of an issue, on account of once the collection happens, the collected's *dead*, but in the rare instance a Collector makes a play and misses, it can make their second try a bitch. And if, after you're collected, you're unlucky enough to wind up a Collector yourself, that ability to sense the one who collected you never fades – it gnaws at you for all eternity."

"Wait – you're telling me I'm like some kind of asshole compass? That you're gonna follow me to the dude who screwed us over?"

"I wish it were that simple," I said. "But for you to sense Danny, we're going to have to get you close to him. Which means we need to find out where he's gone off to – and to do that, we need to figure out what he's playing at."

"How we gonna do *that*?"

"I'm not sure," I admitted. "But I've got an idea where we can start."

"Well, let's get going, then – we're burnin' daylight! I think it's high time we made this fucker pay!"

I had nothing to say to that, so I just gritted my teeth and nodded. Truth be told, Gio's enthusiasm made me feel like shit. He had no idea what I was about to drag him into. He had no idea he was only here because Danny's plan to appease his Deliverants by getting me to inter his soul had failed. He had no idea that Danny would be as desperate to put him in the ground as I was to bury Varela.

He didn't know because I didn't tell him. Telling him would have only complicated matters, and matters were plenty complicated already. Besides, it wasn't like telling him would've made a difference. Gio here was damned either way – the only question was whether he was going help me extract his pound of flesh before he went. And until that time came, I didn't need him getting cute on me. So I didn't tell him.

Keeping Gio in the dark was the right call – the smart play. But knowing that didn't make me feel like any less a heel for doing it.

Just then, a whimpering alerted me to the fact that our mortician friend had awoken. He looked to have a pretty good goose-egg on his forehead from where he'd connected with the floor tiles, and as I watched, he collected himself into a ball and began rocking back and forth, knees hugged tight to his chest. His eyes were fixed on a spot on the floor six inches in front of his shoes, and he was muttering something to himself, though what it was, I couldn't hear. A prayer, I suppose, if he were so inclined. Or it coulda been a grocery list.

"The hell's the matter with *him*?" asked Gio.

"Cut him some slack," I said. "Poor bastard's had two corpses get up off his table in as many days."

"Well, then, you'd think he'd be getting used to it by now."

I approached Ethan, crouching down beside him and putting a hand on his shoulder. It was a friendly gesture, but he flinched nonetheless. "Listen, Ethan," I said, in the sort of tone you might use to soothe a frightened child, "you did good. You honored your end of the deal, and now I'm going to honor mine. Me and Gio – er, Mr Frolman – are taking off, and my guess is, you'll never see either of us again, OK?"

I don't know if he heard me. I suppose it didn't matter. I'd said my piece – and besides, once we were out of Ethan's life, everything would eventually return to what, in the world of a mortician, passed for normal. That was more than you could say for either me or Gio here, a fact that went a long way toward blunting my sympathy and assuaging my guilt.

Gio, for his part, was busy struggling into the jacket of his burial suit – a jacket that, with the proper support, could've sheltered a family of four. Once he managed to squeeze himself into it, he sat down to pull on his shoes, grunting with exertion as he tried to reach his feet.

"Jesus, dude, it ain't that I'm ungrateful for you bringing me back and all, but next time you find me a body, you think I could see something in a medium? I mean this guy's freakin' *gaaah–*"

At that last, he tossed his loafer to the floor in sudden fright, the intended end of his sentence forgotten. When the shoe hit the tiles, a fat orange-brown cockroach spilled out of it and skittered under the stainless steel mortuary table. Gio recovered quickly, blushing at his startlement and retrieving his errant loafer. I, on the other hand, did not. At the sight of the cockroach, a chill crawled up the length of my spine as though on spindly insect legs, and a cold sweat broke out across my face and neck.

"Hey, Captain Mumbles," Gio yelled toward the fetal Ethan, full of false bluster now in compensation for his bout of fear, "what kind of funeral home are you runnin' anyway? I mean, I know you keep dead bodies and shit in here, but can't you fucking *clean*? You owe better to the folks that come through here than to bury 'em full a roach eggs." Ethan didn't reply – he just rocked and stared at nothing. "Hey, asshole," Gio continued, "I'm *talkin'* to you!"

"Leave him alone," I said, my voice thin and tinny to my ears. "The roach wasn't his fault. You want to blame somebody, you're going to have to take it up with me."

Gio balked at my admonition, wheeling toward me with an eye-roll and a derisive snort. "What, you moonlighting as his housekeeper?"

"Francis," I said, my voice dripping quiet menace, "I'm telling you to drop it."

Something in my tone must've convinced him, because the predatory smile that his chiding of Ethan had brought to his face faltered, and then disappeared altogether. He followed my gaze to the spot where the cockroach had disappeared from sight and stared at it with an expression like clouds gathering. "So that thing," he said, his words devoid now of all humor, "it's like some kinda bad guy or something?"

I shook my head, though my eyes never left the shadowy underside of the mortuary slab. "More like some kind of sign," I replied.

"OK, then, a sign. But a sign of *what*?"

"A sign we're running out of time."

"Get your things," I said, "we're going."

"Everything I got in the world right now, I'm wearing. Where the hell we going?"

I drew my thumb and forefinger across my lips as if to zip them, and then nodded toward the door, still staring at the spot on the floor where the cockroach had been. Truth be told, I didn't know if it could understand what we were saying, or whether my reticence would delay my Deliverants' pursuit either way. What I *did* know was that I wasn't gagging for a repeat of the whole bugs-in-my-motel-room incident, so for now, discretion seemed the better part of valor.

Out in the driveway, Gio caught sight of Ethan's tiny, ancient hatchback. "You're kidding me, right? I seen Matchbox cars bigger than this thing. No way this dude you stuck me in is gonna fit inside that piece of shit."

"Yeah, well, he's going to have to, because it's all we've got."

He eyed the Fiesta up and down and shook his head in disbelief. I had to admit, the car didn't look much larger than his Frohman-suit, and its faded blue exterior was flecked with enough rust to make me wonder if it was structurally sound enough to carry him. As we climbed into it, I heard him mutter something about clowns and sardines, but it was kind of hard to hear him over the squeaking of the shocks.

I thumbed the ignition, and nothing happened. I frowned, and tried again. Nothing still. Three tries later, the old girl sprung to life, but I guess my frown stayed put, because Gio clapped me on the shoulder and smiled.

"Hey, man, lighten up! We ain't neither of us dead yet – we may as well have some fun while we're here! 'Sides, you and me decked out in a coupla kick-ass suits, hunting down the shit-bag who killed me? We're like the fucking Blues Brothers, man! We're on a mission from *God*."

I'll admit, mob stooge or not, I felt sorry for the guy. Poor son of a bitch was wrong on so many counts, I didn't even know where to start. So I didn't. Didn't bother to point out that he and I were dead already, or that if God was the one pulling our strings, He was a supreme deity with one sick sense of humor.

No, I didn't say any of that. Instead, I shook my head at the damned man's pointless optimism and threw the Fiesta into reverse, wincing as it labored backward into the quiet suburban street.

9.

The Shady Acres Rest Home was a sprawling clapboard mansion in the southern style, nestled in the sun-scorched Alabama countryside about an hour's drive from Montgomery. Years of unrelenting heat and humidity had reduced the once-white paint to a blistered patchwork the color of old newspapers, which draped like lace over the ash-gray wood beneath. In the lot beside the building, a few dusty old sedans glinted in the afternoon light – staff, I assumed, because the row of spots marked *Visitors* was vacant until I piloted the Fiesta into the one nearest the entrance.

I climbed out of the car and felt the hot breath of the Gulf breeze against my cheeks. We'd been driving for going on fifteen hours, Gio and I, our only stop three frantic minutes at a strip-mall in St Louis spent swapping the Fiesta's plates with a pair from a navy blue VW Rabbit. Gio spent the first few hours of the drive peppering me with inane questions – about my job, my life, about the places I'd been and the people I'd dispatched. He'd also blathered at length about the guys he'd whacked and the scams he'd pulled working for the Family out in Vegas. No doubt he felt some kind of kinship between us, seeing my job as nothing more than the supernatural extension of his own. But it wasn't – not to me, at least. Unlike

Gio, I took no joy in what I did, and God willing, never would. Besides, thanks to Danny, I already had more friends than I could handle – the last thing I needed was another. So I mostly kept quiet, and waited for Gio to talk himself out. Somewhere around Nashville, road-weariness set in, and he lapsed into a sort of drowsy, companionable silence. I'm not gonna lie, I was grateful for the quiet, but if you want to know the whole truth, I was glad to have some company as well. So long as he kept his yap shut, at least.

"So," Gio said, the Fiesta rocking as he grabbed hold of the oh-shit handle above the passenger seat and hoisted his fat frame out of the car, "you gonna tell me what the hell we're doing here? Besides sweating to death, that is," he added, mopping his prodigious brow with his tie.

"We're here to see an old friend," I replied.

Gio eyed the nursing home with skepticism. "Exactly how *old* a friend are we talkin' here?"

"Old enough."

"This dude gonna know where to find the guy who offed me?"

"No, he's not."

"Then why did we come all this way to see him?"

"Because unless I'm much mistaken, he's going to lead us to someone who might. You got the time?"

"Last I saw, the clock on the dash read quarter to one."

"We'd best get moving, then, unless you feel like waiting around here till next week."

By the look on his sweaty, heat-flushed face, I'd say he didn't much relish the thought of spending the week in such steamy environs. Which was fine by me, because *I* sure as hell didn't – though my reluctance had nothing to do with the heat. No, for me it was more the frickload of angry, crawly Deliverants on our tail that made me reluctant to stay *anyplace* for one second longer than we had to.

Inside, the lobby of the nursing home was quiet. A ceiling fan turned lazily above an empty seating area comprising a rose damask sofa and two matching armchairs, all at least as old and timeworn as the building itself. A wooden reception desk ran the length of the far wall, and behind it sat a plump, silver-haired woman in pale blue scrubs, her nose buried in an Elmore Leonard novel. As we approached, she set the book down and flashed us a tired, perfunctory half-smile that looked as if it had walked into the room only to forget what it was doing there.

"Can I help you, darlin'?" she asked, her vowels stretching pleasantly beneath the weight of her drawl.

"Yes," I said, "I'm here to see Mariella Hamilton."

"And your relation to the patient?"

"I'm her grandson."

"Her *grandson*," she echoed, incredulous.

"That's right."

"What about him?" she asked, raising an eyebrow as she took in Gio's massive frame. "He her grandson, too?"

"No," I said, flashing her my best we're-all-friends-here smile. "But he's an old friend of the family – grew up a few doors down. I'm sure she'd like to see him."

The woman shook her head. "Sorry, darlin', but if he ain't family, he'll have to wait here. The rules, you understand."

Gio made like he was gonna object, but I cut him off. "That's fine," I said. "He'll wait."

The way the woman eyed the two of us, it was clear she didn't believe a word of what I'd said. But then she shrugged, as if deciding she didn't care much either way. "Mariella's in room 2123," she said, her words tinged with weary resignation. "Just follow the hallway to your left until you reach the staircase, and–"

"Thanks," I said. "I know the way."

• • • •

Mariella Hamilton was a tiny, frail specimen of a woman, nestled in the soft white blankets of her hospital bed like a champagne flute wrapped for transport. Looking at her, I couldn't fault the nurse downstairs her skepticism at my claim we were related. Her skin was the color of brown sugar – a far cry from my meat-suit's pasty white – and stretched tight and shiny across her fragile bones. Though she couldn't be a day under eighty, her hair was still largely black, and pulled into a severe bun, so that what few streaks of white were present swirled like creamer through coffee atop the contours of her head. Her eyes were closed, as always, and her hands were crossed atop her breast. Clipped to one finger was a sensor, which ran to the heart monitor that blipped a quiet rhythm from its perch beside the bed – the same rhythm it had blipped, without fail or deviation, for the last twenty-seven years.

I leaned in close and kissed her forehead. Then I took a seat in the chair beside the bed, gathering her hands into my own. I closed my eyes and bowed my head, my lips moving in silent prayer. It was only when the sound of footfalls echoed through the room that I raised my head again, blinking against the sudden brightness as I turned to see the source of the interruption.

Turns out the interruption was a hulking kid of maybe twenty-three, with thick arms, dishwater hair, and dull, close-set eyes that glowered out at the world from beneath a brow that could have sheltered woodland creatures in a storm. He was dressed in the same pale blue scrubs as the woman downstairs, though his were nowhere near as clean, and he was carrying a tray laden with alcohol swabs, a rubber tourniquet, and a handful of needle-tipped test tubes of the type used to collect blood. When he saw me sitting there, he froze. Confusion and good manners played tug-of-war with his face. Eventually, good manners won out, and he smiled, continuing into the room and setting his tray down on the bedside table beside me.

"Sorry to barge in on you like that," he said, his words tinged with the same drawl as the nurse I'd spoken to downstairs. "Mariella here doesn't get company too often. Truth be told, you scared the hell out of me!"

"Did I?" I asked.

"You did, at that," he said, looping the tourniquet around Mariella's arm above the elbow and tapping at one suddenly protruding vein. Seated as I was, the kid towered over me, the scent of soap and sweat and sick clinging to his massive frame.

"So," he said, his eyes never leaving his task, "how is it you know ol' Mariella?"

"Actually, I don't. It's Quinn I'm here to see."

At that, the guy went rigid. Thick ropes of muscle flexed beneath the skin of his forearms, and his jaw clenched in sudden tension. A moment later, he appeared once more relaxed, but it was too late – I knew my words had hit their mark.

"I don't think I know any Quinn," he said, feigning levity. "You sure you got the right room?"

"Yeah, I'm sure I got the right room. Just like I'm sure you know exactly who I'm talking about."

The kid was quick, I'll give him that. No sooner were the words out of my mouth than he'd kicked the chair out from under me. My cheek exploded in white-hot pain as I slammed face-first into the floor, the upturned medical tray clattering to a rest beside me. Then he leapt on top of me, knocking the wind from my chest. He grabbed a fistful of my hair in one meaty hand and yanked, wrenching my head upward and exposing the tender flesh of my neck. My muscles burned in protest at the awkwardness of my position, and I wanted to thrash, to fight, to struggle against his iron grip. I wanted to, but I didn't. It didn't seem prudent, what with him holding a needle to my jugular and all.

"Who are you?" he hissed into my ear. Needle dug flesh, and I squeezed shut my eyes as I fought the urge to flinch. "What are you doing here?"

I opened my mouth, but nothing came out but a sort of dry, creaking noise. The pressure against my jugular doubled, and I tried again.

"I– I was… I was looking for *you*…" I wheezed. I couldn't get any air into my lungs. My head was fuzzy; my vision dimmed. "It… it's me – *Sam*!"

Suddenly, the weight atop me was gone. I rolled over to see the guy crouching awkwardly over me, and staring at me with an expression of shock and bewilderment. The needle he'd been wielding fell forgotten to the floor beside me.

"Sam? Is that really you?"

"Last I checked," I said, dabbing at my blood-pricked neck with one hand.

Two things happened then that I confess I wasn't expecting.

The first of them was he slapped me – hard. Getting slapped by a guy that size is hardly a dainty affair; it was more like getting socked in the face with a two-by-four. My head snapped back from the force of the blow, and rebounded off the floor with a *fwack*. Everything went kinda spotty for a minute, and my cheek burned in remembrance of his hand.

The slap I probably shoulda seen coming. But the second thing? The second thing I wouldn't have predicted in a million years.

The second thing was, the dude grabbed me by the lapels of my suit coat, hoisted me up off the floor, and kissed me like he meant it.

10.

When he finally released me from his grasp, I slumped back to the floor, a bemused grin breaking across my face.

"I've got to be honest with you, sweetheart – that meat-suit of yours isn't exactly my type. But still, it's good to see you, Ana."

"It's good to see you, too, Sam." All trace of her meat-suit's Southern accent had disappeared, replaced by Ana's crisp Balkan tone. She looked at me a moment from behind those dull, close-set eyes, and traced the line of my jaw with one thick, calloused finger.

Then she slapped me again.

This time, I wasn't so surprised. I turned my head in time with the blow, so this one was like getting smacked *gently* with a two-by-four. But hell, she hadn't killed me yet, which by my reckoning meant things were going better than expected. Then again, the day was young.

Ana Jovic was without a doubt one of the best Collectors the world had ever seen. In the fifty-four years I'd known her, I'd never once seen her falter in her task; she did every job with quiet efficiency, neither hesitating nor belaboring the kill – and never, *ever*, missing her mark. It was Danny who'd discovered

her back in '57, possessing unwary travelers between collec-
tions and living feral among the ruins of her old village – a
burned-out farming community thirty miles east of Sarajevo.
And it was Danny who suggested, as he put it, that we "bring
her in" – that we invite her to join our little Collectors' sup-
port-group/cabal. At first, I was reluctant – the girl was wild
and uncontrollable, living like an animal off the land – but once
I gained her trust and heard her tale, I realized we couldn't not.

See, Ana was born in 1931 to a family of ethnic Serbs in
what was then Yugoslavia. When the fascist Ustaše seized
power in '41 and declared Croatia an independent state, they
set out to purge their nation of Serbian influence in the interests of cultural purity. The Ustaše called it ethnic cleansing, but
it was genocide, pure and simple.

In February of '42, Ana's village was overrun by an Ustaše
death squad. The men, they rounded up and shipped to work
camps. The women, they raped. The children, they shot dead
in the streets. Ana, even then a resourceful child, fled into the
woods, seeking refuge in the icy mountain wilds. The rest of
her family was not so lucky. Ana watched from afar as, along
with the rest of the townspeople, her mother and father were
slaughtered, and the home that had been in her family for generations was pillaged and vandalized. Something in her
snapped, then, and that frightened little girl made a choice that
sealed her fate forever.

For her home was not the only thing her family had passed
down through the generations: it was said that Ana's family had
the Gift – that hers was a line of mystics dating back to Roman
times. Of course, Ana had thought little of the stories, or of her
mother's teachings; after all, it seemed that nothing ever came
of them – never once had she seen any evidence that they were
any more than family lore. But once the men had come and
killed her family, Ana thought differently. Ana came to believe.

She spent a month out in the woods before the demon came, and in that month, the soldiers had all gone. Their places had been taken by Croat families who set about rebuilding the town and claiming it as their own. They were not to blame for what had happened, but at that point, Ana hardly cared.

Now, summoning a demon is a difficult task – one that the most powerful of mages might try their whole lives in vain to accomplish. It is blood magic of the most potent and dangerous kind. That Ana managed it at all is impressive; that she did it at the age of eleven is unprecedented. And the creature she summoned was no mere foot-soldier, but a demon of the highest order. He was so taken with the young girl that summoned him, he decided that rather than simply smite her for her impudence, he would offer her a deal: her soul in return for whatever she desired.

What she wanted was her parents back – but as the creature told her, that's beyond even the most powerful demon's reach. But of course, he said, there were other options – other ways for her to rectify the wrongs she had endured. At first, she wouldn't hear them, but her demon was both patient and persuasive. So in the end, she settled for revenge.

When the demon finished with that town, there wasn't a person left alive. He'd torn flesh from limbs, and ripped still-beating hearts from panicked, sweat-slick chests. He had bathed in the blood of innocents. And all at the behest of one frightened little girl.

Of course, that frightened little girl had assumed that there'd be comfort in what she'd done – that once she'd avenged her family, she'd find some measure of peace. But she couldn't live with the knowledge of the damage she had wrought. For weeks, it ate at her, until finally she couldn't take it anymore. So she did the only thing she could think to do. She wandered back into her once more ruined town, her once more ruined home. With bloodied hands, she wrenched a shard of glass from the shattered window in her family's empty parlor. And, lying on the floor of what was once her bedroom, she sliced deep into the tender flesh of her wrists, only to find that, for her, oblivion was not in the cards.

Her body died, of course, but Ana herself remained. She honed her abilities as a Collector, but between jobs she would return to the village she had twice seen destroyed. Maybe it was penance; maybe it was to remind her of who she'd been in life. Whatever her reasons for returning, it was clear the place was poison to her soul. But Danny and I, we changed all that. We brought her in. We spirited her away. We flattered ourselves with the thought that we were helping fix this damaged creature out of the kindness of our hearts, but the truth was anything but. We were all of us beyond fixing – and of the three of us, Ana was the only one with the courage to admit it. Which is probably why we both fell so hard for her.

"So," she said from behind her boy-mask, "are you going to tell me what you're doing here?"

I rubbed absently at the spot on my cheek where she'd slapped me, palm rasping against two days' stubble. "I told you, I'm here to see Quinn."

"And you expect me to believe that?"

"Honestly, I don't give a damn what you believe."

"Sure you do, Sam – you always have. Tell me, in the twenty-seven years since Quinn was shelved, how many times have you come to see him? Once? Twice?"

The truth was more like a half a dozen, but still, I knew it wasn't enough. Not for Ana. Not for Quinn. "I don't see how it's any business of yours," I snapped.

"I suppose it's not. Except that you never seemed to give a damn about what happened to Quinn, and now out of nowhere here you are, and on a Monday, no less – the very day I always visit. It does cause a girl to wonder."

She was right, of course, about why I was here – that it was her I was here to see – but she was dead wrong about me and Quinn. I didn't stay away because I didn't give a damn. I stayed away because it hurt too much to see him like this. I stayed away because I couldn't help but feel responsible. I stayed away because I was a coward.

See, Quinn was a mistake – *my* mistake. I'd collected him myself in Belfast, back in '72. Like the rest of our little cabal, Quinn was a contract kill. Belfast back then was at the height of the Troubles by spring of that year, clashes between the Unionists and the IRA had reached a fever pitch. Between the bombings and bouts of open war in the streets, hundreds of innocent lives were lost, and thousands more were injured. One such innocent was Quinn, who lost an eye and both his legs when a car bomb detonated a few yards from where he stood. At the time, he was a scholarship student at Queen's University, working toward a degree in engineering. Quinn was from a working-class Catholic family, and his father had died when Quinn was still a child; it had been his dream that his studies would one day allow him to support his widowed mother. But when a roadside bomb ended that dream, Quinn was forced to find another way.

The deal he made was simple: his mother would be taken care of, in return for his immortal soul. When I came to collect him, he didn't protest, didn't fight – he just closed his eyes and smiled. And when I wrapped my fingers around his soul and his lifetime of experiences washed over me, I wept at his decency, his tenderness – at the cruel acts of heartless men that had led him to my grasp. So when I heard that he'd been forced into Collection, it was only natural that to me we bring him in.

Truth be told, I don't know what tipped off the higher-ups to the fact that he'd been disobeying orders and consorting with other Collectors. Maybe he'd been acting oddly. Maybe one of the dead-drops we used to communicate had been compromised. Maybe it was just bad luck. What I *do* know is that when they found out, they brought the full weight of hell down on him. They tortured him for days – and you'd best believe that demons know a thing or two about inflicting pain – but still Quinn never talked; he never gave us up. Maybe if he had, they'd have spared him – allowed him to continue his existence as a Collector.

But he didn't. He wouldn't. And in punishment for his unwavering loyalty to those he loved, hell's response was merciless.

Once our demon masters tired of hearing him scream, Quinn was shelved – stuffed into a useless body decades from expiring. He was still fully aware, but trapped, unable to summon the strength to leap away. The only release for a Collector who's been shelved is the death of the vessel in which they're ensnared. By that time, though, it's usually too late – the shelving nearly always drives them mad. And of course, the vessel in question is mystically protected – no amount of violence, either physical or magical, will cause Ms Mariella Hamilton to expire before her time.

So how is it I know all this? Easy – Lilith told me. And from what I heard from Ana and Danny, they got the same spiel from their handlers. What I *don't* know is whether we were told because they suspected we were involved, or whether Quinn was simply made example of to every Collector in existence. Not that it really matters. Quinn's shelving broke something inside me. I withdrew into myself, hitting the bottle pretty hard and focusing on whatever collection was at hand, but I couldn't keep the guilt at bay. Ana didn't understand that what I was doing was trying my best to cope – she saw it as callous and uncaring.

And that's when Danny made his move. Somehow, he convinced Ana that it was me who had hung Quinn out to dry. I hadn't the faintest idea what he told her, or whether he himself believed it. I guess it doesn't really matter what he believed, because either way, it spelled curtains for our little club. Ana and Danny rode off into the sunset, leaving me and Quinn behind. I guess sometimes friendship is a bitch.

"I admit," I said, "it wasn't *only* Quinn that brought me here. I wanted to see you, too – make sure you were OK."

Ana eyed me with suspicion. "Why wouldn't I be OK?"

"Ana, I talked to Danny."

"Ah," she said. "So *that's* why you've come – Danny told you he and I were over."

"That's right."

"And you came running all the way to Nowhere, Alabama just to see if I needed a shoulder to cry on? Why Samuel, I'm touched."

"It's not like that. I'm not here to get you back."

"Get me *back*? I wasn't aware you ever *had* me."

"You know what I mean."

"I assure you, I do not. You and I, we had our fun, Sam, but I know full well your heart belongs to someone else."

Elizabeth. She was talking about my wife, Elizabeth. "She was a long time ago," I said. "Lifetimes now, it seems. And you know as well as I do I'm never going to see Elizabeth again."

"True," she said, "but that doesn't make you love her any less. I mean, you damned yourself to an eternity in *hell* to save her, Sam – how could I possibly compete with that? How could anybody? Besides, with you and Danny, it was never about loving me – it was about fixing me, *possessing* me. I swear, I wish the two of you would get it through your heads that I'm not some delicate little flower to be sheltered and protected. It would have saved us all a world of hurt."

"I told you, Ana – none of that is why I'm here."

"Then why, exactly, are you here?"

"I'm here because Danny's in some kind of trouble."

"And you think that you can help him."

"Something like that."

"You do so like to play the savior, don't you, Sam?" Her eyes drifted over to the woman lying still beside us, to the Collector trapped within. "It's a shame you're so goddamn lousy at it."

"I don't have time for this verbal sparring bullshit," I said. "Danny's missing, and I aim to find him. Now are you going to help me or not?"

She stared at me for a long moment, eyes narrowing in thought. "Why, Sam, I misread you! You're not *helping* Danny – you're *hunting* him. What, pray tell, did he do to piss you off so much?"

I considered lying to her, but at that moment, there was a rasping in the corner. A massive, bulbous wasp – too large by half for Alabama, but dead-on for the jungles of the Amazon – was skittering along the joint between ceiling and wall. The dry rat-a-tat of its wings against the plaster was like a death rattle. I wondered how long I had before its friends arrived.

"He stole something from me," I said. "A soul that I was sent to collect. And now I want it back."

"He stole a soul."

"That's right."

Ana shook her head in weary resignation. "Daniel, you idiot," she muttered, more to herself than to me.

"You don't sound too surprised."

"I wish I was. Truth is, I've seen something like this coming for a while, now. It's why he and I are no longer together. Although even *I'm* surprised he would have brought you into all of this…"

"All of *what*? Ana, what the hell is Danny up to?"

"Sam, Danny's a junkie."

I don't know what I'd been expecting her to say, but that sure as hell wasn't it. "Come again?"

"You heard me fine the first time. He's been skimming for a couple years now."

Jesus – skimming? This shit with Danny was even worse than I thought.

The skim-trade is big business in the demon world. It's sort of a black market for happy memories. Demons like to play all big and scary and superior, but the truth is, when it comes to humankind, the Fallen are jealous as all get-out. See, when they fell, they were removed from the light of God's grace, and doomed to an eternity of darkness and despair. Skimming's their way of reversing that – for a time, anyway. If a demon with the proper set of skills can get his hands on a human soul before it's interred, he can shave off tiny fragments of life experience. This process is, of course, forbidden in the underworld, and it's dangerous as hell – word is, one slip of the hand and the soul could crack, releasing enough raw energy to level a city block. But done properly, those skimmed fragments provide a high no demon could attain on their own: the high of love, of *life*; the warm embrace of a moment in God's grace.

"But I thought skim was just for demons," I said. "I didn't think they'd deign to deal to humans – alive or otherwise."

"That's mostly true, I guess – but they've got to get their product somewhere, right?"

I frowned. "You're saying Danny was funneling them souls? But why? How'd he get involved?"

"About three years back, he was approached by a demon who runs a skim-joint outside of Las Cruces. Somehow – I don't know how – he'd found out about Danny's relationship with me, and he exploited it for all it was worth. He said it would be a shame if our handlers found out about us – especially when such a discovery could be so easily avoided. He offered us protection – that, and access to all the creature comforts we could ever want. In return, all he asked for was a day or so to tinker with whatever soul Danny had collected. Once he extracted what he needed from the soul, he returned it to Danny for interment, and no one was ever the wiser. The system worked well enough for a while – and I confess, distasteful as the demon's protection racket was, the nights Danny and I spent dining and drinking in the finest hotels without fear of discovery were among the happiest I've ever known. But then somewhere along the way, Danny's method of payment changed."

My face twisted in disgust. "Do you have any idea how fucking stupid you two were not to simply break it off with one another? What if you'd been caught? Or what if Danny's demon-friend fucked up and cracked the soul Danny was assigned to inter? What do you suppose his handler would do then, huh? You want him to end up like Quinn? 'Cause make no mistake – if he were caught failing to perform his duties as a Collector, that's *exactly* what'd happen."

"Of *course* it was stupid, Sam. I knew it; Danny knew it. But can you even remember what it's like being happy – even if for just a moment? Danny knew the risks, and as he told me a thousand times, even if he was caught, he wasn't hurting anybody but himself. Of course, when he started using, everything changed. He retreated into himself, and shut me out entirely."

"So when your gravy train runs out, you up and bail, huh?"

Her eyes flashed with sudden anger. "You're a bastard, you know that? You have no *idea* what it was like. You have no idea what that shit *did* to him. When he was skimming, it's like he wasn't even there – and when he came down, it was even worse. He was hollowed out. A ghost. After a year of trying to reason with him, of begging him to give it up, I couldn't take it anymore. So finally, I left. You know a thing or two about leaving, don't you, Sam?"

I let that comment pass. "Still, Danny's actions don't track. I mean, the bigwigs only tolerate the skim-joints because they stay below the radar – they don't disturb the status quo. You said yourself, they *borrowed* Danny's souls, they didn't *steal* them. So where's the upside in having Danny snatching Varela?"

"How the hell should *I* know? Maybe demand is on the rise, and the usual methods for obtaining skim can't keep up. Maybe the recent unrest between heaven and hell has disrupted the skim-joint's regular supply, forcing them to look elsewhere. Or maybe Danny's just desperate. Maybe he needed a fix, and figured you for the sucker he could take it from."

I shook my head. "You know full well only a demon's got the reflexes to pull a successful skim. Danny wouldn't stand a chance – he'd crack the soul, and blow his meat-suit all to shit."

"That's assuming he's still in his right mind."

"Come on, Ana, this is *Danny* we're talking about. Junkie or not, you know he's working some kind of angle."

"Maybe. But I certainly couldn't tell you what it is."

I thought a moment, played the angles in my head. "This demon who's been pulling Danny's strings," I said, "he got a name?"

Ana's gaze, which until now had met my own, dropped. She stared at the floor a moment, and when she spoke, her tone was scarcely more than a whisper.

"Dumas," she said, her voice tinged with shame and regret. "The demon's name is Dumas."

11.

"So," Gio said, "you gonna tell me what the hell happened back there?"

He twisted in the Fiesta's passenger seat to look at me, his worried frown rendered sickly green by the pale dashboard light. Our tires clattered against the blacktop as we barreled west on 20, the speedometer pushing eighty as I chased the sunset that had long since dipped beneath the horizon before us. The lights of Shreveport were fast receding in the rearview, which meant that there were damn near two states between me and my meeting with Ana. In my opinion, that was still a couple states too few. I pressed the pedal to the floor mat and felt the whole car shudder as the needle climbed to ninety.

I guess I couldn't fault Gio for his concern – I looked a wreck after my tussle with Ana. My suit was a rumpled mess. My hair was mussed from when she'd yanked back my head. Dried blood crusted around the pinprick in my neck. Besides, I'd barely said five words since we'd left the rest home – I'd been so rattled by what Ana had told me, I didn't trust myself to speak. And even if I did, I sure as shit wasn't going to spill my guts to Gio. Not when it was that touchy-feely sharing bullshit that left me feeling like this in the first place.

I guess Ana's betrayal shouldn't have taken me by surprise; after all, as far as she was concerned, I'd betrayed her long ago. And God knows Danny's screwed me over more times than I can count. But I'd always thought of Ana as being better than that.

Turns out, I thought wrong.

See, most demons have themselves a nasty sense of humor, which means when you cut yourself a deal with one, you'd best be careful what you wish for. Ana knows that better than anyone. She thought when she cut her deal to avenge her family that she was exacting justice. But there's no justice in the slaughter of innocents – there's only pain and remorse. Ana didn't realize that until it was too late, but you can be damn sure her *demon* knew. Now, that bastard already had her soul by way of payment regardless of what she wished for, but still he couldn't help but twist the knife by turning her into the very thing she most despised – by convincing her to kill. And since twisting the knife is what hell is all about, the powers that be used the same sadistic logic in determining her punishment. Having been unable to live with the fact that her revenge had driven her to become a vicious killer, Ana was condemned to kill for all eternity as a Collector.

My story isn't so far off from her own. In life, I was a decent man – or so I thought. But then my wife fell ill, and I was offered a deal: essentially, my wife's life for my own. What I didn't know was that, before the demon took my life as payment, he would strip me of everything I held dear: my decency, my compassion, my respect for human life. Much like Ana's did to her, my demon turned me into a killer – a heartless bastard – and the kicker is, he did it with such ease that for years after my death, I wondered if maybe that was who I'd always been. It took a long time for me to realize it wasn't – that I'd simply been so desperate, so focused on saving

Elizabeth, that I hadn't spared a thought about what that goal might cost me. In the end, her health returned, but she couldn't live with the person I'd become. She left, and took our unborn child with her. Looking back, I couldn't even blame her. By the time that evil son of a bitch was done with me, I was but an echo of the man Elizabeth had married – hollow, empty, cold. And when finally, I lay broken and alone, that fucker delighted in my misery, laughing at the ruined man that I'd become.

That demon – that fucking *monster* – was named Dumas.

Ana knew my story, of course, as I'd known hers. Which means she knew how much she and Danny getting into bed with Dumas would hurt me. Maybe in her mind, I deserved it. Hell, maybe I even did. Either way, it didn't make it hurt any less.

But like I said, I wasn't going to say any of that to Gio. And since I couldn't think of anything else to say, I said nothing – a nothing that, so far, had stretched on for going on eight hours.

"OK, if you don't wanna talk about it, could you at least tell me where we're going?"

"Las Cruces," I said.

"Las Cruces? As in New Mexico?"

"That's right."

"Is that where we're gonna find our guy?"

"Maybe. Maybe not. I don't know."

"Then why the hell are we going there?"

"Because it turns out Danny's involved in some pretty nasty shit – sort of the undead equivalent of drug running, I suppose. Las Cruces is where his employer's at."

"Ah, I gotcha – you think maybe we can shake him down, make him tell us where this Danny guy's been hiding."

"Something like that," I lied. I didn't have the heart to tell him the truth: that it wasn't Danny I was really after. That as much as I'd like to see Danny pay for what he'd done, recovering the Varela soul was my only real priority. That there was a chance Danny wasn't in Las Cruces at all – that he'd simply left the soul there and moved on – and this errand I was dragging Gio on would bring him no closure, no justice, no peace of any kind.

Only even *that* was a lie – it isn't that I didn't have the heart. I didn't tell him because I didn't yet know whether or not I'd need him, and so I had to keep him motivated – invested in a common goal. I didn't tell him the truth because if I did, I couldn't use him anymore.

I guess Ana was right about me after all: I really *am* a bastard.

"So this boss-man we're going to see," Gio said, "he a reaper-type like you?"

"Dumas? No, Dumas is nothing like me – he's a demon."

Gio looked impressed. "A demon, huh? He got, like, horns and shit?"

"No," I said. "The monster shtick is strictly for the foot-soldiers. The higher-ups, they've got the juju to alter their appearance – to change the way your eye perceives them. They all look pretty much like you or me. But then, I thought you would've known that."

"Why the hell would I have known that? It ain't like I've ever met a demon before."

"Of course you have."

"The fuck're you talking about?"

"Gio, how do you think you ended up here?"

"I dunno – I mean, I guess I done some shit I shouldn'ta done. Ain't that sorta how this works?"

"Sure, for some. But that alone isn't enough to get you collected. No, to get collected, you've either got to be full-on Hitler bad, or you've got to make yourself a deal with a demon. And you, my friend, are the latter."

"But that don't make no sense! If I'da made a deal with a demon, wouldn't I remember it? If I'da made a deal with a demon, wouldn't I at least have gotten something out of it?"

I shook my head in disbelief. "You think you *didn't*?"

"What – you're saying that I *did*?"

"Gio, before you wound up working for the Outfit, what kind of shit were you pulling?"

Gio hedged. "Oh, you know, a little of this, a little of that."

"Yeah, my guess is emphasis on *little*. The way I hear it, you were nothing but a two-bit thug. I'm guessing some mugging, a hold-up or two, maybe a little smash-and-grab, right?"

Dude was frowning something fierce, now. When he spoke, his tone was sullen, petulant. "I did all right."

"Sure you did," I said, "but you've got to admit, that sort of stuff doesn't exactly make you Outfit material, now does it?"

"I... I guess not."

"Only one day, a guy comes along, says he'll make your dreams come true – all you've got to do is come work for him, and he'll take care of the rest. Next thing you know, you're living large, and you can't believe your luck – but you aren't about to question it, because you're afraid that if you do, it's all going to go away. Am I close?"

"A little too," he admitted.

"That guy you met – he make you shake on it?"

He thought on that a sec. "Yeah."

"Demon."

Gio fell silent for a while, mulling over what I'd just told him. Then he heaved a sigh and shook his head. "Shit," he said, "it ain't like I was ever in line for the pearly gates anyway – not after all I done. The way I see it, I still came out ahead."

"Yeah, only now hell's got all of eternity to try to change your mind."

We spent the next mile or so in silence. When Gio finally broke it, his tone was absent its usual bravado. He sounded small, fragile, afraid. "What's gonna happen to me? When this is all over, I mean."

"You're asking what hell is like?"

"Yeah."

"I couldn't say."

"You mean you're like forbidden?"

"No, I mean I couldn't say. Hell is sort of like a tailored suit of bad. Everybody's is a little different, and everybody's is designed to deliver the punishment that best fits them. For me, hell is right here, right now – it's this world, this life, this thankless task. For you, I couldn't say."

"That don't give me much to help prepare for it."

"Sorry, but that's all I've got. And even if I had more to tell you, it wouldn't help. There's just no preparing for what you've got coming."

"Jesus, dude – your bedside manner *sucks*. You *trying* to scare the shit outta me?"

"I'm *trying* to tell you the truth," I said. It came out harsher than I intended. I took a breath and tried again. "Look, if you want to know what hell is really like, you've got to look inside yourself. Hell is your worst fear, your deepest insecurity, laid bare for all the world to see – again and again, for all eternity. You think you can psych yourself up for that, then be my guest. But if you want my advice, I suggest you enjoy what little time you've got left."

"Speaking of," he said, "I got myself a special lady in Vegas I wouldn't mind seeing one last time before I'm dead for good. You think once we finish with this demon guy, we could maybe swing on by?"

"No," I said.

"Right. Figures."

And then, for a while, we said nothing.
For a while, we both had nothing left to say.

12.

"Collector!" she said, her voice echoing off the dingy bathroom tiles. "You want to tell me what it is you think you're doing?"

I shut off the tap and looked in vain for a paper towel, instead settling on shaking the rust-scented water from my hands. We were at a truck stop an hour west of Abilene, in a stretch of countryside so brown and dead that, but for the occasional patch of scrub brush, it might as well have been on Mars. It was pushing three in the morning, and though there were a couple guys in the parking lot catching some shut-eye in their big rigs, the inside of the truck stop was deserted. Gio was outside, gassing up the Fiesta, which meant that in here, it was just me – well, me and Lilith, now.

I watched her in the dingy mirror as she strolled barefoot from the bathroom stall, eyeing her new surroundings with distaste. She was clad in a sheer black evening gown rendered transparent by the fluorescent lights overhead. For a second there, as I stood looking at her, I forgot my own name.

I closed my eyes and swallowed hard, and in dribs and drabs, my composure trickled back. "What I'm doing, Lily, is my job."

"Is it, now? Because I was under the impression you've not been so concerned with doing that of late."

I sighed. "So I guess you know about Varela, then."

"As a point of fact, Collector, I know almost *nothing* about Varela. I know that you have thus far failed to collect him. I know my superiors are less than pleased about that fact. I know that when it came time for me to find you, you were on some kind of fucking field trip when you should have been out handling your business. So tell me – what else is there I ought to know?"

"Nothing – I'm handling it."

"That's funny, because last I saw you, you told me it had already been handled."

"Yeah, well, there were some extenuating circumstances. Nothing you need to worry about. I've got it under control."

"You do." Lily, incredulous.

"Yes, I *do*."

"Tell me, does your definition of *under control* include the undead soul in the fat-suit waiting outside for your return?"

Shit. Gio. Maybe it was wishful thinking, but I was hoping I could keep him off her radar. Oh, well – too late now to do anything but play it cool. "As a matter of fact, it does. And how the hell'd you even know? You can tell just by looking at him that the body he's wearing isn't his?"

"Of *course* I can," she snapped. "That getup he's parading around in may be enough to fool a monkey like yourself, but I assure you, any creature not once bound to your precious mortal coil will see him coming from a mile away. Now I think it's time you stop playing around and tell me exactly what is going on."

So I did – or sort of did, at least. I told her about tracking Varela through the jungle, and the fact that when I found him, he was dead. I told her that Varela's soul'd been missing, which meant he'd died by a Collector's hand. I told her that I'd tracked down that Collector, and taken back what I thought was Varela's soul – only to find that it was not. And I told her that I aimed to hunt down that Collector once more, and take back what was rightfully mine.

What I *didn't* tell her was that I knew the Collector in question, and that I'd landed in this mess because apparently he and I had a score to settle. I couldn't see the upside in her knowing. As pissed as Lilith was at me right now, for the moment she and I were on the same side. But if she thought I'd brought this on myself, she wouldn't hesitate to sell me out. So my choice was either keep her in the dark, or spend the next few decades on the shelf. Not much of a choice, if you ask me.

"So," she asked when I was done, "you've no idea why this Collector targeted you?"

"Nothing concrete. But if I had to guess, I'd say a demon put him up to it – I haven't been too popular among the Fallen since I killed Merihem and Beleth."

She cocked her head a moment, trying the theory on for size, and then she nodded. "That does make a certain sort of sense – a great many in the Depths were incensed they didn't get to see you burn for what you'd done."

"Those two got what was coming to them," I said, perhaps a bit too defensively.

"Perhaps. Perhaps not. But the question as to whether your actions were justified has little bearing on the predicament in which you currently find yourself. I assume I needn't remind you what your punishment will be if you fail to bring Varela home."

"No," I said. "You needn't."

"Good. What I *will* remind you of is the fact that your failure would also reflect poorly on me, as well as attract a great deal of attention to the both of us that I would just as soon avoid. And if that happens, you can be sure that I will take my time in turning you over to them so that I can dole out a little punishment of my own. Pleasure and pain are inextricably linked, Collector, and I assure you, though I prefer the former, I am every bit as proficient in the latter. By the time I'm finished with you, you'll be *begging* to be shelved."

"Let's hope it doesn't come to that."

"I'd suggest you do a little more than *hope*."

"I told you, I'm working on it. Don't count me out just yet."

"I wouldn't dare," she said. "So, the gentleman outside – his is the soul you stole back from this rogue Collector, thinking it to be Varela?"

"That's right."

"And now he's to serve as your dowsing rod."

"Something like that."

Lilith smiled. "I confess, Collector, I'm impressed – that borders on clever."

"I have my moments."

"Yes," she said, "you do. I only hope for your sake you have enough of them." And then she said something that completely floored me, and put the lie to the cool confidence that oozed from her every pore. "Tell me, Collector, is there anything you need of me?"

That one question was enough to let me know that Lilith was afraid – that she was feeling the pressure as surely as was I. That one question scared the shit out of me. Because Lilith wasn't exactly the helping-others kind – not unless her ass was on the line.

"That depends – you got any idea how to locate a missing soul?"

"If he were a living human, perhaps, but unfortunately for the both of us, the only dead person I've the ability to locate is you."

"And I'm guessing talking to the higher-ups isn't going to help."

"No, it most certainly would not. I'm afraid that my superiors are among those who would like to see you burn for what happened in New York. They've been ordered to stand down on that regard, but I've no doubt that they would leap at the chance to get at you another way. What I will do, though, is keep an ear to the ground; perhaps I can learn something of use about your little Collector friend – such as where he's gone off to, or what he intends to do with the stolen Varela."

My little Collector friend. Right. Of course, having Lilith dig into the whole Danny thing was less a help than it was something else for me to worry about, but I couldn't tell her that. So instead, I just said thanks.

Lilith turned to go, and as she did, a fat, black bug crawled out of the sink-drain beside me. It was followed by some sort of improbable, spindly-legged thing the color of dry leaves, and then two iridescent blue-gray beetles, who wedged themselves in the drain trying to both claw out at once. As I watched in growing horror, a blood-red centipede slipped past them, its many legs scrabbling for purchase against the yellowed porcelain basin.

"Lily, wait," I said, not taking my eyes from the swelling ranks of insects rising in the sink beside me. "There is one other thing."

"Yes?"

"Any chance you could call off my Deliverants a while? Just until I sort this out."

She smiled at me, then – a sad, wan smile, surprising from her in that it was more sympathy than pity. "Would that I could, Collector, but I'm afraid Deliverants fall outside of hell's dominion."

"Outside of hell's dominion? What does that even mean? If hell isn't in charge of them, who *is*?"

"Pray you never find out," she said.

Pray. Right. 'Cause that's been working well for me so far.

"Oh, and Collector?"

"Yeah?"

"Whatever it is you plan on doing – do it soon."

And just like that, she was gone.

13.

By the time the sky began to lighten in the east, I was exhausted. My skin was twitchy, my limbs heavy and ungainly. My stomach was a roiling mess. I couldn't blame it, really. Aside of a Dr Pepper and a bag of Doritos picked up at the truck stop a few hours back, I hadn't eaten much in days – and that shit only barely qualified as food. Gio'd insisted we needed something; I guess I shouldn't have left him in charge of picking out the something that we needed.

Not that the crap we'd eaten bothered *him* any – dude was slumped open-mouthed and snoring in the seat beside me, same as he'd been the past two hours. I confess, I was more than a little jealous. My eyes were bleary and itchy as hell, and my lids were getting pretty heavy – every couple of minutes, I had to fight to keep them from crashing down. It didn't help that this stretch of road was nothing more than two dull strips of sun-bleached blacktop split by a couple feet of bare dirt and surrounded by mile after mile of flat, brown desert. Add to that the lonely graywash of the predawn half-light, and the fact that we hadn't seen another car in hours, and it was pretty tough to stay awake. I felt like I was stuck in the borderlands between day and night, between sleep and wakefulness – the sole witness of a world no one else would ever see.

At least the quiet gave me time to think. Problem was, my thoughts were all questions and no answers. I wondered what the hell Dumas was playing at, having Danny take Varela's soul. I wondered if I was going to track Varela's soul down in time to save my hide. I wondered if marching into a skim-joint full of demons who hated my living guts with no real plan and no protection was going to get me anything but evicted from this skin-suit. I wondered if my eyes were open.

The problem with that last one is that if you have to wonder, it's a good bet that they're not. Too late I realized my chin was resting against my breastbone, and my eyes were watching nothing but the backs of my lids. I jerked awake, the bitter tang of adrenaline biting at the back of my throat. While I'd dozed, the Fiesta had drifted across the barren center divide, its headlights slicing across the oncoming lane and illuminating the desert beyond.

With knuckles white, I wrenched the wheel clockwise. Once more, the Fiesta careened over the median strip, shocks squeaking in protest all the while. Then she leapt back onto the pavement, dragging undercarriage and loosing a flurry of sparks. Tires squealed as I brought her parallel with the roadway, the Fiesta's rear-end swinging wide and then finally skidding into place. I let out a breath I hadn't known I was holding and willed my panicked heart to slow.

And that's when I realized we were no longer alone on the road.

He was a withered old man, rail-thin and barely clad, hunched over a gnarled gray walking stick that was really nothing more than a bit of driftwood. He stood inches from the Fiesta's speeding bumper, so close in fact, the headlights passed by him on either side. It was too late to stop – too late to avoid him. At that moment, I was nothing more than a passenger, watching in terror as two thousand pounds of glass and steel hurtled toward his fragile, awkward frame.

But I didn't hit him – or, at least, the *Fiesta* didn't. Quick as death, the old man raised a hand, and suddenly, the car was still. Unfortunately for me, though, *I* wasn't. I guess Gio was smart enough to belt his fat ass in, but I never cared much for seatbelts myself, they being a little after my time among the living. So when the car stopped dead, I shot out of the driver's seat and plunged full-on Superman through the windshield. I heard a sickening crack – bone or glass, I wasn't sure – and then I was soaring through the chill morning air. I hit the man, and then flew *through* him. Not as though he was some kind of ghost, though; more like I was an angry toddler, and he was a playmate's stack of blocks. He just, I don't know, *fell apart* around me, and next thing I knew, I was eating dirt.

I have no idea how far I must've slid along the ground, getting bit and clawed by rocks and twigs along the way. Felt like a fucking mile. All I know is, when I stopped, the world around had disappeared in a cloud of reddish dust, thick like fog in the sickly glow of the Fiesta's headlights, and every molecule of my borrowed body was letting me know just how much they didn't like this sudden turn of events. I tried to move. It didn't take. And that's when the fucker grabbed me.

If I'd been thinking clearly, it wouldn't have made much sense – I mean, I *felt* the old man fall apart when I flew into him. And truth be told, *grabbed* doesn't begin to cover what he did to me. I mean yeah, he took a fistful of suit-coat and all, but then he lifted me like I was nothing, and tossed me like a rag-doll into the desert. I heard a rib crack as I hit the ground, and my right shoulder popped like a drumstick pulled from a roast bird; the arm attached went slack and numb. I bit my cheek so hard on impact, blood poured red-black from between my lips. Before I could so much as take a breath, he was on me again, rolling me over and yanking me close. I screwed shut my eyes and prayed. I was sure that he would kill me. I only prayed he'd do it quick.

But he didn't. Instead, he spoke, with a voice like wind through autumn leaves, a voice that seemed to come at once from everywhere and from nowhere at all.

Where is it?

At first, his words didn't register, so disturbed was I by their timbre, their unearthly quality. And it wasn't just his words – his whole *body* seemed to rustle and quake, his every movement a disquieting susurrus.

Disquieting, and familiar.

With a sinking heart, I realized where I'd heard that sound before.

In a camp full of dead men at the heart of the Amazon rainforest.

In an anonymous motel room outside of Springfield, Illinois.

I forced open my eyes, and saw the old man's face inches from my own. But it was not a face at all, and this *thing* was not a man – nor was it like any demon I'd ever seen. No, this creature before me was more a vulgar sketch of a man, rendered in a teeming mass of writhing, scratching bugs. What I'd taken to be weathered skin of dusky bronze was nothing more than a living coat of roaches, their constant motion allowing the occasional glimpse of ropy muscles rendered in blood-red millipedes, which pulsed and flexed around stick-bug bones. The man-thing was clad in a tattered robe of massive, velvet-backed spiders, giant, gleaming ants, and a dozen other varieties of crawly things I'd never before seen. Its hair and scraggly beard were a wriggling mat of gray-white maggots, which occasionally tumbled with a patter onto my face and chest. And from beneath a brow of twitching locusts, the man-thing glared at me with slate-blue beetle eyes.

The creature cuffed me in the ear, shaking me from my reverie and pasting my face with a thick smear of crushed insects. Then I was struck by a fresh wave of agony, rippling outward from my suddenly swelling ear, thanks to what I could only assume was a wasp's sting.

You shall listen when I speak, it said. *You shall answer when I ask. And you would be advised to do it soon, before I tear this rotting body limb from limb. Now where is it?*

"Wh-where is *what*?" I stammered, my panicked, addled brain not catching on to what my gut already knew. But the beast was having none of it – it pulled me closer to its repulsive visage, its hot breath like rot and death.

Don't play coy with me, boy. You know I'm here for the Varela soul.

"You–" I said, fighting back the bile that rose in my throat as the creature's stench invaded my sinuses, "–you're my Deliverants?"

At that, the man-thing shuddered and hitched, a hundred-thousand insect wings fluttering as one against each other. I'd never heard so horrible a sound in my entire life. Never so horrible a sound as that abomination laughing.

I'm afraid, Samuel, that on that point you are quite mistaken. These creatures – these shepherds – are but humble servants, lending form to that which in this realm is formless. Just as that decaying sack of meat you're wearing lends you form.

"No," I said, revolted at the very thought. "You and I are nothing alike."

You dare balk at that? You who have for so long been granted asylum in my realm? How dare you speak to me this way?

As the creature seethed with fury, a kernel of a plan began to take root in my mind. Not a *good* plan, mind you, but then, I wasn't in a position to be picky.

"I'll speak to you any goddamn way I please," I spat, every syllable sagging under the weight of my contempt. I'll grant you, on the face of it, goading this thing didn't seem like the best idea ever. But the way I figured it, this fucker was gonna kill me either way. Either I could stick around and get tortured until it figured out I didn't have what it was looking for, or I could piss it off, and maybe make it kill me quick. Sure, it'd hurt like hell, but once this vessel was dead, I'd be reseeded somewhere else. Where, I didn't know, but the way I saw it, *anywhere* was better than here.

You think your God has any power to damn me? Me, who reigned while he was but a babe in his crib, and this cesspool you call existence was but a glimmer in his eye? Your God is nothing more than a seditionist – a pretender to the throne. For eons before him I ruled, and my dominion was Chaos – the Great Nothing from which this filthy rock you call a home emerged.

"You expect me to believe that shit? Man, every demon worth a damn likes to spin himself a yarn about how he's the biggest, baddest creature in the land, and ain't a one of 'em is telling the truth. Now, the bug thing's neat and all, but why don't we cut the crap. You're no more an Old God than I am – you're nothing but a scavenger. So save your parlor tricks for someone who gives a shit."

I steeled myself for my inevitable eviction from this meat-suit, but the death blow never came. Instead, the creature laughed that horrible, rasping laugh. The sound set my skin crawling, and made this meat-suit's fillings ache.

Nothing but a scavenger, it said, shaking its nightmare head as it did. *I suppose I am, at that. And for that, I have your precious God to thank – he and that Fallen brat of his. Those two bickering little snots carved up my glorious empire of Nothing, taking what they wanted and leaving me only the narrow border of the In-Between to claim for my own. And angry though I was to be left with their table-*

scraps, for a time, it was enough. After all, the living had the good sense to honor me, to pay a tithe in return for safe passage through my realm. Never before had there been subjects in my domain, and I admit that I was flattered. But now the old ways have been forgotten, and with them, so too have I been. Now, such forgetfulness may be unavoidable in the living, but I assure you, I've no intention of allowing another of your kind to forget. No, over you, I have dominion, and as such, I demand your fealty. So I suggest you tell me where the Varela soul is before I'm forced to lose my patience.

"I don't have it," I said.

Lies!

The creature roared, and once more tossed me into the air. I slammed into the ground a good thirty feet from where I started, and for a moment, everything went white. The man-thing leapt after me, covering the distance in one insectile bound. Then it grabbed me by the lapel and slapped me hard across the face. I felt the swell and burn of another fresh sting, but this time, it was just another white-hot point of light in my constellation of suffering.

Do you think that I don't know what you are doing? Do you think I'll stand by and allow it to happen again? Were it not for the Great Truce, for the rules to which we three agreed, I would not abide the Nine at all. But now it seems that truce is crumbling, and with it my patience for your games. I assure you I will not abide a tenth.

The creature grabbed my wrist and squeezed. My wrist bones ground sickeningly against each other. My stomach roiled with sudden nausea. My vision dimmed. I shrieked, and damn near fainted.

"I swear to you, I have no idea what you're talking about – I'm not trying to *do* anything! The soul you're looking for was stolen – stolen by another Collector! Maybe he's the one you're looking for! All I want is to get it to where it belongs!"

That's precisely what the other said. I suspect the both of you are lying – lying to protect each other. Lying to buy yourselves time. But I assure you, it will not do you any good.

"The other – you mean Danny? You know where Danny is? Just tell me, and I promise you, you'll get your soul."

I fear you misunderstand the nature of our relationship, Samuel – it is I who makes the demands. You may persist in this lie all you like, but I assure you, I will not be taken in.

"That's great, except I'm not lying."

Even if you aren't, it hardly matters. The soul is in your charge. If you speak the truth, then your negligence is no less an affront to me than would be your rebellion. And for that, you must be punished.

The creature plunged its hand into my chest, grasping tight my soul as I had done to so many in my time.

No – not like I'd done.

This was worse. So much worse.

The man-thing squeezed, and what I felt was so awful it made all the pain I'd ever experienced seem like a fucking spa treatment. Death itself was but child's play compared to this. To being swallowed whole by Nothing.

A horrid emptiness pressed in on me – chilling, absolute. The muted colors of the pre-dawn desert seemed a thousand rainbows strong compared to the terrible void that engulfed me. My thoughts were stripped away – my very sensations – until I found myself longing for the agony of my broken and bloodied physical self.

Until I longed to feel anything at all.

As I plunged ever deeper into the abyss, cast alive into the creature's unholy In-Between, I heard its voice as if from somewhere high above.

Three days, it said, so quiet I could barely make it out. Though the words were as light as the last scraps of Being that surrounded me, and my self was but a fading memory, I knew exactly what the creature meant.

And just like that, the Nothingness lifted.

I was in the desert.

I was in the desert, and I was alone.

14.

"Sam!"

A single, barked syllable. Urgent, it seemed, but I couldn't make sense of what it meant, and anyways, it was so very far away. My eyes fluttered open for a moment, only to be assaulted by grit and wind and morning light. Then my lids came tumbling down. I didn't see the point of stopping them.

"Goddamn it, Sam, stay with me!"

I felt a slap across my face. The words seemed louder now, their meaning more apparent. I recognized my name, at least, if not the person saying it.

"I swear to Christ, Sam, if you die, I'm gonna fuckin' kill you."

Gio. Right. The tough-guy cadence was a dead giveaway. What I didn't know was why he was making such a fuss.

And then it all came back. The desert road. The sudden stop. My little chat with the old man.

No, that wasn't quite right. That thing was *old*, but not a man. It was a monster, a horror-show, a walking abomination – a wretched beast that claimed it was a god.

God or not, that thing had plunged me into Nothingness – horrid, empty, complete – and given me an ultimatum.

Three days, it had said. Three days to find the soul that Danny had stolen from me and lay it to rest.

Three days before the Nothing was forever.

That last thought got me moving. I sat up, or tried. It didn't take. Gio was saying something, but I was having trouble hearing him. I once more opened my eyes. The world was kind of blurry, and a little gray around the edges, but at least this time they stayed open. Seemed like progress to me.

A sudden lurch, and I was off the ground. Gio wheezed and grunted as he hauled me over to the ruined Fiesta, cursing all the while. My head lolled back, and I spied the patch of dirt that I'd been sprawled out on. The desert sand was darker there.

Dark like rust.

Like blood.

We reached the car. He tossed me in. Like the plot of land I'd left behind, his hands and shirt were slick with blood – my blood. Gio's face was a mask of concern. I tried to tell him not to worry, that I'd be all right, but the words died on my lips. I couldn't find the breath to speak, and my chest hurt like crazy – a sharp, burny sort of pain. After a couple minutes of struggling to speak, I forgot what I was trying to say in the first place. And a minute after that, it didn't matter.

I was once more asleep.

A prickle in my sinuses, a sudden burning in my throat. My eyes fluttered open, and consciousness returned. Gio sat, expectant, beside me, a vial of smelling salts cracked open in his hand. The backseat of the Fiesta was littered with gauze and tape and spent tubes of ointment. I think a good half of that ointment wound up on my face, slathered over my numerous contusions and leaving me a sticky mess. My ribs were now taped, and though it still hurt like hell to breathe, the pain was of a more manageable sort. My right arm was in a sling – the shoulder back in place, it seemed – and the wrist the creature'd squeezed throbbed in time with the beating of my heart. *No big,* I thought, *this meat-suit was a lefty anyway.*

"Wh-where…" My voice sounded thick and wet and wrong. Gio must've thought so, too, because he frowned.

"Round back of a twenty-four-hour pharmacy." He caught me eyeing the gaping hole in the Fiesta's windshield, and smiled. "Don't worry; nobody saw us pull in, and I didn't steal this shit or nothin' – I bought it with cash outta the morgue dude's wallet. How you feelin'?"

"Peachy," I croaked.

"Yeah, you look it. You wanna tell me what the hell happened back there?"

"Long story."

"Seems to me, we got a while."

No, I thought, we don't. But what I said was, "You remember the bug back at the mortuary?" My Ms sounded like Bs. My Gs rattled like phlegm in the back of my throat.

"Yeah?"

"I just tangled with a few thousand of his friends."

"Wait – you're telling me *bugs* did this to you?"

"More like a bug *monster*, but yeah."

"A bug monster? As in, a monster made of bugs?"

"Pretty much."

"Shit." He looked stricken, and cast a furtive glance from side to side. "This bug monster – you think it's comin' back?"

"If we don't track down what Danny took, and soon, you can count on it."

He swallowed hard, and did his best to put on a brave face. It wasn't terribly convincing. "Guess it's a good thing I patched you up then. You gotta be in tip-top shape so you can kick its insect ass the second time around."

I laughed. It hurt.

"Listen," he said, "speaking of patching you up, I got some good news and I got some bad news."

"OK," I said, wary. "What's the bad news?" The way I was talking, it sounded more like *Wazzabanooze?*

"The bad news is the trip through the windshield broke your nose. I was hoping when you came to that you'd be able to muddle through as is, but to be honest, you don't sound so good. Which means I'm gonna hafta straighten it – and *that* is gonna smart like hell."

"Then what the hell's the *good* news?"

"The good news is, you ain't gonna be conscious long to feel it."

Before I could reply, he grabbed my head in both hands, his thumbs on either side of my nose. Then he jerked them to one side. I heard a sickening crunch, and let out a wail. Then, for a while, I didn't hear anything at all.

When I next came to, the sun was getting high overhead, and I was surprised to find myself peering through an unmarred windshield at a good acre of gleaming candy-apple red. A quick look around, and I realized I was sitting in the passenger seat of a classic Cadillac convertible – '58 or '59, I think – complete with red leather interior, sparkly paint-job, and chromed-out tailfins. The ragtop was down, but the old girl wasn't going any-where; she was just sitting in what, apparently, was a mostly empty strip club parking lot. (Sorry, *gentleman's* club, according to the awning over the front door – though if the airbrushed mural of a pair of legs extending outward on either side of the entryway was any indication, it didn't look like the sort of place in which a gentleman had ever actually set foot.) Gio was try-ing his best to rectify that – he'd popped the steering column with the Fiesta's tire iron, and was currently trying to strip a couple wires with his teeth. The mangled heap of the Fiesta sat beneath the strip club's darkened neon sign a good twenty spots to my right. Every once and a while, Gio glanced over at it, as one might toward a jungle cat on the verge of pouncing.

"Gio," I said, noting as I did that my voice had lost some of its thick, wet quality of earlier this morning, "you want to tell me what the hell you think you're doing?"

"What's it *look* like I'm doing? When you had your little tangle with the bug monster, the Fiesta took a fucking beating. Now, that don't really bother me none, on account of she ain't mine, and she was a piece of shit to begin with. But if I had to guess, I'd say our good pal Ethan's probably reported her stolen by now, which means we gotta steer clear of any legal entanglements – and it seems to me a giant fucking hole in our windshield is the sort of thing the five-oh might notice. Bottom line is, you wanna make it to Las Cruces, you and me are gonna need another ride."

"Yeah," I said, eyeing the Caddy's sparkle and shine and eye-catching lines, "it'd suck to attract any undue attention to ourselves."

"Look, make your smart-ass jokes all you want. But it's almost nine in the morning, and this place's been closed for hours. Which means whoever owns this beauty was drunk enough he probably cabbed it home. I bet he spends half the day sleeping off his hangover. That gives us plenty of time to get the hell outta Dodge 'fore he wakes up. By the time he realizes this baby's missing, we ain't even gonna be in the same *state*. And you gotta admit, Sam – this Caddy is a work of art. We'd be nuts not to take it."

"Gio, no. This car's too damn pretty not to be missed, and too rare not to be noticed. Pick something else – like maybe that nice, nondescript Civic over there."

"Hey, you got to pick the last one, remember? And if you got a thing for penny racers, that's your deal. But I barely fit into that fucking thing, so there's no way I'm gonna help you steal another one exactly like it – not when there's a ride this cherry just sittin' here waiting to be picked."

"Seriously, Gio – stop this, now."

But Gio didn't listen. He just glanced over at the Fiesta yet again, and redoubled his efforts to get the Caddy running.

"Did you hear me? You are *not* to boost this car!"

"Damn it, Sam, I ain't your fucking sidekick, OK? Truth is, you *need* me, and I say this Caddy is ours! The way I see it, any douchebag who'll leave a ride this fine sitting in a strip club parking lot is askin' to be taken down a peg. And it ain't like it's gonna kill you to loosen up and live a little – hell, *you're* the one who told *me* I should enjoy what little time I had left. So if you want my help on this little revenge-trip of yours, you're gonna hafta shut up a sec so I can concentrate!"

"I think you misunderstand the nature of our relationship," I said, unintentionally echoing the creature's words to me last night. I opened the Caddy's massive door and stepped unsteadily out onto the blacktop of the parking lot. "You don't get to call the shots. You want to go it alone, maybe steal yourself a shiny ride, hole up somewhere, and wait to see if hell forgets to hunt you down, that's your business – and I promise you it won't end well. But if you want to come with me and make the guy who killed you pay, you'll do as I say and pick another fucking car."

I leveled my gaze at Gio, trying to imbue it with as much bad-ass as I could muster. At the time, I was pretty pleased with the result, because he was staring back at me in wide-eyed terror. Of course, I didn't realize it then, but that terror had nothing whatsoever to do with me.

"Look, Sam, I get what you're saying – really, I do. But this really ain't the time to discuss it. How 'bout you get in the car, and we can talk about it on the road?"

"Are you even listening to me? That's the *last* place we're going to talk about it! Get it through your fucking head – I am not leaving this parking lot until you pick another car!"

"You won't be saying that in a minute," he mumbled, more to himself than to me.

Something clicked with me then. His jangled nerves. His furtive glances. His sudden desire to leave. At first, I'd chalked it up to the rush of stealing such a cherry ride, but it was something more than that.

"Gio," I said, "what'd you do?"

"Look, can we just go?"

"Not until you tell me what you did."

"Well, I figured we can't ditch the Fiesta without people taking notice – it's all beat to hell and fulla blood. The cops are bound to think some serious shit went down, and we don't need that kind of attention. So I handled it."

"Handled it? Handled it how?"

But before Gio could answer, the morning calm was torn apart by an explosion that set the Fiesta soaring skyward, and threw me ass-over-teakettle into the waiting Cadillac. I wound up wedged head-first into the passenger-side footwell, my torso pinned between the seat and dash. It was hell on my ribs, but at least it kept my face from scraping against the floor mat. I tried in vain to catch my breath, but the force of the blast had knocked the wind from my chest and left me gasping like a fish on a trawler's deck. I must've been flopping like one too, as I struggled to right myself – but at that, at least, I had some success. After a moment's thrashing about, I wound up sitting sideways across the bench seat, one foot braced against Gio's pudgy face, and my back against the passenger door. You'd think a shoe against your cheek is the kind of thing you might take notice of, but if Gio did, he didn't show it. He was too busy staring at the pillar of thick black smoke that spiraled skyward from the twisted remains of Ethan's Fiesta.

Charred bits of scrap and glass rained down upon us from above, but still, Gio just sat there, stunned. Through sheer force of will, I drew a breath – as hot and thick as tar – and barked a single, desperate syllable.

"GO!"

My voice sounded tinny and far away to my ears, which still rang from the crack of the blast, but that single syllable was enough to goad Gio into action. He sparked the ignition to life and threw the Caddy into gear. Then he laid on the gas and we squealed out of the parking lot, the scent of our tires against the blacktop lost in the charred stench of the twisted wreck we left behind.

15.

We were twenty minutes from Las Cruces when I realized we were not alone.

The strip club was a good half hour behind us, though between the heated bickering, the withering silences, and the bouts of justifiable paranoia that flared up with every speed trap that we'd passed, it felt like twice that long. It was a good thing Gio got the Caddy running when he did – a fire engine and a couple of squad cars went screaming past us in the oncoming lane before we'd gone four blocks from the strip club parking lot, and by the time we reached the highway, a column of smoke a mile high cleaved the morning sky and no doubt drew the attention of every law-enforcement type the city over.

I'll admit, as near as I could tell from the passenger seat, the Cadillac handled like a dream, and as the sun crested overhead, sending the temperature into the seventies, cruising with the top down was a little slice of heaven. The stretch of highway leading upward from West Texas to Las Cruces runs alongside the Mesilla Valley – a fertile floodplain four miles wide, blanketed with lush green farmland and dotted here and there with fragrant pecan groves. It was a pleasant respite from the hostile no man's land we'd been driving through, but I was so damn furious at Gio for the attention he'd drawn our way – and so damn worried about getting snagged by the cops before we managed to track down Varela's soul – I couldn't properly enjoy it. So instead, I sat there needling him, oblivious to the danger lurking a couple feet behind us.

"Seriously, Gio, what the hell were you thinking?"

Gio said nothing. He just grit his teeth and drove, his fingers white-knuckled on the wheel. I wasn't surprised; I'd asked him that at least a dozen times in the past half hour.

"What, you're not talking now? Come on, Smart Guy – I'd *love* for you to fill me in on your master plan."

At that, he wheeled toward me, his eyes glinting with anger. "Fuck you, Sam. If it wasn't for me, you'd be bleeding to death in the fucking desert right now. And has it even occurred to you that if you hadn't decided to hold your impromptu little Q-and-A back there instead of letting me do my thing, we'da been long gone by the time the Fiesta blew? So don't go crapping on my plan – *you're* the one who went and screwed it up."

"You think the fact that we were there when it happened was the only flaw in your otherwise genius plan? You're even dumber than I thought. Unless you somehow managed to vaporize the Fiesta, they're going to eventually get the VIN off of it, which means they'll be able to track it back to Ethan and to Illinois. Ethan's no doubt smart enough to leave out the whole walking-dead angle, but you can be damn sure he'll give them our descriptions, and once they know we crossed state lines, the Feds'll get involved. Next thing you know, every cop from here to California's got eyes out for us. And here we are, cruising around in a bright red stolen car the size of a fucking aircraft carrier. You know what? My bad. In retrospect, it was an *awesome* plan."

Gio's borrowed face went red with rage, and he lobbed back a profanity-laced retort, but I didn't pay him any mind. I was preoccupied by the strangest sensation at the nape of my neck – a sudden niggling intuition that something was not quite right.

At first, I had trouble putting my finger on exactly what it was. Not a tingle, to be sure, and not a sudden chill. But as a Collector, I've learned to trust my instincts, and in that moment, my instincts were insisting we were not alone. And in retrospect, that insistence felt not unlike a cowboy boot to the back of the head.

When the kick connected, I pitched forward, and smacked my face into the dash. It hurt like hell, and my vision went spotty, but at least I remained conscious, and my nose stayed where Gio'd put it.

I saw a blur of snake skin out of the corner of my eye, this time heading in Gio's direction. He yelped, and the Cadillac swerved left. Beside us, a car horn blared.

Gio tried to correct, and went too far. We barreled toward the barbed wire fence that separated the dirt shoulder from the green-tinged farmland beyond. *Shit*, I thought – *two cars in one day? You've got to be kidding me.*

But this time, it wasn't meant to be. I heard a string of curses, delivered in a drawn-out Texan twang, and then an arm shot out from the back seat and grabbed the wheel, yanking it to the left. Our bumper missed the fence post by scant inches, and then Gio slammed the brakes, bringing the Caddy to a skidding halt on the shoulder.

"Jesus H. Christ, that was a close one! I mean, shit, I didn't want that bitch to take ol' Bertha here away from me, but that don't mean I want to go and wreck her!"

I turned toward the source of the statement to find a paunchy, denim-clad sixty-something sprawled across the back seat and fanning himself with a sweat-stained Stetson. A thin cotton blanket that had until moments ago no doubt covered him sat discarded on the seat beside him. He had a shock of white hair atop his head, and a dusting of stubble to match. Gin blossoms colored his nose and cheeks, and his eyes were rimmed with red. As I watched, those eyes widened, and he suddenly twisted around, hanging his head over the side of the car and puking.

Normally, in my world, that's a sure sign of possession, but if the smell coming off this dude was any indication, this time it was the result of way too much tequila. The odor of sick aside, I was relieved that the head-kicking portion of the program was apparently behind us. The shape our passenger was in, he didn't pose much of an immediate threat, so while he was busy purging the contents of his stomach, I wheeled on Gio and tried my best to conjure death-rays with my eyes.

"You have got to be fucking *kidding* me," I whispered. "You didn't check to see if the car was *empty* before you boosted it?"

"How was *I* supposed to know he was sleeping it off in back? With that blanket on, he looked like a pile of junk."

I touched my good hand to the back of my head. "That pile of junk almost took my fucking head off – and damn near got all three of us killed."

"Yeah, but look on the bright side," Gio said, smiling. "If he's here, there ain't nobody around gonna report this baby stolen."

The bright side. Right.

This day kept getting better and better.

Eventually, our cowboy friend's heaving ceased, and he flopped back onto the seat, wiping his mouth with his sleeve.

"Well, hell," he said. "I guess you boys are going to have to take me back now, aintcha?"

"Come again?" I asked, flummoxed. I suppose the more well-behaved among you might not know this, but in my experience, carjackings don't typically elicit such blasé responses.

The man saw my confusion and frowned. "Boy, I don't want to tell you how to do your job, but ain't you repo types just supposed to take the *car*? Jolene's made it pretty clear she wants her half of what I got, but she sure don't seem to want nothin' to do with *me*."

Gio opened his mouth to say something then, but I silenced him with a glance. Then I turned to our new friend and gave him my best not-a-car-thief smile. "Listen, Mr – I'm sorry, I didn't catch your name."

"That's because I didn't throw it, son. Name's Roscoe McRae. As in founder and CEO of McRae Oil, and soon-to-be-ex-husband of one Mrs Jolene McRae. But then, I would've expected you to know that."

"Of course, Mr McRae. Listen, Mr McRae, we're sorry to have troubled you, but we were only doing our job. The agency led us to believe the car would be unattended."

"You're sorry to have troubled me."

"Yes."

"You were only after the car."

"That's right."

"And you think taking the only thing that I got left in this world that brings me any joy wouldn't have *troubled* me?"

"Sir," said Gio, the word dropping unfamiliar from his lips, "if you don't mind my asking, what the hell were you even *doing* back there?"

Roscoe looked at Gio like he was the kid in class you had to keep away from the paste. Then he shook his head and laughed. "You a car guy, son?"

"A little," Gio admitted.

"Ain't no *little* about it – either you *is* or you *ain't*. Me, I been a gear-head since long before I could even reach the pedals, and I always told myself that when I made my fortune, I was gonna get myself a Cadillac – a real one, mind, not one of them silly SUVs all the NBA players cruise around in these days. Took me damn near forty years to manage it, too. So if you think I'd leave this beauty unattended in a strip club parking lot just 'cause I had a little too much to drink, you got another thing coming. Bertha here deserves better'n that – just like she deserves better'n getting auctioned off to the highest bidder so Jolene can buy herself another of them ugly stoles she never even wears. As if she ain't got useless crap to spare now that she's maxed out all my credit cards."

Gio looked chastened. Me, I felt too shitty about the whole affair to bother gloating. *I told you so* is all well and good, but it wasn't going to get us out of the predicament Gio's dumb-ass call had put us in. "For what it's worth," I said to Roscoe, "I'm sorry."

"Ah, hell, son, it ain't your fault. You been nothin' but nice to me since I woke up, and that's even granting that I kicked you in the head. You're so polite, it's almost hard to believe someone went and beat the snot out of you." Roscoe's gaze slipped from my bruised and swollen face to the rocket-ship lines of his beloved Bertha, and his eyes shone wet with tears. "Almost."

He shook his head as if to clear it, and when he met my gaze again, his eyes were dry. "Ain't no use crying, I suppose. You gotta take the hand the good Lord gave you, and do with it the best you can. Tell you what – how about the three of us go and grab a little breakfast, and then y'all can drop me at a bus station so I can head back home. That bitch can wait a spell to get her filthy mitts on Bertha, and I could use a little grease to soak up what's left of this tequila."

After a moment's consideration, I agreed. After what Gio and I had put him through, it seemed to me the least that we could do. And hell, if an hour or so of playing along meant that we could drive this baby free and clear a couple days, then it was time well spent.

So Gio pulled back into traffic, and we continued on our way. I was oddly cheered by Roscoe's presence, and I was heartened by the fact that he believed us to have a legitimate claim to take his car. This quest to recover Varela's soul had thus far proved to be quite the pain in my ass, so it was nice to finally catch a break.

Of course, the problem with being damned is there's no such thing as a lucky break. And as much as I liked Roscoe, I had no idea at the time what a lousy idea it was to let him tag along. If I knew then the cascade of awful *that* call would kick off, I swear I would've given the man his car back on the spot. Reunited with his precious Bertha, Roscoe could've been on his merry way, and me and Gio would've been free to hitch a ride the last twenty-odd miles into town – no harm, no foul.

But I didn't know. So instead of making the smart play, I carried blithely on – oblivious to the disaster that awaited.

16.

If it weren't for Rosita, none of this shit would've happened.

Don't get me wrong – I'm sure that she's a lovely person. And if she isn't, how the hell would I know? I've never even met the woman. But if she hadn't gone and plopped her diner smack in our fucking way, we wouldn't have wound up in such a god-damn mess.

I guess I should've known better, but at the time, all I was thinking of was getting rid of Roscoe without a hitch, and the hand-painted "Rosita's Diner – Nothing Finer!" billboard made the place look divey enough you just *knew* they could fry up a mean egg. Plus, the stretch of I-10 just south of Las Cruces was nothing but farmland and trailer parks, which at the time made Rosita's seem like a godsend. I figured we'd stop long enough to pour some coffee into Roscoe, get him a bite to eat, and call the guy a cab, and that would be the end of that. Hell, I was even going to pay. OK, fine, *Ethan* was – but still, a gesture's a gesture. The way I saw it, it was the least that I could do. But unfortunately, that's not how things shook out.

Just the sight of the place as we pulled up was enough to put a smile on my face. Rosita's was built around an old Valentine Industries lunch counter – those squat little red-and-white diners so common to the Southwest in the decades following the Second World War. Sure, the paint had faded a bit, now more rust-and-sand than red-and-white, and the original railroad car design had been expanded over the years with a series of squat cinderblock additions, painted white and wodged on here and there at random. But still, the sight of the old diner, and the salty-sweet scent of its well-tended griddle, brought me back – back to a time when Danny was a trusted friend, and every meeting with Ana crackled with the spark of possibility. Back when Quinn was a smiling, happy child who dreamed he'd one day be an engineer, building cities out of blocks in his mother's tidy Belfast garden.

I should've known right then Rosita's would be trouble. Those times are long gone now. Ain't nothing going to bring them back, and I'm a sentimental fool for wishing otherwise.

Our problems started in the parking lot. Two black-and-whites, parked nose to tail – their engines running, their drivers chatting amiably over paper cups of coffee. Another cruiser sitting vacant in the lot. We hadn't seen them before we pulled in because the bulk of the parking lot was tucked out of view around back of the rambling hodge-podge structure. In retrospect, I should've realized they'd be here – there wasn't anyplace else nearby for folks to go, and it's not like the cops along this stretch were all that busy. A little all-night place like Rosita's probably topped up their thermoses for free – a small price to pay for a guaranteed police presence in the wee hours of the morning. Helps to keep out the riff-raff – riff-raff who might otherwise be inclined to rob the place. Problem is, it also works on riff-raff like Gio and me, who are just looking for a bite to eat.

Gio was the first to spot them. He'd been regaling Roscoe with stories of car-thefts gone awry, repurposed – for the sake of conning Roscoe – as repossessions one and all. They'd been getting on like fast friends, laughing and cursing and bragging loudly to one another in the way that both cowboys and gangsters do. Then we rounded the corner of the building and Gio clammed up mid-sentence – his posture jerking ramrod straight, his hands suddenly at ten and two on the wheel. The Caddy rocked on its suspension as he slowed it to a crawl. The way he was acting, he may as well have lit a fucking flare.

"Uh, Sam?"

"I see them," I replied through gritted teeth. "Keep driving."

Gio had us rolling at about a half a mile an hour. Ants were zipping past us on the ground below. "A little faster than *that*," I snapped.

Roscoe glared at me through narrowed eyes. "You boys want to tell me what the hell is going on?"

"Nothing," I replied, perhaps a bit too quickly.

"Nothing – right. That why you're trying your damndest not to catch the cops' attention?"

"Roscoe," I said, my voice as calm and even as I could manage, "this is really not the time."

"But–"

"I said *not now*. I like you, Roscoe – I do. Which is why I'm going to ask you nicely to please shut your fucking mouth before I'm forced to do something we'll both regret. Sit tight and I promise you that everything will be just fine. Or don't, and see what happens."

At that, the color drained from Roscoe's face. He looked from the cops to me and back again as though wondering whether he should try to make a play, but my words must've had their intended effect, because a moment later his shoulders sagged, and suddenly he looked old and frail and deflated. Satisfied, I nodded at him and turned in my seat, facing once more forward. We're just three friends out for a drive, I thought as loudly as I could, hoping against hope the cops would pick up on the vibe.

"Gio," I said, "get us out of here – quietly."

Gio obliged, piloting the gigantic Caddy on an excruciating lap through the lot and heading out the way we came. I prayed they hadn't noticed us. I knew that in this parade float of a car, they couldn't not.

What I *didn't* know was whether they had traced the Fiesta back to Ethan yet, and if they *had*, whether the Feds had managed to distribute our descriptions. I told myself they couldn't possibly have worked that fast – that as far as these dudes knew, we were just a carload of guys who, on second thought, didn't want to brave the twenty minutes' wait it'd take for a table to open up.

Yeah, I didn't really believe it, either. And even if I did, it didn't matter. Eventually, the BOLO would go out on us, and when it did, there wasn't a question in my mind these boys would remember having seen us. Which meant soon enough, every copper in Las Cruces would have eyes out for us – and that would damn sure put a damper on my plan to track down Dumas.

After what felt like a freakin' hour, we cleared the diner's parking lot, the Caddy's whitewalls crunching as they gripped the gritty desert road. I set my jaw and forced myself not to hazard a glance back, so loath was I to meet the gaze of the officers who were almost surely staring after.

"Either of y'all feel like telling me what *that* was all about?"

We were weaving through the patchwork farmland on the outskirts of town, Gio turning left or right as I instructed. Fields of onions and green chilis raced by on either side, rustling gently in the morning breeze and filling the air with their vegetal scent. Gio hadn't said a word since we'd left the diner parking lot, and apart from the occasional directional command, neither had I. That was OK, though – Roscoe had been talking enough for the three of us, peppering Gio and me with question after fruitless question.

"You boys in some kind of trouble?"

"There," I said to Gio. "On the left."

Gio nodded. Coming up on our left was a massive, leaning barn, the wood bleached gray by sun and age. A pair of rutted tracks, overgrown with fragrant desert sage, led from the shoulder of the road to the place where the barn door once hung, though it didn't hang there any more. Now the entrance was a gaping maw that led into the darkness beyond – a darkness dappled here and there with narrow beams of sunlight, which streamed in where the roof had rotted through.

The Cadillac rocked along the dirt track and disappeared into the gloom. Inside, the air was close and thick and sickly sweet; a thin sheen of sweat sprung up across my borrowed skin, plastering my clothes to my frame. Gio cut the ignition, and I hopped out of the car, watching from the doorway of the barn to ensure we hadn't been followed. For a time, I heard nothing but the beating of my meat-suit's heart. Then Roscoe broke the silence – his voice low and quiet and full of fear.

"You boys ain't repo men, are you?"

"No," I said, "we're not."

"So you're what, then? Car thieves? Common criminals?"

"Something like that."

"Ah, come on, Sam – tell him!" This from Gio.

"No."

"Why the hell not?"

"For one, telling him won't go well. Believe me, it never does. And for another, it's not safe."

"Seems to me, he's involved now whether we fill him in or not – so what's the harm?"

"You're not getting me," I said. "I mean telling him isn't safe for *us*."

Gio blinked in disbelief. "After all you been through today, you're afraid of *Roscoe* here?"

"I'm afraid of a lot of things," I said. "Unnecessary complications, for example – which is *exactly* what Roscoe here would be if we told him. Simply put, he doesn't need to know."

Roscoe looked from me to Gio and back again, squinting against the darkness. "What? What aren't you telling me? What don't I need to know?"

"We're Grim Reapers," Gio blurted. "We're on a mission from God!"

"Excuse me?"

I sighed. "Ignore him, OK? Gio – shut the fuck up."

But Roscoe wasn't about to take my advice. "Grim Reapers," he said. "Great. I fall asleep for a couple hours, and I'm abducted by a couple of goddamn loonies!"

"I'm being serious!" Gio insisted.

"Oh. Good. You're being serious. In that case, I believe you. Does that mean I can go?"

Gio bristled at Roscoe's sarcasm, but I just frowned and shook my head. "I'm sorry," I said, not unkindly. "But you've seen us. You know where we are. What we're driving. I can't let you walk out of here – there's too much at stake."

It was then that Roscoe noticed what I'd been doing. While we three had been talking, I'd popped the trunk, and riffled through it until I found what I was looking for – a length of yellow nylon rope of the kind used to tether the trunk closed when transporting oversized loads. Given the loft-like spaciousness of the Caddy's trunk, I'm guessing its use would be limited to packing up other, smaller cars.

"Sam, no," Gio said, his voice strained by sudden alarm.

"Gio, shut up and mind the door. The last thing we need now's another witness."

Gio's face twisted into a silent plea, visible even in the

murky half-light. I held his gaze a moment, and with obvious reluctance, he did as I said, shuffling over to the doorway and standing guard.

I coiled the rope around both hands, and pulled taut a two-foot length of it between them. Roscoe's eyes widened in fear, and he tried to back away, but the Caddy blocked his path.

"Don't," he said. "Please."

"I wish I didn't have to, but there isn't any other way."

"I'm begging you, don't do this. Just take the car and go – I won't tell a soul, I swear!"

"I'd like to believe you, but right now, I can't take that risk."

"But I got *grandkids*."

"I'm sorry," I replied. "It's nothing personal."

I was on him in a flash. The whole time, Gio never turned around – unwilling or unable to, I'll never know. For a little while, old Roscoe put up quite a fight. But eventually, Roscoe wasn't fighting anymore.

When the deed was done, I slammed the trunk, and climbed into the driver's seat. The keys I'd found in Roscoe's pocket, so this time, no hotwiring was necessary. I slid them in and thumbed the ignition, and the old girl sprang to life.

"C'mon," I said. "We're going."

Gio shrugged then, looking tired and drawn, and plopped heavily into the passenger seat. I backed the Caddy out of the barn, leaving nothing but gloom and silence behind.

17.

"I don't see why you had to do it, is all."

"I told you, Gio – he would have been a liability."

"A liability! A liability *how*? Maybe if you'da taken a sec to properly explain the situation, he'da wound up on our side!"

"Explaining the situation to his satisfaction was going to take a hell of a lot longer than 'a sec' – and chances are, he wouldn't have believed me anyway."

"*I* believed you fine," he said, his tone that of an insolent child.

"Yeah, but *you* I brought back from the dead – and in another body, to boot. That goes a long way in the convincing-you department."

"Still," Gio replied, "you didn't hafta to get all drastic."

"I'm sorry – is the hell-bound mob enforcer going *soft* on me?"

Gio bristled. "I ain't going soft – I just liked the guy, is all."

"Oh, for Christ's sake, Gio – it's not like I *killed* him. And once we get to where we're going, I promise I'll let him out of the trunk, OK? I just can't have him making trouble if we run into any more cops."

Gio muttered something, but I didn't catch it.

"I'm sorry – what was that?"

"I *said* he's probably hot in there. We shoulda given him a bottle of water or something."

"The guy is bound and gagged, Gio – what the hell's he going to do with a bottle of water?"

"I guess," he said, but he sounded unconvinced.

"He'll be fine. Besides," I said, glancing down at the real estate circular – picked up at a convenience store a few miles back – that sat open on my lap and then back up at the street before us, "it looks like he won't be back there much longer; we're here."

Here, in this case, was Cuesta Verde Estates, a tidy little development a few minutes north of downtown Las Cruces – or, at least, it *would* have been a tidy little development, if the project hadn't been abandoned years back when the market tanked. The ad in the circular promised *"SEVERAL UNITS AVAILABLE! PRICED TO MOVE! FINISH TO SUIT!"* – all music to a would-be squatter's ears. I counted twenty-four homes on the single, winding drive, ranging in state from finished, just inside the charming flagstone sign that marked the entrance of the development, to skeletal frames draped in Tyvek and sheets of plastic as the pavement gave way to fifty feet of dirt track before vanishing into the desert beyond. Only the first three or so looked to be occupied. The rest sat vacant, their many *FOR SALE* placards swaying gently as one in the warm desert breeze. I checked the clock in the dash. It was barely 2pm. That meant what few people actually lived here were likely all at work or school or wherever.

For now, the neighborhood was ours.

I piloted the Cadillac down the empty street, past the well-tended yards of the occupied houses, and into a stretch marked by heat-cracked earth and overgrown by desert scrub. Here and there, the pavement jutted a couple feet to the left or right of the main drive, and the curb followed suit, curving to accommodate these tiny on-ramps to nowhere. They were no doubt intended to allow for future development should the need arise; I'm sure whoever plotted out Cuesta Verde saw modest taupe houses on every tenth of an acre for miles around, on streets named Mesa and Arroyo and the like. Now those preparations for expansion were nothing more than a painful reminder of headier times too far gone to even hope that they'd return.

"There," I said, nodding at an unfinished house around the bend from the entrance to the development, obscured from view of the occupied homes by the two that came before it. "That's the one."

Gio heaved a sigh that sounded like a balloon deflating. "I still don't see why we can't stay at a motel."

I shot him a look that would've made a small child cry. Gio just blinked back at me from amidst a pile of crumpled cellophane wrappers and empty Coke cans – his face full of crumbs, his expression blank. "Well, for starters, I just spent the last of Ethan's cash on food – food that was *supposed* to last the three of us at least a day. And I'm sure the cops've flagged Ethan's credit card accounts by now, which means we even try to get a room, they'll be on us in minutes. Then there's the matter of the stolen Caddy and the pissed-off Texas oilman in the trunk, which as far as I'm concerned makes parking anyplace where there's witnesses a pretty crap idea."

"Hey, it ain't *my* fault I ate all that shit – this dude you stuck me in was fuckin' *hungry*. 'Sides, Roscoe's gotta have a little dough on him, right?"

"Not a dime. I checked his wallet – plenty of plastic, but any cash he had went the way of the G-string last night."

"Figures you'd kidnap the only oil exec on the planet that ain't carrying a fat wad of bills. So fine, a motel's out, but that don't mean we gotta stay in a total *shithole* – I mean, they're trying to sell these places, right? Which means they gotta have a model home around here somewhere. You know, with lights and AC, and running water so I could maybe take a shower? I mean, *this* place ain't even finished – it's like a fucking tent with siding."

"Yeah, but it's out of sight, and it's got a garage where we can stash the car. The model home was around front, near the ones where people live, and it didn't have a garage – you think nobody's going to notice if we move in?" I shook my head. "I'll tell you, man – it's a good thing you had a deal with a demon to fall back on, 'cause on your own you're kind of lousy at being a criminal."

"Geez, Sam, didn't nobody ever tell you words can hurt? Like, imagine for example I said, 'Funny, you talkin' smack about how I do my job, 'cause from where I'm sitting, it looks like you suck so bad at doing yours that *you* had to come beg *me* for help'? That'd kinda sting, wouldn't it?"

"Cute," I snapped. "Real cute. Now how about you work off that bag of Funyuns you devoured by getting that garage door open so we can park this boat inside, huh?"

"Wow," he said, hauling himself up out of the bench seat and trotting up the driveway, "sounds like somebody needs a hug." Gio's tone was pissy, but I caught the hint of a smile at the corner of his lips as he yanked up the garage door and beckoned me in. Despite myself, I wound up grinning back at him. Then he flipped me off.

I drove into the waiting garage, shaking my head as Gio slid the door shut behind me.

God help me, I thought, I'm actually starting to like this guy.

"Looks like we're clean," Gio said. "For now, at least. Gotta say, Sam, in my line a work, I've swept for bugs a time or two – but before today never the creepy crawly kind."

I was sitting cross-legged on the bare plywood subfloor of our new squat, reading the copy of the Las Cruces *Sun-News* I'd picked up on our snack run by the light of the afternoon sun. Or, rather, that's what I was *trying* to do. Gio'd barely given me a moment's peace. Reading near Gio was like reading in the company of a dog – he couldn't seem to comprehend that what looked like me just sitting there ignoring him was me actually fucking *doing* something.

I'd kept him busy a few minutes checking the house for Deliverants – but it was a small place, and wide-open on the inside, so it didn't take him long. The fact there weren't any was heartening. I guess my buddy the bug-monster figured he'd give me a little latitude to go along with my marching orders.

Not like that latitude was going to do me any good if I couldn't find five quiet minutes to formulate some kind of workable plan. I'll tell you, between Gio's yammering, and Roscoe screaming his fool head off in the bathroom, it was a miracle I didn't kill them both. I mean sure, I'm not strictly speaking supposed to dispatch folks willy-nilly, but it wasn't like the water I was in could get any *hotter*.

Least, that's what I thought at the time. One of these days I'm going to learn that when I think to myself it really couldn't get much worse, I am never, *ever* right. *Much worse* is sort of hell's stock in trade, and I'm an idiot for forgetting that, even for a moment.

"You figure this Danny jackass has got a plague of locusts on his tail, too?"

I shook my head. "Crows."

"Come again?"

"The creatures stalking Danny would be crows."

Gio snorted. "Gotta tell you, dude: you wound up with the shit end of *that* stick."

"You think?" I asked. "Seems to me, I'd rather run into a bunch of pissed-off insects than an equal number of angry crows. Those fuckers are smart, and nasty when pressed."

Gio fell silent then, for like a whopping ten seconds. I should've known it wouldn't last.

"So what exactly are you looking for?" he asked.

"I don't know," I snapped. "I'll find it when I see it."

"This research shit would go a hell of a lot faster if you had an iPhone, you know."

"Phones should have cords," I said, "not television screens."

"Next you're gonna tell me a woman's place is in the home, right? I know you're older than you look, Sam, but you might wanna try gettin' with the times – it's a brave new world out there! Besides, everybody says print is dead anyway."

"Yeah, well so am I – and for that matter, so are you. So how about you make like it for a bit and clam up so I can read?"

Gio raised his hands as though surrendering. "Hey, you wanna be a crotchety old fogy, that's your business. I'm just saying a little Google access would make your life a whole lot easier."

"Hey, I've got no problem with technology, but a Google search can't help me any if I don't know what it is I'm looking for. And all I need to make my life a whole lot easier is a few minutes of peace and quiet." I nodded toward the bathroom, where old Roscoe was shouting himself hoarse. "You think maybe you could shut him up?"

"I ain't about to whack him, if that's what you're asking."

"What are you, new? If I wanted Roscoe dead, I would've killed him myself back at the barn. I was thinking something more along the lines of bringing him a beer and a bite to eat from what's left of our stash. And toss me that pack of smokes, while you're at it."

"Aw, come on, Sam – you're not really gotta light up in here, are you? Didn't nobody ever tell you secondhand smoke kills? The last thing I need right now is lung cancer on account of your nasty-ass habit."

"You're kidding me, right? You're worried about *lung cancer*? Gio, you'll be lucky if you last the fucking week – and if by some miracle you're walking around in Mr Frohman's body any longer than that, it'll be your heart that gets you, not your lungs."

Gio looked nonplussed. "Still, dude, it's all of our house. Can't you take it to the porch or something?"

"Gio, this house isn't *any* of ours – and if I drag my ass outside to smoke, somebody might see me and call us in. You want to spend your last days on this earth in jail?"

At that, he looked chastened. "I'm just sayin' – a little consideration for your fellow housemates would be nice. Besides, it's the twenty-first century – who smokes anymore?"

"Oh, for Christ's sake. Toss me my fucking cigarettes – I'll crack a window, and blow the smoke outside, OK?"

"You know what? Go ahead. Not like you give two shits about anybody but yourself."

He chucked the pack at me, and then sulked over to the bathroom door, a gas station burrito and a Santa Fe Pale Ale in hand. I unwrapped the pack and tapped out a cigarette. Then I fetched a matchbook from my pocket and struck one alight. But as I raised it to my waiting cigarette, I paused.

Lung cancer? Seriously? Guy was off his fucking nut.

I sat like that a minute, marveling at Gio's unrelenting ridiculosity, the match flame a scant inch from my unlit smoke. Eventually, the flame guttered and died. I thought about striking another, but something stopped me.

Ah, fuck, who am I kidding? Some*one* stopped me. That's right – the bad-ass soul collector skipped a much-needed smoke to spare a damned man's feelings. Least I *hope* that's what it was. Better to admit that I'm a marshmallow than that I was swayed by the dumbest argument this side of *the devil made all the dinosaur bones and stuck them in the ground to deceive us*.

Jesus, am I going soft? I mean, shit – if I want a smoke, I should just *have* one, right?

Right?

Eh, I thought. Maybe later.

Then I shook my head and set the pack aside, cigarette and all.

18.

"I don't get it," Gio said, struggling to keep a grip on the local section of the newspaper, which was flapping like a flag in a hurricane now that the Caddy was on the open road. For the moment, it was just he and I — we'd left Roscoe tied up and screaming back at the squat. It was safer traveling without him, and not just a little quieter, too. Or rather it would've been, if Gio could've kept hold of the goddamn paper. "What exactly am I supposed to be seeing?"

"Halfway down, under the thing about the fire."

"'AREA MAN FOUND WANDERING IN DESERT'," he read.

"That's the one."

"Yeah, but what about it? All it says is that this dude was found naked and babbling late Sunday night somewhere off of Canyon Point Road."

"He's our guy."

"The hell you mean, 'He's our guy'? You think Naked Dude's the demon dope-peddler you been looking for?"

"No. But I think he can help me find him."

"Yeah? How?"

"Because I'm pretty sure Dumas's skim-joint is where he was coming from when they picked him up."

Gio frowned. "I thought you said this skim shit was only for demons and undead-types like you and me – that the living wouldn't get nothing out of it."

"It is. Only those removed from the light of God's grace are susceptible. The living would be unaffected."

"Removed from the light of God's grace, huh?" His thick brow bunched with worry. "Is that what I am now?"

I hesitated for a moment, then bit the bullet and told him the truth. "Yes." What else could I have said?

He swallowed hard and tamped down his emotions. When he looked at me again, he was a little drawn, a little pale, but once more calm and collected. "So what the fuck would Mr Richard Shaw of Chilton Drive, Las Cruces have been doing there?"

I sighed, tried to explain. "When you're out on a heist, you ever drive your own car?"

"Hell, no – you're on a job, you want something disposable. A car that, once you ditch it, it can't be traced back to you."

"Exactly – and for a demon, it's no different. See, skim-joints are strictly verboten in the demon world, because they rely on a steady supply of human souls to make their product – souls destined for hell, sure, but souls nonetheless. Now, ideally, the skimmer shaves off what they want and then passes the soul on to meet its ultimate fate, so nobody's the wiser. But if there's a fuck-up in the skimming process, that soul could be destroyed. The destruction of a human soul is a violation of the Great Truce between heaven and hell, and if either side were seen to be condoning such an act, the result would almost certainly be war – which means skim-joints are an affront to God and the devil both. So the *last* thing any demon wants is to get caught coming out of one. An easy way around that is to possess some unsuspecting bastard for a few hours and ditch him when you're done – sort of the demon version of a getaway car. See, unlike me, all demons – be they the lowliest and most monstrous foot-soldiers, or the higher-ups that look like you and me – have bodies of their own, so when they possess someone, it's more like remote projection. Snatching a vessel to hit a skim-joint means their true selves can be safe and sound half a world away. On the off-chance their vessel's killed, they wind up right back in their own body – no harm, no foul. Only the hardcore skim junkies ever bother to show up in person; the way I hear it, the high's better if you're present in the flesh."

"Yeah, I gotcha – but if they wanna keep things on the DL, why wouldn't they just kill the dude when they were done with him? I mean, what's to keep the guy from blabbing?"

"Well, for starters, demonic possession is pretty traumatic. The vessel usually doesn't remember much in the way of specifics – just the odd image, scent, sensation. Besides, even if he *did* remember, who in their right mind would *believe* him? And remember – Dumas's skim-joint would attract a fair bit of business, so this wouldn't exactly be an isolated incident. If all Dumas' patrons started killing vessels left and right, the white hats would be bound to notice, and that's the last thing anybody wants."

"The white hats? You mean, like, *angels*?" Gio's face had taken on the kind of inner light usually reserved for kids waiting up to catch a glimpse of Santa Claus.

"That's right. Only we're not talking harps and feathers – these are more the angry Wrath of God types. Believe me," I said, thinking back to my own tangle with an angel months before, and the swath of destruction across the length of Manhattan that had resulted, "angels are not to be trifled with."

That inner light faded, replaced by something closer on the reverence scale to fear. "Still, I don't get why you're so sure this Richard dude's our guy."

I smiled. "Easy. Demons got themselves a nasty sense of humor. They've pretty much got their pick of living vessels, but usually they've got a reason for choosing the one they do. Sometimes, they'll snatch a priest, make him speak in tongues at Mass to fuck with him. Sometimes, they'll take some buttoned-down old schoolmarm and ditch her at a leather bar. Or sometimes, when they need to hitch a ride, they'll pick a guy because they think his name is funny."

"What's so funny about Richard Shaw?"

"Nothing in particular," I admitted. "But what do you want to bet he goes by Rick?"

Richard Shaw's home was a low-slung yellow brick ranch in a quiet residential neighborhood about a mile north of the university. A pair of live oaks on either side of the pebbled front yard shaded the house from the light of the afternoon sun. I pulled the Cadillac into the short concrete drive, coming to a halt beside a beige Buick LeSabre adorned with a Jesus fish and a sticker for the local Christian station (*REJOICE in the Lord!*). Looks like whatever smart-ass demon decided to take himself a ride in a Rick Shaw got a twofer in the fucking-with-mortals department.

Though the day was bright and clear, and the temperature a balmy seventy-five degrees, every window in the house was closed, and the blinds were drawn as well. Three days' worth of newspapers sat untouched atop the stoop, and the letterbox beside the door was overflowing.

I scaled the porch steps and knocked.

Nothing happened – unless, of course, you count me and Gio shuffling awkwardly from foot to foot in our filthy funeral suits like the most unlikely, bedraggled missionaries ever while we waited for the door to open as *something happening*.

I knocked again. Still nothing.

"Mr Shaw?" I called. "I was wondering if we could have a moment of your time."

Inside I heard a scuff of feet on tile. A twitch of curtain revealed a glimpse of darkened living room as Shaw appraised us from inside. "Go away!" he cried, his voice plaintive and unsteady.

Gio looked from the door to me and back again. Then he patted his prodigious stomach and smiled. "You think maybe if I do the Truffle Shuffle, he'll let us in?"

"You're not helping," I replied under my breath. Then, louder toward the door: "I assure you, sir, we'll only be a minute; we just have some questions about what happened to you the other night."

"I told you people a dozen times already – I'm not talking to reporters! Why can't you all just leave me alone? Isn't it enough you ruined my life, you… you… *bunch of jerks*!"

Bunch of jerks. My, but that one stung.

Time to try a different tack.

"My associate and I are not reporters, Mr Shaw – we're Federal Marshals."

Gio looked at me like I'd sprouted a second head. "We're *what* now?" he muttered.

I shrugged my best *roll with it* shrug. Gio responded with what can only be described as a harrumph.

There was a *thunk* as the deadbolt disengaged, and the door opened a crack. The chain was still set, and Shaw peeked out under it, wary but hopeful. He was a slight, small-boned, thirty-something man in a pink polo shirt and iron-creased jeans over off-brand tennis shoes of gleaming white. His features were delicate bordering on feminine, and he had wide, pale blue eyes that, from the lack of lines surrounding them, appeared unaccustomed to the doubt that now darkened his face. "Federal Marshals?"

"That's right," I replied. "I'm Marshal Hutchinson, and this is my associate, Marshal Starsky. Now if you would please let us in, I believe we could shed some light on what happened to you Sunday night."

"But how do I know you're *real* Marshals, and not reporters *pretending* to be Marshals so I'll let you in?"

I sighed and dug Ethan Strickland's wallet from my inside coat-pocket, flipping it open and waving it at him as though it meant a damn. When he reached for it to take a closer look, I yanked it back. "Mr Shaw, attempting to handle a law officer's badge is a federal offense."

"Oh. Of course," he said, withdrawing his hand as visions of prison time danced in his head. "And please, call me Rick."

As Shaw closed the door, and disengaged the chain, Gio leaned in close, a grin plastered on his meaty face. "A federal offense, huh?"

"Hey, it *could* be."

"You're a fuckin' piece a work, you know that? And Starsky? Really? Why the hell couldn't *I* be Hutch?"

The door swung open once more, this time all the way. "Please, come in." We complied. Once we entered, Shaw ducked his head outside, casting furtive glances left and right before shutting the door behind us. "Sorry about the mess."

I looked around. Aside of a smattering of cellophane candy wrappers on the coffee table, the Spartan living room was immaculate. A floral couch sat beneath a simple wooden cross. Two royal blue recliners faced it from across the coffee table. No knick-knacks, no TV, and not a speck of dust in sight.

"Please, sit down," he said, disappearing into the kitchen around the corner. "Can I get you anything to drink?"

"Beer, if you have it," Gio said, as we both settled into the recliners.

"I do *not*. Alcohol is the devil's gasoline, and I for one like to keep the great deceiver's tank on E. Besides, I thought officers couldn't drink on duty?"

"That's only in the movies," I replied, and shot Gio a look that could've shattered glass.

"Ah," he said. "Well, I shouldn't be surprised. As Reverend Bellows always says, fiction *is* lying. So: apple juice or Fresca?"

Gio mimed gagging, and I punched him in the thigh. "Water would be fine," I said.

"Water it is," he said. A couple minutes' puttering, and he returned carrying a tray laden with drinks, and a crystal dish of hard candies.

"Care for one?" he said, grabbing a handful and unwrapping them with all the eagerness of a meth-head looking to score. "They're sugar-free. Even still, I usually limit myself to two a day – Jesus hates a glutton – but this week has left me out of sorts. As if I need to tell *you* that, after my outburst at the door. I'm *so* sorry you had to witness that; my language was inexcusable."

"The hell're you talkin' about?" Gio asked. "You mean when you said *jerk*?"

Shaw colored. I fought the urge to punch Gio in the leg again.

"You have to understand," Shaw said, "I'm simply at the end of my rope. I haven't slept a wink in days. My Mabel took the girls up to Branson to stay with their grandparents as soon as we returned home from the police station – she scarcely said a word to me that whole ride home, and now she won't even return my calls! Of course, normally in times of crisis, I'd find solace in the church, but once my story hit the papers, my congregation wanted nothing to do with me. I've been asked not to attend services until further notice. They gave away my choir solo to that cow Lorena Wilkins. Now I hear there's even talk of excommunication! I know the good Lord never presents us a challenge we can't handle, but right now, I don't see how I'm going to manage!"

He popped three candies into his mouth and crunched away at them with zeal. The way they sounded, I was less worried about his mental state than his teeth.

"Mr Shaw," I said.

"Rick."

"Rick. I understand this is a difficult time for you, but if we could ask you a few questions about what happened Sunday night–"

"But that's just *it*! I have no *idea* what happened Sunday night. One minute, I'm putting the girls to bed, and the next, it's hours later, and I'm wandering like a Jew through the desert, naked as the day God made me! Mabel said I got up in the middle of First Corinthians and walked right out the front door, but I swear I don't remember doing it – and to this day, I haven't the faintest notion what became of my clothes."

"Believe it or not, that's not uncommon in cases of this type. What we need to know is if there's anything at all you can tell us about your missing hours. Sights, smells, general impressions. Any detail you remember, no matter how small, would be a great help to us in our investigation."

Shaw slumped in defeat. "I wish I could help you – really, I do. But I've been over that night a thousand times, and I've no memory of it at all. If you don't mind my asking, what, exactly, are you investigating? What could have *done* this to me?"

"Demon," Gio muttered, but not quietly enough. Shaw's eyes went wide with sudden fear and disbelief.

"Worshippers," I interjected. "Demon-worshippers. We've been tracking them across the lower forty-eight for months. They've got a nasty habit of drugging people and luring them out into the desert for their weird-ass ceremonies. Word is, they're trying to conjure up a demon. But you've got nothing to worry about, Mr Shaw. Once they strike, they're unlikely to return to the same target a second time, and the fallout from the drugging aside, they shouldn't pose any future threat to you or your family. They're just a bunch of misguided nuts with no more idea as to how to call a demon than you or I." More you than I, I thought. I mean, I'm not a crack conjurer or anything, but I know a couple blood rites that'll summon in a pinch.

But Shaw found no comfort in my words. Instead, he looked pale and drawn, and his hand trembled as he reached for another batch of candy.

"I wouldn't be too sure of that," he said.

"Excuse me?"

"I *said*, I wouldn't be too sure of that. See, there is *one* thing that I recall from Sunday night – only it seemed so crazy, I assumed it was a dream."

"And what's that?"

"An awful stink, the likes of which I'd never smelled before. But even still, I know *exactly* what it was. Deep down, I guess I always knew."

"Knew *what*? What was it that you smelled?"

"Brimstone," he said. "The devil's stench."

19.

"So, do demons really smell like brimstone?" Gio asked once we were back on the open road.

"Not any demon *I* ever met. Though I once knew one who wore *way* too much Drakkar."

"Then why the hell'd we hightail it outta there so quick?"

"Because that doesn't mean it's not a clue."

"I don't follow."

"Well, it seems to me if it wasn't the *demons* that reeked of sulfur, maybe it was the place they took him to."

"You sayin' you know where that is?"

"Nope," I said. "Not yet."

"Then where the hell're we headed?"

"Library."

"*Library?*"

"Yeah, you know – big building, lots of books. They were all kinds of popular back in the day when people actually used to read. Don't worry, you'll like it – they have Google."

"Thanks, smart-ass. What I meant was, *why* are we going to the library?"

"I'm working on a theory," I said. "One that's gonna take a

157

little research to confirm. Believe me, when I know something, *you'll* know something, OK?"

Gio fell silent for a moment. "Hey," he said finally, "you think Shaw's gonna be all right?"

"Hard to say. Seems to me, it's fifty-fifty whether or not his wife comes back – and I'm pretty sure his spot on the choir is gone for good. But my guess is, he'll be OK."

"Yeah? Why's that?"

"He's got faith," I said. "And once the dust settles, his faith is going to be stronger than ever."

"How the hell you figure *that*? The poor bastard just got bitch-slapped by the universe – you really think it's gonna *help* his faith?"

"I don't see how it couldn't. The way I see it, even the most devout among us have their moments of doubt. Enough bad shit happens to good people in this world to rattle even the churchiest of Christians, and you can't tell me that a hardcore atheist doesn't plead with God to make it stop when he's got the bed-spins after a couple drinks too many. It's human nature – we're all of us stumbling in the dark, latching on to whatever brings us some measure of comfort and security, no matter how fleeting. Only Shaw managed to stumble into something bigger and scarier than himself – the kind of something his precious Bible's been warning him about all his life. Doesn't matter much the book was written by a bunch of clueless saps just like him, trying to piece together the unpieceable; once the shock of his encounter wears off, he's bound to start seeing his no-good-very-bad day as a big fat confirmation of everything he's ever believed."

"The way you talk, you almost sound like you're *jealous* of the dude."

"Jealous? No. If, in all of this, he loses the woman that he loves, he's gonna be hurting something fierce. That seems to me like way too high a price to pay for what he's getting in return. But a guy like Shaw? My guess is whatever happens, he'll accept that it was simply meant to be. God's plan and all that crap."

Gio snorted at that last. "Don't put much truck in God's plan, do you?"

"And you're what – surprised? Tell me, Gio, where did God's plan ever get *you*?"

"Hey, I can't complain. I did OK for myself – good job, nice ride, a pretty lady to come home to every night."

"Dude, do you even *hear* yourself? You're on your way to *hell*."

"That ain't God's fault. I'm man enough to take responsibility for what I done. Ain't nobody to blame for where I ended up but me." He squinted appraisingly at me from the passenger seat and shook his head. "But hey, you feel like the big man's gotta take the fall for your fuck-ups, that's between you and Him – it ain't no business a mine."

"No," I said. "I chose this path. But if God's plan hadn't included killing the woman that I loved, maybe I wouldn't have had to."

A pause, long and awkward. Neither of us eager to break it. Finally, Gio did. "The deal you cut – it was to save your *wife*?"

I clenched my jaw, gripped the wheel so tight it hurt. "Yeah."

"I'm sorry, man. I didn't know."

"Don't sweat it," I said, willing the aching in my chest to cease. "You couldn't have known."

"Was she, like, *sick* or something?"

"Do we have to talk about this?" I snapped.

Gio flushed, fell silent.

I let out a breath and willed the pounding of pulse in my ears to slow. "Tuberculosis," I said, once the knee-jerk flush of anger had subsided. "Diagnosed at nineteen, if you can believe it. Her whole life ahead of her, and then bam. For a couple years, she got off light. No sign, no symptoms. We started thinking hey, maybe we can make this work – after all, most folks with TB go their whole *lives* without ever getting past the latent stage. But then the coughing started, and she went downhill quick from there. This was in the days before a cure, mind you, and the two of us were poor as dirt. All we had was each other. I couldn't afford to give her the kind of care she needed, and if we'd thrown ourselves at the mercy of the medical community, they would've locked her ass away – another lunger off the streets, safe to rot within the walls of some decrepit sanitarium. So I did my best to take care of her at home – but of course, it wasn't enough. And when I got sick of watching her slowly drown in her own blood, I did what I had to do to save her life."

When Gio spoke, his voice was small, unsure – as if he didn't know if he should respond. "Did it work?"

The roadway blurred. I raised a hand to my eyes, and wiped away the moisture with my sleeve. "Yes."

"Hey, that's somethin', right? I mean, you two got to live out your happily ever after for a while before you got collected – didn't you?"

Happily ever after? Yeah, that's how I thought my deal would play out, too. But it very fucking *didn't* – Dumas made sure of that. See, part and parcel of my deal was, I was at his beck and call – required to do his bidding at a moment's notice, day or night. At the time, I didn't know he was a demon; Dumas had fashioned himself in the image of a gangster, which made me a gangster's errand boy. For months, he pushed me and he pushed me toward a life ever more dark and violent and despicable, until finally, I pushed back and killed him. Well, I *thought* I did, at least – turns out bullets aren't so effective when it comes to killing demons.

But the fact he couldn't die doesn't absolve me of his murder; when I pulled the trigger, I thought I was ending a human life, and that level of moral corruption doesn't come without a price. The blood I spilled that night served to seal my deal for good. And of course the fucker played dead just long enough for me to tell Elizabeth what I'd done. She couldn't stand the man that I'd become, and so she left – left me broken, alone, afraid – and took our unborn daughter with her.

I suppose Dumas could've had me collected then, as I lay reeling from the loss of the woman I traded everything to save, but he didn't. Instead, he made sure I stuck around long enough to see Elizabeth find someone else – and to watch our daughter grow inside her, knowing full well that I'd never get to meet her, hold her, *know* her – before he sent the meanest, most vicious Collector hell had to offer to deliver me to my fate. By then, the pain of death seemed like a respite. Sure beat the pain of a life without Elizabeth.

Or, at least, that's what I thought at the time.

Now, of course, I know better. Now I know that I'll be living without Elizabeth for eternity. I'm sure the thought would bring a smile to that shit-bag demon's face, maybe put a little spring in his step.

So *happily ever after*?

"Not exactly," I replied.

20.

"Hey, Sam? I think I got something."

We'd been at the library maybe twenty minutes. The first five of them I'd spent online searching the local paper's database for any mention of sulfur or further instances of naked wandering. I spent the next fifteen wrestling with the fucking microfiche machine, because it turns out if you want to read more than a line or two online, you have to pay for it. Gio watched over my shoulder for a while as I cursed and scowled and occasionally rapped the obstinate piece of junk on its side in an effort to get it to work, all to no avail. When he tired of chuckling at my expense, he returned to the bank of computers on the far wall, leaving me to stew in peace.

I craned around in my seat to face him, and in so doing, knocked a spool of microfilm onto the floor, where it dutifully unraveled. I'm pretty sure I heard the old lady making bake-sale flyers at the photocopier snicker. "I swear, Gio, if you're calling me over there to watch another video of a monkey dancing, I'm going to be pissed."

"No monkey this time, honest. Stop fucking with that thing and come over here, would you?"

Turns out, Gio *had* found something: a series of hits about an old hospital nestled in a narrow box canyon a few miles outside of town. Abandoned since the Fifties, its sandstone façade was crumbling and decrepit, and it had been all but reclaimed by the desert that surrounded it. He had enough windows open to make my head hurt – I think people born into the digital age must be wired differently to process so much shit at once – but most of the hits were pretty useless: a piece from the local historical society, too dry to bother reading; a couple hikers' websites, chock full of photographs of the hospital and the surrounding desert; a video piece from the local NBC affiliate on the perils of teen drinking that highlighted a story of a kid who, several years back, fell to his death from a window of the abandoned structure while he and a bunch of his friends were out partying in the desert. I began to wonder what the hell Gio dragged me over here for.

But as I read, there were others that were more illuminating. The minutes from a city council meeting in which the purchase of the old hospital was discussed. The results of a formal land survey – complete with map – submitted to the city by the developer, who declared his intent to build a resort upon the land in question, to take advantage of the natural sulfur springs that bubbled up from beneath the canyon floor. And the subsequent announcement on the city's website that all construction of the resort had ceased due to lack of funds.

For each of them, the developer was listed as Walter Dumas.

I clapped Gio on his borrowed shoulder, and fought the urge to do a little end-zone dance. His meaty face broke into a grin. "Nice work, Gio – this is *perfect*."

"So what now?"

"Print it. Print it all."

It was dusk when we arrived back at the squat, and the house was submerged in shadow, the nearest working lights

over two blocks away. The second we pulled into the driveway, I heard Roscoe screaming "*HELP!*" over and over again,
to no one. He must've been carrying on like this a while; his
voice was hoarse, and his calls sounded more rote than
plaintive, as though his heart wasn't really in it anymore.
He picked up a bit when he heard us coming in, but when
he spotted me through the open bathroom door, he slumped
against his restraints, and his shouting ceased. Seeing him
there, glaring at me in petulant defeat from atop the un-
plumbed toilet, he looked for all the world like a child
sentenced to a time-out.

"Oh," he said. "It's you."

"You been shouting like that the whole time?"

"No," he said, too quickly.

"I'll take that as a yes. Don't worry – it doesn't bother me
any. It's just there's no one around to hear – you really
could've saved your breath."

"You two are gonna kill me, aren't you?"

I laughed. "Roscoe, if we were going to kill you, you'd be
dead by now – if only to save ourselves the trouble of carrying
your ass around. Look, I know this sucks, OK? But tonight,
I've got some business to attend to, and once that's done, me
and Gio will be on our way. So just sit tight a while, and everything's gonna be just fine."

"Fine. Right. Says the guy who thinks he's a Grim Reaper."

"Roscoe, look at me. Whatever it is I think I am, I'm telling
you, it ain't your time to die. Now, maybe I'm nuts, or maybe
Gio was just fucking with you, but either way, I promise you
you'll be just fine, OK?"

He locked eyes with me a moment, and then he nodded.
"Shit," he said, though it sounded more like *SHEE-it*. "I guess
I believe you. And it ain't like I got nothing better to do, I sup-
pose. But do an old man a favor, would you?"

I smiled. Roscoe had no way of knowing it, but I had a few decades on him easy. "Name it," I said.

"Whatever damn-fool thing you're fixin' to do tonight, you be sure to get it done and come back in one piece. Last thing I need is to die strapped to a toilet 'fore my divorce is even finalized – then that thieving devil-woman would wind up with *everything* insteada just half."

I smiled. "It's a deal."

"Oh, and one more thing – if it ain't too much trouble, that is."

"Yeah?"

"I could sure as hell use another beer."

"So what's the plan?" Gio asked, once I got Roscoe settled down.

Gio and I were in the midst of a convenience store feast, polishing off the last of the junk food we'd picked up that morning and washing it down with lukewarm beer. Truth be told, it was making me kind of queasy – or maybe that was the thought of what I was about to do.

"The plan?"

"Yeah – like, are we goin' in guns blazin', or what?"

"Last I checked, Gio, we didn't actually have any guns."

"You know what I mean. Whaddya use to take down a demon, anyway? You stake 'em or some shit? Hit 'em with holy water? There some kinda prayer you gotta say?"

I shook my head. "None of that stuff works."

"Then what does?"

"Aside of a mystical object designed specifically to kill a demon? Pretty much nothing."

A pause. "You got one of those?"

"Nope."

"Know where we can find one?"

"Nope."

"So what the hell're we gonna do then?"

"*We're* not going to do anything. *You're* going to stay here and babysit Roscoe, while *I* go out there and see what I can find out."

"So lemme get this straight: I'm supposed to sit here on my hands while you go pokin' around a demon crack-house fulla scary monsters that want you dead with no strategy, no backup, and no weapons of any kind?"

"Yup."

"Actually, you know what? My end of this plan don't sound half bad."

"You sure?" I asked. "Because it's not too late to trade."

Gio laughed. I took a pull of beer, and wished that it were something stronger.

"Listen," I said, "there's a damn good chance I won't come back from this–"

"Aw, come on, man, don't talk like that."

"– and if I don't, you let him go and then you *run*, you hear me?"

But Gio shook his head. "No need, man. You'll come back. And Sam?"

"Yeah?"

"Make sure you come back."

21.

Plumes of red-brown dust billowed outward from beneath the Caddy's wheels as it barreled through the hilly landscape north of town. I hadn't seen a paved road in over twenty minutes, and the steering wheel struggled against my grasp like a living thing. Storm clouds gathered over the mountains to the east, blotting out the rising moon, and the breeze was thick with the heady scent of creosote resin – a sure sign of coming rain. As darkness descended over the desert, my world shrank to whatever was illuminated by the jitter of my headlights as I jounced along the uneven dirt drive.

Even with my map, I damn near missed the entrance to the box canyon. A stand of cottonwoods obscured its entrance, their thick foliage creating the illusion of a solid mass of rock when really it was cleaved in two. But something in the way the breeze disturbed the leaves gave me pause. A rock shelf should have sheltered them, but instead, they whipped about as though they were in a wind tunnel – which, upon closer inspection, they were.

I ditched the car behind a thicket of tamarisk and plunged into the canyon. Lightning flickered in the distance, providing snapshots of the world around me. The entrance to the canyon was maybe twenty yards across. The canyon floor sloped down-ward, dense with scrub brush and mesquite, and strewn about with massive hunks of rock. A narrow ribbon of dirt, more trail than road, wound through it all, and disappeared into the noth-ingness beyond. And, without so much as a flashlight to guide my way, so did I.

Mindful of the fact that the darkness that enveloped me would provide me little in the way of camouflage to the keen eyes of any watching demons, I clung to the edge of the trail, taking shelter among the underbrush. It was slow going, and I stumbled more than once, tearing the knee of my suit pants and scraping the hell out of my palms. An hour in, the rain began, plastering my hair to my scalp and my clothes to my weary, borrowed frame, but I pressed onward, grateful that the noise of it would serve to mask my stumbling gait.

Eventually, the ground began to rise, and above, the pitch-black shadows of the canyon walls gave way to the softer purple-black of storm clouds. A smell like rotten eggs hung in the air, mingling with the scent of desert rain. My pulse quickened, and I scanned the darkness for any sign of sentries or booby traps or the like, but as far as I could tell, there weren't any. Doubt crept in, and I wondered if I'd been wrong in coming here – if I was wasting my time chasing down a flimsy, dead-end lead as all the while the clock ticked down to Nothing.

No. Dumas was here.

He had to be.

It was the graveyard I discovered first: several dozen simple wooden crosses encircled by a low iron fence, and jutting at odd angles from the uneven canyon floor. They'd once been painted white, it seemed, but a good long while out in the desert sun had seen to that; now they looked as gray and dead as the bones they served to mark.

Beyond the graveyard sat a smattering of squat, stone ruins, built upon a series of rock terraces carved into the crook of the canyon, and linked by a winding set of stone steps. The smaller outbuildings scattered at the bottom of the incline were reduced to just a couple crumbling walls, but the large main building that presided over them was largely intact – and its windows flickered with candlelight.

Looked like this was the place, after all. I wished like hell I had some kind of weapon; all of the sudden, this plan of mine didn't seem like the best idea.

I scaled the steps, noting as I did the iron bars that still graced the framed-out, glassless window holes of the ruins that I passed. The bars seemed somewhat out of place on the windows of a hospital – not to mention, this campus was way too small to have required such a large cemetery on its grounds.

That's when it clicked for me. What I was looking at. The town historians could call this place a hospital all they wanted – but this far out of town, with bars on every window and a goodly cache of bodies in the ground?

This place was no hospital.

This place was a sanitarium.

Isolated. Reinforced. Impossible to escape. A prison in which to stash the terminally contagious, so that the healthy people of Las Cruces could go about their days unburdened by any worry about suffering and death. Once upon a time, I sold my soul to Walter Dumas to keep my Elizabeth from winding up someplace just like this. It's only fitting that I'd find him here tonight.

As I approached the base of the main building, I abandoned the easy going of the stairway in favor of the rocky slope beside it. I skirted the building at a crawl, freezing every time I slipped and sent a cascade of pebbles pattering to the canyon floor, listening for any evidence I'd been spotted.

But that sign never came. My approach, it seemed, was unde-tected. And as I circled the building, a hand against the coarse stone wall to guide my way, I discovered something. Or, rather, I discovered *nothing* – a patch of even deeper black within the darkness that enveloped me, a void where a wall was supposed to be.

I felt around. It was a hole in the foundation, big enough to accommodate a man. Provided, of course, that the man in question didn't mind sucking in his gut and squirming under a clutch of wobbly rocks held in place by the barest hint of crumbling mortar, and each large enough to squeeze the breath from his lungs should they dare to fall.

Lucky for me, I was just such a man.

I tried feet-first, but no dice – the hole was maybe three feet off the ground, and once I stuck my legs inside, I couldn't reach anything to push off of to propel myself inside.

Shit. Looked like I was going to have to go in head-first.

The wall was damn near two feet thick. Chunks of masonry clawed at my clothes and skin as I scrabbled through the hole, leaving behind the subtle illumination of the canyon and plunging into darkness so complete I couldn't see my hands in front of my face. Stone shards sharp as glass bit into my palms. Phantom colors danced before my eyes, blotches of blue and red and yellow-green. I clenched shut my lids, but the blotches remained. My meat-suit's brain trying to make something out of nothing, I suppose. Not so different from how I'd be spending my eternity, if I didn't track down Varela's soul in time.

The wall ended. I spilled forward. A good ten feet of empty space, and then I slammed into the packed-dirt floor. For a moment, I just lay there, struggling to reclaim the breath that had been knocked from my lungs. Then I pushed myself up off the floor and took stock of where I was.

There really wasn't anything to see. I mean there *really* wasn't anything to see. The room I was in was windowless, and as dark as the hole through which I'd entered – I couldn't tell if it was ten feet across, or a hundred. Somewhere in the darkness, water dripped, and the air was cool and damp, raising goosebumps on my exposed skin.

My hands splayed out before me like a blind man's, I staggered forward, disoriented by the utter lack of light to guide my way. The ground was uneven, and scattered with detritus – the brittle crunch of paper, the ankle-rolling *clink* of glass vial against glass vial. Occasionally, my way was barred – the cold iron of an ancient boiler, which reeked like blood and rust; the dry creak of old bed-frames, their springs whining in protest as I shouldered a stack of them and nearly sent them crashing to the ground – and I was forced to feel my way around. The going was slow and laborious, and despite the cold, an acrid sweat sprung up across my face and neck – sweat borne of concentration, and of mounting fear.

As I plunged deeper into the dank basement of the sanitarium, I noticed something: a strange, thick, scratching noise like sandpaper against wet wood. I stopped and listened. The sound was rhythmic and oddly repellent, and for the life of me, I couldn't tell where it was coming from. Suddenly, though, I knew exactly what it was – my every muscle tensing as realization dawned.

It was breathing.

Breathing, but not human.

OK, I thought, no big. You're just blind and defenseless in a creepy, creepy basement with what is almost certainly a big, scary demon. So what say we see about leaving said basement before big, scary demon decides to earn that big and scary.

I forced myself to take one step, and then another. It wasn't easy. My meat-suit's every instinct was leaning more toward curling up into a ball and crying. Of course, this meat-suit's former occupant asphyxiated in his own home when all he had to do was crack a window, so as far as I was concerned, its instincts didn't count for much.

I inched across the room, hoping to spy something that would signal a way out. My progress was so halting, and the room so very dark, that at times I felt as if I was walking in place. And all the while, the sickening sound of the demon's breathing enveloped me, reverberating off the distant walls until it seemed to come from everywhere, and from nowhere at all.

My foot came down on something soft and slick and alive – arm or leg or fucking *tentacle* for all I knew – and it recoiled beneath me. I pitched forward, falling to the floor. My heart banged out a drum roll in my chest as a massive, unseen hulk shifted noisily beside me in the darkness. But then it settled down again into what I assumed was a skim-induced slumber, the awful meter of its breathing like the devil's own metronome. And once I managed to stop trembling, I picked myself up off the floor and continued on.

At the far end of the basement was a staircase. Well, half of one, at least. The bottom five steps had rotted out, and the sixth, which spanned the space between the two supports at chest height, appeared to be on its way – it was spongy and smelled sickly sweet like fallen leaves after a rain. But at the head of the stairs was an open doorway, through which spilled the faintest hint of candlelight, so one way or another, I was getting up there.

I placed my palms atop the sixth step and pressed, testing to see if it would hold my weight. It sagged and crumbled like wet paper. I wrapped my fingers around the edge of the one above it and pulled until my toes lifted off the ground, and the wood began to crack. Not great, but good enough. The only problem was, I had no leverage – I'd left my sling back at the squat, but thanks to my tangle with the bug-monster, my right arm wasn't of much use. And there was no way I was going to be able to hoist myself up there on the strength of my left arm alone.

After a moment's consideration – and another few moments of trying to talk myself out of it – I decided I had no choice but to go back and retrieve a bed-frame from the pile.

Back through the stifling darkness.

Back past that unseen *thing*.

With a steeling breath, I retreated from the faint illumination of the doorway above, plunging once more into the absolute black of the basement. The creature in the darkness shifted, and its breathing hitched and skipped – its sleep turning fitful perhaps as the skim left its system?

I did my best to ignore it. My best wasn't very fucking good. Like trying to catch some Zs on an inner tube while the lifeguard's screaming "*SHARK!*", only maybe not as relaxing.

I found the bed-frames by pure sense-memory, all the while knowing when I passed them last, I'd been close enough to trip over whatever it was that slumbered beside me. I held my breath, lifted a bed-frame off the pile. Rusted springs shrieked like harpies. I froze, and my eyes clenched shut, some lizard-brain part of me seizing up as I waited for the killing blow.

It never came.

I turned and took a step, bed-frame in hand. My right shoulder ached like hell from the recent dislocation, the joint oddly loose and wobbly. At least I hadn't disturbed the sleeping Whatever, I thought.

And that's when everything went to shit.

A chitinous click beside me, a rustle like a snake uncoiling, and once more, the breathing hitched.

And then stopped.

And then sniffed.

I told myself that I was nuts. That I had to be mistaken. But there was no mistake. Silence, and then two sharp inhalations – rapid, regular – as though the creature was sampling the basement air around it.

Maybe it sensed an intruder. Maybe it was just hungry. But either way, I sure as hell wasn't going to stick around to find out.

I abandoned any pretense of stealth, my dress shoes clapping against the dirt floor as I sprinted toward the stairs. The bedframe squeaked in time with every step, a vulgar parody of sensual passion. I didn't have the time to find that funny. Behind me – hell, all *around* me – the darkness came alive with squirmy, whispery movement, as the creature behind me roused itself and unfurled.

Christ, how big *was* this fucking thing?

Demons come in all shapes and sizes, but most that interact with humankind at least loosely play by the rules of our physical world. If I had to guess, though, I'd say this fucker didn't venture out of the Depths all that often, because whatever the hell it was, it resisted any kind of sense-making. It seemed to fill the darkness, to encircle me without actually giving chase; its size increased with every passing second. I could feel the strain of my poor meat-suit's brain as it tried to make sense of the contradictory input it was being given. The sensation fell somewhere between migraine and amateur lobotomy.

But still, God bless it, that meat-suit kept on running.

Again, that chitinous click, like some horrid beak clacking shut – right behind me, and also to my left and right, and maybe above. I grit my teeth and kept on going.

A faint susurrus of whispered words jabbed into my brain like an ice pick, unknown to me but awful nonetheless. A threat, I thought.

No – not a threat, exactly. More like an invitation.

I was pretty sure I oughta pass.

I slammed the bed-frame against the ruined stairs, the metal feet digging into dirt floor and rotten wood as I wedged it between them. Something cold and slick wound its way around my waist – a tendril seemingly of darkness itself. I kicked and scratched, and scrambled up the makeshift ramp, rusty springs piercing my skin. The creature bellowed – aloud or in my head I wasn't sure – and drew closer, as if intoxicated by the scent of fresh blood.

My hand found the doorframe at the head of the stairs and gripped it, pulling me toward the faint candlelight. The creature tightened its grasp. I locked my gaze on my knuckles, ghostly white in the scant illumination. The pressure in my meat-suit's brain eased, the visual input a balm against the senselessness of the creature at my feet. Behind me, the creature snapped and clicked – in hunger, perhaps, or maybe in anger.

I glanced backward toward it, and the strength of its assault intensified, yanking me backward toward the darkness that enshrouded it. My fingernails dug into the doorframe, splinters plunging into the tender flesh beneath them.

And suddenly, I realized how this game was played.

I tore my attention from the beast that held me, and once more focused it on the door, the hall, the blessed candlelight. That candlelight was my tether to the rational world, and as I fixed my gaze on it, the demon's grip on me slackened. It squealed in frustration, mirroring the squeal of the bed-frame beneath me. Heartened by its cries, I kicked and thrashed – my foot connecting against something hard and brittle behind me, which caved in with a sickening *crack*.

Suddenly – briefly – I was free. As I pulled myself through the doorway, something wrapped around my ankle, and despite myself, I looked back. I caught a glimpse of translucent gray flesh, the glint of jet-black eye – a ruined beak of brownish red. Pain erupted behind my eyes, and I fought to keep from yelling – unwilling to give away my position to whatever else lurked in this godforsaken place.

It dragged me back toward the doorway, toward the darkness, toward its shattered, snapping beak. I skittered backward along the dusty floor, finding no purchase with which to stop myself.

I found no purchase because I wasn't looking. I wasn't looking because I was too busy trying to reach the mirror.

It was but a shard of mirror, really, jagged-edged and dulled with age. It lay on the floor a few feet to the right of the basement door – tantalizingly close. As the creature yanked me backward, I snatched at it.

Glass bit into the meat of my palm, into my fingertips, but I held on to that mirror as though my life depended on it. I'm pretty sure it did.

As I slid through the doorway toward the creature, I twisted in its grasp, angling the mirror as best I could to pierce the darkness of the basement with the hallway's candlelight.

The creature thrashed, recoiled as the light struck it – but it didn't let go. It still had me by one shoe, my leg dangling off the side of the stairwell, shaded from the reflected light by one rotted joist.

I kicked at the heel of that shoe with the toe of the other, over and over again – still sliding backward, toward the pressing darkness.

Finally, my shoe came off, a sacrifice to the angry beast. I flopped back into the hallway with a thud. Then I crab-walked backward a few feet away from the basement door, my meat-suit's survival instinct and terror working hand-in-hand to get me the hell away from there and further into the protective candlelight.

Don't get me wrong: spent and shaken as I was, I appreciated the help. But at that point, it wasn't strictly necessary.

The creature was gone – swallowed by the darkness below.

22.

Upstairs, a quiet cacophony, like a nightmare cocktail party heard through a shared wall. Myriad drips, drops, and plinks as the torrent outside found its way into the decrepit structure – pooling in depressions, leaking through cracks, pouring off of jagged ledges where the first-floor ceiling had caved in. Dozens of voices, some raised, some quiet, talking all at once in tongues both foreign and familiar. The thud of heavy footsteps above – shuffling, skipping about, and unless I was mistaken, dancing. The crackle of a warped and timeworn record from somewhere far away, playing Patsy Cline at half the speed and twice the warble. And the snap and hiss of candles in the damp.

The hallway I was in extended the length of the building, stretching into murky nothingness to either side of me. The floor and walls were blackened and peeling, as if from fire. The ceiling – plaster, by the look of it – sagged in places, and was entirely absent in others, mildew and yellowed water marks blossoming here and there the length of it.

I picked a direction at random, my one stocking foot stained with ash and soot as I scuffed along the empty hall – wary, alert. I'd never seen the inside of a skim-joint before. I don't know what I'd been expecting from a place demons go to get whacked out on moments stolen from the humans they profess to despise – something speakeasy-er, I guess – but this sure as hell wasn't it. This place made your average crack house look like the Ritz. But hey, I'm sure the rent was reasonable.

Beside me was an open door. I ducked inside. A small, square room, with bare wood floors and a ceiling of rotting plaster. In one corner was a candelabrum, anchored to the floor by tiny termite hills of wax, a halo of soot dancing on the wall behind it in the shifting candlelight. In the other corner lay a man. Many men, in fact – though in reality, this thing was not a man at all. His visage shifted as he slouched, eyes fluttering, against the join of the two walls, alternating between a half a dozen human faces at random. His lips moved as he lay there, muttering in a voice that shifted tone to match each face, as though the lot of them were in conversation, each talking over the other in an unintelligible stream of syllables.

Though he lay there helpless and twitching, this creature was no doubt a powerful demon, and one accustomed to dealing with humankind. Demons of the lesser orders are unable to alter their appearance in the eyes of man; their gruesome physiognomy is merely a reflection of their own corrupted natures. Should they desire to walk among the living unnoticed, they're forced to take a living host – and even then, if they possess that host too long, their nature will begin to warp the host as well. And powerful demons who do not deign to interact with humankind – like, I suspect, the beast I left downstairs – simply do not bother to alter their aspect to accommodate human perception, leaving puny human minds like mine to piece together something that makes sense out of the nonsense that they're given. But this guy, even ensconced in whatever skim-trip he was on, maintained some semblance of human appearance. Granted, without a conscious, focused will, the shapes didn't hold for long, but never did he slip from displaying a human form – never did he offer a glimpse of his true nature. That meant power. That meant danger. That meant I was glad he was asleep.

The man-demon shifted in his slumber, and his arm, which had previously rested across his stomach, flopped to the floor. His shirt-sleeve was rolled up to the elbow, and the tender flesh of his forearm was pocked with track marks – though no needle could mark a demon's flesh for long; the injury would heal itself before any scarring could occur. And indeed, these marks weren't from a needle at all, but from countless shards of skim. One such shard was in there now, like a jagged bit of colored glass inserted just beneath the skin – I could see it flickering below the surface like lightning contained within a cloud.

He rolled and kicked a leg, like a junkyard dog dreaming of glorious pursuit. His eyes flashed open, locked on mine. His hand lashed out and wrapped itself around my leg. Dark fire – the fire of the Depths – flickered across his arm, and the room seemed suddenly engulfed in their all-consuming flame. It spread outward from his being like the halo of soot from the candles across the room, fluttering like weightless silk as it expanded. Then his lids slammed shut, and the dark fire dissipated. The demon was once more asleep.

I pried my leg from his grasp and retreated to the hall. There was nothing for me in that demon's room. I wondered if there was anything here for me at all. If I was a fool to have even come. But it was too late for such concerns – I was here. Committed. There was nothing else for me to do but see it through.

As I continued down the hall, I peeked into the rooms I passed, finding some empty, and others flush with three, four, even five demons – most of them foot-soldiers, leathery black and hideous. Some lay still in dream, while others swayed in time with the music, or gestured wildly as they conversed with whoever had a guest-spot in their skim-trip memory. Not a one of them showed any interest in me; occasionally, one would glance my way, but their gazes slid right off of me like I was furniture.

I couldn't help but wonder what it was like: these fallen angels, these creatures of the Depths, subjecting themselves to human experiences, sensations, emotions, all in the name of feeling closer for a moment to the God that had forsaken them. And I wondered what it must feel like to come down from that, and realize you were once more removed from the light of God's grace. It must be horrible – a shock akin to their initial fall. It wasn't hard to see why they – or for that matter, Danny – might get hooked. Why they might keep on coming back.

At the end of the hallway was an empty doorframe crumpled outward at each side, as though something too large to pass through it had decided to force the issue. Beyond the doorway, a staircase led upward. Its banister was of dubious integrity, but the stairs themselves, bowed and scarred though they were, looked broadly feasible. They groaned and popped under my weight, but they held, and so I headed up.

As I climbed the stairs, the strains of music I'd heard below grew louder. Through the scratch and hiss of the weary old vinyl, I heard Patsy's lament.

… *I'm crazy for trying, and crazy for crying… and I'm crazy for loving you…*

Sounded like her week was going about as well as mine.

The entrance to the second floor was barred by a cave-in just inside the stairwell door; through the starburst pattern in the inlaid safety glass, I saw a pile of rubble four feet high. With luck, I thought, the third floor won't be similarly afflicted.

It wasn't. The third floor, like the second, still had a door –

a heavy wooden affair inlaid with safety glass – but its top hinge had separated from the doorframe, which left it hanging at a nauseating angle that prevented it from latching. Slowly, carefully, I pushed it open, listening for any indication the movement had been noticed. Apart from a redoubling of the record's volume, I heard nothing, so I slipped through the doorway, and eased it shut behind me.

The stairwell door opened into a broad room, from which a hallway like the one on the first floor extended. A pile of splintered timber along one wall looked like it had once been some kind of desk, suggesting this had maybe been a nurses' station. There were candles everywhere – on the floor, atop the rubble of the desk, in the nooks created by the crumbling of the failing walls. An old Victrola cabinet sat in the center of the room, the Cline record spinning beneath its propped lid. Deep gouges furrowed its mahogany frame in sets of four parallel lines each, as though some demon had taken a swipe or two at it in a fit of pique. Apparently skim-trips weren't all wine-and-roses after all.

I heard a low, huffing breath to my left, like a city bus laboring up a hill. Close – too close for my tastes.

I spun around. Behind me, hidden from view around the corner as I'd entered the room, was a demon. A *massive* demon, sitting beneath a jagged hole in the ceiling, through which poured a torrent of desert rain. Given the size of this monster, I couldn't help but think that hole must be how it had gotten in.

The demon was maybe ten feet across, and standing no doubt would've been twice that high. Its skin was the sickly, glistening white of a creature raised belowground; its body was segmented and striated, like that of a grub. Thick horns of yellow-white protruded from its head on either side, stretching for several feet before curving slightly downward and terminating in two nasty-looking points that scratched the rain-soaked walls. Two rows of six eyes each, milky white in the absence of that trademark demon fire, were wet from rain and tears both. The creature sat with its legs hugged to its chest, rocking back and forth like a child. Its ropy neck flickered like the man-demon's arm had flickered, indicating skim. In one hand it held a wildflower, brilliant purple in the candlelight.

As it turned its gaze toward me, its awful face broke into a smile.

It extended an arm toward me – an arm that nearly spanned the length of the room – and offered me the flower.

And with a voice as terrible as damnation itself, it said, *"Daddy?"*

Something in my meat-suit snapped then, and I tore out of the room at a sprint, leaving a puzzled child-demon in my wake. Animal panic coursed through my veins, obliterating reason. I ran like I had the devil at my heels, and as far as this hunk of meat was concerned, I guess I did. I ran past countless rooms like the ones I'd peeked inside downstairs. I ran past demons large and small, their utterances an awful chorus, egging me on. I ran until I reached the far end of the hall, and then my sock-clad foot came down on something sharp, and I stumbled, sprawling into a room brighter and warmer than those I'd seen so far. It was the mirror image of the one that I'd just fled, but this room was not in ruins. Its ceiling was intact, its walls unmarred, and, improbably, a fire crackled in an earthen fireplace along one wall.

I looked around in puzzlement at my surroundings, my heart still thudding in my chest. Beside me, atop an expensive-looking woven rug, sat a high-backed leather chair and a small side-table in the Mission style. A stained-glass lamp on the side-table cast colored shapes around the room, despite its cord dangling frayed and incomplete a foot from its base. Beneath the lamp was a snifter half-full of amber liquid, around which was wrapped a fat, bejeweled hand. The hand, in turn, led to a cuffed wrist, which led to a suit-jacket of bland gray. The jacket was wrapped tightly around a rotund, sweaty man, whose eyes danced with black fire, and whose mouth was curved into a predatory grin.

"Hiya, Sammy," said Dumas. "It's about time you showed up."

23.

"You – you knew that I was coming?"

Dumas snorted, and took a sip of his drink. "You think an operation like this, one that pisses off the Big Guy and the Adversary both, and we wouldn't have any goddamn *countermeasures*? Please – we've been monitoring your progress since before you even reached the canyon. Sweet ride, by the way."

"If you knew I was coming, why didn't you kill me hours ago? Why let me get this far?"

"I considered it, of course – but honestly, what would it have accomplished? You would've just wound up in another body and come back to pester us all over again, like the little gadfly you are. Besides, I've always had a soft spot for the souls I've corrupted – you little tykes are so adorable with your eternal suffering and *why-me* whining and your sad little puppy-dog eyes. So call me sentimental, but I decided this time I'd give you a pass."

"A *pass*? You call my tangle with that thing in the basement a *pass*?"

"What, Abby? Abby's harmless. Well, to *you*, at least – her tastes run more toward the living, the younger and fresher the better. Besides, if I hadn't made things a *little* challenging, you wouldn't feel like you'd accomplished anything getting up here, and just imagine what that'd do to your self-esteem! I'm about building up, Sammy, not tearing down."

"Big of you," I said.

"Isn't it, though?" He made to take a pull of his drink, and then stopped short. "Oh, hell – where are my manners? Care for a drink?"

"No, thanks."

"Probably for the best. Stuff's made from the blood of the Chosen – it'd likely eat that monkey-suit's insides right out of you. Still, it *is* delicious – and damn hard to come by these days. One of my clients had a case lying around since the last Great War. Traded it for a slice of nun who'd had a genuine religious experience before she died. Course, the way things have been going of late, this stuff won't be rare much longer, so I figure I may as well drink up! Now, Sammy, you want to tell me what brought you all this way? Some unresolved daddy issues, perhaps?"

"Don't play coy with me – you know damn well why I'm here. I came for Varela."

"And Varela is...?"

"Play dumb all you like," I said, "but I'm not biting. I underestimated you once before; it's not a mistake I'm likely to repeat."

"Really? Because I was of the impression you're not a man who learns from his mistakes – you're always far too certain you're in the right. But let's say for the sake of argument that I *do* know who this Varela is. What makes you think I'd hand him over to *you*? I mean, I allow you into my place of business out of the kindness of my heart, and this is how you repay me? By issuing orders and expecting me to snap to? It seems you've forgotten your station in this world, *Collector* – you're in no position to make demands of me. You'll be lucky if I don't kill you for your impudence."

"By all means, go ahead. As you said, I'll simply be reseeded elsewhere – and when I am, I'll be sure to tell my handler where she can find the missing Varela soul."

At that Dumas sat upright and set his drink down on the table. "Wait," he said, leaning forward in sudden interest, "you're here about a missing *soul*?"

"As if you didn't know."

"I *didn't* know."

"Cut the bullshit," I spat. "I know all about your arrangement with Danny Young. I know he's been funneling you souls in return for skim. And I for damn sure know that Danny stole Varela's soul. Now, I've seen enough of your operation tonight to know that business is booming. So what happened? The souls Danny was assigned to collect couldn't keep up with demand? Or was Varela some kind of special order?"

Dumas scowled, his face flushed with anger. "Boy, if I were you, I'd watch your tongue. You don't understand half as much as you *think* you do."

"Then by all means, enlighten me."

He downed his drink and wiped his lips with the back of his hand. "First off," he said, gesturing around the room with his empty glass before setting it on the table, "we ain't in the business of taking special orders – the product we got is the product we got. Partly 'cause we gotta keep a low profile if we wanna keep this operation running, and snatching souls to fill requests would attract all kinds of unwanted attention. Also partly 'cause it's not necessary. A skim-trip ain't so much about the specific *experience* being relived; it's about the *feeling*, the sense that the Maker's in His heaven and all is right with the world. All you need for that's a soul that ain't been all the way corrupted, and believe me, we got scads of 'em just stacking up, Danny Young or no."

I nodded toward the empty glass beside him, my face a mask

of disbelief. "So you're telling me the nun-soul you traded for that you came by honestly?"

Dumas chuckled. "I'm not sure *honestly* is the right word, but yeah, she arrived via the usual channels. Guess a pious life's no guarantee you'll get measured for your wings and harp once your final bell has tolled." He saw the doubt in my eyes and continued. "Don't look so surprised, Sammy! Hell's fulla decent people who couldn't hack it without a little assistance from the likes of me – you of all people should know that. And believe me, you're better off not knowing what she bargained for; the whole affair would turn your stomach."

I thought a moment about what he'd said, but the math still didn't add up. "The fact remains that Danny works for you, and that he stole the soul I'm looking for. I'm supposed to believe those two things are unconnected?"

"Believe what you want, Sammy – and someday, you'll have to fill me in on how you've come to know so much about who I do and don't associate with – but the truth is, Danny doesn't work here anymore."

"He doesn't." Skeptical.

"No, he *doesn't*. Fact is, the boy got sloppy – unreliable. Became a liability to the organization. So I had to let him go."

"If that's the case, then what the fuck would Danny want with the soul of some drug kingpin that wasn't even his to take?"

"Wait – don't tell me this Varela you're looking for is *Pablo* Varela? As in head of the Varela drug cartel?"

For the life of me, I couldn't tell if he was shining me on, or if his surprise was as genuine as it seemed. "So you *do* know of him," I said.

"Of *course* I know of him," he replied. "I'm a big fan of his work! That bastard is as nasty as they come; well, *was*, I suppose. A shame that someone of his talent would be struck down in his prime…"

"Yeah, I'm all broken up about it. Only now that I know you're such a fan and all, I'm forced to wonder if maybe you had Danny take his soul as a little keepsake – you know, so you could stick it in a glass case beside the ball from McGwire's go-ahead run or whatever."

"Are you nuts? Leaving aside for a moment the fact that Danny no longer works for me, you know the kind of attention it'd attract to my operation, snagging the soul of a rising talent like Varela? And anyways, if *any* of the Fallen has McGwire's go-ahead run, it'd be Mammon; he's the one who cut McGwire's deal."

"OK, so assuming for a second you're telling the truth–"

"Why, Sam, that *hurts*."

"–and Danny *wasn't* working for you when he stole Varela's soul, what could he possibly want with it? You think he might be trying to score a skim-fix on his own?"

"Doubt it. Even if he's desperate, the kid ain't *stupid*, and to try and process a soul all by his lonesome with those pathetic monkey reflexes of his, he'd hafta be. Besides, Varela was as twisted as they come – there's not much point skimming off a soul as corrupted as his. No, what Danny'd want if he were jonesin' is a soul with a little decent left in it. So either he took Varela just to fuck with you, or..."

Dumas's eyes got a faraway look in them, and he fell silent for a moment. Then he shook his head and muttered, "Well, I'll be damned," more to himself than to me.

"What?" I asked. "What is it?"

"I do believe I figured out what ol' Danny Boy might be up to. And if I'm right, you're not the only one that crazy fucker played."

"I don't understand."

"That's all right," he said, a rueful grin gracing his face. "I'm beginning to."

Dumas got to his feet, clapped me on the shoulder.

"Come with me," he said. "There's something I think you need to see."

24.

The rain beat down on my face and neck, and made treacherous the stone steps that we descended. These steps were narrower than the ones I'd followed up to the main building, and they hugged the craggy canyon wall, making their path unpredictable and the going slow. The warmth and light of Dumas's fireplace were but a distant memory, three stories and a world of wet away. Dumas led me downward through the darkness, looking dry as ever, as though the rain didn't dare to dampen him. It was an illusion, of course; Dumas looked dry for the same reason Dumas looked human – because that's how he *chose* to look.

Me, I looked like a drowned rat, my one shoe-clad foot squishing with every step, and my bare sock soaked clean through and caked thick with mud. Figures I'd wind up coming to the desert on the one fucking night it rains. Next time, I'm bringing a slicker and some rubber boots – provided I survive long enough for there to be a next time.

"Where exactly are we going?"

"Servants' quarters," Dumas replied.

"Yeah, I can see why you'd want to tuck 'em out of sight," I said, glancing back toward the main building behind us –

191

its crumbling façade barely visible through the pounding rain. "You'd hate to ruin the lovely ambience you've got going on back there."

"What, you didn't like the rug? I thought it really tied the room together."

At the base of the slope up to the main building, Dumas jagged right, disappearing from view. I'd been figuring on a left-hand turn toward the constellation of outbuildings I'd seen on my way in. Visibility being what it was, I had no idea where Dumas had gotten off to, so for a moment, I just stood there like an idiot in the rain.

"Hey, Sammy – you comin' or what?"

Turned out Dumas was standing in a natural alcove in the rock maybe eight feet high, and barely wide enough for two men to stand side-by-side. At first, the alcove didn't seem to be that deep, and then I realized that what I'd taken to be the inside wall was in fact a heavy iron door, so thoroughly corroded by the elements that it looked as natural as the rock walls that surrounded it.

At the center of the door was a wheel – a wheel as rust-caked as the door itself. It would've taken a dozen Strong Man competitors and a can of WD-40 to move that thing an inch. Dumas spun it like a pinwheel in a stiff wind. And with a shriek like the cries of the tormented, the door swung inward.

Stepping inside, it was apparent this wasn't so much an alcove as a cave. A well-trodden dirt floor led inward from where we stood, pocked here and there with strange stone outcroppings the color of sun-bleached bone. Torches hung on the walls at regular intervals, casting long shadows of the rock formations, and causing the corridor before me to writhe like a living thing as their flames licked at the stone ceiling above. The air was thick with oily smoke; it burned in my throat and made my eyes water. But beneath its tarry bite was another scent, sour and unpleasant: a sulfurous reek that seemed to emanate from the very walls.

"Abandon hope, all ye who enter here," I muttered.

"I know, right?" Dumas replied, his eyes dancing with mirth in the torchlight. "I was thinking of having a doormat made special."

We proceeded down the natural corridor. Rooms branched off from it on either side – some sealed with iron doors of their own, some nothing more than bare rock arches leading into darkness. It was warm inside – too warm. Between the fumes, the heat, and the ever-shifting firelight, I felt dizzy, ill, disoriented. But if Dumas noticed, he paid no mind, instead leading me down, down, down toward God knows what.

No, I thought. About this, God has no idea.

Over time I became aware of a peculiar sound, low and rumbling like machinery. It built and built upon itself until it was damn near unbearable, a horrid oscillating pressure in my eardrums that made my eyes blur and my temples throb like the early stages of a migraine. I tried to hide my discomfort from Dumas. It worked about as well as any of my plans thus far.

"You hear that, Sammy? That's the sound of *commerce*. Of product being made. I tell ya, it's music to my ears…"

"Yeah," I said, trying to smile, and winding up with more of a pained grimace. "Catchy."

He nodded toward a door up ahead, another iron job that, if anything, was heavier and better reinforced than the one through which we'd entered. "You wanna see?"

I didn't. I told him so. He showed me anyway.

I really shoulda seen that coming.

When he heaved open the door, the sound doubled in intensity. The pressure in my eardrums seemed to spread. My intestines fluttered like I'd eaten a bad burrito, and the fillings in my meat-suit's teeth began to ache. It was all I could manage to keep my feet. Dumas was mock-oblivious, clapping one arm over my shoulder and ushering me through the doorway, his features ablaze with malignant delight.

The room was small and dark, and the air inside was thick with sulfurous steam; it billowed outward through the open door like hot breath on my face. No torches graced the close stone walls. Aside from the firelight that spilled in through the open door, the only illumination came from somewhere in the center of the room, a ghostly gray light that appeared at first to emanate from the very steam itself. But as the steam dispersed, I caught a glimpse of the machinery behind the awful racket – and the true source of the room's sole light.

It appeared to be some kind of massive lathe, sitting at table height and fastened to the floor with bolts as thick as my arm. A hodge-podge of tarnished brass fixtures – wheels, knobs, cranks, and levers – jutted from its cast-iron shell, and several grime-caked gears transmitted power to the spindle from a thick rubber belt that extended upward to a diesel engine above, running at full bore and fixed to the ceiling by a series of heavy chains. Angling downward from the ceiling, as well as upward from the floor below, were several copper pipes, which snaked their way around the room from a cistern in the corner and converged on the object mounted on the rapidly turning spindle.

The object itself was scarcely larger than an acorn, and obscured from view by the steam that billowed off of it – steam generated by the water jetting toward it from the copper pipes. But as it turned, it flickered with familiar light, and beneath the clamor of machinery, I could just make out the melancholy wail of its song.

It was a soul. A human soul, reduced to a mere commodity by Dumas and his ilk.

The machine's attendant – a hulking mass of demon-flesh clad head-to-cloven-hoof in thick, coarse leather – threw a lever, and the engine chugged to a halt. The spindle slowed and stopped, and, with a squeak of turning valves, the flow of water petered out as well. My head was grateful for the silence. My heart ached to see a soul treated so callously as this.

The machinist shook free of his gloves and stripped off his mask – a grotesque parody of the face beneath rendered in leather and brass, with a lens of amber-colored glass where the demon's sole eye proved to be. Don't get me wrong, the demon beneath was hardly a looker – picture a rabid, mangy, cyclopean Rottweiler, and you're more or less there – but that mask? That mask was the stuff of nightmares.

"Nice getup," I said.

The dog-beast eyed me with the sort of disdain you'd expect from a blue-blood stepping over a puking wino. "Boss," it said with a voice a good octave lower than any human one I've ever heard. "There some kind of problem?" The words seemed unwieldy in the creature's mouth, as if it were unaccustomed to speaking in a human tongue, and though it was speaking to Dumas, its eye never left me. The eye itself was black and glistening and rimmed all around with red. Its corners were crusted with dried mucus, sickly white against the creature's pitch-black face. I could see my reflection in the surface of that eye, smaller and more frightened than I maybe would have liked.

"Problem? Nah – just giving Sammy here the nickel tour!" Then, to me: "You wouldn't know it to look at him, Sam, but old Psoglav here is the best skimmer in the business. A real surgeon with his blade. Ain't that right, Psoglav?"

Psoglav said nothing, instead plucking said blade up from where it lay atop the stilled lathe – so quickly that I scarcely saw him do it – and testing the set of its edge against the ash-gray callus of his thumb. The blade itself was flat-topped like a chisel and very fine, with a tapered stem and a handle fashioned from what appeared to be a human bone. I confess I didn't like the way Psoglav was looking at me while he held it.

Psoglav smiled at my obvious discomfort, flashing what looked to be a set of crude iron teeth jammed willy-nilly into his mottled gray gums, and then his hand flicked out at me, placing the tip of the blade under my chin so fast I didn't even have time to exhale, much less react. Every muscle in the demon's body was tensed, but the blade barely grazed my skin. Still, it was sharp enough to draw blood – I felt it dripping warm down my chin.

I wanted to move. To recoil. Hell, to take a fucking breath. But Psoglav could kill this meat-suit with a lightning flick of his wrist, so I didn't dare. Instead I stood there, bleeding in the darkness.

"This monkey," he said to Dumas, who seemed for all the world not to notice the drama unfolding before him, "he our new Collector?"

I said nothing. Dumas answered, "Perhaps."

The pressure on the blade increased ever-so-slightly, and my bleeding quickened. The damned thing was so sharp, though, I barely even felt it.

"I hope for his sake he proves more reliable than his predecessor."

Dumas smiled. "You hope no such thing. I know you're still chomping at the bit to have a go at Daniel, and it looks to me like you'd be more than happy to exact your revenge on Samuel in his stead." He paused, and when he spoke again, his voice was full of steel. "Though if I were you, Psoglav, I wouldn't."

Though Dumas's words were conversational enough, Psoglav's eye widened in sudden fear, and faster than my own eyes could even register, he recoiled. The blade gone, I raised a sleeve to my bleeding chin and resisted the urge to collapse into a puddle on the floor.

"My apologies," Psoglav said – to Dumas, though, not to me.

"Think nothing of it," Dumas replied, the tone of levity in his voice restored.

"With your permission, boss, I think maybe I should return to my work."

"Of course, of course," Dumas replied. "The machinery of capitalism stops for no one – not even me."

We took our leave of Psoglav, and Dumas shut the door behind us. I heard the diesel engine cough and sputter, and then roar to life once more. Soon, the awful racket of the lathe's turning resumed.

"That Psoglav's a real charmer," I said, dabbing at my chin.

"Oh, he's a tad excitable, I'll admit, but he's damn good at his job."

"Not a fan of Danny's, huh?"

"Seems there's a lot of that going around lately. Although in Psoglav's case, I'm not surprised. Most of the Collectors in my employ can't stay far enough away from him, but Danny? Danny pestered poor Psoglav any chance that he could get. Always asking questions, bugging him to watch the skimming process, and generally following him around like some yippy little toy dog. Maybe Psoglav worries you'll pick up where Daniel left off."

"He's got nothing to worry about. I'm never going to come work for you" – *again*, I added mentally – "and what's more, I'm pretty sure you know it. So you wanna tell me what that little dog-and-pony show was *really* all about?"

"I just need you to understand the skill required to maintain an operation such as this, and the consequences of any lapse in said skill, so that you can begin to understand the severity of the situation in which we find ourselves."

I thought back to my showdown with the bug-monster, and let out a single, barking laugh. "I'm pretty sure I understand the severity of my situation."

"And I'm just as sure you *don't*. See, Psoglav is a rare breed – a creature of such speed and single-minded focus that you'd think he'd been conjured for the sole purpose of extracting skim from souls."

"Yeah? And?"

"And he's the fourth such beast to hold that post."

"I don't follow."

"What I'm saying, Sam, is that human souls are as volatile as they are fragile, and that for all of his talent, Psoglav, like his predecessors, is not infallible. Sooner or later, he *will* slip. Perhaps he'll simply tire of his task, and his attention will wane. Perhaps one of the thousand tiny shards kicked off during the skimming process will find its way around his leather armor and send him on an unintended little trip. Perhaps he'll simply sneeze. It doesn't much matter what winds up causing Psoglav to slip; what matters is that when he *does*, he'll take this cave and maybe half the canyon with him. Just as his predecessor did to my operation in Nepal, and as his predecessor's predecessor did to the house I ran in Cook, Australia. It's why I'll only ever put a skim-joint at the ass-end of nowhere; I learned my lesson back in San Fran in '06."

I thought back. "What the hell happened in '06?"

Dumas laughed. "Sorry, Sammy – sometimes I forget how pathetically short a span you monkeys get to live. I meant 1906. My skimmer cracked that one but good; between the shockwaves and the subsequent fire, over three thousand of your kind perished. Of course, they figured it was an earthquake, and I guess it was, at that – the buffoon cracked that soul so bad he disturbed the very plates beneath the ground, and leveled a city in the process. Since then, I've made it a policy to steer clear of urban centers, and to never, *ever* start a skim-joint on a fault line."

"Big of you," I said.

"Just good business," he replied, oblivious to my biting tone.

A thought occurred to me. "You said three thousand of my kind were killed that day, but what about *your* kind? What happens to Psoglav, and to your customers, if this place blows?"

"You mean do they *die*? Why, Samuel, are you concerned my little tale might dent your rep as the first to kill a member of the Fallen in millennia?"

"Hardly. Just didn't square, is all."

"Oh, come now, you're a resident of hell – what's the harm of copping to the sin of pride? And anyways, your reputation is intact; a cracked soul has never, to my knowledge, killed one of my kind. It does *sting* like a mother, though, I'll tell you that – the blast can strip flesh from bone and limbs from bodies, and those closest to it usually slink off to a quiet corner of the Depths for a century or so to nurse their wounds and try to grow back what they've lost. Even still, some of them never come back quite right; my San Fran skimmer's blind for good, and the poor bastard's now got the reflexes of a tree sloth."

"A real heartbreaker, that."

Something tickled at the back of my mind, and I found myself thinking back to the mess that was last year's Manhattan job. See, what happened was a bigwig seraph by the name of So'enel decided to go rogue and incite a war between heaven and hell. To do so, he conspired to mark an innocent soul for collection – a major no-no according to the Great Truce – and since it was *my* handler the shitweasel was conspiring with, I was the one dispatched to do the deed. Lucky, no?

But even less lucky was Mu'an, the messenger-demon who served as go-between for Lilith and So'enel. Once their plan went south, So'enel endeavored to eliminate any evidence of his involvement – and since Mu'an fell solidly into that category, the seraph sent a cadre of his angelic lackeys to shut him up for good. They caught up to Mu'an at Grand Central, and unleashed a holy fury the likes of which the modern world had never seen. Mu'an escaped with his life – barely – but the force of the angels' attack nearly wiped the terminal off the map. To this day, the government considers the blast an act of terror, and no fewer than three dozen extremist groups took credit for it. I wondered how many would take credit for the ferry boat in Maine that foundered a couple days back after an explosion ripped a hole in the hull and killed half the passengers on board; just the latest in a growing list of angel-on-demon violence.

"The blast that results from cracking a soul," I said, "it sounds a lot like an angel's wrath to me."

At that, Dumas cocked his head, and then he smiled. "I suppose you *would* have some experience in that regard, wouldn't you? Quite the bit of business you got mixed up with in New York. Yes, I suppose they aren't dissimilar – both unleash the power of the Maker's might, His grace, His wrath. In many respects, the human soul is a far greater font of power than even the greatest seraph can tap into – after all, you monkeys are, for reasons that to this day escape me, the Maker's most favored little playthings. But humans lack the capacity to channel such power, and even the best of you are touched by sin, which blunts the damage to my kind. An *angel's* wrath," he said, as if trying on the word for size, "is more directed, more controlled... and because it's not occluded by darkness, far more deadly to their Fallen brothers."

"Why are you telling me all this? I don't believe for a second you've even the slightest affection for me, and yet here you are, pulling back the curtain when you probably should've sent me packing. So what gives? What's your angle?"

Dumas sighed and ran a hand through his thinning hair. For the first time since I'd arrived, he looked concerned. "My angle? Same as it ever was, Sammy. I'm a businessman, pure and simple, and as such, I have to protect my interests. And right now, Interest Numero Uno is keeping my ass off the white-hat's hit-list. I don't know if you've been keeping score, but it's open season on the Fallen out there. Our Chosen brothers are spoiling for a fight, and they'll jump on any excuse to send a little wrath our way. Normally, that's no concern a mine. I run a quiet operation here – keep my head down and my profile low. Only all the sudden here comes Danny Young with a yen to misbehave, and the more ruckus he makes, the worse things're gonna get for me. See, whether or not he's operating on my behalf, the fact remains he was once in my employ, and as such was privy to all manner of sensitive information – information that, left uncontained, could lead the feather-and-harp brigade right back to me. So when you wandered in from the desert asking questions about all things Danny, I figured shit – why not point Sammy in the right direction, see if maybe he can catch him? He does, and that's two problems off my plate. Problem Two is you, in case you ain't been keeping up."

"Hold up a sec. You say you wanna point me in the right direction – does that mean you know where Danny *is*?"

"Would that I did, Sammy; it'd save us both a hell of a lot of trouble. But I'm pretty sure I *do* know what he's *planning*, and more importantly, what'll happen if he succeeds. If that happens, the stupid bastard's gonna unleash a disaster of Biblical proportions – one that'll make my skimmer's slip in San Francisco and the subsequent destruction look like a goddamn kitten sneezing."

"OK then, spill: what the hell is Danny playing at?"

Dumas answered my question with one of his own: "Tell me, Sammy – what do you know about the Brethren?"

25.

"The Brethren?" I repeated. "Not much. I mean, I've heard the stories. A group of Collectors who, centuries ago, banded together and found a way to break hell's bond of servitude. Of course, they're nothing but a fairy tale – a Collector's pipe dream."

"A fairy tale," Dumas said, smiling. "Right."

"I miss something funny?"

"Funny? No, not too," he said. "Come on – this little tour of ours ain't done."

Dumas led me deeper into the cavern. The corridor, so broad at its outset, dwindled until it was more fissure than tunnel, and could no longer accommodate the intermittent torches that had marked the way thus far. Dumas snatched the last of them from the wall – a concession to my human eyes, no doubt – and took me by the elbow, dragging me reluctantly into the narrow, winding pass.

The walls pressed close as, sideways, we squeezed through. A time or two, stone outcrops dug into my back and chest as I forced myself through a particularly narrow spot or around a tricky corner, Dumas's light all but disappearing ahead of me as, despite his apparent girth, he pressed onward without incident. When that happened, I was left alone with my thoughts, my fears, my shallow hitching breath – all three of them threatening to spiral out of control and leave me panicked, trapped, damned to be stuck here in the darkness until the clock ran out and the bug-beast came to claim me. But that thought alone was enough to keep me moving, and eventually, the passage widened. Not much, mind you – the walls in this new, smaller chamber were maybe three feet across, and the ceiling here was low enough I had to stoop – but after the sidewalk-crack we'd slipped through to get here, it may as well have been Montana.

As I cleared the fissure, brushing filth from my lapels, Dumas turned to me and smiled. For a moment, with the torchlight glinting off his eyes and yellowed teeth, he looked every bit the demon that he was. "Welcome to the monkey house," he said.

"Excuse me?"

"The monkey house. This is where I stash the Collectors in my employ. Out of the way, so they can fling their poo or whatever it is they do without troubling my Fallen employees or bothering the clientele."

I looked around. By the torchlight, it looked like the cavern continued on another seven feet or so and then terminated. Three low openings, each shored up with rotted four-by-fours, extended outward from the room on either side – two left, one right. I ducked my head to see inside the one beside me. It was no larger than a coat closet, and apart from a heap of blankets in one corner, it was empty.

"They're rarely occupied," called Dumas, his stentorian voice echoing off the close stone walls. "Save for Danny, none of my Collectors ever had much interest in sticking 'round once the job was done. Not all of them are as eager as Danny was to sample the product, so most of them are outta here as soon as

204   THE WRONG GOODBYE

the soul they brought's done processing. But Danny was another matter. Danny liked to stick around. I always figured he
came back here to fix, that the ramblings on the wall were
nothing more than skim-induced delusion. Stuff's awful to
come off of – for your kind in particular – and it'll fill your head
with all manner of wacky shit you'd be hard-pressed to explain
once you finally touch down. Truth is, I never thought much
of it. But you factor in these ramblings with his interest in
watching Psoglav ply his trade and his theft of the Varela soul,
and a pattern emerges." He gestured toward the doorway fur-
thest back. "That's the one you want. That's where Danny
staked his claim."

Once I crawled inside, I could see why. It was bigger by half
than the other I'd seen, and set a little ways apart, providing
some small measure of privacy. At first, of course, the room was
black as pitch, but as Dumas shimmied in behind me, his torch's
light crawled up the walls – first illuminating the bare military
cot that took up much of the chamber's floor, and then the tat-
tered photo of two strangers I presumed were he and Ana that
rested on the framework of the door. And as the light climbed
toward the ceiling, I realized the walls of Danny's chamber were
covered with writing – writing of all shapes and sizes, in a dozen
alphabets and at least twice that many languages. I recognized
Arabic and Hebrew, Sanskrit and Akkadian – all scratched onto
the wall with charred bits of wood or pointed rock – but most
of the tongues were foreign to me. They looked to be the work
of a crazy person, with no rhyme or reason to their placement
– some scrawled over older snippets, some halted halfway
through; some flecked with blood as if the scribe's hand had
split at the effort required to mark the stone. It was hard for me
to imagine Danny had done all this. It was hard to imagine *anyone* could have.

"What *is* all this?" I muttered.

"Folklore, mostly. Tales transcribed centuries ago from the oral tradition. Or, more accurately, fragments of tales. See, these stories were thought lost to your kind, and for good reason – the forces of heaven and hell aligned to purge them from this Earth, for fear of the damage they could cause."

"And these stories," I said, "they're about the Brethren?"

"Yes. Most of it's nonsense, of course – an oblique passing reference, a half-heard conversation written down a hundred years after the fact. But some of them are quite specific. Dates. Places. Descriptions of rites the likes of which I've never seen. And it's the latter, of course, that our Daniel seemed most interested in – they're the ones writ large across the wall."

My eyes settled on one black char inscription scrawled atop all the others, and wrapping around three quarters of the room. The script itself was crude and angular, though if that was Danny's doing, or the appearance of the language itself, I didn't know.

"What is this," I asked, "Phoenician?"

"Close," Dumas replied. "It's Ancient Aramaic. Predates Biblical Aramaic by nearly five hundred years."

"Can you read it?"

The look he gave me, you'd think I just insulted his mother. "It says: 'As the worlds drew thin, the unclean spirit was cleaved, which in turn summoned forth a Deluge that purged the Nine of sin, and cast their bonds of slavery aside.' Or, you know, something to that effect."

"What the fuck is that supposed to mean?"

Another look, this one like I'm the kid in class who eats the paste. "What does it *sound* like it means?"

"It sounds like Danny aims to crack Varela's soul and wind up a normal boy," I replied – glib, dismissive.

Only Dumas didn't take it that way, which, truth be told, kind of freaked me out. "Yeah, that's what it sounded like to me, too. Only it don't say 'crack,' it says 'cleave.' As in fucking rend asunder."

"The hell's the difference?"

"The difference, Sam, is all the difference. That shit that went down in San Fran? That was on account of a 'crack.' A mean one, yeah – the worst I've ever seen – but the soul we cracked was only damaged, not destroyed. I think that Danny's aiming to *destroy* Varela's soul, and that's a whole other ball of wax. We're talking split-the-atom bad. Worse, in fact. 'Cause 'cleave' ain't the scariest word up on that wall."

"OK, I'll bite – what is?"

"Deluge."

"Deluge." Me, playing parrot; skeptical.

"Yep."

"Like, *the* Deluge? As in Noah and a giant fucking boat?"

"The very same," he said. "Well, more or less."

"Meaning what?"

"Meaning I don't know crap about some bearded jackass collecting zebras or whatever, but there ain't a civilization worth a damn that doesn't have a flood myth of some kind. To this day, Hindus tell the tale of Manu, who saved Mankind from the rising waters of an apocalyptic flood. Ancient Mesopotamians had Utnapishtim, a man who survived the Deluge only to be granted eternal life. You people got that Noah deal. Point is, the particulars may not agree, but when you add up everything that *does* agree, it looks to be that once upon a time there was a big-ass flood."

"And you're telling me it was the Brethren and some weird-ass soul-cleaving mojo that caused it? What about the whole 'God sent the flood to purge the Earth of Man's wickedness' thing?"

"Hey, I ain't sayin' for sure that's not how it went down. Like I said, this shit's been buried deep by the good guys and the bad guys both, and the only folks who've got the juice to answer that are like a mile above my pay grade. But it seems to me if your precious God sent the flood to wash away Man's wickedness, he did a pretty fucking lousy job. And as far as the whole soul-mojo angle, it's not as crazy as it sounds. All magic worth a damn requires sacrifice – an infusion of life's essence to get the gears a-turnin'. That's why the mystics of your species always use blood to kick-start their little parlor tricks. Sometimes, sure, animal sacrifice will do, but you and I both know human blood is where it's at if you really wanna get anything done. And a feat of the kind we're talking about – breaking the bonds of eternal damnation, dropping off the radar of heaven and hell both – that'd require more juice than even a genocide's worth of blood could muster. That'd require *real* power. Power like what'd be unleashed if you destroyed a human soul."

"Why Varela, though? Why's the soul got to be unclean?"

"Could be because it's hell's bond he's trying to break. Could be it doesn't have to be at all. Probably Danny's just going by what he's read – which ain't the worst plan, since the Brethren seemed to pull it off."

"So you're saying this could *work*? Danny does his little song and dance and busts open Varela and he's free?"

"Maybe. Maybe not. Seems to me it doesn't matter – what matters is Danny *thinks* it will. Once he shatters that soul, it won't matter to the millions he'll be killing whether his hoodoo was successful."

"But it can't be that easy to destroy a soul, can it? I mean, it's not like he can just whack it with a hammer, or every time some yahoo thrill-seeker's parachute failed to open, *boom* – apocalypse."

"True enough," Dumas conceded. "Only a demon-forged in-strument would be capable of inflicting the kind of damage

Danny's after. And I'll admit, they're hard to come by. But the boy's already gotten this far – you think we ought to leave it up to chance he falters now?"

It was a fair point. Actually, from where I was sitting, it was a seriously *unfair* point, but given that I'm damned and all, that made me more inclined to believe it. I looked for any sign Dumas was putting me on with all of this, but if he was, it didn't show. And truth be told, it jibed with what I'd seen these past few days; after all, the bug-monster'd said, "Were it not for the Great Truce, for the rules to which we three agreed, I would not abide the Nine at all. But now it seems that truce is crumbling, and with it my patience for your games. I assure you I will not abide a tenth." So it sounded to me like the Nine and the Brethren were one and the same. And that Danny was gunning to be number ten. Only Captain Crawly had it in his head *I* was the one causing problems, which didn't really bode well for me – particularly since I still didn't have the faintest idea who the hell he was, or how he fitted in to all of this. And the rotten cherry on top of this shit sundae was if I didn't stop him, not only would I wind up chillin' in oblivion, but millions of people would die horribly. How'd that old poem go? "Fear death by water."

Too fucking right, I thought.

"So the Brethren are real, and Danny's obsessed with them, and he stole Varela's soul to recreate an ancient mystical rite that, if he's successful, would bring about a second Great Flood and wipe out civilization as we know it?"

"That's about the size of it, yeah."

"Shit," I said.

"Yeah," Dumas replied. "Shit."

"So – what now?" I asked.

"What're you asking me for? You know what I know. You

wanna stop the guy, you're gonna hafta figure out the rest all by yourself."

"I thought we *both* wanted to stop the guy."

"Yeah, and I just gave you all the help I can."

"Says the guy who knew about Danny's cave-man ramblings from the get-go and did fuck-all to stop him going rogue."

"You gotta understand, Sammy, coming down off a skim, you tap into something. Something greater than yourself. Something greater than the soul you're skimming off of. It's like, for a little while, you're tapped into the whole of human experience or some shit. Past, present, future – who knows what the fuck you're gonna see or why? Call it chance, call it the hand of God – from where I'm sitting, they're the same damn thing. But whatever you call it, I just figured that's where Danny got all this – and hell, maybe it was. I didn't think for a second he understood a word of it. Yeah, maybe I fucked up, but if I start poking around now and then the shit goes down, it only increases the odds it all leads back to me – which is precisely what I'm trying to avoid. So sorry, champ, but you're on your own. But hey – there's a chance you'll come through and save the world. A very, very narrow chance."

"Thanks."

"Don't mention it," he said, and then he smiled. "Hey, I think you and me, we just had a breakthrough in our relationship. Hashing things out all civil-like – me not killing you, you not killing me. Feels good. Feels *right*. Feels like maybe we oughta hug it out."

He spread his arms. I shook my head.

"Suit yourself. How 'bout a word of advice instead, on account of how we're such good friends now."

Friends my ass, I thought, but what I said instead was: "I'm listening."

"If it were me tracking Danny down, I'd be trying my damndest to figure out where worlds draw thin."

"Yeah. That'd be more helpful if I had the tiniest idea what the fuck it even meant."

Dumas shrugged like *what're you gonna do?* "Hey, you know as well as anyone that the whole of Mankind's prophecies and scripture amount to nothing more than a ten-thousand-year-old game of telephone. Half the time, they don't mean shit at all, and the other half–"

But before he finished his thought, there was a muffled boom from somewhere overhead, and the very cave around us shifted, raining dust upon us both and forcing me to steady myself with one hand against the wall. The movement was unthinking, reflexive, and of course it was my bum arm I reached out with; when my palm connected with the chamber wall, a jolt of queasy, white-hot pain shot up my arm, settling in my shoulder and throbbing like an impacted molar.

Another boom, right on the heels of the first. This one loosed more than dust – the darkness above rattled as small rocks bounced off the walls on the way down, and then a not-so-small rock whizzed past my head in the darkness, parting my hair and damn near doing the same to my skull before burying its pointy self six inches into the dirt at my feet.

"The hell?" I said. "Did Psoglav–"

"No," Dumas replied, his face set in a frown. "If Psoglav had cracked a soul, he'da brought the whole damn cave down. And whatever that was, it came from outside."

"It couldn't have been the storm," I said, thinking aloud, "lightning doesn't make the fucking ground shake. Besides, it sounded like a goddamn bomb went off. It sounded like…"

Dumas watched me talk myself out. Then he supplied the same words my brain had. "An angel's wrath? That what you were gonna say?"

I said nothing, my mouth moving for a second like that of a dying fish before I took notice and closed it. Dumas was glaring at me now, and the frown that graced his face deepened into something harsher, angrier, more sinister. His squat, round frame seemed to swell until he dominated the narrow room, and his eyes raged with black fire. "*You* did this."

"What? No! Why the hell would you think–"

"Why? Gee, Sam, I don't know – maybe because when you came marching in here, you were pretty sure stealing Varela from you was *my* idea. Maybe because you blame me for the eternal predicament in which you find yourself. Maybe because despite all the havoc that you wreaked in life, and in the decades since you up and died, you still fancy yourself a Good Guy, and thought turning stoolie on me would be your fast-track into the Maker's good graces. And here I thought you and I were getting on so well."

Dumas, a full head shorter than me when we crawled in here, dropped the torch he'd been carrying and grabbed me by my lapels, lifting me until I was a good foot off the ground and we were nose to nose. The room seemed to elongate as the torch lit it from below. Dumas's face had elongated as well – to twice its normal size, it seemed – and when he spoke, I saw his mouth was now filled with row upon row of blackened, jagged teeth. "Tell me, Sammy," he said, his striated, spiked tongue lashing at his front teeth with every word, and rasping out the sibilant in my name, "did you ring up one of your angel-friends before you sauntered over here, maybe let 'em know where you were going? Did you promise to deliver me if they'd make your missing-soul problem go bye-bye?"

My feet cast wild shadows as they scrabbled for purchase, but it wasn't any use. "I didn't – I swear!"

He slammed me into the rock wall behind me. My head hit

so hard I thought I'd puke. Then I did puke, so, you know, yay for being right.

"I think you're lying to me, Sammy," he said, and slammed me into the wall again, so hard my vision swam. Not that I minded much. In the best of times, Dumas wasn't much to look at, and these weren't the best of times. From what little I could see through the darkness and the circling cartoon birds, Dumas's current visage put Psoglav to shame. "But it hardly matters, does it? Either you called in the cavalry, or you were so fucking incompetent in getting here they tracked you. You'll pay dearly either way, I assure you. But now, unfortunately, I have to delay the pleasure of flaying you alive, so I can deal with this fucking mess you've made. Don't worry, though – I'll be back before you know it."

A leathery rustle, the click of claws on stone, and Dumas was gone – gone so quickly that he was through the narrow aperture of Danny's hovel and out of sight before I even hit the ground.

Which I did.

Hard.

And then got whacked square in the back by a stone the size of a fucking cantaloupe falling from above.

This week was not my favorite ever.

The cantaloupe brought friends. Like half the fucking roof. Shit pelted me like this was a game of dodgeball and I was the last kid standing, only harder, meaner, and from above. OK, maybe it wasn't so much like a game of dodgeball as it was a game of try-not-to-get-stoned-to-death. I'd never played that one before, but I hoped to God I'd catch on quick.

Got up. To my knees, at least. Felt like an accomplishment, till I got knocked back down. Figured maybe up wasn't the way to go. Figured instead I'd stay low.

I protected my head as best I could with my bum arm. The

tendons in my shoulder hurt like hell, holding it up like that, and the old bean still got clocked a couple times, but I deflected enough blows to stay conscious, so we'll call that a win. Tried to snatch the torch with my good arm, but the steady rain of dust from above proved too much for it, extinguishing the flame.

That was OK. I'd seen darkness aplenty those past two days. I was starting to get used to it.

What was harder to get used to was the constant battery outside – like London in the fucking Blitz – and the deadly hail of rocks it set upon me.

A stone dagger shook loose from the ceiling and sliced along my side, through fabric and skin both. The wound burned white hot, the only light in the room – and I could see it even when my eyes were closed. Hurt enough it made me lower my shield-arm for a moment. Then a quick shot to my temple reminded me why that was a bad idea.

A crushing blow from nowhere set off fireworks in my kidney. Something inside me went all wet and loose. I'll be pissing blood if I get out of here alive, I thought. The notion didn't fill me with warm fuzzies.

Now, I know what you're thinking. You're thinking why didn't I let nature take its course and say sayonara to this poor pathetic meat-suit? After all, just two days back I was rooting for the bug-monster to kill me, so why not? Why bother busting ass for the privilege of wandering smack into the middle of an angel/demon grudge match when I could take my chances with reseeding and hope I wind up possessing someone hale and hearty and way the fuck away from here? And believe me, I get where you're coming from. But there's a couple things I'm privy to that you're not.

Thing One: dying fucking hurts.

Thing Two: dying *really* fucking hurts.

How bad does dying hurt? So bad that even if shit's hitting the fan full-on and you've got no other choice, you still stop and check the math to make sure it don't add up another way. And yeah, OK, I'll cop to trying to goad the bug-monster into killing me, but there were extenuating circumstances – namely the fact that I was (mistakenly, as it turned out) pretty sure he was going to kill me anyway. So I wasn't so much rooting for death as I was for him to make it quick. Big difference.

Besides, the key to a successful reseeding is luck, and lots of it. Luck's the difference between winding up in a millionaire meat-suit with a private jet or an invalid in an adult diaper without enough spare juice to raise his head, let alone allow you to hop hosts.

Now do I strike you as the lucky type?

Yeah, that's what I thought – which is why most times I'd just as soon take my chances in the here and now, regardless of the crappiness of said here and now.

Sick of getting pummeled, I crawled toward where I figured the door was, but ran into Danny's cot instead. I started to turn around, and then I got me the beginnings of an idea, so I stopped. My fingers traced the cot's metal frame until I found the hinge. Then I folded it in half and climbed under. It was a tight fit, me hunched inside my makeshift A-frame tent, but it was better than being crushed to death. It was, at best, a temporary solution; the way this place was filling up, I had to get through that crawlspace and into the outer chamber fast if I wanted to keep this meat-suit breathing.

I tried sliding the whole shebang forward, toward the door. Too damn many rocks in the way. I looped my hands around the frame and lifted, figuring I'd use it all umbrella-like and knee-walk over, but the uneven terrain required all fours to maneuver, which is to say I tipped over and wound up on my face.

I won't lie – tipping over hurt. Hurt enough it took a sec to realize I wasn't getting pummeled anymore. I could hear shit falling, sure – louder every second, in fact, suggesting this room wasn't going to be a room much longer – but it was no longer reaching me. Seemed the cot had gotten wedged against the wall, building me a little fort. But by the creaking of its frame, it wasn't going to stay wedged for long.

I clawed over rock and dirt and the still-hot cinders of the torch, mindful not of the scratches and burns I inflicted on myself in the process, only of the door, of freedom, of *away*. A few seconds of blind groping and I found it. The aperture was narrower now, and riddled with loose stone, but there it was.

There it was.

A sound like a thousand hoofbeats as the ceiling caved in, and the darkness around me imploded. I dove for the passage as the cot crunched beneath the sudden weight. Hot, stale, dusty breath chased after me as all the air in the heap of rock that used to be a room was expelled along with me. And then the ceiling of the crawlspace popped overhead like a crack spreading through glass, the sound zipping past me in the darkness and letting me know I wasn't out of the woods yet.

I scampered through the short passage and into the slightly larger outer chamber of Dumas's so-called monkey house, only realizing I'd left the crawlspace behind when the echoes of its collapse reverberated off the walls around me. All I wanted was to collapse as well, bloodied and spent as my egress from Danny's burrow had left me. But the muffled booms of the angels' continued onslaught, and the constant patter of pebbles on the dirt floor, suggested that wouldn't be prudent. Suggested that Danny's hidey-hole was only the beginning. Suggested that if I didn't get my ass out of these caves and into the open desert air, my ass was gonna get a whole lot flatter.

So I kept moving.

Finding the fissure that connected the monkey house to the main cavern wasn't easy. Damn thing was only sideways-me wide, and in complete darkness, every nook and cranny in the cavern wall felt like pay dirt. I must've circumnavigated the chamber twice before I finally found it, and beat to hell as I was, squeezing through was no mean feat. But, halting though my progress was, it was progress, and eventually, I spilled from the crevice, tumbling to the dirt floor and squinting against the sudden light.

Sweet Christ, was I sick of falling down.

Turns out, though, much as it hurt, that fall was lucky as all get-out. Not like it was strategy or anything – I was just beat up enough I was having trouble supporting my own weight, is all – but still, it was lucky nonetheless. 'Cause when I fell, I wound up hunkered behind one of them rock formations that juts up from the floors of caves – stalagmite or stalactite, I can never keep them straight – and so I managed not to run afoul of the angry angel.

I should've known that this light I stumbled into was too bright, too white – too pure to be cast by torches alone. Should've recognized it for what it was. Because I'd seen light like this before. Breathtaking. Painful. Glorious. Deadly.

The light of God's grace.

The light that emanates from His most trusted servants – and from His deadliest assassins.

Most times, were you to spy an angel topside, you'd never know it. They, I don't know, seem to dim their natural light, and project a sort of vague suggestion of human form that your eyes slide right off of. I mean, you register the basics. Eyes? Check. Hair? Check. Two arms? Two legs? Yup and yup.

But if I were to ask you what *color* those eyes were, or was the hair cut long or short, you'd have no earthly idea. Which makes sense, because an angel is a celestial being; there ain't nothing *earthly* about 'em.

This guy, though, he wasn't bashful. Wasn't subtle. Wasn't hiding his true nature. Which, quite frankly, means me saying "guy" wasn't quite accurate. But junk-having or not, tall and hulking as he was, "guy" and "he" seem closer than the alternative. Seem as close as this earthly, imperfect language of ours is gonna get.

The angel stood naked in the middle of the hall, lit from within and shimmering like a mirage on the horizon. Like pavement on a hot day. Like a reactor on the verge of meltdown. He was eight feet tall if he was an inch, and he was so beautiful – and so goddamn terrifying – I didn't realize until I heard his captive speak that he was not alone.

The voice I heard was low and rumbling, and in a tongue I did not speak – a tongue I *could* not speak, full of sounds no human could ever hope to make. Though the canyon beyond the cave raged with sounds of battle – screams of anger and of agony, and countless explosions far less muffled than before – that voice cut through them all, and reached my ears as though from mere inches away.

The voice was Psoglav's.

The horrid dog-beast was on his knees before the angel – a posture of necessity rather than penitence, given that the angel had in his hand one of Psoglav's wrists, which he held twisted over Psoglav's head, keeping him immobile and in no small amount of pain. Though if Psoglav's acid tone was any indication, the hold still left him somewhere shy of accommodating.

The angel struck out with his free hand – a chopping blow to Psoglav's throat. An awful gargling sound, and Psoglav fell silent. The angel spoke then, its words in the same tongue as the demon it questioned, but where the latter's words sounded horrid and perverse, the former's were melodic and well-modulated – serenity itself.

Then, when Psoglav failed to answer, instead spitting at his captor's feet, the angel ripped off Psoglav's arm, which kind of put a damper on the Zen of the moment.

Psoglav roared in agony. I'm talking shook-the-fucking-walls roared. I thought my ears were going to bleed. Thought the place was going to come down around me. But the angel didn't even flinch. Instead, he smacked Psoglav across the face with his own severed arm, spewing gore across the cavern wall, and asked his question again.

Psoglav, now free of the angel's wrist-hold on account of the wrist the angel was holding being no longer attached to him, picked himself up off the floor and launched himself at the angel – marshalling every ounce of strength and speed he had – his iron teeth bared for attack. If the angel had a face, I might've thought Psoglav aimed to bite it off.

But he never got the chance.

The fastest goddamn demon I've ever seen, and he didn't even come close.

Oh, sure, he started well enough, rocketing off the ground faster than my human eyes could follow. But a funny thing happened on the way to biting his Chosen brother. Two things, actually. The first was that Psoglav slowed to a halt in mid-air, his snapping maw scant inches from its intended target. The second was that the angel, I don't know, *expanded* – growing bigger, taller, brighter – until he seemed less a person than a tiny, white-hot sun.

It happened so fast, I nearly failed to react. Nearly. But when the corona created by the angel-sphere engulfed Psoglav and then collapsed back in on itself, I hit the floor, hiding behind my stalagamabob and burying my face in the dirt.

Then the angel loosed God's wrath, which set the very air around me ablaze, its blinding white light searing my retinas despite their being protected by closed lids and rock and dirt, while my ears rang with the most beautiful and terrible sound I'd ever heard. Once upon a time, a girl with cause to know told me it sounded like a chorus of children, painful in its beauty, and that strikes me as close to right as anything I could come up with. But even that can't do it justice, because the whole of human experience has yet to invent the words to describe such agony, such ecstasy – and given the animal terror with which I trembled upon hearing it, I pray they never will.

I pray they'll never have to.

I pray this infant war between heaven and hell dies in child-birth.

Because the alternative is too frightening to imagine.

I've no idea how long I spent, curled fetal behind that stone outcrop and weeping like a child, but when I came to my senses, I was alone. Aside from the charred black husk I assumed was once the demon Psoglav, the cave was empty – deserted – and most of the torches had burned out. All was still and quiet – not just in the cave, but in the canyon beyond as well. After the hue and cry of war, I felt as though I'd been struck deaf, but what few torches remained lit cracked and popped as they burned through the last of their accelerant, and as I found my feet and staggered along the cavern's gentle upslope, my shambling gait echoed off the limestone walls.

I walked without thought, without fear of discovery, with no intention but to be free of this subterranean hell and to feel fresh air upon my face. I suppose if I had the energy, I would have wondered who'd won, and whether I'd be greeted by a pissed-off Dumas or a legion of wrathful angels upon surfacing.

I'd have wondered if it was day or night, or whether I'd been out an hour or twenty-four of them – the latter of which would leave me right screwed with regard to the bug-monster's deadline.

But I didn't wonder any of those things. I was too tired. Too sore. Too bruised and bloodied to even care. And God help me for saying so, but as much as my every movement hurt – as much as I wondered where I'd find the strength to even take another step – the momentary absolution from caring bestowed upon me by my pain was bliss.

For maybe the first time since I shuffled off the mortal coil, I felt free.

26.

You know the problem with self-delusion? It doesn't matter if your escape-hatch from reality is drug or drink or – in my case – exhaustion born of repeated brutal ass-whuppings; whatever the method, the comedown is a bitch. It's a lesson I've been privy to plenty in my life, but damn if this particular comedown didn't blindside me all the same.

Maybe if I'd stuck with the plan – get topside, feel the wind in my face – it could've been avoided. Though looking back at how it all shook out, sticking to the plan would've likely led to nothing more than two days spent wandering in the desert before Big 'n' Buggy came to get me. But speculating now's irrelevant. My plan went out the window the moment I saw the soul.

It was the flicker I was aware of first: a pale gray-white playing across the right-hand limestone wall just up ahead, like moonlight reflected off of water. As I approached, I realized the light was coming from across the hall, spilling through the doorway left empty by dint of someone or something tearing the heavy iron door that once sat there clean off its hinges.

The doorway, I realized, led to Psoglav's little machine shop

– the withered, pitch-black heart of Dumas's whole operation. And that light was someone's soul, left forgotten by the
so-called good guys and the bad guys both.

But not by me.

I suppose on some level I must've known it was foolish of
me to care. That even if I *could* lay the soul inside to rest, it was
doomed to an eternity of torment – and Danny's failed Gio-for-
Varela bait-and-switch sure as hell taught me the point was
moot, since my Deliverants wouldn't accept it anyways. Still, I
couldn't just leave it there. A damned soul is still a soul; it deserved better than to be cast aside like so much garbage.

Inside, the room was dark and quiet. The soul was still seated
in the spindle of the massive lathe, and cast long shadows of the
nightmare machinery on which it sat. The diesel engine that
hung above the work surface was cold and quiet, and reeked of
motor oil and overuse. Its scent did little to mask the pervasive
stench of sulfur from the cistern in the corner, and from the
copper pipes that snaked away from it, dripping rotten-egg
water in plinks and plunks onto the lathe at random intervals.

As I approached the soul, I noticed its surface was cross-
hatched with scratches, and around it, the work surface was
littered with tiny, glimmering shards. A fine layer of vaguely
iridescent dust blanketed the lathe, glinting dully in the grime-
caked nooks and crannies of the machine's many knobs and
gears. Too much dust to've been kicked up by this one soul. A
shudder ran along my borrowed spine as I wondered how
many tiny human moments had been reduced to dust at the
hands of that fucking monster and his machine. I wondered if
those souls could feel the pain of those moments' absence as
they whiled away forever in the depths of hell.

I felt a sudden urge to destroy the implement that wreaked
this havoc. It wasn't enough that Psoglav had been reduced
to cinder; I needed to ensure his subtle blade never parted

memory from soul again. But as I cast about for it, I realized it was nowhere to be found. Not atop the lathe. Not on the floor around it. Not in the many pockets and loops that graced Psoglav's discarded apron.

It was then I realized I was not alone.

Just a subtle crunch of foot on gravel. Topside, I might never have heard it, but down here, where all was still as death and stone walls amplified even the faintest of noises, it may as well have been a gunshot. But like a gunshot, I couldn't quite tell from which direction it had come. The room was so shrouded in shadow, there were hiding places enough for a half a dozen would-be attackers, and as the sound bounced off the walls, it seemed to come from all of them at once. And it was that moment's hesitation as my brain sorted out the likeliest spot for someone to hide that did me in.

Don't get me wrong; I got the answer right. The sound came from behind the squat bulk of the cistern. It's where I would've hid. It's where my assailant did. But the time I took to get to that conclusion was time enough for them to close the gap between us.

I wheeled, too late. Electric pain as a white-hot needle pierced my neck. For a half-second, I wondered if it was the pain of Psoglav's subtle blade. Then all of the sudden, I was a little girl.

Yeah, I know how it sounds. But it's the fucking truth. One minute, I'm getting ambushed in a demon's lair, and the next, I'm on my belly underneath my bed – a darkened flashlight in my trembling hands, my heart racing beneath my favorite flannel nightgown.

A creak of hardwood floor, and then another. Stocking feet beside the bed. Familiar. Familial. Adrenaline prickled through my system, chemical fear steeling my tiny frame. Whatever minuscule part of me was still Sam reflected back to another girl, another time – this one locked inside a wooden trunk in

Amsterdam. But who she was, or how I knew her, I couldn't recall. Those thoughts were too far from reach. Those memories belonged to someone else.

The stocking feet shuffled away, my stalker leaving – or so I thought. I relaxed a little, my fear subsiding.

Prematurely, it seemed.

Rough hands, strong and calloused, grasped my ankles and dragged me from my hiding place. I let out a squeal of sheer terror as those same hands lifted me up off the floor and hurtled me toward the bed. For an endless second, I flew through the air as though gravity had no dominion over my tiny frame – my nightgown flapping, my pigtails trailing out behind me, the flashlight clattering to the floor. Then I hit the bed and bounced so hard it rattled on its frame, and sent stuffed animals flying in all directions.

Dad was on me in a flash, roaring like a cartoon monster and tickling my ribs until I roared too, with laughter. I clamped my hands over my mouth, determined not to give him the satisfaction, but mischief glinted in his eyes, and he grabbed both my ankles with the crook of his elbow like a headlock, and set to tickling my feet. It was too much for me to take. I thrashed and thrashed, but his grip was like iron, and I couldn't break free. I guess I must've been shrieking something fierce, too, because before long, Mom poked her head in, her frown of mock-disapproval not quite hiding the amusement that crinkled her nose and the corners of her eyes.

"Raymond," she said, her tone stern, "you were *supposed* to be putting Gabriella to bed."

"Oh!" he said, feigning surprise and lifting me once more off the bed. He held me up so we were eye-to-eye and leveled an appraising gaze my way. "Is this my Gabby? I thought it was an intruder – I found her hiding under the bed with a flashlight."

"If this is how you handle intruders, I think we've got more to worry about than a daughter up past her bedtime." Mom turned her attention to me. "What on earth were you doing under there, anyway?"

"Reading," I said.

"Reading," she echoed, one eyebrow going up.

"Mmm-hmm," I said. "Sylvester and the Magic Pebble. Almost finished it, too."

"You hear that, dear?" Dad said. "Our four-year-old was up late *reading*. Thank God we put a stop to *that*."

"She'll be cranky in the morning," Mom said.

"You seem pretty cranky *now*," he replied, but there was no malice behind it.

Mom once more arched an eyebrow, and said, "I do, do I? Well, then, don't expect to be staying up past your bedtime with *me* tonight, mister."

Dad laughed at that, though I had no idea why. Grown-ups can be so weird sometimes.

"All right, kiddo – time for you to go to bed."

"But I'm not sleepy!" I replied. As I said it, though, I realized it wasn't true; a yawn hit me out of nowhere, and I tried my best to stifle it, to no avail.

"Sure you're not," he said. "But how 'bout you try anyway, as a favor to your old man."

He tucked me in and kissed my forehead. Then he headed for the hall, flicking out the bedroom light as he went by. The hall light was still on – that's how Mom and Dad always left it; that's the only way I slept. When he reached the doorway, he turned around, silhouetted by the golden hallway light.

"Sleep well, kiddo," he said, and in that moment, I knew I would.

In that moment, the small, forgotten part of me that was Sam Thornton felt safer than he'd ever felt before.

• • • •

It didn't last.

Jesus Christ, did it not last.

Don't get me wrong – those few moments I spent nestled snug in my bed, the soft glow of the hall light a gentle reassurance that Mom and Dad were just a room away, were second only to the first time I'd laid eyes on my Elizabeth. Before her illness. Before my cursed deal. Before everything I ever cared about was stripped from me, and my life became a literal, unending hell.

But those moments of feeling snug and protected were few indeed – and hell wanted me back.

The first sign this world was slipping from me was the hall light. One moment its calming presence shone like the light of God's grace, and the next... it was simply gone.

I'm not talking gone like someone flicked it off. I'm talking gone like the very concept of light was torn free from the fabric of reality. Like my room was swallowed whole by some nightmare beast. Like any sense of security I'd been clinging to was ripped from my chest and devoured right in front of me – a feeling amplified by the horrid slavering sounds that seemed to fill the sudden darkness. They crept up on me, first so faint I had to strain to hear them – my body stock still, the covers pulled over my head to keep away the pressing dark – but soon, it was as though they were coming from right beside the bed. And something else was happening, as well: the bed seemed to come untethered from gravity, pitching and roiling like a ship on choppy seas. Only instead of the ocean's roar, what I heard was the wet, wrong sounds of smacking lips and gnashing teeth, and the squeak and crunch of floorboards rending.

Whatever lurked in the darkness was coming closer.

Whatever semblance of sane reality this room represented was flying apart at the seams.

And I experienced it all not as a Collector who'd grown accustomed to such horrors, but through the eyes and mind of a frightened little girl.

At first, I was paralyzed. I couldn't even bring myself to draw breath. I was too terrified to draw the attention of whatever it was that made those noises in the darkness.

So instead I lay there with the covers over my head willing the room's vertiginous yawing to stop.

But then I heard it draw a breath, and then another, as if whatever the darkness hid was sampling the air around it – air that no longer smelled of dust and fabric softener and Mom's pot roast, but instead of rust and rot and death – and the noises intensified. A whisper of motion surrounded me, like when Dad dragged our cooler down to the water's edge when we went to the beach. Like the scales of a snake scraping across each other as it uncoiled.

The unseen creature was surrounding me.

I mustered whatever steely reserve this little girl contained, and drew the blankets down, uncovering my face. My tiny hands were balled into fists, still clutching the blankets for dear life as my eyes strained against the black. But it was no use. Whatever was out there could've been six miles, six feet, six inches from my face, and I wouldn't have known the difference.

I heard an awful clicking noise that seemed to come from everywhere at once, and the image of a basement in the desert – of a ruined brown-red beak – bubbled to the surface of my mind.

The monster in the dark whispered to me, then. Not a threat, exactly. More like an invitation. It seemed to speak not in language but images, each somehow imbued with a tone of lurid suggestion – of it feasting on my flesh, of it subsuming me, of me joining countless others of the eaten in an eternity of torment, of oneness, of experiencing the beast's relentless hunger. Those countless others called to me as well, their throaty, lustful whispers assuring me it only hurts a moment, that soon I'll see how fun it is down down down where they are, all I have to do is let the creature (Abyzou they called her in reverent tones) take me taste me eat me end me and oh how lovely it will be!

Though my mind had once proven closed off to such suggestion, world-weary and guarded as I'd then been, little-girl-me was guileless and unprotected. The desperate pleas of the consumed held me rapt, revulsion and morbid curiosity forcing me to listen – and the more attention I paid them, the more voices joined the chorus. Some begged, some threatened, some cajoled, but all to the same end: to partake of my flesh, my innocence, my life. And as the pressure they exerted on my fragile mind increased, I was horrified to realize I was tempted to give in, if for no other reason than to get them all to stop.

But they wouldn't stop – I knew they wouldn't.

And then I remembered my flashlight.

To this day, I don't know if it was the part of me that was still Sam who forced that thought to the forefront and latched onto it like the life-preserver it was, or if in that moment, I was rescued from oblivion by a little girl. I suspect the latter. Because even if that little girl was nothing more than an echo, the woman she'd become now dead and gone, that little girl still thought she had her life ahead of her – which was more than I could say. And I can't deny the surge of confidence I felt in the moment I made up my mind to fight – confidence born of faith, of trust, of a belief that in the end, good will triumph and the monsters will slink back empty-handed to their closet lairs. God knows I don't usually think any such thing. God knows I normally have cause to know better.

I'm just glad I didn't know any better right then.

I cast the blankets off. Mom's hospital corners yanked free, and, with a sudden snap of flapping fabric like a flag in a strong wind, the bed linens disappeared into the void. Apparently, whatever was out there didn't want to afford me the protection those blankets bestowed.

That was fine by me. I wasn't the one who needed protecting.

The bed pitched and shifted beneath me like a bull trying to buck a rider. My world seemed to spin like a house caught in a tornado. It tied my stomach into knots and made even the simplest movements monumental acts of will. Debris swirled around me – debris that had once made up my room. One by one, the floorboards tore free, disappearing into the oppressive black as my covers had. Bent nails and wood splinters loosed in the process tore at my nightgown, and the tender flesh beneath. My stuffed rabbit, Mr Fluffy, whacked me in the face and caromed away too quick for me to catch. My child-heart felt a pang of sorrow as he was lost to the darkness.

Clutching the bottom sheet in one clenched fist, I swung my legs off of the bed. For one terrifying moment, my tiny feet found nothing, and I worried my plan was all for naught – that too much of the floor had torn away, and the flashlight had long since been swallowed by the abyss. But then my toes touched something solid, and my confidence returned.

I said a prayer and let go of the bed. The insane yawing cast me to my hands and knees. Around me, the voices of the creature's victims redoubled their efforts, shouting screaming begging threatening pleading until my only thought was *make it stop make it stop make it stop*.

But it didn't stop. It wouldn't stop, unless *I* made it stop.

Fingers splayed, I dragged my palms across the floor, groping wildly left and right in a desperate attempt to find the flashlight. All around me, the darkness was alive with the voices of the damned, and the creature's wretched slithering.

My right hand bumped hard round plastic. My left ankle was ensnared by something cold and wet – tongue or tentacle I wasn't sure – and I yelped, my fear redoubling. My fingers closed around the flashlight as whatever grasped my ankle yanked me backward, an obscene mockery of my father's playful act.

I rolled onto my back, wielding the flashlight before me like an unignited lightsaber. Then the floor under me ended, and I was falling.

No – not falling. Swinging at the end of this appendage. Dangling over the gaping maw of this blasphemous creature – this beast that would consume me, that would make me part of it forever.

I thumbed the flashlight's switch.

The darkness shattered.

It was as though I'd switched on a bank of floodlights – as though I'd turned on the sun.

For a moment, I saw a tangle of mottled gray flesh, a gaping rust-colored beak – a wet, pulsing black gullet. Then the creature shrieked – my whole world shaking – and, in a wisp of oily gray-green vapor that put me in mind of rot, of sickness, of death, it simply ceased to be.

Just like that, all was silent.

Silent, but not still.

When the creature vanished, I was released from its grasp, and felt a sudden strange sensation – like falling, only upward. Despite myself, I dropped the flashlight, so disoriented was I by what was happening. It fell not upward with me, but down, and I soon left its blinding glow behind. But I did not fall in darkness. Phantom images swirled around me, a zoetrope of paths taken and not taken, of experiences long forgotten and lives never lived. For a time, the little girl and I were one, our experiences intertwined – every possible iteration of both our lives projected all around us as though in mockery of the path toward damnation we both chose. But slowly, that little girl and her experiences bled away, and with her, her sense of hope, of faith, of happiness.

Above me, something glimmered, like the surface of the ocean seen from below. Consciousness, I thought. I rose toward it without control, without volition, at once aching for the reality I'd abandoned, and for the fantasy from which I'd been so violently torn. All around me swam the demons of my past, the horrors of my present, the false promise of futures never realized. They reflected off the shimmering membrane above, funhouse images that seemed to mock the man I'd become.

Right before I broke the surface, I heard someone call my name, in a voice as beautiful as love, as sad as heartbreak. That one "*Sam?*" carried with it years of bitterness and sorrow, now long behind. That one "*Sam?*" somehow suggested eventual acceptance of who I was and what I'd done that fell somewhere short of forgiveness, and yet still seemed a kindness of which I was not worthy. That one "*Sam?*" conveyed an eternity of peace and happiness forever marred by my absence – an absence for which I, now made aware of it, would never forgive myself.

When I heard that solitary "*Sam?*" I wept like a child.

For the voice that spoke it was Elizabeth's.

27.

"Sam?"

I couldn't breathe.

My lungs burned in my chest. My limbs prickled from lack of oxygen. Blind panic gripped me, and I thrashed about like a man drowning.

"Sam!"

I heard her call my name. My Elizabeth, I thought for a moment, but it wasn't – not this time. Was it Ana? I wondered, feeling a pang of guilt at the notion – or rather, at the thrill that coursed unbidden through me, so soon after being in the presence of my life's true love. But it wasn't Ana, either. The voice was unaccented.

I opened my eyes, a monumental force of will, but everything was blurry and blue-black. I suppose that should have worried me, but it seemed secondary to the fact I couldn't breathe.

"For fuck's sake, Sam, would you hold still?"

A hand on my chest. Small. Dainty. Strong as a goddamn ox. It pinned me to the ground with such force, my panicked thrashing all but ceased. Then another hand cupped my jaw and, with forefinger and thumb, squeezed, forcing open my mouth. Only then did I realize why it was I couldn't breathe.

Two fingers in my mouth. Instinctively, I fought, but the fingers' owner paid me no mind. Instead, she carefully tweezed out the dry, scratchy bolus that blocked my airway, and tossed it to the dirt beside me.

I gulped air into my lungs, and the world around me steadied. My vision cleared, and I realized I'd seen vague blue-black because vague blue-black was all there was to see. I was lying in a small clearing on the canyon floor, the first faint tinge of morning light just bright enough to blot out the stars above, but not enough to allow me to make out the details of my surroundings.

I rolled over to one side, a dry cough rasping against the tender flesh of my throat. It felt like it'd been stuffed full of twigs. I poked at the ball that lay beside me, and realized I wasn't far off – it appeared to be made of feathers, bone, and sinew, bound together with coarse twine.

Then I realized the arm I was propped up on was the one I'd dislocated – and yet it held my weight. I sat up – my kidneys not protesting, despite the beating they'd just taken – and rolled my shoulder joint a couple times to test it. It felt fine.

"Feeling better, Collector?"

Lilith. I should have known. Who else could have found me way the hell out here?

I spat, or tried. My mouth was dry as dust, and tasted like death. Believe me, I wish that were a colorful exaggeration, but it isn't – and sadly, on this count, I'm in a position to know.

"Actually, yeah," I said. "Though I could do with a mint. How long was I out?"

"A day, I'd say, give or take a couple hours."

The news hit me like a fucking mallet. An entire day gone. Which meant I only had one left.

Lilith caught my wide-eyed panic, mistook it for anger. "Don't look at me like that – had I not come along to rescue your sorry undead ass, it would have been a week. Quite a mess you've landed yourself in. Two dozen of the Fallen slaughtered at the hands of their Chosen kin – the first overt offensive since the Great War. And the rumor in the Depths is you're to blame."

"How's that, exactly?"

"They say you led the Chosen here, though there's some debate as to whether that was by incompetence or by design."

"It wasn't me."

She looked dubious. "You were the only one Dumas's seers detected; no one else was sensed entering the canyon. It's possible they followed you without your knowledge–"

"It *wasn't* me," I repeated.

"Fine," she said, showing me her palms. "It wasn't you. Then who?"

"Whoever doped me up and left me here to rot," I said. "Danny, I'm guessing."

"But why? Why would he do such a thing? What would he stand to gain by inciting a new war between heaven and hell?"

"He doesn't give a shit about the war. What he needed was a distraction so he could steal Dumas's skim blade."

"To what end?"

"Believe me," I told her, "you don't want to know."

My body was wracked by a sudden coughing fit. I doubled over, hacking till I damn near puked. When I was done, the ground in front of me was littered with mottled gray feathers.

"Here," she said, passing me a leather canteen. "Drink this." I did. It was filled with coarse red wine, which burned my savaged throat as it went down, and filled my belly with warmth. I shivered at the sudden shock of it, only then realizing how chill the night air around me was.

"Are you cold?" Lilith asked. I nodded, wine dribbling down my chin as I drank. "I believe I can remedy that." She snapped her fingers, and from her thumb and forefinger sprung a single dancing flame. She touched it to a rough-hewn, makeshift structure of scrub brush and gnarled wood beside me, about the size of a small coffee table – a structure that looked suspiciously like an altar – and, with a dry crackle, it caught fire, casting an ever-shifting circle of orange light across the canyon floor. For a moment I was blinded, and sat huddled by its warmth, seeing little of the world around me. Then, as my eyes adjusted, I realized there were shapes all round us in the darkness, lying immobile in a perfect circle at the edge of the firelight's glare.

I peered at them, struggling to see. A coiled snake. A bird of prey. A jackrabbit lying on its side, one ear jutting skyward. Possums, prairie dogs, armadillos, assorted sundry lizards – all gathered around us like they'd come to watch, to see what disturbed the quiet of this desert night.

But they hadn't come to watch, and they didn't see a thing. They were all still. All silent. All dead.

Lilith caught me eyeing them and smiled, though her smile was tinged with sadness. "Sadly, all magic requires sacrifice," she said. "These creatures gave their lives to bring you back. Willingly, I might add. I simply bade them come and come they did, so eager were they to assist me in my task. You should be honored."

"Right," I said. "I'm sure they came on account of I'm such a great guy, and had nothing whatsoever to do with the fact the woman calling them is the embodiment of seduction itself."

"You flatter me, Collector," she said, in a husky tone that sent a shiver of longing down my spine.

"Just a statement of fact. And I see we're back to 'Collector' now."

"Excuse me?"

"As I was coming to, you called me Sam."

She laughed, then. Good Lord, did Lilith have a laugh. "I

wouldn't get used to it, were I you. I was merely trying to guide you safely back to the land of the living – or, at least, what passes for it in your hobbled, damned existence. Said journey is not without its peril."

"Yeah, I gathered that right around the time I almost got noshed on by some angry calamari. I'm guessing that wasn't just some harmless nightmare."

"Nightmare, yes. Harmless, no."

"Had you been calling me long?" I asked, perhaps too casually.

Lilith cocked her head quizzically. "I suppose." My face must have dropped at that, because she followed it up with a some-what put-out, "Why – should I *not* have brought you back?"

"No – it's not that. It's just... as I surfaced... I thought you were someone else, is all. My Elizabeth."

"*Your* Elizabeth? My word, Collector – don't tell me after all these years you still cling to the pathetic delusion of the living that is *love*. You've been around long enough to learn that love is nothing more than chemical attraction – meat at-tracting meat for the purpose of making more meat. Don't get me wrong – with human life as short and pointless as it is, one can hardly blame them for fooling themselves into think-ing there's something more to it. But you of all people should realize there's not – and that thinking otherwise leads to naught but damnation and regret."

"You're wrong. Love isn't some kind of chemical accident – it's an expression of faith. Faith that somehow, despite the odds, there's something more to life than living in fear and dying alone."

"Ah, yes – 'God is love' and all that rot. Tell me, have you ever really stopped to think about what that means? Love is cruel. Love is vicious. Love inspires people to kill, to maim, to torture. Love ruins lives, fells cities, destroys civilizations. If you ask me, love's not all it's cracked up to be. But then, you shouldn't *have* to ask me – you should only have to reflect on where love has gotten *you*."

"I have no regrets," I said.

"Then you're a fool."

We sat in silence for a while, me rubbing my limbs to re-store circulation after God knows how long lying exposed to the cold night air, and Lilith dressing and roasting one of the carcasses that encircled our little camp. I didn't realize how hungry I was until the meat spit fat into the fire, and filled the night with its scent. I was so hungry, in fact, I didn't dare ask what kind of meat it was, for fear it'd put me off my ap-petite.

Whatever it was, it was delicious, or I was hungry enough I couldn't tell the difference. My throat hurt like hell with every swallow, though, thanks to the ball of feathers, bones, and flesh Lilith'd lodged in it while I was out.

I nudged the ball with my foot. Lilith watched me, but said nothing.

"The fuck *is* this, anyways?"

"Buzzard, mostly. Consider it a calling card of sorts. A focal object for the spell that brought you back from the depths of your skim-induced slumber. A spell that, you'll note, has the pleasant side-effect of healing body as well as mind. You're welcome, by the way."

I tried to muster up a thanks. It wouldn't come. "A calling card?" I asked. "A calling card for whom?"

Lilith frowned, as if considering not telling me. Then she sighed, her decision made, and the frown lifted. "I suppose, Collector, we've come far enough together you've a right to know, regardless of what my superiors may think on the mat-ter. Two days ago, you asked me to call your Deliverants off, and I told you I could not – that they fell outside of hell's dominion. Deliverants are creatures of the In-Between: the border that separates heaven and hell, life and death, being and not-being. The In-Between is both vast and membrane-thin, an infinity of nothingness contained in such a perfect join between worlds one can scarcely see the seam. The denizens of heaven and hell both are forbidden passage through the In-Between, and yet humankind must venture through it when they leave their world of rot and impermanence for the next – whichever *next* that proves to be. Which is why both sides are forced to employ your kind – and the filthy carrion creatures that assist you – to facilitate the journey. For you see, Deliverants are not the *only* inhabitants of the In-Between."

Realization dawned. "Collectors. You're talking about Collectors."

"Yes."

My thoughts turned back to the horrific visage of an old man, rendered in teeming, hungry insects. To a patch of earth dyed red with blood. To a horrid, rasping voice – which I now realized spoke a truth as terrible as the vulgar sketch of humanity from whence it came.

These creatures, it had told me, *are but humble servants, lending form to that which in this realm is formless. Just as that decaying sack of meat you're wearing lends you form.*

Over you, it said, *I have dominion.*

"Lilith," I said, bile rising in my throat as my repaired meatsuit crawled with terror and revulsion, "who did you call? Who put me back together?"

She hesitated for a moment, reluctance borne of fear. "It calls itself Charon."

"And this Charon – he's the ruler of the In-Between?"

"Yes. Are you all right, Collector? You look pale."

How she could see that in the dark wash of pre-dawn blue, the flicker of firelight, I don't know – but then, I reminded myself for perhaps the thousandth time, Lilith is not so human as she appears to be.

It would seem neither of us are.

"I'm fine," I said.

"You look anything *but* fine."

Fuck it, I thought. She'd been straight with me. I may as well return the favor. "This Charon," I said. "I met him. In the desert, on the night that we last spoke. He damn near killed me."

"And yet he came when summoned to heal you this night," she said. "Most interesting."

"He told me I had three days to return the Varela soul to him, or he would plunge me into Nothingness for all eternity. My guess is, he only healed me so I could complete my task."

She considered it. "Perhaps," she said, frowning. "Though I'm forced to wonder, why you? Charon could have just as easily called on any of your kind. I suspect there is a reason you, specifically, were chosen. Perhaps Charon's developed a certain affection for you."

I thought back to our meeting in the desert. To the biting anger in his tone, the seething fury of his assault. "Not likely," I said.

"Then perhaps you serve a purpose in his plan. A being as powerful as he no doubt sees a great deal more of the board than do such lowly pawns as you or I."

"Exactly how powerful *is* this Charon?" I asked.

"How do you mean?" Lilith replied, suddenly cagey, as though there were something in my tone she didn't like.

"When we met in the desert, Charon claimed he was an Old God. That my God is nothing more than a pretender to the throne. A seditionist. A fraud."

"And this troubles you?"

"I don't know. I suppose it does."

"Why?"

"It's hard to explain," I said. "But to me – to all of humankind – the very existence of a loving God is the greatest comfort we could ever know. Even," I added ruefully, "for those of us removed from His good grace. And the thought that He might've stolen his throne – taken it through violence or deceit like a common criminal – robs me of that comfort. It makes him no better than the rest of us."

"Oh, Collector, when are you going to learn? For all of your moralistic hand-wringing – about your role in this world, your perceptions of my actions, or the origins of your precious Maker – existence is not as simple as all that. There are no good guys, no bad guys – just a giant fucking mess, and a bunch of damaged beings trying to muddle through as best as they can. Perhaps your Maker did steal his throne. Perhaps Charon is lying – you'd be amazed at how many beings like myself have carved out a chunk of history passing themselves off as a deity to one religion or another. Only the Maker Himself could tell you for sure who's been lying all these millennia, and in case you hadn't noticed, He's been quite silent of late. Either way, who are we to judge? We're each of us nothing but frauds and liars. I mean, look at you! You fancy yourself a decent man, but if that's the case, then how did you wind up here? How did any of us? There is one thing I do know, though: whatever Charon is, he does not abide insubordination. You'd do well not to cross him."

"That much, I gathered."

"So what do you intend to do?"

"Same as before," I said. "Track down Danny. Find Varela's soul."

"Have you any idea where he's gone?"

"Where worlds draw thin," I muttered, remembering the inscription on his hovel wall.

"What's that supposed to mean?"

"I wish I knew."

"Well, then," she said, "you'd best go get that rotund dowsing rod of yours and find out. It seems you've one day left."

28.

Problem was, my dowsing rod was gone.

By the time I hit the edge of town, the sun hung high over-head, baking cracks into the earth and obliterating all trace of the numbing chill of desert night. I'd stripped my filthy, tat-tered suit coat off during the ride, letting it flutter away on the breeze to be claimed by the desert. Once a somber, tasteful black, it'd ended up as dun-colored as the arid wasteland in which I left it – as dun-colored as the once-red Cadillac I drove. I chucked my one remaining shoe as well, this dead man's dress socks stuffed inside. Even barefoot and in rolled-up shirt-sleeves, I was sweating, and I could feel my face and neck begin to burn under a sun that shone as hard and bright as a lamp without a shade.

The Caddy creaked as though arthritic when I braked to a halt in front of the squat, its brakes and shocks no doubt as full of grit as my eyes and clothes, as the lines and creases of my skin. The paved driveway was soft and hot beneath my feet, scorching my soles as I stepped out of the car and setting me high-stepping toward the door.

Inside, the squat was still and dark, and stuffy as well – the air heavy and ill-smelling from the breath and sweat of people too long confined. "Gio?" I tried to call, but my voice came out a dry croak. "Hello?"

My feet made little sound as I padded through the skeletal interior of the half-finished house. I strained to hear any signs of life, but there were none. The Gio I knew was not a slight or nimble man; surely, if he were here, I'd hear him. And what of Roscoe? That old coot couldn't go ten seconds without shouting his fool head off.

No. They were gone. They had to be. Hell, I'd told Gio to do exactly that before I'd left. Of course, I hadn't realized by doing so I'd be consigning myself to an eternity of Nothingness. Without Gio, I had no way to locate Danny. Without Gio, I was toast.

I strolled the house less cautiously now that I'd convinced myself there was nothing there to find. I remained convinced of that right up until a bloodcurdling scream pierced the air – so loud and so close, if I'd been wearing socks, I would've jumped clean out of them.

I turned and caught a glimpse of denim-clad fury. Then a wide, rectangular something swung downward toward me, blotting out my field of vision. I threw my hands up to block the coming assault, but I was too late. The rectangular something connected with my face in a squish of poky bristles and a plume of stale, woody house dust.

I sneezed – which maybe, on reflection, doesn't do justice to the ferocity or effectiveness of the fwacking I'd received. I mean to say I sneezed *a lot*.

"Sam?" drawled my attacker, his thick Texas accent somehow finding a second syllable I never knew *Sam* had. "Sam, is that you?"

Next thing I knew, I was the unwitting recipient of one hell of a bear-hug, the old man levering me off the floor with his prodigious gut and squeezing so hard I couldn't find the breath to sneeze.

When I'd last seen Roscoe, he'd been tied to the toilet, pleading for his life. Guess absence really does make the heart grow fonder.

"Jesus, Sam, it's good to see you!" he said, once he finally released me from his grasp.

"Thanks," I said, brushing myself off and trying to get the tickling in my nose under control. "What the hell'd you hit me with?"

"Push broom," he said.

"And you were gonna what – sweep me to death with it?"

He scowled at me, faux anger hiding embarrassment. "By the look a you, you could maybe use a decent brooming. And besides, it was all I could find by way a weapons in this place. A man gets mighty paranoid, holed up too long alone."

"Alone? Roscoe, where's Gio?"

"Left late yesterday, and don't you go blamin' him for it, neither. The both of us done thought you were a goner, an' yet that boy stayed anyways, for as long as he could stand."

"If you both thought I was dead, what're *you* still doing here? I told Gio if I didn't come back, he was supposed to let you go."

Roscoe did a little soft-shoe, showing off his unbound limbs. "You see anythin' keeping me here? I stayed because I *wanted* to. Was the only way I could get that boy to go. He said someone oughta be here in case you came back."

"No offense, Roscoe, but *why*? I mean, I appreciate your sticking around and all, but we *kidnapped* you. We tied you up. Why on earth would you decide to help us out?"

"Figured I owed you," he said.

"How's that?"

"Now, Sam, I ain't the most religious man, but I do believe the good Lord sent you two boys to rattle my cage a bit, shake me off the path I was on. I made some decisions I ain't proud of lately – decisions that wound up with me passing out piss-drunk in a strip club parking lot. And even then, I didn't see I'd hit rock bottom. But then you two jokers come along, and of all the cars in the world you coulda jacked, you wound up taking mine. You and Gio, you showed me ain't no good can come of the life that I was leadin', and aside a sticking me in the trunk a while, you boys treated me just fine. Least I can do to show my thanks is help you two find your own way."

"That's sweet and all, but I've gotta tell you, me and Gio are no messengers from God. We took your car because it was pretty and it was there to take – and believe me when I tell you, we had no idea you were passed out in back. And unfortunately, as far as finding my own way, there's nobody who can help with that but Gio, and he's long gone."

Roscoe shook his head and smiled. "Just 'cause you don't *know* the good Lord sent you don't mean it ain't so. And as for finding Gio," he said, nudging me with his elbow like we were co-conspirators, "maybe I can help with that. 'Fore he left, he gave me a message to give to you."

"Yeah?"

He screwed up his face, like he was trying to get it right. "'Though she is blind, she has the sight. Her visions, they are always right. Into the future, she will peek, and put you on the path you seek.'"

I blinked at him a moment. Wondered was this some kind of joke. But if it was, he wasn't letting on. "Roscoe, what the fuck am I supposed to do with that?"

"How the hell should *I* know? You two are the spooky Reaper types. Thought maybe it was like some kinda magic words or somethin' – 'specially after he made me say it back so many times, till he was sure I had it right. Figured it'd mean something to you. Foolish a me, I guess. Sounds more like some bullshit psychic-hotline jingle than anything else."

Well, I'll be damned, I thought. That's *exactly* what it sounded like.

"Roscoe, you're a genius!"

He laughed. "Ain't nobody accused me a that one before. You sayin' you know where you can find him?"

"No, but I've got an idea. I'm afraid I'm gonna need a favor, though."

"The car?" he asked. I nodded. "Take her," he said. "Me and Bertha, we had a good run, but there's only one woman in this world for me, and that's my Jolene."

"The same Jolene you called a thieving devil-woman not two days back?"

"Hey, ain't none of us're perfect, Sam. And the fact is, you can't help who you're meant to be with – or, for that matter, who you're meant to be."

Truer words were never spoken.

"You want a lift somewhere, at least?"

Roscoe squinted at me and cocked his head. "Look at this Grim Reapin' sumbitch, up against some kinda scary deadline, God knows what-all nipping at his heels, and he's still got manners enough to offer me a ride. You know what, Sam? You're all right. And speakin' of, I'll be all right too – don't you worry none for me. Now, git."

We shook hands and parted friends.

Then I headed north, following the breadcrumbs Gio left behind.

Las Cruces to Las Vegas is eleven hours on a good day, I-10 cutting a jagged northwest diagonal out of southwestern New Mexico and clear up to the southernmost tip of Nevada – bisecting Arizona like a through-and-through. Eleven hours of khaki-colored desert interrupted only by the occasional, reluctant green that accompanied human settlement, jutting from the arid soil like weeds through a sidewalk crack. Eleven hours between me and my only hope of finding Danny.

I made the drive in nine.

Not bad, I'll admit – but I could've shaved off another half hour if I hadn't had to stop for gas, money, and a change of clothes. I was so focused on my task, I damn near forgot this battleship of a car ate gas like Gio's meat-suit went through Ring Dings. But somewhere outside of Tucson, the engine started sputtering, and I realized the needle was on E.

And me without a penny to my name.

Took another ten minutes for me to spot a truck stop, and by then, poor Bertha was on fumes. I doubt she could've gone another mile. Hell, I thought she was going to quit long before she did, but that old girl took pity on me. I was grateful. I'd spent far too long in the desert the past two days to relish the thought of hoofing it.

The truck stop was huge: three acres of fresh-lined pavement, pumps, and gleaming big rigs, all rippling in the late morning heat. At the center of the automotive sprawl loomed a massive central building trimmed in red neon piping and boasting a lunch counter, a convenience store, a set of jumbo-sized car wash bays, and – if the signs were to be believed – shower facilities both hot and clean. Why in God's name *hot* was a selling point six inches from the surface of the sun was beyond me.

I pulled the Caddy up to a pump out of sight of the main building next to a municipal truck stacked high with orange traffic barrels and caked with hot-mix asphalt. The faded state seal stenciled across the side of the truck bed read *Ditat Deus*. *God Enriches*, if my rusty Latin served. Though as I watched the trucks belch black diesel fumes into the cloudless sky and set out across the lifeless earth, I didn't see much evidence to support that claim.

Even in the shade, the pavement burned my soles. I trotted barefoot to the door, thinking inconspicuous thoughts. Turns out, I needn't have bothered; bare feet aside, I wasn't any rougher around the edges than half their clientele.

The store inside was more Walmart than 7-Eleven. Everything from tube socks and trucker caps to televisions and toaster ovens, the latter two made special to plug into a truck's cigarette lighter. The clothes – mostly novelty Ts and off-brand jeans – weren't much my style, but they were tempting nonetheless. Still, tough to walk off with a whole outfit hidden in your pants, so instead I settled on pocketing a hammer and a flat-head screwdriver. Wish I could've snagged some aloe vera while I was at it; after two hours of being chased westward by the sunrise, the back of my neck was hot enough to fry an egg. But all pharmacy items were on a rack up by the register. Guess they didn't want the truckers lifting the No-Doz.

The signs for the showers led me down a long, narrow white-tiled hallway, cracked here and there and yellowed with age, but clean enough not to put the lie to the signs outside. As I pushed through the swinging door to the men's locker room, I heard the sound of running water. The locker room was only slightly wider than the hall, with two benches running parallel to one another in the center, and a wall of lockers on either side. To my right, a doorway led to a series of toilet stalls, a wall of sinks and mirrors opposite. Another doorway on the far left of the room led to the showers, if the steam billowing through the aperture was any indication.

Sounded like at least a couple of them were running, which I was psyched about. Meant I'd have me some selection. Occasionally, one of the showers' occupants let slip a line or two of Skynyrd, neither tuneful nor lyrically accurate. That I could've lived without.

I turned my attention to the lockers. Two banks of small,

square boxes, painted institutional gray. The kind where you put in quarters and take the key, which was perfect for my purposes, since a) you can tell at a glance which ones are occupied, and b) they're by far the shittiest-constructed type of lockers on the planet.

Three of them were occupied. I popped 'em each in turn. A nosy parent with a paperclip would've had more trouble with their daughter's diary than I had with these bad boys. Insert screwdriver in lock and tap with hammer, as easy as you please. Hell, I even had the sound of running water to drown out my hammering, and its sudden absence would let me know if the owners of this crap were coming back. My only worry in the world right then was that these guys would be too short or too fat for their clothes to fit.

I laid out the contents of the lockers on the wooden bench nearest me. Grayed with age and damp and mildew, the bench was bolted to the floor nonetheless. Who'd want to take the fucking thing was beyond me, and that's even granting my only purpose for being there was to steal shit.

I played Goldilocks a second, poked through my potential haul. A pair of cargo shorts, size 48: too big. Bright red shirt, all fringe and piping, and some skinny ink-blue jeans to match: too cowboy. Well-worn pair of boot-cut Levis and plain black T-shirt: just right.

I dressed quickly. The shirt smelled of sweat, but likely far less than did I – and anyways, it fit, or near enough. The pants were maybe a size or two too big, but had a studded belt threaded through their loops. I buckled it, and all was well.

The shoe situation was a tougher nut to crack. I looked to be a twelve at least. But all I had to work with was a pair of steel-toe work boots, pair of cowboys, and a ratty pair of high-tops – nines, tens, and (I shit you not) seven-and-a-halfs, respectively. The tiny high-tops came from the same locker as the tent-like cargos. I wondered how the guy stayed upright.

Cowboy had a travel stick of Old Spice. I slathered some on. Big Dude and Just Right had left their wallets in their lockers; I guess Cowboy left his in his truck. I thumbed through them, fixing to take them both, but something stopped me.

Pictures, encased in those cheap-ass clear vinyl books that you get with wallets – the ones most folks throw out. Big Dude hadn't, though. Instead, he'd stuffed them full of shots of him and his little girls. Smiling, happy. Had a smiling wife, too. In a couple pics, they had themselves a dog – a handsome little mutt, all ears and lolling tongue. Even *he* looked like he was smiling.

I swiped his cash and cards, but left his wallet on the bench. What I took, he could replace. But those vinyl-wrapped pictures were like happy trapped in amber. Like little glinting slivers of skim, only without the nasty comedown. Last thing I wanted to do was deprive Big Dude of that.

The only picture in Just Right's wallet was torn out of a girly magazine. That one I kept.

The wallet, I mean. Jesus.

I strolled out of the locker room whistling before one of them shut off the tap. Grabbed some jerky, bottled water, and a pair of flimsy flip-flops, and brought them to the counter. Told the kid behind the register to grab me one of the pre-paid cell phones hanging up behind him, and paid for fifty bucks in gas. Then I said, "Fuck it," and had him ring up some aloe vera while he was at it.

I was in and out in less than seven minutes, and long gone before the shouting started. Of course, I didn't realize at the time I'd just taken a star turn on no fewer than two dozen security cameras, or that the cops who'd spotted us lowriding through the Rosita's parking lot would ID me from that footage right around the time I stopped in Phoenix to take a leak. I didn't know that they'd tie Bertha – and by extension, me – to the explosion at the strip club, or that a piece of shrapnel containing the Fiesta's VIN would lead the Feds to Ethan's doorstep around the time I hit the Nevada state line. The way I hear it, Ethan's breathless (if not entirely sensical) statement to the Federales tied a bow around the whole damned affair and set some junior G-man salivating at the prospect of nabbing the nefarious perpetrator of a real-live transcontinental crime spree.

Said perpetrator being me, in case that wasn't clear.

But like I said, I wasn't aware of any of that. I just drove blithely on toward Vegas, as one by one the pieces clicked into place.

As I pushed open the storefront door, I was greeted by the sound of crashing surf. After two days of wandering in the desert like some latter-day Moses – you know, if Moses were undead and damned and playing for the black-hats and, OK maybe it ain't the best comparison after all – I thought maybe God was mocking me. Then a pan-flute sounded, and I spotted the boom box on the counter by the register. Propped against it was a CD case that read *Reaching Elysium: Divinity Through Relaxation*. That's when I knew for sure that God was mocking me.

The place wasn't much to look at. Outside, it was a bland commercial storefront in a bland commercial district of Las Vegas, cut off from the glamor of the Strip – and the benefit of its tourist dollars – by the Las Vegas Freeway. Sandwiched as it was between a nail emporium and an all-you-can-eat Chinese buffet, the reek of chemicals and cooking oil seemed designed to speed what little foot-traffic might happen by on their way without a second glance. Not that a second glance would've done much good. The sign over the door was cheap,

hand-lettered, and simply read: PALMISTRY TAROT DIVINA-
TION PSYCHIC READINGS LOST ITEMS FOUND. No name,
no phone number, no punctuation. But from what I could dig
up online on my piece-of-shit cell phone, the place had been
in business for five years, and the ratings I'd read were glowing
to a one. Maybe there was more to the place than its appearance would suggest.

There fucking oughta be, I thought, or I just spent half of
my last day on Earth running down a bogus lead.

It was Gio who brought me here. With that stupid rhyme
he made Roscoe memorize. With something he said back in
Las Cruces. *This research shit would go a hell of a lot faster if you
had an iPhone*, he'd told me. *A little Google access would make
your life a whole lot easier.*

So I took his advice. Googled as much as I could remember
of Roscoe's poem. Turned out, it really *was* a jingle – not for a
psychic hotline, but for a real, live psychic hailing from Gio's
old stomping grounds. She had an ad in the online edition of
the *Las Vegas Weekly*, sandwiched between one touting the
loosest slots in town, and one the loosest women. So if this
lead didn't pan out, maybe I'd spend my last remaining hours
on one of those.

Inside, the shop was dim and close, the air-conditioned air
thick with musky incense. The walls were lined with shelves
stacked high with crystals and candles, charms and amulets,
books of spells and jars of herbs. The ceiling was draped with
fabric – an ornate batik in blue and purple. The tapestry was
not quite as large as the dimensions of the ceiling itself, and
was set at a forty-five degree angle to the room so that yellow-
stained acoustical tiles showed in all four corners.

At the center of the shop was a table and two chairs. The
table was small and round and covered in raw silk of vibrant
orange. Atop it sat a deck of Tarot cards and a wooden incense

burner filled with ash. The chair nearest me looked to be one scavenged from a dining set. The one opposite the table was a threadbare lime-green wing-backed armchair.

In the armchair was a woman. Damn near seven *feet* of woman.

Honestly, I don't know how I'd missed her. Her stillness, perhaps, or the fact that her garish outfit blended into the chromatic assault of the room at large. Though she was seated, she and I were nearly eye-to-eye. Her naked shoulders were even with the top of the chair back, and the yellow head wrap that hid her hair dimpled the tapestry above. She wore a scant halter of the same yellow as the head wrap and a pair of low-slung Daisy Dukes. The outfit would've been revealing on a woman half her height. Dark brown and well-muscled, she sat cockeyed on the armchair, nestled in the crook of wing and backrest, one arm slung across the chair back. Her broad shoulders and strong jaw bordered on masculine. A good six inches of cleavage tipped the scale the other way. Her legs were crossed at the knee such that one of her platform heels touched the floor, while the other dangled a ways off the ground, her shin a long diagonal. A pair of oversized Jackie O sunglasses hid her eyes from sight. As she tilted her head toward me, I caught a glimpse of my own matched-pair reflections staring back at me – twin strangers who stirred in me neither memory nor sentiment.

"Can I help you, sugar?" she asked. Her voice was husky and well modulated. She spoke without looking at me, her head angled slightly as though listening carefully to my every move.

"You're Lady Theresa?"

"That's right."

"Then I believe you can. I'm looking for someone," I said, and before I could continue, she raised a hand to hush me.

"Darlin', ain't we all." She gestured toward the seat opposite her, cut the deck on the table. "Please, sit down."

I sat down. She drew herself upright, and swung her legs around to face me. Seated across from her, I felt like a child. She shuffled the cards with a showman's flourish, and laid one down – a man and woman intertwined. The Lovers. "The first card dealt represents the question you've come to ask," she said. "It would seem yours centers on a matter of the heart."

"How can you tell?"

She smiled. "The cards know all," she said, misunderstanding my question.

"No," I said. "What I meant was, your ad claims you're blind. How can you tell what card you just laid down?"

"Ah – I see. You're a skeptic. Of course, when I say, 'I see,'" she said, sliding down her sunglasses to reveal a tangle of mottled scar tissue surrounding eyes clouded white by cataracts, "you understand I'm speaking figuratively." She slid her glasses back up on her nose. "The cards speak to me," she said. "In fact, I'm pretty sure they speak to everyone. Most just don't listen well enough to hear them."

She laid down another card, this one above the first. A woman among the clouds with a staff in each hand, surrounded by a wreath of some sort – or perhaps an ouroboros, a serpent eating itself. "The World," she said. "It represents an ending, completion – or perhaps the culmination of a quest."

To the left of the first card she placed The Devil, in which a winged, horned demon held captive a man and woman, chains biting their naked flesh. She claimed it represented ignorance, obsession, lust, and hedonism. I thought it was a tad more literal than that.

To the right she placed Judgment, which depicted an angel sounding a trumpet, while below, gray figures rose up from stone tombs. What she said of it I didn't hear – I was too entranced by the background image of the card itself. For far behind the rising dead was a massive wave, cresting high above them all.

Below The Lovers, rounding out the cardinal points, she laid the card of Death.

I'd seen enough. I pushed back from the table, my chair toppling as I rose suddenly to my feet.

"Is something wrong?" asked Lady Theresa. Her voice and manner were calm, as though I hadn't just freaked out and knocked over my chair. In fact, her only physical response was to slouch against the wing of the chair – legs once more out to one side, right arm draped casually over the chair back so that her hand hung out of sight.

"I don't have time for this," I said, my voice shakier than I would've liked. "I'm looking for Francis Giordano. Do you know where I can find him?"

I'll tell you, for a blind chick, she could *move*. One second, she's stretched out like a housecat in a patch of sunlight, and the next, I'm flat on my back. The table that had until recently separated us was now upturned, and cards lay scattered across the floor. One platform heel ground against my Adam's apple. And that arm she'd draped so casually over the chair back had returned holding a sawed-off shotgun that, unless I was much mistaken, had until recently been Velcroed to her chair back.

"Listen to me, you son of a bitch – you ain't taking my Gio from me again, you hear? You tell your people he's *my* man, and hell can't have him."

Oh. Good. He told her, then.

I tried to argue. To explain I wasn't here to collect him. But that was kind of hard, seeing as how she'd stuffed the barrel of the shotgun in my mouth. So instead, I settled for thrashing around like an idiot and making frantic *mmmmfthftfh*ing noises.

"Damn *right* you should be scared. Now, I understand your

kind can't die, but you feel pain the same as anybody else. So I want you to remember something before you come sniffing around here for my man again, OK?"

I *mmmm*ed some more. I guess she took it as a good enough response.

"I want you to remember what buckshot tastes like."

I watched her finger tighten on the trigger. Felt a sudden rush of warm dry air, cutting through the chilly air-conditioned shop like a knife. Something hit the ground behind me, and then the gun went off, my world disintegrating in a sudden roar of thunder.

It took me a couple minutes to realize I wasn't dead. A couple more before I could bring myself to open my eyes. My face stung like hell, but a quick check indicated everything was more or less where it was supposed to be. The left side of my face was pretty scraped up, and my ears were bleeding, too, but all in all, a shotgun blast to the face wasn't as bad as I'd anticipated.

Then I saw the crater in the floor beside me – ruined tile and pitted subfloor – and realized she'd missed.

I tried to piece together what had happened. Saw the shop door still swinging open, two paper bags of groceries lying just inside. One was upright, and stuffed to overflowing. The other was on its side, its contents scattered across the floor. A pool of milk spread slowly out around it like a photo-negative of someone bleeding out in an old black-and-white horror movie.

Lady Theresa was lying on her back beside me, her shotgun out of reach. She seemed content to let it stay there. Of course, it's not like she had a choice, what with Gio sitting on her chest.

The boy looked good, I'd give him that. Maybe being on the lam suited him. He'd ditched his funeral duds, swapping out his suit for a pair of navy blue Bermuda shorts and a silk bowling shirt. Looked like he'd had himself a shower and a shave as well. Lady Theresa, however, looked a little worse for being tackled. Her hair wrap had come undone, setting loose a good two feet of unruly Afro. Her sunglasses sat crooked on her head, leaving one pale white eye exposed. And she looked *pissed*. From all the gesticulating the two of them were doing, it was clear they were having a discussion, and a heated one at that. But my ears were ringing like Notre Dame at Christmas, so it took me some serious concentrating before I could piece together what they were saying.

"– I mean Jesus fuck, Ter, what the shit were you *thinking*?"

"I was *thinking* I was saving your fat ass, darlin'. How was I supposed to know this guy was friendly?"

"I told you keep an eye out for him!"

"No, you told me to keep an eye out for some dude in a suit all beat to shit. This guy strolled in all healthy-like in jeans."

"Yeah, well, thanks to you, he looks halfway back to beat to shit."

"I'M FINE," I said, from like a thousand miles away.

"Fine, huh?" asked Gio, smirking. "Then why the hell're you yelling?"

"I'M YELLING?"

"Yeah."

"AM I STILL?"

"A bit, dude."

"OH. DID YOU MISS ME?"

"For the sake of politeness, let's say yeah. Hey," he said, nodding toward the still-upright bag of groceries, "you wanna beer?"

"GOOD LORD YES."

29.

"So," I said, washing down a bite of chips and salsa with a swig of Dos Equis, "when'd you realize you had the sight? Uh, the ability to divine, I mean," I added lamely.

Theresa laughed. "You gotta loosen up, honey – ain't no need to dance around the fact I'm blind. I mean geez, you try to shoot a guy *once*, and he gets all worried about offending you."

"Funny, that," I said.

We were sitting in the back room of Theresa's shop, me and Gio on a thrift-store dinette set, Theresa lounging in an oversized beanbag chair in the corner. The room was draped all over with richly colored fabric just like the front room of the shop. An oversized lava lamp sat in one corner, next to an air mattress and a pile of blankets. A galley kitchen with a mini-fridge and a toaster oven occupied one wall. The sink was piled with dishes, and a pair of toothbrushes lay next to it. Looked to me like Gio had been crashing here, and his woman with him.

My hearing was back to maybe fifty percent, and a few minutes' cleaning up my face in the shop's restroom revealed only minor cuts and scrapes beneath the blood. I'd emerged to discover Gio'd laid out a snack-food feast, as well as the promised beers.

I hadn't realized until I saw the food how hungry I was. And after twenty minutes of shoving food into my face, I'd only just begun to slow. Guess skim really takes it out of you. No wonder Danny had looked like shit.

"As for my ability to sense what lies behind the curtain," Theresa continued theatrically, "I guess somehow I've always known."

Gio snorted.

"Something funny?" I asked.

"Just the fact she's fulla shit," he replied. "Ter can't see the goddamn future any more than she can see your hand in front of her face."

"You're kidding me."

"He's not," Theresa said.

"But the cards—"

"— are marked," she finished. "You notch the edge ever so slightly with your nail – usually suit on the right-hand side, card value on the left. Something my daddy taught me when I was a kid. Got me kicked out of Binion's more than once."

"More than once? I was under the impression once you get kicked out of a casino, you're never let back in."

Theresa smiled. "That's mostly true," she said. "But the first time they kicked me out, I was a lanky boy of twenty-three. One of the benefits of starting out a Terrence and becoming a Theresa is you get a do-over on the mistakes you make in youth. Or a second chance to make them all over again."

Ah, so that explained her height, her voice – her broad, well-muscled frame. But right then, I was far more curious about the hand she'd dealt me before the shooting started, and the reading she'd doled out. "The cards you laid down today – did you pick them?"

"Nope," she said. "Never do, and today's deal was no different; they came up how they came up. All I did was read 'em."

"Then it's time to burn those cards – they hit a little close to home for my taste. If *you* didn't select those cards, something else did, and whatever that *something else* is, your deck – and by extension, you – are now on its radar. Even if you *weren't* harboring a fugitive from hell," I said, nodding toward Gio, "that kind of attention is best avoided."

Theresa shivered at the thought, crossing her arms and hugging them tight to her chest. "You got it, darlin'. If I'da thought for a second any of this shit was real, I'da stayed good and far away. Fact is, my daddy was a confidence man, and in a way, I suppose, I was taking after him when I opened this place. He always said the mark of a good grift is folks walk away feeling like they're the ones getting something out of it, and by that measure, this gig of mine is as good a grift as you'll ever find. Folks want to believe. They want the comfort of knowing there's a plan for them. But believin's hard. You can't just tell 'em what they want to hear – you gotta make a show of it. My pop, he was all about blending in, looking like the marks he set his sights on. For me, that ain't never been an option. But in this business, being peculiar's more an asset than a liability. Folks find Otherness mysterious, hard to fathom; it's that mystery that helps 'em believe. And baby," she said, extending her arms as if inviting appraisal, "if you want Other, I ain't nothing but. But that's all this gig has ever been: a grift. If I could see the future even a little, you can be damn sure I would've ducked when that shitfuck decided to break a bottle across my face."

"Jesus," I said. "That's how you got your scars?"

Theresa nodded, her massive, parted Afro bobbing as she did so. "Once upon a time, I was a showgirl at The Flamingo."

Gio interjected. "Topless dancer, she means."

"Funny – you never seemed too hung up on my title back then," she said. And then, to me: "It's where we met. Gio was a regular. This was, of course, before he had boobs of his own to look at."

"Hey, gimme a break," Gio said. "I didn't pick this body – Sam did. And believe me, hon, these things ain't half as fun as yours."

She arched an eyebrow, and then laughed.

"Anyways," she continued, "it used to be they'd walk high-rollers through the dressing room, introduce 'em to the girls. One of the perks of a big bank account, I guess. One night, they bring this fella through – finance minister for some Po-dunk country I'd never heard of – and he and I get to talking. Before me and Gio got together, this was. After the show, we headed back to his suite, have a couple bottles of Dom, fool around a little. I thought we had a lovely time. And so did he, until he popped backstage on my night off to ask after me, and some catty-ass bitch who'd been coveting my spot on the weekend show for months spilled the beans about my former dick-having. Two nights later, I'm walking out to my car after a performance, and *BAM* – lights out. Crazy fucker would've killed me, too, if Gio hadn't seen."

"So what happened?" I asked.

"I took care of it," Gio replied.

Theresa said, "Took care of *him*, you mean."

"I took care of *both* of you. Believe me, if it were up to me, I wouldn't'a done him so quick. But what was I gonna do – let you bleed out while I took my time on him?" Then, to me: "I snapped his fucking neck right quick, and then I stuffed him in my trunk and drove Theresa to the ER."

"Sounds reasonable to me," I said, and I meant it. In life, I wasn't what you'd call a violent man. But I learned the hard way that even a man not prone to violence will kill if it's to protect the woman he loves. Even if it means that woman can never look at him the same again. In that sense, Gio's a hell of a lot luckier than me.

"Damn right it does," he said. "'Course, the fucker got pretty ripe out in the parking lot, on account of I stayed by Theresa's bedside for the better part of three days. But we been together ever since. A shame I had to ditch that car out in the desert along with the body, though – that rotting bag of shit managed to take Ter's sight *and* ruin a cherry '73 Mustang. I'm talking Mach 1 fastback in Grabber Orange with a spoiler and a side-stripe. Better coffin than that assweasel ever deserved."

"Boys and their cars," Theresa said. You could damn near *hear* her sightless eyes rolling behind their tinted lenses. But she was smiling when she said it – a wan smile tinged with sadness, but a smile nonetheless.

"OK, I've got to ask," I said. "You told me you don't believe in any of this supernatural stuff, and yet when some stranger comes walking in here claiming to be your dead boyfriend, you welcome him with open arms. How the hell does *that* work?"

"My dear Samuel, are you of all people going to get all hung up on looks? The way Gio tells it, this time next week, you won't look like this at all. You'll be halfway around the world – another body, another job. And yet you'll still be you. I'll admit, when Gio walked into the shop, I was skeptical, but blind or not, it didn't take me long talking to him before I saw the truth. Flesh and bone ain't who you are – it's what's within that counts."

I hoped to hell she was right – that this time next week, I was still somewhere in the world. Right that sec, though, I wasn't counting on it.

"Listen, Sam," Gio said, "not that I mind hanging out and shooting the shit, but don't we kinda have a job to do?"

Theresa sighed. "Gio, do you really think Sam had forgotten why he came? The boy was just trying to be polite."

"We've come far enough, me and Sam, he oughta know he don't gotta wear kid gloves with me."

"If you think he was doing it for you, then you're even thicker than that body you're borrowing. He was doing it for *me*. See, Sam here plans on taking you away from me, and he don't expect you to come back. Not rushing you is his way of letting me have a few more minutes with you before I lose you all over again. Only there's one thing Sam didn't count on."

All the sudden, I hoped to hell that beanbag chair wasn't hiding another sawed-off. "Yeah?" I asked, resisting the urge to duck. "What's that?"

"I'm coming with you."

Gio balked. "The hell you are!"

"I'd like to see you try to stop me, love. You forget, I know where you're going. You leave me here, I'll only follow after."

I scowled. "Wait – what do you mean, you know where we're going? *I* don't even know where we're going."

But Theresa didn't reply to me, instead saying to Gio: "You're up, love. It's time to tell him about the crows."

"I been doing some poking around, in case you made it back. Thought I'd see if I could track down this Danny character."

"Uh huh," I said, smiling ruefully. "In case I made it back."

"OK, so sue me – I didn't actually expect you'd walk out of that skim-joint alive. But I figured if I could keep an eye on where Danny was, I could stay a step ahead of him, keep him from collecting me a second time."

"Not a half-bad plan," I admitted.

"Thanks. So anyways, I remembered what you told me 'bout *his* bugs being crows, and that gave me an idea. An idea that led me to *this*."

The laptop was slow and ancient, the YouTube video grainy. A well-quaffed bottle blonde behind a desk emblazoned with the call-letters KABC. She sat frozen mid-blink as the laptop struggled to load the video, a graphic of a common crow hovering to the left above her.

Finally, the video began.

"For over thirty years," she said, her words rendered tinny by the tiny laptop speakers, "the corner of Cesar Chavez and Mednik Avenues in East Los Angeles has been home to one of the largest Dia de los Muertos processions in the nation, attracting observers and participants from all around. This year, however, it seems a whole *new* crowd is interested in joining the celebration. And what could be a more appropriate addition to the Day of the Dead festivities than a murder of crows?"

The image shifted. Now the screen displayed a busy intersection, two four-lane roads crossing beneath the diamond-bright midday sun. The camera was angled from one corner of the intersection to the other, its focus trained on a vibrant mural of the Virgin of Guadalupe, her hands as ever in prayer, the whole of her surrounded by radiant light.

Of course, she was hard to see past all the crows.

They perched along every inch of the stone wall on which the mural had been painted. They sat atop the streetlights and the power lines. They hopped along the sidewalk, heads cocked, as though looking for a tasty morsel dropped by the passersby. As though looking for the soul Danny owed them.

The piece cut again, this time to a chain-linked parking lot, flush with cars. The fence was packed with crows – silent, unmoving, and sitting damn near wing to wing.

Another cut. Now we were looking at a city park, a baseball diamond worn to dust by countless pairs of running feet. Crows pecked lazily at the infield dirt, and speckled black the outfield. The fence behind home plate looked to be made of them – dark feathers gleaming in the sunlight, that shine amplifying their movements and creating the impression that the clamshell canopy itself was squirming, twitching, alive.

The anchorwoman had been talking the whole time, but of course I hadn't heard a word. When I tuned back in, I heard her say, "...officials are baffled as to the cause of the recent infestation, which stretches from McDonnell to Vancouver Avenues west to east, and has been reported as far north as Dozier Street and as far south as the Pomona Freeway. Local business owners have expressed concerns about the animals' impact on foot traffic, but Animal Control insists they pose no threat – and organizers of the upcoming Dia de los Muertos celebration assured KABC tomorrow's festivities will proceed as scheduled."

Dia de los Muertos. The Day of the Dead. A holiday that dates back to an ancient Aztec practice – to a time when humankind was young, and magic commonplace. A holiday on which it's said dead souls return to walk amongst the living, and the living attempt to draw back the veil of death, inviting communion with those they've lost.

If that wasn't *where worlds draw thin*, I didn't know what was.

I shut the laptop lid, clapped Gio on the shoulder. "Nice work. Now let's go get that son of a bitch and end this."

"But, Sam..." he said, his jowly face tinged with worry. "Those things... they're waiting for me. Is it wise for me to just go waltzing in there?"

"They're not waiting for *you*, they're waiting for your *soul*. Your soul, as delivered by Danny. They won't take it any other way – they can't."

"You sure about that?" asked Theresa. The question had some steel behind it.

"If they could take his soul, he'd be gone for good already. I interred his soul once before, thinking it was the Varela soul Danny swapped it for. It didn't take."

"When the time comes," she said, "you best not be thinking you can trade my Gio to get this Varela back."

"I wouldn't dream of it," I said.

"You try, you won't be dreaming ever again, you hear me? I'll find a way to end your ass for good."

"Ter!" Gio admonished.

"No," I said, "it's fine. Theresa, you have my word I won't hand Gio over to Danny." As for ending my ass for good, Theresa would have to get in line.

"How do I know your word is worth a damn?"

"You don't. But my word is all I've got."

"The hell it is," Gio said. "You got us. Now let's roll."

We grabbed the shotgun. We grabbed the chips. We grabbed some cash from Theresa's register, and as many Red Bulls from the fridge as we could carry.

We were in such a goddamn hurry to get the hell out of Las Vegas, we blew a stop light at the corner of Twain and Dean Martin. Then we hauled ass onto I-15 south toward Los Angeles, oblivious to the traffic camera that snapped picture after picture of our departure.

30.

We were a mile north of Chino on 60 when I spotted the tail. *The* 60, I supposed they'd say out here on the left coast, but I was born back east, so no *the* for me. Just one black-and-white, a Statie I suppose, pulling out of one of those spots they don't like you swinging U-turns through and sliding into traffic two cars and maybe fifty yards behind us.

"Dude," said Gio, who was riding shotgun, "we've got company."

"Be cool," I replied. "He'll leave us be." And at the time, I actually believed it. I'd been speeding pretty seriously until I spotted him, but when I did, I'd eased off the gas, and coasted by at barely seventy. I figured if his lights weren't on yet, he'd just hang behind us a while by way of warning, and then leave us alone. I didn't realize at the time the traffic cam in Vegas slapped a big, fat arrow at the end of the dotted line of mayhem half a country long that indicated where we were heading – one that resulted in the Feds putting out a BOLO for us that stretched from Sacramento to the Rio Grande.

Five minutes after we picked up our first Statie, two more slid in behind him, all quiet-like, so as to not spook us. It spooked us.

"Uh, Sam? Our company's got company."

"Yeah, I see 'em, Gio – I'm not *blind*," I snapped.

"Hey!" This from Theresa, in the back.

"Sorry," I said through gritted teeth, my hands at ten and two on the wheel.

Three minutes later, we picked up a few more – two sliding into traffic from the Nogales Street entrance in Rowland Heights, and a third swinging through a turnaround at damn near sixty miles an hour.

I kept the needle right at sixty-five, and my eyes on the road before me, trying my damnedest to come up with some kind of workable plan. I was running out of time, and not just with the cops. The sun had already dipped below the horizon, and the sky ran the spectrum from goldenrod above to the deepest crimson as it met the western horizon. I'd heard tales of the smog in LA being responsible for some beautiful sunsets. I had no idea if it was the cause of this one. What I do know is it was the most gorgeous one I'd ever seen – which seemed fitting, since I had a little under four hours to get the Varela soul back and stop Danny from unleashing an apocalyptic flood; chances were, it was the last I'd ever see. For all its beauty, that sunset proved unsettling, if only because the amber hues above reflected dully off the white side-panels of the cop cars behind me, and the ensuing gold-and-black put me in mind of a swarm of angry bees. These past three days, I'd had enough run-ins with angry insects to last a lifetime.

As I drove, I watched the cop cars in my rearview multiply. They were still hanging back a bit, and they'd yet to fire up their lights – but they were creeping up behind us. If I had to guess, I'd say they were hoping to take us by surprise, end this chase before it started.

Funny; I kinda hoped to do the same.

I ran through the angles in my head. The way I figured it, they couldn't use a spike mat to pop the Caddy's tires, because there were other motorists aplenty on the road. Not as many as I'd expected though, this close to LA, which meant they'd likely closed the onramps once they spotted us. They were biding their time... but to what end? Not to get an unimpeded crack at us; they didn't seem to be shunting any of the traffic already on the freeway aside. So why?

A low *whump-whump-whump* from somewhere in the distance gave me my answer.

A helicopter.

I fucking *hated* helicopters.

No, really: I hijacked one once – long story – and it was nothing but a grade-A ass-pain, up to and including when I had to ditch it in the middle of Central Park. But at least I now knew what was holding the boys in blue at bay: they were waiting for their air coverage. Waiting to have eyes on us. Once that happened, there was little we'd be able to do to shake them. Which meant the time to move was now.

I put the pedal to the metal – or, in this case, to Roscoe's custom shag floor mat – and the Caddy's engine sprang to life. Seventy-five. Eighty. The cop cars dropped back a ways, caught by surprise after ten plus miles of traffic law observance. Eighty-five. Ninety. By the time the lot of them found their accelerator pedals, I'd put a hundred yards between us – and at least a half a dozen cars.

Suburb after suburb blurred by, nothing but green foliage and rooftops half seen over the highway's noise barriers. Places with names like Hillgrove, La Puente, Hacienda Heights. Exits on a highway, nothing more. The skyline of Los Angeles glinted in the distance like some dark gemstone against the blood-red velvet of the sky.

One hundred miles an hour. One-ten.

Cops behind us. Danny, with luck, ahead. And night falling fast. Three days whittled down to three hours.

One way or another, our exit was coming up.

"Gio?"

"Yeah?"

"You're a car guy, right?"

"Sure – why?"

I took a long look in my rearview. "Behind us, we got a mid-nineties Ford pickup; a minivan – Dodge, I think; a Corolla; a Hummer; an Impala. Which one's got the best side airbags?"

"How the fuck should I know?"

Not the most helpful answer ever, so I took a different tack. "If it were you, and you had to roll one, which would you rather be in?"

"I dunno – the Hummer?"

Good enough for me. Only douches drive Hummers anyways.

"Cool. Grab the wheel. On my signal, be prepared to put your foot on the gas. And no matter what, don't slow down, you hear me?"

Gio wrapped one sausage-fingered hand around the wheel. "I hear you," he said. "What's the signal?"

"Me dying," I said. His eyes widened. "Don't worry, though – I'm coming back."

I twisted in my seat, locked eyes with the Bluetoothed asshat in the Hummer. He was wearing a powder-blue polo shirt with a popped collar and a pair of oversized aviators, and he was chattering away at whoever was on the other end of that phone call like his life depended on it. I focused on him with every ounce of attention I could muster. And then I hurled my consciousness at him with all the strength I had, like he was the nerdy kid in a game of dodgeball.

For a moment, all went black, and the cacophony of the freeway melted away. In that moment, my world was just a sickly nothing, a morbid amuse-bouche to whet my appetite for what Charon had in store for me if this idiot plan of mine didn't pan out. And then all the sudden, *BAM*, I'm puking all over Asshat's center console – the reflex action of any newly possessed meat-suit – while some jaded phone-sex worker asks me through my Bluetooth headset if I've been a bad boy.

Not yet, I thought – but I'm about to be.

I tugged Asshat's seatbelt. On and locked. Rolled down the driver's side window, and chucked his aviators and the piping hot macchiato in the center console out of it. I eased off the accelerator, and watched the cops expand in my rearview until they were a car-length or two behind. Up ahead, the Caddy swerved wildly as Gio tried to drive it riding shotgun, while the lifeless Jonathan Gray meat-suit lolled to one side in the driver's seat.

One shot, Sam, I told myself. You only get one shot at this. You'd better make it count.

Right before I made my move, Asshat got wise to what I had in mind for him and his precious Hummer, and from whatever dark recess of his mind I'd stuffed him into, he started screaming at me to stop. I didn't listen. Instead, I jerked the wheel as far right as it'd go. The Hummer's tires squealed as the vehicle swung perpendicular to the roadway.

Then rubber once more gripped pavement, and the Hummer flipped.

That first roll was the longest second of my life. The Hummer was so tall, and the speed it had been traveling so fast, that it got three-quarters of a rotation around before it ever touched the ground. I went from right-side-up to upside-down to sideways as smooth and silent as if I were underwater – and then my world exploded in shattered glass, spent airbags, and rending metal as the passenger side slammed into the roadway.

I didn't have much time. I tried my damndest to ignore Ass-hat's myriad cuts and scrapes, the shuddering of the Hummer as it skidded along the freeway, and the shriek of steel on pavement. Instead, I visualized the meat-suit I'd left back in the Caddy. The way it moved. The way it smelled. The way my thoughts rattled round its brain. See, every meat-suit's different. Every one I've ever inhabited has left an imprint on my soul, and in every one of them I've ever abandoned, I've left a little of what makes me *me* behind. It's one of the bitches about being a Collector – eventually, subjugating vessel after vessel chips away at you until there's nothing left but a ghost, a shadow, a feral creature that knows nothing but this cursed existence. But today, I was counting on that fact to save my ass.

See, hopping bodies is a bit like picking a lock. You need to hit all the right tumblers on your way in, or no dice. It takes concentration, focus: two things in short supply when you find yourself smack-dab in the middle of a traffic accident.

OK, maybe "accident" is the wrong word. But who's ever heard of a "traffic on-purpose"?

Anyways, I was banking on the fact I'd been in the Jonathan Gray body long enough – and left it recently enough – it'd be like coming home. That my key could find the lock in total darkness. That I could stroll on in without whacking my shin on his metaphorical coffee table, or some shit.

Gimme a break – metaphors aren't my strong suit.

Lucky for me, crazy-ass stunts like this one *are*.

I closed my eyes. Stretched my consciousness. Latched onto the meat-suit in the Caddy like it was a life-preserver. I'm pretty sure it was.

The transition was fast. Crazy fast. Almost no time at all spent in the Nothing that stretched between. Which is why, even as I was doubled over the Caddy's driver's side door puking, I could feel the impact of the cop cars slamming full-bore into the roof of the Hummer.

Holy hell, was it a sight to see. The Hummer was lying on its side in the road, its undercarriage facing us. When the cops slammed into it, it leapt a few feet off the ground and lurched toward us as if by magic, the remainder of its airbags deploying and filling the cabin like oversized popcorn. Then a cop car launched over it, twisting sideways in the air in a strangely balletic turn, and two others, trying to flank the automotive carnage, slammed into the concrete barriers on either side, loosing a flurry of sparks. One flipped, one didn't, and when all was said and done, the Hummer, two dozen cop cars, and God knows how many civilian vehicles were unwitting accomplices to our escape.

Eh. The civilians were likely all locals, and they were headed into LA proper. This probably ain't even the worst traffic they've seen this week. I just hoped the douchebag in the Hummer was OK.

But we weren't out of the woods yet. The night was filled with the sound of sirens, and the low *whump* of the chopper was getting louder. I scanned the sky, and saw it slide in over the roadway behind us, a spotlight surveying the pileup behind us – but then, on orders from below I assume, its spotlight swung our way, a jittery circle of white tracking across the empty freeway, reflecting off the dotted yellow lines. Its wasp-like body tilted after it as though chasing its own light.

So much for shaking them.

I laid my hands on the wheel as my meat-suit's urge to vomit subsided, and felt Gio yank it wildly to the right. I kicked his foot away from the gas, and yanked the wheel back. "Gio, what the fuck are you doing?"

"Atlantic Boulevard!" he shouted.

"What?"

He waved the chicken-scratch directions he'd copied down from the laptop back in Vegas. "This is our fucking exit!"

Fuck. More like *was*. By the time I got the message, we were past it. I yanked the wheel. Hopped the curb. Ran across a triangle of exhaust-browned grass, took out a smallish shrub. Hopped another curb, and wound up back on track.

Above us and about seventy yards behind, the helicopter followed, its spotlight skittering over us every now and again, only to slide off once more with a jerk of the wheel, a random tap of gas or brake.

The exit ramp ended at a light. Perpendicular to the exit was a broad commercial stretch, four lanes of traffic surrounded by strip malls, sidewalk storefronts, and auto dealerships, their brightly colored signs pushing back the falling night. The ocean to the west had doused the sun's blaze by now, leaving the sky overhead that starless royal blue that passed for dark within spitting distance of any major city. Beside me, Gio shouted to be heard over the oppressive din of the approaching chopper, and gesticulated wildly. Though I could barely hear him, my eardrums throbbing from the thrumming of the helicopter's blades, the gist was clear enough. Our destination lay on the other side of the intersection.

The light was red. Traffic flowed past us in both directions, dense and steady. But waiting for the green was not an option.

I laid on the horn, and goosed ol' Bertha into action. She leapt forward like she'd been born to, and we shot out into the intersection like a bullet from a barrel.

Horns blared. Shouted curses peppered us in Spanish and English both. The chopper gave chase a moment, and then pulled back, mere inches from a tangle of power lines. The streetlight to its left was not so lucky – it wound up a fine dice as the helicopter peeled away. Sparks rained down. The mangled streetlight pole toppled, yanking free a phone line as it fell. Amidst the swerving, honking chaos, the chrome and steel seas parted. I saw my opening and took it. For a moment, I thought we were gonna make it. But the moment didn't last.

You wanna know the problem with goddamn U-Hauls? I'll tell you what the problem is: the fucking "U". I mean, sure, most truckers the country over are jacked up on coffee or meth or Pixy Stix or whatever, and not a one of 'em you encounter on the road has had a full night's sleep in weeks, but at least they know how to drive their fucking trucks. I've seen the commercials late at night on cable; they've got to go to school and take a test and everything. But all you need to drive a U-Haul is a license and a bunch of shit to move, and it seems to me neither of those qualifications is a reliable indicator of your ability to successfully pilot fifteen tons of truck and cargo down a busy city street. Which is to say, OK, I ran the fucking light, but I still maintain that bastard should have swerved the same as everybody else when the streetlight came down, and he never would have hit me.

He did, though. Hit me. Well, hit Bertha, at least. Smack in the rear right tire. Spun us around like this behemoth of a vehicle was nothing more than a children's toy, leaving the three of us clinging for dear life so as to not get thrown.

Could've been worse, though. If I hadn't seen him and cut left at the last minute, Theresa would've wound up pasted to his grill. I'm guessing getting Gio's woman killed would've made him a whole lot less cooperative – and, you know, I would've felt bad and stuff, too. So thank God for small favors.

Anyways, when our Sit'n Spin stopped going round, we found ourselves facing back the way we came. The chopper hovered wobbily above the off-ramp, its rotor damaged – more keeping watch than giving chase. That bought us some time till the cavalry arrived. Seconds, not minutes.

The Caddy was straddling a low hedge in front of a Staples

and a Taco Bell, and tottering like a seesaw. Woozy and out of sorts as I was from the crash, all I could think was what kind of an idiot drops a Taco Bell smack in the middle of one of the largest Mexican populations in the country? I mean, I like Chalupa Supremes as much as the next guy – preferably with some of that caulk-gun guac they put on 'em if you ask – but seriously? Putting a Taco Bell here is like plopping a Red Lobster on the coast of Maine. The sight of it depressed me so, I half wondered if I should let Danny do his thing, and wait for the rising waters to wash the world clean.

But of course then I wouldn't be around to enjoy it. So to hell with it, I thought – let's go save the world.

Again.

Problem was, the Caddy wasn't moving. I must've thumbed the ignition a half a dozen times, but she just sat there, engine ticking, refusing to move.

Poor Bertha, I thought. She gave her all. Of course, every war's got its casualties – I hoped to God Bertha would be the only one tonight. I stole a glance at Gio and Theresa, and muttered a silent prayer to that effect. I'd lost enough friends in my life already.

Yeah, I called them friends. Shut up.

I glanced at the clock on the dash – an old, round analog dealie with light-up numbers at three, six, nine, and twelve. The second-hand was stopped dead, and the display read nine-thirty. Which meant I had no more than two hours and change before Charon plunged me into Nothingness. And that's assuming bug-monsters are on Pacific time.

"You two OK?"

"Yeah," said Gio, though he didn't sound it.

"Never better," said Theresa. "Did you really die back there?"

"This body did," I said. "But only for a sec."

"A sec. Right. 'Cause that's a lot less fucked up than dead for good."

"Not *saying* it's less fucked up. But from where I'm sitting, it's sure as hell *preferable*. Looks like we're on foot from here. You up for it?"

"You askin' 'cause I'm blind? That's discrimination, friend."

"Actually," I said, "I was asking Gio."

But Gio didn't hear me. He was just sitting there, one hand to his chest, his face pained and slick with sweat.

I put a hand on Gio's shoulder, tried to rouse him. "Gio?"

"I can *feel* it," he muttered, more to himself than to me.

Theresa leaned forward, put a hand to Gio's cheek. "Feel what, hon?"

"I can feel his hands around my soul! Clawing, gouging, tearing it free of my flesh... Jesus, Sam, is this what it's like to be collected?"

"Afraid so. And when we take you, we feel everything you've ever felt – up to and including your collection. Which means that's what it feels like *to* collect as well."

"But why... why didn't I *remember*?"

"Shock," I said. "But that particular get-out-of-jail-free card only comes up once a deck – next time, you'll feel it, and you'll remember."

"If there *is* a next time," Theresa said.

"Right," I said. I didn't have the heart to tell her sooner or later, there was bound to be a next time. "But right now what matters is that feeling means Danny's close."

Theresa cocked her head and frowned. "Let's hope he's closer than those sirens," she said.

I listened for a moment. She was right. They were distant, but approaching fast. "We need to move."

We set out at a trot past the strip mall down a gently curving street that some overzealous city planner likely thought of as "organic." Arc-sodium orange from the streetlights lit our way past low-slung ranches on modest lots, and put me in mind of faded sepia photographs, pale golden-hued mementos of better times that never were. The night air was cool and crisp, low seventies at most, and was alive with mariachi music, spiced meats, and something more sinister – the faint ozone scent of magic. At first, we saw no signs of celebration save the makeshift altars set out on stoops and sidewalks: votive candles, marigolds, children's toys, and sugar skulls surrounding pictures of the departed both young and old – the flowers, sweets, and trinkets intended as *ofrendas* to the dead. But as we ran – me out front, the shotgun held tight to my chest so as to attract less attention, Gio and Theresa hand-in-hand behind me – we happened upon passersby bedecked in their Dia de los Muertos finery: their outfits a garish funhouse reflection of their Sunday best, their faces painted up as skulls, or hidden behind ornate *calavera* masks. As they made their way westward toward the festivities, they laughed and hooted and whooped, and shot off rapid-fire Spanish at one another. If they noticed us, they gave no sign. It was as if *we* were the spirits that walked invisible among them.

Invisible to *them*, perhaps, but not to all. For all around us – on every streetlight, every rooftop, every fence post and power line in sight – were the jagged silhouettes of thousands upon thousands of crows. Their heads turned as one as they tracked our progress, their ink-black eyes unblinking as they watched us pass.

We'd lost the chopper when we abandoned the commercial strip right off the freeway and disappeared into the relative darkness of the neighborhood beyond, but it hadn't given up on us. It hovered low over the rooftops, its searchlight tracing out a grid below. Searching. Probing. Advancing ever toward us. But the costume-clad around us paid it little mind. Even blocks away, the music from the festival was loud enough to drown out the thrumming of its rotor, and perhaps the sight of searching helicopters was all too common to the residents of LA.

"What exactly are we looking for?" asked Theresa. "Uh, metaphorically speaking, of course."

"I'm not sure," I admitted. "Gio, where are we going?"

He considered the question, his face sweat-slick and deathly pale. "That way," he said, indicating the direction most of the foot-traffic was headed – the direction of the festival.

Theresa frowned. "How do you know?"

"'Cause my gut is screaming bloody murder to run the other way."

"Yeah," Theresa said, flashing a wan smile, "you never were one to listen."

We pressed on. As we did, what had begun as the odd passerby coalesced into a crowd. Into a party. Into a sea of deathly faces staring back at us. The neighborhood to our right gave way to a city park, its rolling lawn flush with people dancing, its parking lot a makeshift marketplace where booths sold sugar skulls and loaves of *pan de muerto*, cheap sombreros and *calaca* figurines.

The rooftops of the booths and tents were alive with crows – silent, watching. Tree limbs sagged beneath their weight. Occasionally, some celebrant would snap a cell phone pic of them, the flash piercing the night and reflecting off the liquid black of their feathers – but still, they did not move. They remained as stock-still as the Yeomen Warders who stood guard before the Tower of London, Charon's own dark sentinels of the In-Between.

"Why come here?" Theresa said. "What attracted your Danny to this place?"

"Belief is a powerful thing," I said. "If everyone you see here tonight believes a little bit – even if it's only in that deep, primal place in their mind that still fears the dark and makes them cross themselves when lightning strikes – that this night provides a window between the land of the living and of the dead, their combined force of will is enough to nudge the universe such that it's closer to being so. Believe me when I tell you," I said, my thoughts turning to my encounter with Abyzou in the nightmare realm I'd traveled through to return from my unintended skim-trip, "you have no idea what might be pressing up against the glass right now and looking back at us. Or how easy it might be to crack that glass and unleash a cleansing fury on this world. And I hope to God you never find out."

"Dear Lord," she said, "I bet *you're* fun at parties."

Gio clutched his chest and took a knee. A woman in a tattered orange ball gown and a matching veil looked down at him as she pressed past us through the crowd, a churro in each hand. As she noted his obvious distress, her bone-white painted face creased with worry.

Her eyes met mine, her intent clear – does he need help? – but I shook my head and smiled what I hoped was a reassuring smile, the shotgun tucked behind my back out of her line of sight. She hovered for a moment until Theresa took Gio by the elbow and helped him to his feet, and then she disappeared into the teeming throng.

"You OK, hon?" Theresa, her voice tinged with worry.

"We're close," he said, sucking wind like he'd just run a marathon, his face gray and slick with sweat. "Too close, if you ask me."

I caught a glimpse of flashing red and blue two blocks to our east, and shook my head. "Not close enough," I said.

"Could he be masked? Mixed in with the crowd?"

"I doubt it. The kind of ritual he'd be working would require space. Someplace where he wouldn't draw too much attention. Somewhere he wouldn't be disturbed."

"So... somewhere like that?"

My eyes tracked to where Gio was pointing. Diagonal across the park from us stood a construction site, three-odd floors of half-finished building – all concrete, steel girders, and plastic sheeting, which billowed like curtains in the breeze. It was surrounded by a high chain link fence topped with three lines of barbed wire, which slanted outward overhead. Floodlights shone at ground level to deter any would-be trespassers. I shouldered through the horde of celebrants to get a better look, drawing my share of half-hearted Spanish curses – and shouts of alarm from those few who noticed the shotgun in my hands. One passerby, who looked for all the world like an undead bullfighter, shouted *"¡Escopeta!"* and panic rippled through the crowd. As I've said, I don't know a lot of Spanish, but that's one word I understand. Means shotgun. Means our chances of staying hidden in the crowd just dropped to nil. So I said to hell with hiding, and took off full-bore toward the building – the crowd parting before me, Gio and Theresa following close behind.

When we reached the fence, I saw the building was of a peculiar structure. Something about it set my Spidey-sense a-tingling, though at first, I couldn't put my finger on why. Then I spotted it: a sign, graffiti-spattered and bolted to the chain link fence, proclaimed the site as the future home of Asphodel Meadows Condominiums, with a projected completion date of three years back. The sign was illustrated, showing an artist's rendering of the completed building – six stories tall and complete with landscaping, rooftop pool, and smiling, happy tenants. And from the angle of the illustration, it was clear the footprint of the building was a five-pointed star – also known as a pentagram.

A pentagram is a common focal object for all manner of mystical rights. Upright, it's said to represent the wounds of Christ. Inverted, the pentagram is the sigil of the demon Baphomet, long rumored to be but one aspect of the Morning Star himself, also known as Lucifer.

No telling from where I stood which way this pentagram faced. But it was fucking *big*. Which meant it was capable of channeling some serious power.

And lest I think it was a coincidence I stumbled upon a giant fucking pentagram in the middle of this Dia de los Muertos celebration, the name of the place had Danny's fingerprints all over it. He always was a cheeky motherfucker.

According to Greek myth, Asphodel Meadows is the land in the afterlife dedicated to the dead whose lives straddled the boundary of good and evil without ever tipping to either side. Guess that classics education of his was finally paying off. But this building, if it were his, represented *years* of planning, investing, careful construction – maybe *decades*. The Danny I knew couldn't be counted on to plan lunch.

I was beginning to think I'd never really known Danny at all.

Something else about the building troubled me, but it took me a sec to figure out what it was. The buildings across the street were covered in crows. Ditto the ones on either side, and the three barbed wires that topped the fence surrounding it. But despite the fact this place – with all its nooks, crannies, and exposed girders – should have been a perfect roost, its every perch was bare.

Then I noticed the birds perched atop the fence weren't watching Gio, Theresa, and me like the others. To a one, they faced away from us.

They were looking at the building.

At Danny's mammoth pentagram.

I couldn't help but feel they were waiting for me to do something. I wished to hell they'd tell me what. Because if the red and blue that spilled across the crowd on either side of us was any indication, I didn't have much time.

The music cut out to the angry protests of the deathly crowd nearest the stage, who were not yet wise to the crazed gunman in their ranks. Over the PA, one of the boys in blue insisted they disperse. He said they were in danger. That there was a killer in their midst. Both those things were true enough, I suppose – they *were* in danger, and God knows I'd killed plenty – but tonight, at least, the killer they should be worried about wasn't among them, but hidden somewhere within the skeletal frame of the building before me.

The crowd reacted, some with jeers, and others with blind panic. A mob of cartoon skeletons, threatening to bubble over into chaos. Police cruisers dotted every intersection in sight – parked at harsh diagonals in the centers of the intersections, their lights and sirens a vulgar parody of the festivities they'd interrupted.

Officers, ten feet apart, had formed a line along Cesar Chavez Avenue to the north, and pushed southward into the crowd – no doubt hoping to drive me out. Some of the drunker celebrants taunted them or refused to move, while others fled – by reflex or necessity, I wasn't sure. But though the cops' progress was slow, it was unrelenting; they knew full well the freeway blocked any chance of egress to the south, and no doubt the routes to the east and west were covered. They had me cornered, and it was just a matter of time before they found me.

"Gio, listen – you and Theresa need to get out of here while you can. They're not looking for you. You can use the crowd for cover. Just leave, and don't look back."

"Fat fucking chance, dude."

"Gio, don't be an idiot – there's nothing more you can do for me. And remember, if you can sense Danny, Danny can sense you. If you encounter him, he won't hesitate to collect you."

"I ain't leaving you."

"Damn it, Gio, don't you get it? I've been *using* you. No matter what happens tonight, things aren't going to end well for you. Stopping Danny won't change that. The best you can hope to do is extend the time you've got. Because once it's done, there'll be hell to pay."

"You think I don't know you've been using me? Shit, Sam, that's all anybody *ever* does. We use each other to get ahead. To pass the time. To cure the boredom, kill the pain. Half the time, ain't even nothing wrong with that. Shit, you see this lady here? A daily dose of her, and I feel like a better man than I got any right to. I done my share of nasty shit, Sam; you know it as well as I do. You think I don't know how this'll end for me? Some part of me's suspected all my life. Truth is, I don't mind." He took Theresa's hand in his own and smiled, his eyes wet with tears that wouldn't fall. "Just knowing there's a heaven's good enough. But if you think I've come this far to give up now, you're fucking nuts."

Theresa laughed. "Baby, if you ain't noticed, fucking nuts is our boy Sam's specialty." Then, to me: "But he's right. We see this through."

"You don't have to," I said, but she raised a hand to stop me.

"I go where my man goes."

Great, I thought. The cops are closing in, and I'm off to stop a modern Deluge with a blind chick and a dude who needs a breather when he climbs a flight of stairs.

This should go well.

"OK, first we've got to find a way in."

Turns out, there wasn't one. Sure, the fence had a gate and all – one of those slidey deals with rollers and a track, big enough to drive a dump truck through, but it was fastened with a chain as thick as my arm, from which dangled a stainless steel padlock the size and shape of a child's lunchbox. Disc tumblers, not pins, which meant I'd need an hour and a decent set of tools to pop the fucking thing.

"Hold this," I said, handing Gio the sawed-off. "I'm going over."

"The hell you are," he said. "That barbed wire's gonna tear you all to shit – and no way the two of us're gonna be able to follow."

"Speak for yourself, Tons of Fun," said Theresa.

"Oh, excuse me," Gio shot back. "I'm sure you'd scale the fence just fine once I point you at it."

I eyed the barbed wire, the crows wing-to-wing atop it. "Give me your shirt to toss over it, and I'll be fine."

"You kidding me? I ain't giving you my shirt. Then I'm standing here half-naked with a fucking shotgun when the fuzz shows up. Ain't you ever seen an episode of *Cops*? It's always the shirtless dude who gets arrested."

"Oh, for fuck's sake, boys – quit arguing!"

Theresa, who'd been feeling around the fence while we two bickered, grabbed the shotgun from Gio and made for the gate. Before I could shout at her to stop – that lock'd stop a load of buckshot without so much as getting scratched – she unloaded two quick blasts. They pierced the night like thunder, and set the crowd screaming. I only hoped the echoes were enough to mask its origin. Somehow, though, I doubted it.

But she hadn't shot the lock. She'd shot the metal track the gate's rollers were seated on. Ripped a hole clean through it. Then she grabbed the corner of the gate and pulled. Freed of its track, the gate swung outward until the chain halted it, leaving a triangle three feet wide at its base to squeeze through.

"You boys wanna hurry this along? We don't have much time until the cops get wise."

We crawled through the narrow aperture. Theresa first, then me. Gio was last, and it's a damn good thing – the opening was so narrow, we had to grab his arms and pull. Once he was through, we yanked the gate back into place. Maybe it'd take our pursuers a couple minutes to realize where we'd gone.

Unfortunately, it didn't take Danny that long to figure it out.

"Sam?" he called down from somewhere high above – the voice unfamiliar but the accent unmistakable. "Sam, is that you? So nice of you to stop by, mate! Of course, if you hoped to get the drop on me, you'd have done better to leave the Giordano soul at home – I *can* sense his presence, after all. You may as well have draped yourself in Christmas lights – but then, subtlety never was your strongest suit. I'd suggest you both turn your arses around and bugger off while you can. As I understand it, this ritual can get a little… *unpleasant* for those nearby."

Son of a bitch. I was hoping to approach the place unnoticed – to get the jump on Danny before he ever knew what hit him – but thanks to the fucking coppers' interference, it looked like subterfuge was off the table. I guess the lesson is, if you plan on sneaking up on somebody, don't leave a trail of mayhem half a continent wide in your wake. That, or never stop for breakfast at Rosita's.

Once we'd cleared the gate, we'd taken refuge between a pile of cinderblocks and a heap of warped, discarded lumber, which served to shield us from the building and the street both. From our hidey-hole, I shouted back, "Don't do this, Danny! It's not too late!"

"Would that that were true, old friend. But I fear it's been too late for quite some time."

"I'm coming up!" I said.

"I wouldn't, if I were you. You'll find the path is not without protection."

I took the shotgun back from Theresa, popped the floodlight nearest us. Night engulfed our quarter of the building's lot.

"Come on," I said.

We ran toward the building at a crouch. I kept my eyes on the ground ahead of me, scanning the uneven, sun-baked dirt for obstacles that might trip up Theresa, who ran with one hand on Gio's back. Halfway to the unfinished, plastic-clad first floor, a line of pale gray dust cut across the earth. It stretched out to either side of us, and wended its way around the building in a ragged circle.

Alder ash, I assumed. Part of an ancient Celtic rite intended to shield those inside from the underworld's reach. Explained why the crows were keeping their distance. I scuffed my feet along the dirt to break the circle as we crossed the threshold.

When the circle was broken, the crows atop the fence took flight as one, and lighted on the skeletal building frame.

"A-a-ah! It's impolite to crash a bloke's party, Sam, and doubly so for bringing unwelcome guests with you. And in your case, I fear, the penalties are steep."

The floodlights surrounding the building cut out just as we pushed aside the opaque plastic sheeting and ducked into the building. The sudden darkness was stifling. A hand out to halt Gio and Theresa, I crouched low against a concrete support, waiting for my eyes to adjust.

The structure was scarcely more than a shell. Steel girders and molded concrete provided a sketch of the building the architect had intended – the building it would likely never become – but it was absent any touch of warmth or light. The floor was a vast slab of concrete, broken here and there with squares of black both large and small – no doubt to run conduits for plumbing, wiring, air conditioning and the like through. In our case, they were simply pitfalls to be avoided, lest this mission of ours end with us bleeding out in a basement courtesy of a compound fracture.

The elevator shaft was empty – a square column of concrete stretching from floor to ceiling in the center of the massive

lobby, its doorless passageway a deeper dark among the shadows. There wasn't even so much as a cable running up it one
could climb – not that Gio could have, anyway. That left no
way up but the stairs.

There were two sets of them, to the left and right of the elevator, set along the lobby's outside walls. Gio jerked his head
to indicate the nearest of them, and I nodded my assent. Taking Theresa by the hand, he inched along the wall toward it,
and I followed close behind.

Turned out, the first stairwell was a bust. A good six feet of
construction detritus clogged the stretch from ground floor to
first landing – scraps of two-by-fours, twisted lengths of copper
pipe, jagged hunks of concrete run through with rebar – making any attempt to scale the stairs impossible.

Gio indicated the second set of stairs. But this time, I shook
my head. If that's where Danny wanted us, it was the last place
I planned on being. I was through underestimating him.

I scanned the room, spotted what I was looking for: a ladder.
Then I braced it against the edge of a goodly patch of darkness
on the ceiling – an aperture intended, I suspect, for an air duct
– and began to climb, the sawed-off clanking dully against the
rungs as I ascended.

When I reached the top, I paused, scanning the second floor
for any sign of danger before I climbed off the ladder. Then I
whispered for Gio and Theresa to follow. For about the thousandth time today, I questioned the logic of bringing a blind
woman into this. And for about the thousandth time today, I
decided it didn't much matter; if we failed, she was as good as
dead anyways – washed away with the rest of humanity in the
next Great Flood.

It wasn't a comforting thought.

Whatever her handicap, Theresa was lithe and silent as a cat
scaling the ladder. Gio was another story altogether. By the

time he reached the top, he was huffing and puffing like he had a bone to pick with some little pigs, and he didn't so much climb off the ladder as collapse beside it.

"Jesus, dude," he whispered. "Your buddy couldn't finish the goddamn elevator? And did you bother to look down when you climbed up here? There's a hole just like this one right below it, and I'm pretty sure it don't stop there – if the ladder'd slipped, we woulda wound up in the second subbasement or some shit."

"I told you, neither of you have to come."

"And I told you, you ain't getting rid of us that easy. Now, let's go kick some bad-guy ass."

He rolled over and scrabbled to his feet, and then muttered, "The fuck?"

"What's wrong?"

"Dunno." He leaned down, groped at his leg a sec. "No big," he said, waving his hand at me like I could see for a damn by the faint light filtering through the plastic sheeting from outside. "Just got tangled in some wire, is all."

"Gio, don't move."

But it was too late. From somewhere in the darkness, I heard a tinkle of shattered glass.

And then, the room began to shake.

"Gio," Theresa whispered, "what the hell did you do?"

I grabbed the wire from his hands and followed it. It terminated in the center of the room, its end tied around the jagged neck of a wine bottle, which had until recently been perched precariously atop a folding chair. But it hadn't contained wine. The black stain that spread across the floor beneath the chair smelled of iron. Of death. Of blood.

I noticed something else, then, too. A pattern on the floor, encircling the chair and the growing stain. It glowed a sickly green, intensifying as the blood soaked into the concrete. At first, my mind could make no sense of its elaborate symbology, but as the glow intensified, it resolved itself before me. It was less a language than a sort of stylized image, one that conveyed greed, temptation, seduction, absorption – followed by a hollow eternity of oneness, of torment, of relentless hunger.

I might not've recognized the language in which it had been written, but I realized at once what these symbols said.

Abyzou.

"Guys," I shouted, all pretense of stealth abandoned, "we need to move!"

I ran back the way I came. From behind me came a horrible rending sound, as if the very fabric of reality had torn apart.

And then a sickly wet slithering of tentacles against concrete.

And then the chitinous clicking of the demon's beak.

"Don't look at it!" I shouted.

"Don't look at *what*?" Gio replied in alarm.

"No problem on my end," Theresa said, though the bravado in her voice rang false.

I came upon the conduit so fast, I damn near fell in. Then Gio and I hoisted the ladder up through the hole, and tried to brace it against the one above.

But we were too late. A tentacle lashed out from the darkness, glistening in the watery light filtering through the plastic sheeting from the street, and swatted the ladder. It clattered across the room and skittered off the unprotected edge, tearing loose a sheet of plastic and toppling to the dirt lot a floor below. When it hit, it loosed a flurry of surprised shouts, and a *pop-pop* of startled gunfire. The police were closing in.

I aimed the sawed-off at the darkness, and it thundered in my hand. Then another tentacle wrapped itself around its barrel and yanked it from my grasp.

A wet dragging sound filled the air as Abyzou approached. I caught a glimpse of glistening gray skin, and felt a sudden pressure in my mind. Join us, it said. Join us and never be alone again. Luxuriate in ecstatic, excruciating want for all eternity.

I clutched my hands to my head, and tried to shake the thoughts. Only when I pressed tight my eyes did they ease, but even then I couldn't banish them. Beside me, I heard Gio whimper and hit the ground.

"So hungry," he muttered. "It's *so* goddamned *hungry...*"

But there was no fear in his voice. Instead, he sounded full of sorrow. Sorrow and longing.

I fell to my knees. I knew if I didn't do something soon, Gio would succumb, and he'd forever be one with this queen bitch of the underworld. But for the life of me, I couldn't muster the will to stop her.

"Jesus Christ," Theresa said, "what the fuck is wrong with you two?"

A wet *fwack* like hitting a waterbed with a baseball bat, and the cursed creature squealed. The pressure in my mind suddenly eased. Another couple, and I once more found my feet. I opened my eyes, and the pressure once more intensified, though not so badly as it had before. And what I saw amazed me: damn near seven feet of Afroed black woman going to town on a massive, squid-like hell beast with a length of rebar like it was some kind of unholy piñata.

If Abyzou had an ass, Theresa was seriously kicking it.

"You boys OK back there?" she yelled. Her voice was hoarse from exertion, and she was covered in green-black gore, but I could swear her tone was positively cheery. And still, she kept on swinging.

"Getting there," I managed. "You?"

"Right as rain." *Fwack.* "This bitch keeps trying to show me something," she continued. "I can feel her rattling round my brain, trying to trick my eyes. Sucks for her they ain't worked in years."

"That's my baby!" Gio cheered, though when I looked at him, I found he was facing in the wrong direction, his eyes buried in the crook of one elbow.

"Now, you boys got a job to do. I got this chick."

"You sure?"

"Hell yes, I am. I'ma teach her a lesson for hitting on my man."

Gio protested, but he was no help to her down there and knew it. So reluctantly, he came with. Since Abyzou had relieved us of our ladder, we were forced to take the stairs. I'd hoped we'd already avoided – or, in the case of Abyzou, triggered – any protections Danny'd enacted, but if I'm being honest, I knew damn well we hadn't.

Each floor was separated by maybe twenty steps, with a landing in the middle. The stairwell was molded concrete, with no handrails, no windows, and nowhere to hide should trouble come. We crawled forward in utter darkness, worried with each movement some fresh hell would be unleashed. It wasn't until we reached the landing I realized Danny'd been cleverer than that. After all, he didn't need to kill intruders – just delay them. And this latest ploy of his would do exactly that.

See, that last flight of stairs leading up to the third floor was not so dark as the preceding stretch – and with thousands upon thousands of shards of skim to illuminate it, why would it be? Danny'd never struck me as one with much facility for magic, but it looked for damn sure like he'd been studying. God knows what trap he'd rigged up at the base of the stairwell, but summoning Abyzou had been a nifty trick – and this was no slouch, either. Countless shards of needle-sharp skim hovering in the stairwell, aligned like molecules in a crystal, each one aiming a pointy end our way. Each of them was so small, its glow was almost undetectable, but together, their faint phosphorescence reminded me of white-caps on a moonless night, or of an early morning fog.

CHRIS F. HOLM   293

"We have to go back," I said. "We have to find another way."

"There *is* no other way," Gio said. "We got no ladder. We got no time. The cops'll be here soon, and you can be damn sure Danny knows it. Which means he's gonna make his move, and quick. Here, take this."

Something hit me in the darkness. It was Gio's bowling shirt. His Bermuda shorts followed shortly after.

"Uh, Gio – are you naked?"

"Relax, dude – I still got skivvies on."

"If there's a plan here, I'm not following."

"Use my clothes to cover your exposed skin."

I shook my head, and then realized he couldn't see me by the skim's pale half-light. "Gio, this won't work. Skim's too sharp. If you had a leather jacket, maybe, but even then there'd be no guarantee. And if I get so much as pricked, it's lights out."

"You don't get it," he said. "I got *better* than a leather jacket – I got *me*."

"Gio, no. I can't let you do this. You're not among the living anymore – which means you're not immune. This shit will knock you for a serious loop. I got dosed with a single shard, and I damn near didn't come back. God knows what this many will do to you."

Gio sighed, steeling himself. When he spoke, his voice was calm. "I ain't worried about coming back. Long as my lady's here, I'll find my way. And as for God, I sincerely hope he's watching."

He was up before I could stop him. A short, fat man in boxer-briefs streaking wild-armed up the stairs, and screaming bloody murder all the while. The unlikeliest badass I've ever seen – and that includes his sightless lady-friend.

I had no choice but to follow after.

The shards of skim reacted like a swarm of killer bees when

the plane was broken, homing in on him with laser precision. Each pinprick brought with it a bead of blood. Each shard that disappeared beneath his flesh dimmed the staircase slightly. Soon, there was no light left in the stairwell, save that which flickered like distant lightning within his flesh.

The flight was ten steps long. He made it five or six before he fell.

Then he was gone, swallowed by the skim's forced slumber, and I was through.

The set-up of this floor was different from the other two. For one, half the damn ceiling was missing. Broken concrete exposed steel girders and night sky, and afforded me a glimpse of the storm clouds coalescing above us, blotting out what few stars pierced the city's glare. On one distant hunk of crumbling concrete across the roof from where I stood sat a gathering of crows, their outline disconcertingly like that of a hunched old man.

This floor was also the only one to feature any internal construction. Metal studs framed out what looked to be a second, smaller pentagram before me, oriented opposite the one laid out by the perimeter of the building such that its outermost points touched the innermost of the larger one.

Two pentagrams set at odds to one another. Good and evil. Profound and profane. I wondered which the larger represented. I suspected I knew the answer.

Plastic sheeting was tacked over the metal studs, blurring the star-shaped room beyond from view. Beyond the plastic, candlelight danced, the light it cast through the plastic putting me in mind of a lantern's glow.

I pushed aside a sheet of plastic and stepped into the room.

"Sam," said the stranger with Danny's accent, "so nice of you to join us!"

Us.

He said *us*.

Which made sense, on account of he wasn't alone.

She was slight of build, and stunning in all the obvious ways. Sun-kissed hair spilled down over shoulders both shapely and deeply tanned. A spaghetti-strapped tank top of heather gray barely contained a pair of breasts just this side of ostentatious. A glimpse of midriff peeked out above a skirt that started so low and ended so high, in simpler times it would've caused a riot. Her legs gleamed with reflected candlelight, and went all the way to the floor.

In her hand, she held Psoglav's skimming blade.

I turned my attention back to Danny, who was wearing a strapping lad of twenty-five or so, with pale blue eyes and teeth so white they seemed to glow. He looked unperturbed by my arrival. In fact, he appeared the picture of confidence in his yarn-dyed linen shirt and khaki shorts, a pair of leather sandals on his feet. "Who's the skirt?" I asked him. The gnawing feeling in my gut told me I already knew.

"Who's the skirt?" she repeated back to me, her crisp Balkan accent an added barb to her mockery. "Honestly, Sam, is that any way to greet an old friend?"

Ana. I should have known. All the magic. All the planning. Danny never could have managed this without her.

I took a step toward them. Danny raised a hand and waved at me a ludicrous revolver. Seriously, the thing was so big, Dirty Harry would've thought the thing excessive. And the way Danny was holding it, he was just as likely to break his wrist as hit me. But I knew him well enough to realize his carelessness was affected. He could put a round in my chest at twice this distance. So I stopped moving. Stayed put.

"That's a good chap," he said. "You'd be wise to stay outside the circle, or I fear I'll be forced to get quite cross."

I eyed the circle. I hadn't noticed it until he'd called attention to it. The last one I'd seen was alder ash, the sacrifice of the trees' lives enough to protect an entire building from the underworld's reach. This one was smaller, only ten feet across, and made from blood.

"Yes," Danny said, "the loss of life required for this little parlor trick, and the one you encountered downstairs, is unfortunate – but I assure you, I had the good grace to get the poor indigent who unwittingly donated it nice and pissed on decent whisky before I tapped him. In all likelihood, it was a better death than he had coming."

"Yeah, you're a real peach," I said. And then, to Ana: "How can you go along with this? Don't you realize what's at stake?"

"*Go along with this*?" she said. "Why, Sam, you've got it wrong. Do you think our Daniel could have planned a rite so intricate as this? Do you think he has the skills to carry it out? I learned long ago, Sam, no one is coming to rescue me – so I decided to take it upon myself to do so."

Of course. It seemed so goddamn obvious in retrospect. Only Ana could have conjured Abyzou so easily. Only she would have the mystical mojo to pull all this off.

"So it's been you all this time? You who set Danny up as a runner for Dumas? You who sent him to double-cross me?"

"I'm my own man," Danny protested. "My decisions were my own."

"Sure they were. So you're saying it sat OK with you, stealing the Varela soul from an old friend?"

"It was a necessary evil; the ritual requires a truly corrupt soul. The energy it releases upon its destruction breaks hell's bond of servitude as it fuses soul to flesh forever. Hence the young, choice meat-suits – we'll be stuck with them from here on out. And besides, you're one to talk of bloody loyalty. I've not forgotten what you did to Quinn."

"Damn it, Danny – I've told you a thousand times, I'm not the one who got Quinn shelved."

"Yeah, right," he spat. "I suppose Ana *didn't* hear you rat him out, then."

My God. All these years, I'd had it backward. Danny hadn't turned Ana against me. *Ana* had turned *Danny*.

And that's when the pieces clicked into place.

"This building," I said to her. "The design, the construction – the research to get the ritual just right. Inserting Danny into Dumas's operation. Hell, calling in an angelic air-strike so you could get your hands on a grade-A skimming blade… the groundwork to orchestrate all that must've taken *years*."

Ana laughed, short and bitter. "Years? Try *decades*. I first had to pinpoint the exact moment and location of the necessary celestial alignment – no small feat given how deep any mention of this ritual was buried. And even with a Collector's unique skill set, getting money enough was a challenge. Transferring the funds from wealthy meat-suits to procure the land seemed simple enough, but it proved slower than anticipated – I had to do so without raising hackles. And then there was the matter of organizing today's celebration."

"But the Dia de los Muertos has been celebrated in this square for over thirty years."

Ana laughed. "You think that's by *accident*? Every year, this festival has grown, and every year, it's free of charge to all who wish to come. Oh, I'll grant you, the folks who throw it haven't the faintest idea I'm involved – I've been careful to shield both my money and my more arcane influences from public view. And it all culminates in one night, in one moment – after which Danny and I will both be free. Danny, the Varela."

Danny removed from his pocket a swirling, gray-black orb. The Varela soul. I inched forward, but he once more trained his gun on me, and once more I stopped, chastened.

"Danny, don't. Don't give it to her. You have no idea the hell on earth that you'll unleash by going through with this."

Danny smiled then, his youthful expression painful in its naïveté. "Ana's found a way round it," he said. "A spell that'll disperse the energy safely once it's freed us. Those nearest the ritual – like you, perhaps, or the two you've brought – might not fare so well, but I assure you, those beyond the fence will be fine."

"Do you really believe that?"

"Why shouldn't I? Unlike *you*, she's never lied to me."

"No? So it's not possible she's the one who turned Quinn in?" Ana bristled. "The Varela, Danny."

"She said herself she's been working toward this night for thirty years. Tell me, have you known the whole time what she had in store? Or did she only bring you in when she realized she couldn't pull it off alone? When she realized someone would have to stick their neck out to get the tools, the soul, the expertise she needed."

"Don't listen to him," Ana snapped.

"She brought me in five years ago," he said. "But I never thought…"

"What? Never thought that she was using you? That you were nothing but a patsy to her? Maybe that's what Quinn was once, too – or maybe he overheard something he shouldn't have. Twenty-seven years he's spent shelved, and for all those twenty-seven years, she's told you it was me who turned Quinn in, while the whole time she schemed in secret, working toward this night. Tell me, Ana, was Quinn helping you? Did he prove a liability – a loose end in your plan?"

"*Quinn was a mistake!*" she screamed, and then caught herself – her shoulders sagging, her face falling in dismay.

"Ana?" This from Danny: quiet, unsure.

"I never wanted this for him," she said. "He was a friend. Hell, he was scarcely more than a child. I hadn't thought when I asked of him a simple errand it would end so poorly, but then, I had no idea the boy spoke Latin."

"He was Catholic, Ana," I said. "An altar boy. In those days, they all did."

"I'd sent him to procure a manuscript from a monastery in the south of France – a scroll of unknown origin that hadn't seen the outside of the stone reliquary in which it had been sealed in centuries. I'd been tipped to it by a demon contact who swore he'd had a hand in writing it, and his tip was sound; it proved the fullest account of the Brethren I had ever seen. The problem was, young Quinn had seen it too – seen it, and translated its contents – and his enthusiasm at the prospect of escaping this life was too much for him to bear. He wanted to tell the both of you – to attempt the ritual immediately – and try though I did, I could not persuade him otherwise. So instead, I had to silence him."

"Ana," Danny said. "Fuck. How could you?"

"I did what I had to do," was her retort.

"And tonight?" Danny asked. "Have you really devised a spell that will protect against the Deluge, or are six billion fucking people an acceptable sacrifice for your freedom?"

"For *our* freedom," she corrected. "And they won't *all* die. After all, many survived the last. And who are you to say this is a bad thing? It seems to me, a cleansing flood would likely do this cesspool of a world some good."

Danny's face twisted in horror. "So your protection spell–"

"–is one-way," she said. "It will keep us safe from what's to come. It's all I could manage. It's all we really need."

"I'm sorry," he said, to Ana or to me I wasn't sure. But then he threw me the Varela soul, and said to her, "I won't let you do this. I can't."

I dropped the Varela in my pocket. Watched the two of them standing there inside the circle – Danny's eyes brimming with tears, and Ana shaking with rage barely contained.

"You have no right to take this from me," she spat. "But if you don't want to join me, you may prove useful yet."

She was on him so fast, I didn't have a chance to react. She swung the skim blade down hard on his gun hand, its rounded edge connecting with his wrist in a crunch of shattered bone. Then she kicked out his knee, and he toppled forward. With speed and strength that smacked of magical enhancement, she grabbed a fistful of his hair and dragged him backward to the center of the circle. He knelt before her, his arms dangling at his sides, his face a mask of pain. His back arched as her knee pressed against it, the skimming blade poised above his breast.

"What do you say, Sam – do you suppose our boy Danny's soul is dark enough?"

"Ana, don't."

I eyed Danny's gun, which lay ten feet from where I stood – three feet inside the circle. She picked up on my intent and said, "I wouldn't."

"Sam," Danny said. "I'm so bloody sorry."

"Hey," I told him, "you can't help who you love."

He laughed through the pain.

"For what it's worth," she said to him, "I'm sorry, too. But this is my only chance. There's only one way this can end."

I glanced around for a weapon – for anything to end this stalemate. All I saw was the silhouette of Charon sketched in crows – highlighted by the jittery spotlight of an approaching police helicopter, and standing there infuriatingly immobile as if he cared not what went on below.

Or perhaps as if he was incapable of intervening.

Danny tracked the direction of my gaze, and spotted Charon lying in wait. Then he nodded at me almost imperceptibly, as if he understood what must be done. As if giving me his consent.

Such a small gesture – so small, Ana hadn't even noticed it. And yet it was enough to break my heart.

A lump rose in my throat then, and tears welled in my eyes. But I refused to let them spill over. Not when I had a job to do.

"Wait," I said, shouting to be heard over the helicopter's din. "There is another way."

"I'm listening."

"You're going to go through with this regardless – I get that. Big boom. Big flood. But you and I both know Danny's soul ain't dark enough to break hell's bonds; he just proved that by handing over the Varela you need. So I propose a trade."

Ana smiled – feral, vicious. "Varela for Danny, is that it?"

"No," I said. "Varela for my freedom. Danny's, too, for that matter."

"I don't follow."

"It's the circle, right? Those inside break free of hell's bonds, those outside are shit outta luck. So you let me in, and I give you the Varela. You do your thing, Danny and I go free, and so long as we avoid the ensuing flood we walk away as happy as clams."

"You're playing me," she said. "The Sam I know is far too much of a Boy Scout to suggest a thing."

I stepped toward her. The three of us were awash in spot-lights, a second helicopter joining the first. Like heaven's light shining down upon us. "Maybe you don't know me as well as you think."

"I'm too fast for you," she hissed. "You'll never reach the gun in time."

Someone shouted to us through a bullhorn, but their words were lost on the wind. I took the Varela from my pocket and held it out to her. "I wouldn't dream of it," I said.

I stepped into the circle, scuffing my feet along the way.

Dried blood flecked off beneath my soles, and broke the ring.

Ana, realizing what I'd done, screamed in rage, and drove the skim-blade into Danny's chest.

Lines dropped down from above, police in riot gear rappelling from the heavens like God's own army of angels, too late to do anything but watch.

For a moment, the whole world felt as though it bent inward toward Danny's prostrate form, which seemed to vibrate, to hum, his every pore erupting with white-hot light.

So this is how the world ends, I thought. Turns out, it'll be a bang after all.

And in the instant before his soul let loose, bringing forth another flood, ten thousand crows streamed through the open roof, engulfing the lot of us in a fury of talons, beaks, and ink-black feathers.

They swarmed the circle, coalescing into the vast, impossible form of a hunched old man two stories high.

Just as soon as he had formed, he toppled over, engulfing Ana and Danny's tangled forms in his teeming black mass.

And just like that, he disappeared into the Nothingness.

Along with Ana.

Along with Danny.

In the silence that ensued, I cried.

31.

"Good morning, Collector. Nice to see you're amongst the living, so to speak. Though I confess I am surprised to find you here."

A week had passed since Los Angeles. Lilith and I were standing in a cemetery on the edge of Ilford, east London. The sky overhead was the color of slate, and a cool mist beaded up on my woolen pea coat. I looked down at the headstone at my feet. It was mottled with age, and bright green moss clung to one side of it. In weathered letters, it read:

DANIEL ALLAN YOUNG
BELOVED SON
1903–1921

For not the first time, I wondered about my own grave – I'd never seen it. I'd died penniless on the streets of New York, one more John Doe for Potter's Field. Though all of Danny's family money didn't make him any less dead. Now, in fact, it seemed he was a fair bit more.

"I thought I should pay my respects," I said.

Lilith scoffed. "To the man who nearly condemned you to an eternity of Nothingness?"

"It's a little more complicated than that," I confessed.

"It always is." Though this was a cemetery – and mid-morning – Lilith wore an evening dress of bright red, and lipstick to match. Neither showed any evidence of rain. "I knew," she said. "About your little group, and what they meant to you. Truth be told, I was sorry when you and they parted ways."

"You *knew*? Why didn't you ever say?"

"Everyone's entitled to their secrets. And everyone's entitled to those little vices that help them to survive. Regardless of what my superiors might think. We're all of us consigned to this life against our will, Collector. I no more blame you for my fate than you should me for yours."

She raised a hand, caressed my borrowed face. "So tell me," she said, "were you tempted?"

"Tempted? Tempted by what?"

"By your precious Ana's ritual. By the stories of Brethren, and by the freedom that they represent. Tempted to leave this task, this life, this punishment behind."

I thought about it. A simple answer eluded me.

"Yes. No. I don't know. Anyways, the price was far too steep. I couldn't take innocent lives to save myself. I'm not worthy of their sacrifice."

She frowned, but said nothing.

"Lily, why are you asking me this?"

"Because you need to know I would have been, if I were you. And if I'm ever faced with a choice like that, you'd best believe I'm going to take it – no matter what the cost."

"If that's true, then why tell me?"

"We're not so different, you and I. We've both been sentenced to an eternity of torment without even being given a proper chance. The difference is, I aim to do something about it – no matter *what* the cost. And when the time comes for me to make my move, I'd suggest you stay out of my way. Are we clear?"

"Crystal. Only you know what?"

"What?"

"I'm not sure I believe you."

"How's that?"

"Ana did what she did in secret. Convinced her friends to trust her, even as she betrayed them. And in the end, she didn't care who her plans hurt. You, on the other hand, claim not to even *like* me, and here you are trying to ensure I steer clear should you ever make your move. I think you care more about me and my kind than maybe you let on."

Lilith smiled and shook her head. "Perhaps you're right. Or perhaps you simply see what I intend you to. At the very least, we can agree it would be best for both of us if you're never in a position to find out which."

"Fair enough," I said.

"Good. You should know, you did well last night, Collector – word is Charon is most pleased. And as the unrest between heaven and hell descends to all-out war, he is an ally worth having."

"He used me, didn't he? He knew I wasn't to blame for taking the Varela soul. He just needed me to hunt down Ana. To breach the circle, so he could get to her."

"Is that so bad?" she asked. "Some jobs, you send a god. Some jobs, you send a monkey. This appears to have been the latter. Your Ana was quite adept at masking her movements – which is how she managed to waltz into Dumas's skim-joint undetected. And she was a gifted mage – her protections without weakness. Had you not maneuvered yourself into the position that you did, no power in the heavens could have taken her. It seems to me Charon did exactly what he had to do, the same as you. Given the sheer volume of pathetic monkey lives he saved, I'd say you owe him thanks."

"Maybe," I granted. "Still, I wonder–"

But it didn't matter what I wondered. Lilith was gone.

I stayed a while at Danny's grave, and said a prayer for his demolished soul. I wondered what it was like to cease to be, and then I pondered what a foolish thought that was – for who could ever know? My heart ached at the thought that I'd misjudged him – at the thought that he'd simply been victim to his heart in death as he'd been in life. And unbidden, my thoughts turned to Ana – so beautiful, so fierce – who to her last was still that frightened, feral child we'd thought we'd rescued, and never truly had.

I thought of Gio, then, as well, who – after two nights spent shaking in his hospital bed, had at last opened his eyes. I thought of Theresa, who'd never left his side a moment – repaying him in kind for his time spent at her bedside so many years ago. She and I had wrestled him into a cop car amidst the chaos at Ana's cursed building, and disappeared in the confusion – me wearing the body of a cop, the Jonathan Gray left dead for the forensics guys to find. I figured any manhunt would end once they ID'd the body, and then Theresa and Gio were free to disappear. Maybe Gio had a week before hell caught up with him. Maybe he had a decade. And who knows? Maybe they *never* would. Apparently, he wouldn't be the first to beat the odds.

Once I'd taken my leave of Theresa and Gio, I'd set out on a long walk, eventually burying the Varela soul in a sunchoked patch of grass outside a liquor store. Then I plopped myself on a bench across the street and sipped Maker's from a paper bag until my Deliverants arrived to spirit him away. No doubt I drew my share of looks, getting good and sloshed inside my hijacked uniformed policeman, but no one dared challenge me, and I wasn't going anywhere until I knew for sure the Varela job was behind me. I'd never seen Deliverants abscond with a soul before; they arrived in dribs and drabs, eventually swarming the lawn and digging free their package by burrowing beneath it and pushing it skyward. Then they lined up single file and passed it gingerly from back to back until it disappeared from sight. It was morbid and oddly touching, an otherworldly funeral procession. Those who walked past it didn't seem to notice – though somehow, not a one of them crunched a Deliverant underfoot, nor did they stand in the dark procession's path. Perhaps the living are more aware of the magic that surrounds them than they're given credit for.

Tires splashing through a puddle shook me from my reverie, and brought me back to Ilford – to Danny's grave. I turned around to find a massive, dove-gray Bentley parked behind me on the cemetery drive. Somehow, despite its opulence, it didn't seem out of place among the graves beneath the stone-gray sky.

The driver's side door opened. Out of it stepped a man. Bald and broad-shouldered, he had a lantern jaw and a nose that looked like it'd taken a punch or twenty in its time. He wore a starched white shirt, a suit of black, and black leather gloves to match. A pewter cravat hung around his neck, and a matching scarf was draped across his shoulders. He looked at me in this borrowed frame – a rail-thin teenaged boy who'd been struck down by an aneurysm just last night – and said, in an accent that suggested Welsh, "Sam Thornton?"

An icy finger of fear ran down my spine. "Never heard of him," I said, in my best attempt at East End cockney.

"Your accent is bloody rubbish," he said. "And anyway, you're him."

"OK, I'm him," I said glibly, as though the fact he knew who I was didn't terrify me. "And *you* are?"

"Just the hired help. The boss would like to meet with you."

"Who, exactly, is the boss?"

"That's really for the boss to say."

"So I'm to come with you right now?"

"That's right."

"What happens if I don't?"

The big man shrugged. "Find out."

I thought about it. Decided not to.

"No," I said. "I'll come."

The big man nodded once. If I had to guess, I'd say I disappointed him.

He opened the Bentley's rear door. "One condition," I said to him.

"What's that?"

"You got any change?"

The big man cocked his head at me quizzically, and then rummaged through his pockets. I held out my palm, and he dropped three pound coins into my hand. I took two, and handed one back. "Thanks," I said. "I'll only be a second."

I trotted back to Danny's grave and placed the coins atop his headstone.

Then I climbed into the waiting Bentley, and, doors locking, it pulled out of the graveyard, headed toward God knows where.

Acknowledgments

It takes a great deal of work to turn a humble manuscript into a finished, polished novel, and though I'd love nothing more to bask in all the credit, it's hardly mine alone in which to bask. To that end, I extend my deepest gratitude to my agent, Jennifer Jackson, and to the crack Angry Robot team of Marc Gascoigne, Lee Harris, and Darren Turpin, as well as honorary US Robot John Tintera. And though I'll never turn away a compliment for my lovely, lovely covers, it's worth noting said compliments should rightly be directed to Marco once more for the art direction, and to the fine folks at Amazing 15 for making it happen.

Thanks to my parents for their love and support, and to my sister Anna, for occasionally distracting them so I can get some writing done. Thanks also to my in-laws (father, mother, sisters, and brothers), for putting the lie to the stereotype and championing me at every turn. My extended family deserves thanks, too, both for their great generosity of spirit and because I suspect they may well comprise the majority of my readership.

I've been fortunate in my writing career to cross paths with more wonderful people than I could possibly list here.

However, I would like to single out a few of them for providing me support along the way (with sincere apologies to anyone I've missed): John Anealio, Jedidiah Ayres, Patrick Shawn Bagley, Eric Beetner, Frank Bill, Nigel Bird, Stephen Blackmoore, Judy Bobalik, Chris Bowe and the fine folks at Longfellow Books, Paul D. Brazill, Maurice Broaddus, R. Thomas Brown, Bill Cameron, Rodney Carlstrom, Kristin Centorcelli, Joelle Charbonneau, Sean Chercover, David Cranmer and cohorts at *Beat to a Pulp*, the Cressey family, my fellow Criminal Minds bloggers, Laura K. Curtis, Hilary Davidson, Tony DiMarco, Barna Donovan, Neliza Drew, Jacques Filippi, the whole Founding Fields crew, Renee Fountain, Kent Gowran, Janet Hutchings, Sally Janin, Naomi Johnson, Suzanne Johnson, Jon and Ruth Jordan, John Kenyon, Chris La Tray, Jennifer Lawrence, Brian Lindenmuth and the fantastic folks at *Spinetingler*, Sophie Littlefield, Jennifer MacRostie, Dan Malmon, Matthew McBride, Erin Mitchell, Scott Montgomery, Joe Myers, Stuart Neville, Lauren O'Brien, Sabrina Ogden, Dan O'Shea, Miranda Parker, Lou Pendergrast, Ron Earl Phillips, Kathleen Pigeon, James W. Powell, Keith Rawson, Kieran Shea, Julia Spencer-Fleming (and her husband Ross), Julie Summerell, Brian Vander Ark, Jeff VanderMeer, Meineke van der Salm, Steve Weddle, Chuck Wendig, Elizabeth A. White, and Shaun Young.

And, as ever, thanks to my lovely wife Katrina: my co-pilot, my ideal reader, my best friend. A good spouse will pretend not to notice their partner is making it up as they go; only the best of them encourage it.

About the author

Chris F. Holm was born in Syracuse, New York, the grand-son of a cop with a penchant for crime fiction. He wrote his first story at the age of six. It got him sent to the principal's office. Since then, his work has fared better, appearing in such publications as *Ellery Queen's Mystery Magazine*, *Alfred Hitchcock's Mystery Magazine*, *Needle Magazine*, *Beat to a Pulp*, and *Thuglit*.

He's been a Derringer Award finalist and a Spinetingler Award winner, and he's also written a novel or two. He lives on the coast of Maine with his lovely wife and a noisy, noisy cat. He is currently hard at work on the next Collector novel, *The Big Reap*.

chrisfholm.com

Why the Hell?

Portions of this essay first appeared on Do Some Damage, L.A. Noir, and The SciFi Guys, and are reprinted with permission.

The Collector series, it seems, is a tough one to pin down. I've seen it referred to as gonzo pulp. Urban fantasy. Paranormal mystery. Even, to my great surprise, as science fiction, despite the fact there ain't much science to be found within its pages.

Truth is, I don't really mind what people call it, so long as they're enjoying it. If you ask me, though, the Collector series is fantastical noir. But since there's a teeny tiny chance I made that phrase up, I should probably explain just what the heck I think it means.

"Noir" is perhaps the slipperiest term in all of literature. That's in large part due to its muddy origins; our modern use of the term derives from the film noir of the '40s and '50s, which in turn borrowed heavily from the bleak crime tales that began cropping up in the U.S. during the Depression. James Cain, author of *The Postman Always Rings Twice* and *Double Indemnity*, is widely credited as the creator of the modern roman noir. Before Cain, the term was used to refer to what we'd now call Gothic novels, but afterward, the term took on a life of its own.

Thing is, Cain wasn't wild about the label, and those classic film noir flicks? Yeah, they weren't called that then. The title was bestowed upon them by a French critic years after they began popping up in theaters, and the so-called noir canon wasn't really well-defined until the '70s, when critics and cinema historians adopted the label en masse; before then, most of what we consider film noir were simply melodramas. So really, noir fiction is the result of a decades-long game of telephone that bounced from books to movies and back again, with stops on two continents along the way. Now, there's not a lot of agreement as to what it means; like pornography, it seems, most folks just know it when they see it.

The definition that's gotten the most traction of late is noir preservationist Eddie Muller's take on noir as "working class tragedy," due in large part to the fact that it's been championed by no less than Dennis Lehane. "In Greek tragedy, they fall from great heights," sayeth Lehane. "In noir, they fall from the curb."

Now, that doesn't strike me as half bad, but it's more descriptive than prescriptive; a shorthand for where noir's *been*, as opposed to an instruction manual for where it's *going*. For my money, noir boils down to bleak humanism – or, to put it more plainly: shit options, bad decisions, and dire consequences. The difference between Greek tragedy and noir ain't the height of the fall, but the reason: those who fall in Greek tragedy do so because they're destined to; those who fall in noir choose to their damn selves.

In short, free will's a bitch.

But regardless of whose definition you go with, you'll notice something's lacking: namely, any mention of genre. That's because for as much as noir's assumed to be a subset of crime fiction, it's more vibe than subgenre. And, as many an enterprising modern writer seems intent on proving, that vibe is one that plays just as well with fantasy and science fiction as it does with crime.

When I sat down to write *Dead Harvest*, it was the darker aspects of free will I was most interested in exploring. I was raised in a Catholic family, and I've long been fascinated with the Church's teachings on the matter of free will. On the one hand, we're told God gave to humankind, his most beloved creation, the gift of free will, and on the other, that said gift resulted in the humankind's expulsion from paradise, and a taint that's passed to every one of us at birth. We're taught that three-quarters of everything we do – or even think – is sinful, and we should beg forgiveness at every turn lest we wind up burning for all eternity. We're taught that even good people can go to hell if they don't play by God's rules. And we're taught that if they do wind up in hell, it's all their fault.

I'm not trying to knock my family's faith. But being raised in such a faith can scare the ever-loving shit out of you. It puts no small amount of pressure on you to make good decisions, and no doubt has filled the pews for damn near two thousand years of Sundays with folks trying desperately to reconcile their decisions and their beliefs with a rulebook that's both dense and difficult to comprehend. Because by God, if they don't, they're gonna take a fall.

Truth is, the old pulps from which my series draws its tone aren't so far afield from the Church in that regard. I suppose it shouldn't surprise: after all, what were the early pulps if not lurid updates of classic morality plays? James Cain's tales of forbidden romance leading to violence, misery, and regret may as well have taken place in Eden. Chandler's cops and criminals were often cut from the same cloth, while Revelations and the Book of Enoch talk of angels and their fallen brethren. Genesis tells the tale of Sodom and Gomorrah; in *Red Harvest* (whose title I not-so-subtly twisted to suit my own nefarious purposes),

Hammett writes of Poisonville. And speaking of Poisonville, while nearly every culture on the planet has their own flood myth of rising waters sent to wash away the wickedness from the world, Hammett's violent cleansing of that corrupt burg came courtesy of his nameless, unflagging Continental Op – but it was no less awesome for it. And what would any pulp tale be without a decent femme fatale? The Babylonian Talmud first introduced the world to a redheaded, acid-tongued temptress by the name of Lilith, who, in one form or another, has since wreaked havoc in darn near every religious or occult text penned. I'm pretty sure she popped up in *The Maltese Falcon*, too, only then she was known as Brigid O'Shaughnessy. Lord knows she shows up in my series. And believe me when I tell you, you ain't seen nothing yet.

To my mind, the Collector series affords me the opportunity to revisit the roots of these classic archetypes, in what I hope is both a fresh and exciting way. And to drop into their midst a man in Sam Thornton who's not so different from you or I – trying desperately to make his way through the moral minefield that is free will. Sam's neither a bad man nor a perfect one, but even in the direst of situations, his intentions, at least, are pure.

Of course, you know what they say about good intentions...

Meet Sam Thornton.
 He collects souls...

The Collector Book One

Dead Harvest

Chris F. Holm

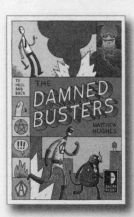

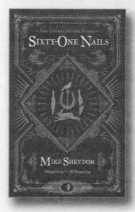

SELL THE DOG

Grab the complete Angry Robot catalogue

ANGRY
ROBOT

DAN ABNETT
- ☐ Embedded
- ☐ Triumff: Her Majesty's Hero

GUY ADAMS
- ☐ The World House
- ☐ Restoration

JO ANDERTON
- ☐ Debris
- ☐ Suited

MADELINE ASHBY
- ☐ vN

LEE BATTERSBY
- ☐ The Corpse-Rat King

LAUREN BEUKES
- ☐ Moxyland
- ☐ Zoo City

THOMAS BLACKTHORNE
- ☐ Edge
- ☐ Point

MAURICE BROADDUS
- ☐ The Knights of Breton Court

ADAM CHRISTOPHER
- ☐ Empire State
- ☐ Seven Wonders

PETER CROWTHER
- ☐ Darkness Falling

ALIETTE DE BODARD
- ☐ Obsidian & Blood

MATT FORBECK
- ☐ Amortals
- ☐ Carpathia
- ☐ Vegas Knights

JUSTIN GUSTAINIS
- ☐ Hard Spell
- ☐ Evil Dark

GUY HALEY
- ☐ Reality 36
- ☐ Omega Point

COLIN HARVEY
- ☐ Damage Time
- ☐ Winter Song

CHRIS F HOLM
- ☐ Dead Harvest

MATTHEW HUGHES
- ☐ The Damned Busters
- ☐ Costume Not Included

TRENT JAMIESON
- ☐ Roil
- ☐ Night's Engines

K W JETER
- ☐ Infernal Devices
- ☐ Morlock Night

PAUL S KEMP
- ☐ The Hammer & the Blade

J ROBERT KING
- ☐ Angel of Death
- ☐ Death's Disciples

ANNE LYLE
- ☐ The Alchemist of Souls

GARY McMAHON
- ☐ Pretty Little Dead Things
- ☐ Dead Bad Things

ANDY REMIC
- ☐ The Clockwork Vampire Chronicles

CHRIS ROBERSON
- ☐ Book of Secrets

MIKE SHEVDON
- ☐ Sixty-One Nails
- ☐ The Road to Bedlam
- ☐ Strangeness & Charm

DAVID TALLERMAN
- ☐ Giant Thief

GAV THORPE
- ☐ The Crown of the Blood
- ☐ The Crown of the Conqueror
- ☐ The Crown of the Usurper

LAVIE TIDHAR
- ☐ The Bookman
- ☐ Camera Obscura
- ☐ The Great Game

TIM WAGGONER
- ☐ The Nekropolis Archives

KAARON WARREN
- ☐ Mistification
- ☐ Slights
- ☐ Walking the Tree

CHUCK WENDIG
- ☐ Blackbirds
- ☐ Mockingbird

IAN WHATES
- ☐ City of Dreams & Nightmare
- ☐ City of Hope & Despair
- ☐ City of Light & Shadow